Nakaa's Awakening

LAND OF MATANG

mining community. It runs from the early 1900s to the interwar years and shows the personal impact of the mining on all the people concerned, including her family members and the Banabans who lived alongside them as their land was ravaged.

The story is by turns sad and uplifting, a complex array of emotions in response to the natural beauty of Banaba and the harsh realities of its exploitation. Stacey spares us nothing, neither condemning nor justifying. The story left me with so many images and ideas. I look forward to the next volume in the series. I highly recommend this book to anyone interested in the general subject area of the Pacific islands, whether or not they know anything about Banaba. It is also an enchanting historical romance!

Jeremy Cooper, Freelance Media Producer, United Kingdom

Naaka's Awakening is the warm-hearted story of Ella Williams and her life on Ocean Island (now Banaba) in the early 20th Century. While her husband oversees the phosphate mining enterprise that brought the family to the island, Ella learns to love the rich culture of the island. Her loyalties are torn when she sees the damage the company is doing to the Banabans' way of life. I highly recommend this story to anyone interested in the impact of European activities in the Pacific, and to anyone who loves to read of new and exotic places. Inspired by true events, and real people, this story held my attention and sent me off on a virtual visit via Google Earth.

I highly recommend this story to anyone interested in the impact of European activities in the Pacific, and to anyone who loves to read of new and exotic places. Inspired by true events, and real people, this story held my attention and sent me off on a virtual visit via Google Earth.

Sally Odgers, Author/Editor, Australia.

"What an incredible story well written. I look forward to the next and the next and the next."

Alice Billing, Australia

Nakaa's Awakening

BOOK ONE

LAND OF MATANG

Stacey M. King

Banaban Vision Publications

GOLD COAST, QLD, AUSTRALIA

Banaban Vision Publications
P.O. Box 6,
Runaway Bay, Gold Coast, Queensland. 4216
Australia
www.banabanvision.com

Publisher's Note: This work is a blend of history, biography and fictional reconstruction. Names, characters, places, and incidents are based on real characters and events which have been combined with the author's imagination to assist in the storytelling.

Book Layout © 2017 BookDesignTemplates.com
Cover by Stacey M. King
Internal images Williams family collection and/or supplied by the author.

Nakaa's Awakening – Land of Matang/Stacey M. King 1st ed.
ISBN 978-0-6485462-3-8

Land of Matang ...

where they dwelt eternally,

was the land of heart's desire,

the original fatherland,

the paradise sweeter than all other paradises,

never to be found again by the children of men.

Sometimes its forests and mountains

might be glimpsed in dreams,

but when the dreamer strove to land

upon its smiling shores,

they faded away before him

and he was alone on the empty waters.

Yet, though Matang was lost forever,

a cherished tradition said that the ancestor gods

had promised to return to their children one day,

wherever they might be...

— Arthur Grimble, *A Pattern of Islands.* 1952

"Most of all they feared the God of Darkness,

The Evil spirit, Nakaa,

who barred their way to paradise after death..."

— Pearl Binder

CONTENTS

PHOTOGRAPHS / MAPS

MAPS

PHOTOGRAPHS

AUTHOR'S NOTE

NAKAA'S AWAKENING is the beginning of the *Land of Matang,* a four-book series based on the epic history of a small remote Pacific Island known as Ocean Island with one of the richest discoveries of phosphate ever found and the four hundred and fifty indigenous Banaban inhabitants who stood in the way of progress.

The storytelling combines history, biography and fictional reconstructions beginning with three generations of the author's family- the Williams- and the hundreds of old family photographs and documents belonging to another time and place back in the early 1900s. Through individual characters, we share their experiences and, at times, conflicting viewpoints as they take us on their journey where people with different cultures, values, and beliefs collide while the international political juggernaut behind the scenes seems unstoppable.

Indigenous words are used to explain some of the storytelling from a Banaban perspective and the original geographical names on the island. The British would later use English phonetic spelling for the four ancestral villages. *Uma* was spelled Ooma, *Tabiang* as Tapiang, *Tabwewa* as Tapiwa, while *Buakonikai* as Puakonikai. Words such as *nei* denote a woman's name, and *te* is the. The letters 'p' or 's' are not part of the Banaban alphabet, and 'b' is used in place of 'p' and the letters 'ti' is pronounced 's'. All other translations are in the Glossary with weights, measures and distance quoted in imperial measures of the times.

This book was inspired by my mother, who has insisted all these years that the plight of the Banabans had to be told. I would also like to thank the retired phosphate industry staff and their families, who gave freely of their knowledge, time and experiences.

This story is far more involved than just the fortunes of a small remote island rich in phosphate. It is a story about people whose lives were entwined and changed forever once phosphate was discovered. To their memories, I hope I have done them all justice.

But most of all, this book is dedicated to an extraordinary people who have endured and will proudly go on.

May you never change...

THE BANABANS

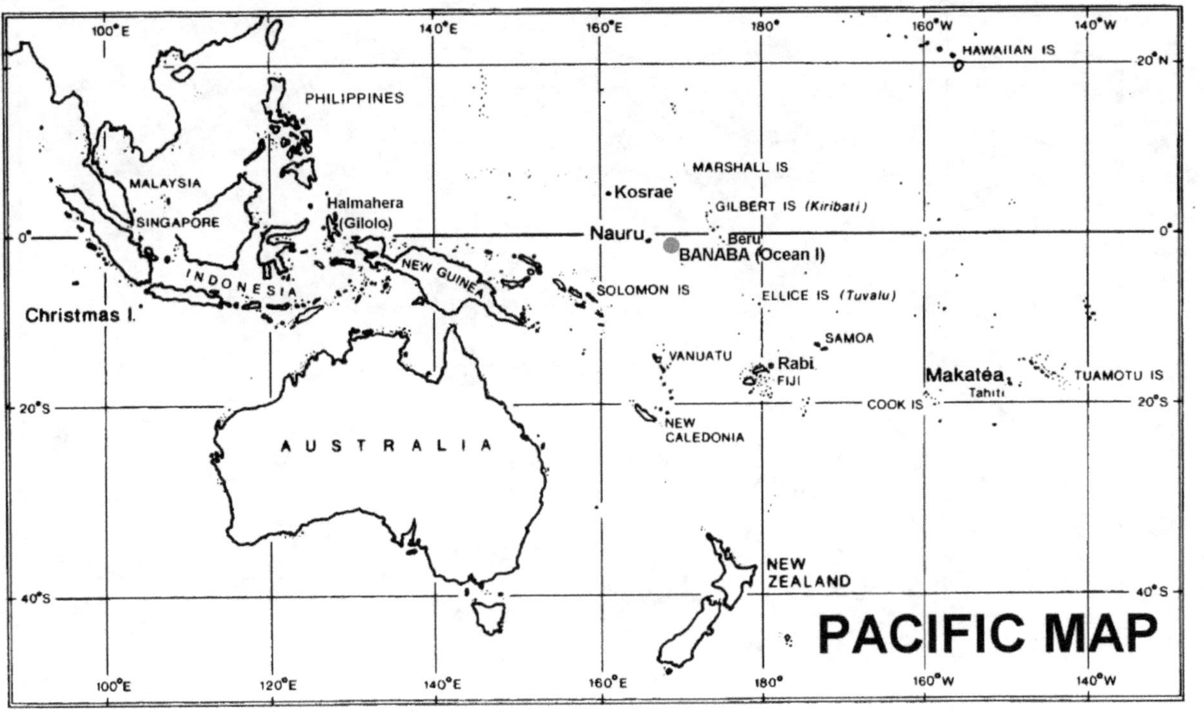

Pacific Map showing Ocean Island (Banaba)

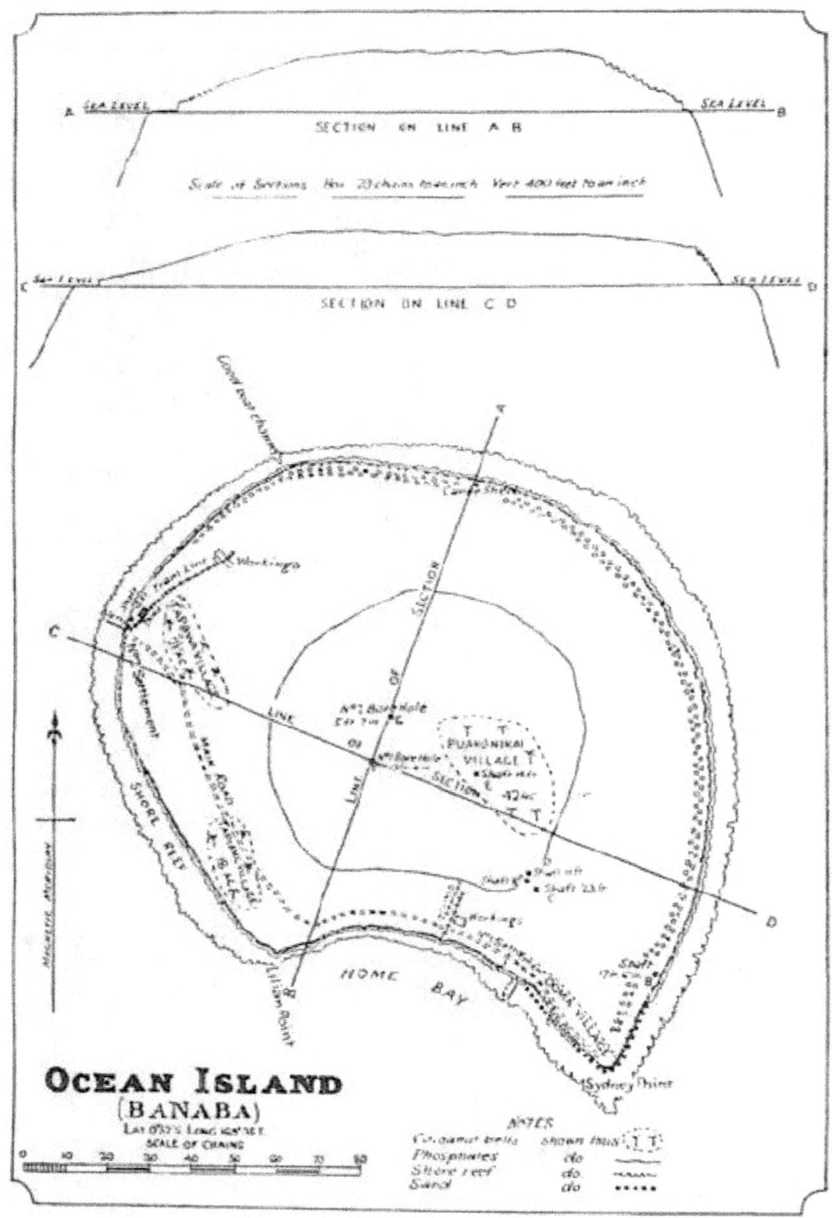

Early Map Showing Phosphate Deposits on Banaba, May 1904

PREFACE

The year was 1992, and it was one of those typical hot Queensland January days when late afternoon thunderstorms brought welcome relief from the heat. As I watched my mother, dressed in black, escort the last of the guests to the front door of our family home, I was suddenly taken aback by the silver gleam from her mane of white hair and the sad realisation that she was now nearing the end of her life. Maybe my great-aunt's funeral and the closing of another chapter in our family's history had brought on my sudden revelation. My mother slowly made her way back to the large family dining table where I was seated, and I could not help noticing how pale and drawn she looked when she stopped to pick up an old sepia photograph from the table.

"They're all gone now, you know," she mumbled, almost to herself, running her fingers over the images captured on film all those years before. "Uma was the last one, and now she's gone too," she lamented, passing the precious snapshot to me before making her way towards the kitchen to make another pot of reviving tea.

Why was I so apprehensive about looking at our family's old photographs that had been stored away and hidden for all these years? I had never discussed my family's background outside the family home for fear my friends would think I was exaggerating. Surely, all those stories I had heard could not be true, I told myself, placing the photograph of my great-aunt, Uma Williams, back with the hundreds of others strewn across the table.

Why was I unable to walk away? Was it just my natural curiosity or the strong bonds of my ancestors that were persuading me to look at my great-grandfather's collection? I let myself be drawn to the faces staring back at me. Some of them I recognised from years ago when I was a young child, their smiles, the various events in their lives captured at that instant, frozen in time. I could remember the tales told to me by my family. The characters they often spoke about really did exist.

I thought of Ella Williams and the stories of her early days as a bride of seventeen when she left her large pioneering family in the country farming town of Bundaberg. How could she have foreseen the loneliness and adventures that lay ahead when her husband John went away to work the guano mines off the Queensland coast for months on end? Ella struggled through the first five years of married life, mostly on her own, with two babies to rear. The tragic loss of her firstborn would leave her devastated, but in true pioneering spirit, she got on with her life. The day her husband John finally arrived back home with the news of his new position on Ocean Island was the day their lives would be changed forever.

Picking up the next photo, my hand suddenly stopped. There's Tetabo, or Tea Tup as my grandmother Gwendolyn called him. He had been their beloved Banaban houseboy. He was just the way she described him; handsome and proud, with his beautiful wife Meri and their son. My excitement grew as more images of Banabans appeared. I had overheard her tales of beautiful natives, palm trees, islands, and her sadness and hushed talk of loneliness, forbidden love and scandal. How could I ever have doubted her?

Now, as I glance down at the gold ring on my finger, the wedding band of my great-grandmother, I feel the bond between us. I know I am part of them, and now it is up to me, a century later, to tell the epic tale of the Banabans as their legend of the Man of Matang becomes a reality. I know it is what they all would have wanted.

1. Ship arriving in Home Bay Ocean Island early 1900s.

CHAPTER ONE

ARRIVAL IN PARADISE

Ella - Ocean Island 1902

Fifteen days of sailing from Australia seemed so far away. The mist suddenly cleared, and the island appeared, rising out of the sea almost as if a large green-encrusted sponge had been set adrift from the seabed below. At that moment the strong westerly winds abated, and the sun's rays broke through the overhanging canopy of clouds. Nothing had prepared Ella Williams for this vision; a tiny tropical isle bathed in a warm glow appeared straight ahead, shimmering on the surface of the vast azure ocean. Ocean Island seemed to be welcoming them to her shores as their steamship drew closer.

Ella brushed aside the long strand of dark hair that had escaped her perfectly coiffured chignon. She could not help feeling the mixed emotions of apprehension and excitement as she thought of why they had come here to this no man's land in the Central Pacific. Her striking green eyes scanned the rich vista to the small island situated only fifty-two miles south of the equator and reported to contain the highest grades of phosphate rock.

She felt terrified at the thought of being so far from home. Of course, if it had not been for the love and loyalty she felt for her husband, she would never have been here in the first place. Her sense of duty to John always came before any personal misgivings.

"Darling, it's time to go." Her husband's voice suddenly broke her reverie.

Ella smiled, turning to greet him. He held their daughter in his arms.

"Did she have a good sleep?" she asked, reaching down to brush aside her daughter's golden ringlets from her weary eyes.

"Yes, she's still half asleep." John Williams smiled down at his precious daughter.

Gwennie was now two years old and had met her father for the first time a few weeks before. Her initial shyness towards him was soon replaced with adoration, and she would not let him out of her sight for the entire boat trip.

Ella leaned over to kiss her face. She liked seeing her husband in his new role as adoring father even if it meant she had lost her daughter's undivided attention.

"Look, sweetheart," Ella said, pointing towards the island, "we're here at our new home."

Gwennie seemed more interested in snuggling into John's broad chest.

"We have to get going," John warned.

Overhead the dark, ominous clouds had begun to close in, plunging the island's beautiful colours into dark shadows. The appearance of Tibbs, the ship's purser, had not gone unnoticed by Ella while John was leading her along the deck.

"Come on, Ella, please, we're here." He sounded unusually chirpy Ella thought when he abruptly stopped.

With his prompting, she reluctantly looked over the side and saw the thick rope ladder dangling from the rail of the ship. All excitement seemed to suck out of her body as her watering eyes were drawn to the sea below and a puny rowboat struggling through the churning waves nearby.

Before she could sound a protest, Tibbs, who was standing next to her, said, "Now Missus Williams, all you have to do, ma'am, is climb down the ladder when that boat gets alongside us." The Englishman grinned, pointing towards the bobbing craft.

Ella looked at her husband in disbelief, ignoring the purser.

"I can't believe it, John! You mean you expect Gwennie and me to climb down that, that... thing?" Her face twisted with horror. "Why can't we use the gangway?"

"Well, ma'am," Tibbs answered, "the gangway is far too dangerous to use today." Apparently noticing her look of shock, he quickly added, "Ma'am I can assure you this is the safest way to land with the westerly coming in."

The sight of her daughter's trusting eyes made Ella pull herself together while her husband wrapped his arm around her shoulder.

Tibbs quickly tied a rope safety harness around Ella's small waist before she had a chance to make any further objections.

"Come on now, ma'am, just hold on tightly to the ladder and do not look down. Just one foot at a time."

While Ella nervously teetered with one leg poised over the rocking ship's side rail, Tibbs was busy strapping Gwennie's little body unto John's back.

Ella peered out over the drop, feeling the rise of nausea hit her stomach. The small craft had now pulled in alongside, dwarfed by the bulk of the ship. She could not help noticing the native men eagerly looking up at her. Momentarily closing her eyes and with all the stubborn inner strength she could muster, she clutched the oiled stained rope of the ladder and lunged over the side.

She felt the coarse sisal fibres bite into her soft flesh as she scampered down the ladder. She was not prepared for the shock of seeing the ship's slimy sidings at such close quarters, and it took her momentarily off guard, her foot missing the rung of the next step altogether. The ship suddenly rolled, and Ella found herself swinging away from the side. In her newfound panic, she stepped right through the rung of the next step, and it caught her behind the back of her knee, tumbling her head over heels.

Her poise was shattered as she unceremoniously struggled with the mass of starched lawn petticoats and her long cotton skirt that was now hanging over her head. The blood rushed to her face while she made frantic efforts to push her garments up. Her fear of falling faded when she felt the pressure of the safety harness cut into her waist.

"Hold on ma'am... I've got you," Tibbs called over the side.

All Ella could think of was what a spectacle she had become helplessly swinging back and fro with each pitch of the ship. John had wanted her to make such a good first impression, and she was putting on a good show for him now.

"Ella, it's all right. We've got you," her husband called, his voice straining on the wind. "Ella, can you hear me?"

Ella thanked God the Almighty she had donned her new bloomers with the fancy lace trim while her face turned an even brighter shade of red. The islanders below were getting a good view now. She started to sob.

"Just try and pull yourself up, ma'am?" Tibbs' voice carried on the next wind gust.

Ella wondered what both of them were doing back up there on the deck. Every time she moved, she was sent tumbling wildly away from the ship again. Through her distress, she suddenly heard a new voice calling to her, a calm, steady voice that seemed to be coming from the boats below.

"Missy, Missy, you orr... e... righte e... me got you."

A feeling of relief washed over her, especially when the end of the ladder stopped swaying. Slowly Ella managed to pull herself back up into an upright position while the almost musical tones of the voice now commanded her full attention.

"Here, Missy Missy... orr... e ... rightee Missy."

Stepping one foot down at a time she descended down... down... and down until finally, she felt strong arms reach out to grab her. There were eight men; six manning the oars and one on the steering oar at the back and another young man who oddly looked so out of place in his ill-fitting clothes among so much bare flesh. She was aware of the bulging chests of the oarsmen when they gently placed her down in the boat among them. Their golden bodies were wet and glistening, and they possessed the most handsome faces she had ever seen.

"Thou blasted Missy, Missy. Me Tetabo, me torks Ingerlish," the clothed young man greeted her, with a great smile breaking out on his face.

Ella noticed his teeth were perfect and gleaming white. His smile was so contagious that flustered Ella let out a nervous giggle. Her head was spinning while her body shook, and her teeth began to chatter, but she was happy to be down off that dreaded ladder. Ella did not have a clue what he was saying, something about being blasted. She hoped he was not talking about guns.

Meanwhile, John, with Gwennie strapped to his back, sailed straight over the edge, never missing a step.

"Ella are you all right?" he asked, noticing the men untying her safety harness. The sight of the young man's dark hands moving around his wife's waist did not go unnoticed, but he knew under the circumstances it could not be helped.

Ella was still trying to compose herself as another wave of nausea washed over her. "I'll be all right, John, as soon as I get to dry land." She tried to smile weakly when the young man moved her towards the back of the boat.

Now with John and herself seated at the back of the vessel, she hardly had time to check on her daughter's wellbeing before their small craft quickly moved away from the protection of the ship's towering side.

"Quick! Hold on…" were the last words she heard from her husband before their boat was picked up by one of the broad sweeping swells rolling in unchecked across the expanse of ocean.

The vessel plunged suddenly downwards into a deep trough, and a high-pitched scream broke through the overwhelming din of the turbulent shore-break. Young Gwennie's angelic face was now transformed into one of utter terror as she again bellowed at the top of her lungs while still secured to her father's back. Their seemingly frail timber craft lifted skywards to catch the next building wave while the oarsmen strained with all their might to prevent them from being overturned into the wild sea.

John felt the intense pain shoot through his ears with his daughter's wails. "Gwennie please, Daddy's here," he tried to console her, but it was pointless. With her piercing screams and the buffeting of the strong onshore winds, his words were lost to the elements.

Ella sat there frozen with fear, watching the sharp, menacing coral reef emerge from the churning white water just ahead. Lord have mercy, she cried to herself, realising they would be smashed to smithereens. Suddenly the craft was violently pitched sideways, throwing her almost on top of John and Gwennie. She fought to grab onto the side of the boat and right herself as the sinister reef suddenly disappeared from view. The vessel was now being hurled straight up into the air, and it was during that moment that Ella caught a glimpse of the island shimmering under bright sunshine once more rising out of the maelstrom around her. Her mind suddenly flashed to her new home and how close she was to her dream.

Leading up to this nightmare, Ella's mind had been on nothing else but Ocean Island. If she and her precious Gwennie and John could only survive the next few minutes, she would be eternally grateful. With their very survival at stake, she did not have time now for the pretty scenery, feeling the murderous jolt when they came crashing down off the side of the enormous wave. With a sudden rush, they dropped back into another deep trough.

The boat seemed to be wallowing clumsily before the oarsmen quickly righted their rhythm to bring the vessel back under control. Ella just had time to adjust her grasp when the onslaught of the next gigantic wave hit them. Her young life flashed before her as she re-alised that they were facing almost certain death out here so far from civilisation in these wild seas. Her new life was just beginning; she was too young to die, she told herself when abruptly her body was flung forward.

They had been married for nearly six years, and out of all those years she had probably been with John for a total of twelve months. He had worked in the various guano mines operating on the remote islands off Australia's Queensland coast. Now, at last, they finally had a chance to be together as a family. She felt like a new bride. She could not die, not now!

Helplessly Ella looked across to her screaming daughter and noticed her husband's face. He looked almost composed under the circumstances she thought, as they were suddenly jerked backwards again. John was always so dependable and in control, but now he could not help them. Their lives were in the hands of the Almighty and these half-naked island men.

"One... Two... One... Two!" the voice of the man on the steering oar hollered continually over the roar of the turbulent waters. The men with bulging biceps immediately reacted each time they caught his count, rowing faster now to prevent the boat from being swamped. Racing down the almost vertical face of the next freak wave the water came crashing over them, flinging the small boat almost totally around.

Ella tightened her vice-like grip. 'This is it!' she told herself, waiting for the water to pull them all under to a watery grave. Her senses were tingling with the smell and taste of the briny sea. She could feel the salt burning her eyes and crusting on her exposed skin.

Miraculously, the half swamped vessel suddenly straightened.

Ella turned her drenched face towards land, trying to focus through her painful stinging eyes on the tall framework of a jetty that appeared between each set of breakers. It looked as though the poor old rickety wooden structure was precariously poised just waiting to collapse into the buffeting sea. Licking the salt from her lips, Ella lifted one hand, attempting to brush wet hair off her daughter's face.

"It's all right sweetheart, we're nearly there," she assured her, her words lost on the wind.

While Ella had been distracted trying to soothe her daughter, she had not noticed their small boat catch one long last wave that was shooting them right past the side of the jetty and her husband's protective embrace as their vessel sped into shore. With a sudden abrupt stop, they hit the small sandy strip in between the menacing reef that fringed the shoreline. Before she realised what was happening, she felt herself being plucked from where she had fallen onto the water covered floor of the boat, while the powerful undertow endeavoured to pull their craft back out to sea.

"Welcome to Ocean Island," her rescuer shouted, quickly carrying her to safety.

Before Ella had a chance to speak or check on what was happening to Gwennie and John, they had already cleared the shore-break away from the driving wind.

"I'm George Cozens, the harbour master here. I assume you're John's wife?"

Ella was still trying to gather her battered and bruised senses when she realised, she was in the arms of a large man. She could feel the hardness of his body as he carried her. Suddenly with a blush of embarrassment, she remembered he was a complete stranger, and she must look an utter mess.

Finding her voice, she stammered, "Yes... yes... that's right, John's... um... wife."

Slowing his pace, he climbed an embankment. "Well, I'm glad to meet you, Missus Williams."

Ella noticed that the large handlebar moustache that gave his face such character moved up and down every time he spoke.

"I know John couldn't be happier to finally have you here with us," he said cheerfully.

His deep voice seemed to match his appearance perfectly, Ella thought, smiling back at the big man as she held on tightly around his thick neck.

"Are you all right, darling?" John called from behind them.

"Yes, I'm fine, John." She was aware that Gwennie had stopped screaming. "Is Gwennie all right?"

John quickly caught up with the big man who was carefully putting Ella down onto the pathway behind the boat shed.

"Gwennie is probably just asleep, but you'd better have a look," John replied, sounding concerned.

After stumbling the first few steps on her worn-out sea legs, Ella rushed to her husband's side. Gwennie's little limp body dangled behind his back. All her earlier hysterics had utterly exhausted her.

"Here, John, we should unstrap her and carry her the rest of the way." Ella was already trying to release the buckles.

Captain Cozens was at her side, supporting the weight of Gwennie's small frame with his big hands. She noticed how he held her ever so gently, concern showing in his deep blue eyes.

"Here, Missus Williams, let me take her. You both must be exhausted. I'll carry her," he insisted, taking her in his arms.

"Darling, are you sure you're all right? You're soaked through."

"I'm fine John, please don't fuss." She was not in the mood for fussing. It had been a long day, a day that had started with so many expectations and had ended on a rather dismal note. All she wanted to do now was to have John and Gwennie organised and settled in somewhere.

While Ella was busy with Gwennie, she had not noticed the large gathering of natives making their way towards them. The crowd was a mass of friendly smiling faces eager to catch a glimpse of the island's new arrivals. Ella stood there, overwhelmed by their enthusiasm. She could not help noticing the meagre coverings of grass they had draped precariously over their loins and private parts. God forbid they were virtually naked.

Ella took in the rest of the spectacle. Flowers were everywhere, in their hair, behind their ears, around their necks and in their hands, making a kaleidoscope of colours that reflected off their gleaming bodies. The women had lustrous ebony hair that hung down the length of their backs. In among all this profusion of colour, the overpowering heady, sickly sweet scent of the flowers and the rich aroma of coconut oil seemed to permeate the air under the sweltering sun.

A hush fell over the gathering when two beautiful women moved forward to garland them with flower leis. Ella noticed there seemed to be a slight commotion at the back of the crowd.

"Oh, here comes your official welcoming party," Cozens warned them at the same time as the gathering cleared a path for two white-clad figures.

Ella suddenly realised the beautiful white dress she had specially bought for this occasion was now a waterlogged rag with starch dripping from the hem. She could feel the sticky goo seeping down into her drenched shoes and pooling between her stockinged toes. Nervously Ella wriggled her feet while trying to brush the untidy mass of tangled hair from her face with a still trembling hand. She noticed her John running his fingers through his short strawberry blond locks and rolling up his damp shirtsleeves. He looked as dashing and debonair as usual.

"Welcome back John, glad to see you made it in safely," the smaller of the two gentlemen announced, while John stepped forward to shake his extended hand.

"Glad to be back, sir." Her husband smiled broadly.

Ella stood silently waiting to be introduced and noticed that Gwennie was still sound asleep in the large Captain's arms. The second gentlemen also moved forward to shake John's hand and make pleasantries.

"Good to see you saved me sending out the rescue party for you," the first gentleman said. Ella noted the touch of sunburn on his fair face.

"It was a pretty lively trip," John said and laughed.

She shuddered inwardly, unable to comprehend the men's light approach to danger, her nerves still raw after her near brush with death.

"Now Williams, where's this lovely wife of yours you've been telling us all about?" the sunburned gentleman asked, walking towards her.

"Mister Ellis, sir, I'd like you to meet my wife." Her husband beamed.

"Missus Williams!" Ellis greeted her, removing his hat and taking Ella's delicate, and still trembling hand. "So glad to meet you. I can see that John is a fortunate man."

She noticed he had a receding hairline even though he was only a young man. She must look a terrible fright, she told herself, feeling the blush rise on her face. The other gentlemen also moved forward, eager to meet her.

"Welcome to Ocean Island, Missus Williams. I'm Naylor. Mister Ellis is our manager, and I'm his assistant. Glad you could join us."

He looked very gallant, Ella thought, watching him remove his white pith helmet, uncovering a head of thick dark hair. He bowed in front of her. Out of the corner of her swollen eyes, she glimpsed more people gathering back along the pathway and heard the men mention that they were to be shown to their house. John had already told her how he had made the necessary preparations to accommodate a few of the men's wives on the island. Two years away from home and loved ones was too long for any man.

"Oh, I'm sorry, I know you must all be exhausted, but allow me to introduce you to our Banaban elders who have come down to greet your family." Ellis pointed to two older native gentlemen who had just arrived.

As Ella was escorted closer to the two men, her eyes were drawn to the striking cream necklaces adorning their dark necks, and she noticed that one gentleman was covered in tattoos the length of his aged body.

John moved ahead of her and spoke some strange words she had never heard before, shaking hands exuberantly with them, their heads nodding in unison.

"*Kona mauri,* Eri! *Kona mauri,* Tabanea!"

It was not until Ella was standing right in front of the two men that she realised their necklaces were not shells at all, but human teeth. While Ellis began her introductions, she felt nausea once again hit her stomach while the trembling in her legs was making her feel weak at the knees. They are cannibals, maybe headhunters, she told herself.

John realised what was happening and placed his arm around her waist. She turned to him with a look of amazement while he squeezed her tight and smiled. "Ella this is Eri and Tabanea, two of the elders of Uma village who have come down to welcome you."

Ella watched as the two old men both nodded and bowed, while the one with tattoos kept repeating, "*Thou tel te blasted, thou tel te blasted.*"

"Tabanea is saying the Banaban greeting he's learned in English for you." John moved closer to her and whispered, "He means, '*thou shall be blessed*', but he's pretty close. Just be pleasant and smile." He turned and replied, "Thank you, gentlemen. Yes, *Kona mauri* gentlemen… *Ko raba,* yes, thank you." He kept nodding his head in acknowledgment.

Ella kept seeing those strings of ugly, yellowing teeth that seemed to be looming ever closer. With all her efforts, she also started nodding, trying to force out a grin.

"I'm glad to see you've already met Tetabo, Missus Williams," Ellis interrupted. "We have assigned him as your house boy, and he's been hard at it learning English. Doing quite well too, if I do say so myself."

"Yeh sur… ee," Tetabo announced proudly.

"He'll be taking care of you and your new home and will be helping you to settle in as quickly as possible," Ellis continued, "so anything you need, please just ask Tetabo and he'll see to it."

He was silent a moment before he went on. "Now I'm sure you're all exhausted after such a long journey. Unfortunately, our new tramway hasn't been completed yet, so I'm afraid you will have to walk up to the house," he added, giving the order for their luggage to be collected.

Her body was beginning to ache all over as the native lads gathered up their belongings. The Captain was close behind them, still cradling a sleeping Gwennie. She was not going to let the pain hold her back as they began the slow ascent up the pathway that cut its way through the surrounding lush vegetation.

They were still being followed by at least half the crowd who had now broken into song. The eerie sound of their beautiful voices and harmonies drifted all around them, while the roar of the surf could be heard carrying up from the sea below. Apparently, they were the new attractions. She would soon find out just how rare white women and children were around these parts.

The pathway was neatly trimmed and swept clean as they passed a native village. The open-sided thatched houses were all in straight lines and looked well cared for. This definitely was not the home of savages, she told herself, looking around in awe. It was beautiful.

"Siree... Missy Missy... see... Uma," Tetabo gushed. Ella did not understand a word he was saying. "See... de... ta *maneaba*." His finger pointed excitedly to a large traditional building prominently placed in the middle of the village.

"Ella, Tetabo is telling you this is his village called Uma, and that's the *maneaba* he's pointing to, or as we call it, the village meeting house," John explained while Ella laughed at Tetabo's *Ingerlish*. She knew she was going to be in for some fun if this was the best he could do.

Ella noticed chickens moving around the grounds while a few pigs browsed on the ends of their tethers looking for the odd bit of food. Their houses were neatly positioned all the way down the slope to the edge of the sea. The tantalising odour of cooking and the strong scents of frangipani and ginger blossoms wafted towards them. The brilliant colour of the hibiscus and poinciana trees contrasted vividly with the lush green profusion of palm trees that precariously arched over the entire village.

It was now late afternoon, and the thick vegetation was filtering the stiff westerly breeze as they moved on. It was still hot, but by the time the sun's rays made the way down through the canopy of leaves, they were in a cooler environment where fine strands of sunlight danced all around them.

Tetabo was keeping them entertained with his English chatter and commentary, and Ella could not help laughing, as she was sure he did not realise half of what he was saying.

John had suddenly turned quiet when they rounded the bend, and a house came into view.

"Hose... him... here, yes... e sur!"

A newly built house stood before them on wooden stumps with a shiny tin roof. A front porch protected the entrance to the front door. But most surprising of all was the lack of windows. In their place were large wooden panels that opened like vertical shutters

"Well?" John asked, waiting for her reaction.

Ella felt speechless. The house was better than the ones back home, and it was all hers. "It's beautiful," she whispered, nodding with approval.

John called, "Come on, don't you want to see inside?" ascending the front steps, leaving Gwennie still sound asleep in Captain Cozens's arms. "Wait until you see the veranda out the back and the washroom," he boasted before disappearing through the front door.

Ella went to take her daughter from the Captain.

"Don't disturb her, Missus Williams. I'll just sit down with her here on the step while you get yourselves organised. The poor wee pet's exhausted," he murmured, rocking Gwennie's little body ever so gently.

Ella smiled at the big man before making her way up the front stairs trying to catch up to her husband.

While she was still adjusting her eyes to the darker interior, John rushed over to her. "Well, what do you think?"

The smile broke on her face before she uttered a word. "I don't believe it!" The house was supposed to be empty, but there were already pieces of good quality timber furniture in place. "Where did you find the furniture?" she asked, amazed.

"I made them all myself, especially for you," he said, leaning down to kiss her cheek. "Wait until you see the bedroom," he added, moving her through the hallway to the back of the house. He would not let her enter the room until she promised to cover her eyes.

"Can I look now?"

"You sure can."

As soon as Ella opened her eyes, she was stunned to see the most beautiful handcrafted timber bed, covered in bedclothes of frilly white lace. He had even made a matching dressing table for her.

"Where? How? You didn't make the bed linen too, did you?" she asked, seating herself on the side of the bed, trying to take in all she was seeing. She had to remind herself she was not dreaming.

"No, I haven't learned to sew yet," he laughed, joining her on the bed. "Well, what do you think?"

Ella kissed him. "It's all just so wonderful. So are you, Mister Williams!"

"Anything for you," he said, lifting her hand to his lips.

"But where did you get all this beautiful linen? It's exquisite," she said, running her fingers over the lace trim on the thick pillows.

"Well, I've been doing a bit of trading with some of the Norwegian seamen aboard the phosphate ships."

"Sir... ee me... yoo... wante... tis?"

There was no mistaking that voice as they both turned their attention to Tetabo standing at the doorway. His arms were laden with suitcases and Ella noted he was smiling from ear to ear.

"Where do you want Tetabo to put all the luggage, darling?" John translated.

Ella scampered to her feet and started to roll up her sleeves. Being the eldest of twelve children, she had always been used to toil, and now it was time to get down to some hard work. There were trunks to be unpacked as soon as they came up from the ship.

"Ella, you don't understand," John said, realising what she had in mind when he saw her rolling up the long sleeves of her poor soiled dress. "You can't do the work; it's Tetabo's job to sort out the house. You're the lady of the house now, and you'll offend him terribly if you interfere." He saw the strange look on her face. "Just tell Tetabo where you want everything, and he'll see to it. Now go and get yourself cleaned up; there's a wash house out the back."

She had forgotten how terrible she must look and, deciding not to argue, thought it better to investigate the washroom. She still did not feel comfortable with the idea of a servant at her beck and call.

The rest of her day was spent in a state of utter bedlam. The enthusiastic Tetabo would not let her lift a finger, and if she heard one more 'Missy, Missy,' pass his lips, she knew she would scream.

Gwennie, after sleeping so contentedly, had woken up full of life and taken an immediate liking to Tetabo. She had already named him Tea Tup, unable to get her little tongue around his name. In between Tetabo's efforts to organise the house, he would drop everything when Gwennie tugged on those terrible old trousers of his and give her his full attention. Ella was soon to learn that children always came first in Banaban eyes.

Their first evening meal had also proved chaotic when women from Tetabo's village started arriving with woven leaf baskets laden with fish and fresh tropical fruits and began to layout the meal on an old grass mat they had thrown down on the parlour floor.

John was finding the whole thing rather amusing and tried to tell her to relax.

Ella, on the other hand, being on the verge of complete exhaustion, was not at all amused but had no intentions of lying down and resting while there was so much to be done.

"Ella, you'll soon learn about island pace. There is no such word as 'time' when it comes to the natives. They will have no idea of what you're talking about."

"But how can you say that when everything the company does is set by the clock? And what about mealtimes?"

"All right, you have a valid point. I'll give Tetabo a watch, and you set him out some type of timetable, and he'll just have to learn to stick to it. But sweetheart, do try and give him a chance. You know he's only trying to help."

John would be back at work with the company, and she would be left to try and organise Tetabo and teach him some proper manners. She did not even have a clue what he was saying half the time.

It was late in the evening before the house was finally silent. Gwennie was happily asleep in the new bed her father had built for her. Tetabo had wanted to stay in case they needed him, but John had insisted on him returning to his village. Now as Ella sat at her dressing table pulling hairpins that held her chignon neatly in place, her hair fell in a long black tendril down her back. She had just come in from the washhouse after preparing herself for bed. The evening meal was still playing on her mind.

"You'll have to tell Tetabo we can't eat off the floor. It's just not done," she told John who was sitting up in bed watching her.

John leaned his masculine frame back against the fluffed-up pillows and wondered what the lads would think if they saw him right now. When you lived and worked with men for so long, you forgot what it was like to have a woman around, especially a lady like his Ella.

Ella picked up a brush and was beginning to count her strokes as she ran it through her loose hair.

"One... two... three..." The glow of the oil lamp next to her threw a soft veil of light, illuminating her body, especially when she lifted the brush with each new stroke.

John had noticed that Ella's face and hands had taken on a real glow during their days at sea. Now as he sat there intent on watching her every move, he could not help imagining that his own wife was looking more like one of the native women with her golden skin and masses of long dark hair, naked breasts, grass skirts and nothing else. John could feel himself stirring just watching her. The long virginal white nightdress covered her from head to toe, though he was sure he could catch a glimpse of flesh through all the gathered fabric, especially with the glow of the lamp silhouetting her delicate shape every time she swung the brush.

"Twenty-one... twenty-two..." she counted slowly, swinging her masses of unrestrained hair from side to side. Suddenly she stopped and turned around to face him. The flickering light caught the gleam of her green eyes.

John's carnal thoughts were abruptly interrupted the instant he glimpsed her striking eyes... she was definitely not a Banaban with those eyes, he told himself.

"John, you haven't answered me," she said, realising her husband was openly staring at her. "We can't keep eating off the floor," she repeated again feeling the beginnings of a blush. She did not like being looked at.

"Yes, darling. How much longer are you going to be?" He wished he could jump from the bed and take her there and then.

"John, you know I do fifty strokes each side," she laughed, quickening her pace.

"Well, hurry up, Ella, I want to go to bed," he said with a slight edge to his voice. He was beginning to get a terrible ache between his legs that needed comforting.

After finally reaching her one hundred strokes, she turned off the lamp on the dressing table and climbed into bed beside her husband, suddenly realising he was bare-chested.

"John, where's your nightshirt?"

Leaving the bed lamp alight beside him, he immediately reached for her, drawing her into his arms.

"You shouldn't be sleeping without your nightshirt on," she scolded while he was busy kissing her neck. The hardness between his legs had not gone unnoticed.

"You'll catch the death of cold like that."

It suddenly dawned on her the stupidity of what she had just said, when the temperature hovered permanently around ninety degrees.

"Ella, you're my wife, it's hot, and I've been living in the tropics for the past two years," he retorted, now running his fingers through her hair.

Ella knew he was losing his patience, and it was her duty to please her husband. She did love him so much, but sex had always been a chore for her, not something a lady enjoyed. She could still hear her mother's words; sex was something a wife endured.

John brought his mouth down onto her lips, kissing her tenderly. She responded to his mouth, trying not to encourage him too much. She did not want him to become overzealous. His passion only seemed to intensify when his hand moved over her small breast out-lined through the fine lawn cloth of her nightgown. As he moved his lips down along her neck, she could feel his fingers tampering with her gown. She tensed as his hand released the blue ribbon tie, expos-ing her naked breast.

"John! What are you doing?" she gasped, clutching for her night-dress, shocked by her husband's unusual behaviour. "What's come over you?"

Suddenly ashamed of himself, John pulled back, realising his mistake. He had to remember that his Ella was a lady. All these years apart from her had left him forgetting his manners. Recovering his gentlemanly composure, he leaned across to extinguish the flickering bedside lamp while Ella quickly secured her garment. In the darkness, his chest was still pounding, and he felt his whole body ache just picturing her naked white flesh, realising he had never seen her uncovered before. Yes, he had been living too long away from her, and all the island's beautiful naked women had him forgetting how to treat a lady. With Ella's encouragement and all the self-control he could muster, he obediently rolled on top of her limp body, lifting up the hem of her gown.

"Darling, I love you, and I promise we'll never be apart again," he whispered in her ear, relieved when he felt her slowly start to succumb to him.

"I love you too," she murmured.

As the sound of the ocean carried on the still night air, Ella dutifully surrendered to her husband's needs, hoping it would soon be over. Why did she have to think this way? She asked herself. Ella knew she loved him, and yes, he was a wonderful man. She just hoped she had not been away from him for too long.

CHAPTER TWO

BANABA

The Rock-Land

In the Beginning:

Millions of years ago, the land sat submerged under the surface of the vast sea. This particular large submarine mountain rose from the surrounding great depths of the ocean floor not far from the Earth's equator. The top of the seamount became encrusted with coral, growing and expanding until it finally broke the surface of the water. Then came the sea birds, landing on the exposed reef as a refuge against the expanse of the ocean. After countless years, the guano deposits or bird droppings began to build upon the coral key, eventually reaching a height of over sixty feet.

For some unknown reason, the mountain submerged back under the sea where it stayed until a great upheaval caused the warping of the ocean floor and once again brought the seamount back to the surface. Because of this powerful phenomenon the mountain now stood at the height of nearly 300 feet above sea level, this time bringing its load of guano back with it, changed by the sea and the forces of nature into what would become phosphorous rock.

On the surface, the mountain tip appeared to be just another new island. But this one was different. Due to the convulsions of the Earth's crust under the seabed, the newly formed island had been twisted and distorted, creating a myriad of caves and tunnels under the surface of the land, making it almost like the texture of a giant coarse sea sponge.

The birds happily came again, this time bringing with them seeds that germinated on the ground. Coconuts washed up against the shores and began to grow. The island soon became covered in thick vegetation, concealing its prized possession of phosphate in the lime rocks below.

Over the centuries that followed, many different people sailed past the island's virgin shores. They hardly noticed it simmering under the hot tropical sun, almost invisible to the rest of the world, and the ancient civilisation that had evolved there over time. It was not until 1804 that a British ship named the island, *Ocean*. It seemed confusing in sailing circles when some of their earlier admiralty charts referred to the island as *Paanopa*. Early European sailors had probably misunderstood the heavily accented Banaban word.

Meanwhile, the indigenous inhabitants, the Banaban people, oblivious to the complexities of the outside world, had a simple existence surviving on the plenitude of fish from the island's waters. The land ownership of this small isle, which consisted of only 1,470 acres, was uniquely complex and tied into their heritage and birthright. A man's status was based on how much land he owned, and no royal or chiefly lineage existed. The Banabans did not know that their strange-looking rocks scattered across their land would one day change their lives and island forever. This change would come with the arrival in 1900 of an *I-Matang*, a white man named Albert Ellis. While the Banabans had no understanding of English, and what this white man was saying, he seemed friendly and very different from the other white men that had come before.

Without any understanding of the island's inhabitants at all, Ellis had them placing their marks together with the new gifted European titles of King, Queen and Chief he had bestowed upon them and added to documents giving his company the authority and sole rights to mine the phosphate on their island for the next 999 years at an annual payment of fifty pounds.

As word spread rapidly through the outside world of Ellis's great discovery, so did the demand for the phosphate. The British government had never been interested in the island before, feeling it was too isolated and miles from nowhere. Now, due to his latest development, the island officially came under the control of the British Empire in January 1901, and the phosphate deposits also became part of the Empire's newly acquired acquisitions. Banaba was now officially known as Ocean Island and the Banaban people never realised the significance of the red and blue cloth that happily flapped in the cooling sea breeze.

No one could have foreseen then just what riches they had fallen upon and the beginning of wealth beyond what any of the Europeans could ever have imagined, while the struggle of the Banaban had just begun.

2. Ella and John Williams with their eldest daughter Gwennie at their new home Ocean Island 1905.

CHAPTER THREE

THE WAYS OF MEN

Ocean Island 1902

John Williams leaned forward on the edge of the straight-backed office chair intent on listening to Albert Ellis speak.

"Gentlemen, we have reached a real crisis point with the Banabans. Unless we can persuade a few of the younger ones to work for us, we're in a real bind." The worry clearly showed on his face.

Ellis had gathered all his heads of departments together in the hope that somehow, someone might be able to come up with an idea to make the local Banaban people see reason.

"Now, as you already know, gentlemen, the Banabans are refusing to gather and load any more rocks." His frustration was so apparent. Stroking his goatee beard, he continued, "We have a ship arriving shortly and no phosphate to load."

"But sir, I thought you'd already made an agreement to pay them for each basket they loaded?" Naylor, his assistant, said.

Harold Pope, the new office clerk, was seated next to John's left and was occupied with mopping the sweat from his brow with his large handkerchief.

John smiled to himself, slightly amused at the newcomer's antics. Obviously, he was not used to the tropics and with that dead-white complexion of his, he had better get used to it in a hurry.

"Well yes, I did, but I've realised that money has no meaning for them," Ellis replied, "and let's face it, they're rather a lazy lot. They'd all prefer to be out fishing and spend the rest of the day sleeping than do any sort of manual work."

Yeah, John thought, old Ellis has a real problem, but who could blame the Banabans. They seemed to be pretty bright to him. It was bloody hot here, so no wonder they wanted to find shelter under the shade of the nearest palm tree.

Captain Cozens looked across to John as they each realised what the other was thinking. Again, both men turned their attention to Ellis, making a point of keeping their mouths shut as Naylor spoke up again.

"Well sir, you personally seem to get on so well with the natives, so surely it's best you try and negotiate with them." Naylor used flattery; it was apparent he did not want to have to be the one to try and haggle with them.

Ellis had got along with the Banabans famously when he had first arrived, but lately, things had not been going his way. His usually calm and collected nature was starting to wane under pressure.

"George, what do you think?" Ellis informally addressed his elder brother who was the manager at the company's other settlement at Tabwewa, situated on the northwest side of the island.

"Well to tell you the truth, Bertie, I haven't got a clue," George Ellis replied. "Until we can recruit more labourers from the outer islands, our hands are virtually tied."

Ellis obviously was not happy with his brother's words and began scanning the faces of the other men seated in the room. His gaze fell on John, who up until now had not offered any suggestions. "What about you, Williams, any ideas?"

John's mind raced as he reluctantly stood up, trying to think of anything that had not already been said.

"Well, it's only a suggestion, sir, but what about sports?" he offered. It was the only thing that immediately sprang to mind.

"Sports?" Ellis questioned; his eyebrows raised. "In God's name, man, what has sports got to do with the Banabans?"

"Well sir," he said, his mind still racing, "it's just that as you know, all the company men here are so sports-minded and maybe we could get the Banabans involved in some sort of game." John could see his idea was not going over too well, so he quickly added, "You know sir, a bit of competition between the villages, except it's who can gather the most rocks instead."

John slowly sat down, feeling rather pleased with himself, even if Ellis did not seem particularly moved with his notion. It was amazing how the brain could come up with ideas when under pressure, he congratulated himself.

His thoughts were suddenly interrupted when George Ellis piped up. "What an excellent idea, Williams."

John turned to look at him.

"You know the villagers over at Tabwewa have always had a certain amount of rivalry with the village here in Uma." The elder brother was suddenly aglow as another new idea came to mind. "If we could promote, or, even better still, ignite that rivalry, it might just play into our hands." He grinned.

Albert Ellis's face also lit up as he started to comprehend his elder brother's words.

"Yes, that's not a bad suggestion, Williams," Ellis said slowly, turning his full attention back on John.

John had a feeling of relief. He had enough problems with his work as platelayer laying all the railway tracks around the island, without getting caught up in this sort of business.

Ellis once again scanned the faces of the men seated before him. Harold Pope was flushed a bright red and seemed distracted as more sweat dripped from his face. "I propose that my brother and I talk to the elders of the two villages in question and pose the idea to them."

Naylor, not one to miss an opportunity, quickly spoke up. "Yes, sir; an excellent suggestion." A look of relief flooded his face.

"Yes, a competition to gather the most rocks." Ellis seemed happier now. "Of course, we'll have to offer some sort of reward," he added, and his voice sounded almost reluctant.

"But sir, you said they weren't interested in money," Naylor eagerly reminded him.

"Well, they've taken a liking to our sugar and jam. That should do!" Ellis replied, looking pleased with himself.

As the tension in the room eased, the men began to relax. No one caught the glance that passed between John and his friend, Captain Cozens. They had never readily accepted the use of the white man's gifts to get what they wanted from the Banabans. It was two years now since Albert Ellis had first discovered the phosphate and the early Banaban hospitality so openly offered them now seemed to be wearing very thin. They had probably just started to realise that the company was really here for good, but being loyal company men, John and Cozens both kept their opinions definitely to themselves.

"Oh, Captain Cozens," Ellis suddenly asked, "how are the finishing touches going with the jetty?"

"Fine sir, we will be finished by the end of this week if the weather holds." Cozens's job relied much on good old Mother Nature.

"Very good; that means your men should be free to help with loading, then." Ellis really sounded brighter now.

After a few more questions to various staff members, the meeting came to a close. John and Cozens had started to make their way from the room when Ellis caught John's attention.

"How's your wife settling in now?"

"Settling in fine, sir, she seems to really like it here."

"Good to hear. I forgot to mention my wife has planned a welcome party for her this Saturday night so she can get to meet everyone." He shuffled through his coat pocket, trying to find the invitation his wife had made out.

"Oh thank you, sir, that's very kind of you and your wife. I'm sure Ella will be looking forward to it very much." John smiled.

Cozens stood there with a big grin on his face, amused at his friend's awkwardness. He knew John was not used to his new social standing since his wife had joined him.

As John took the invitation from the manager's hand, they started to make their way towards the opened door again.

"Before you go, Williams, how's that young Banaban lad working out at home?" Ellis asked.

John noted the tinge of apprehension in his voice; obviously, he thought John was also having some problems. He smiled. "He's not too bad at all, sir, except for the language barrier. Ella seems to be coping with him rather well, and our little Gwennie has taken a real shine to him."

Ellis looked rather surprised. "Well, that's good to hear, especially with all the trouble we're having with them at the moment, trying to get them to work."

"Yes, he seems a pretty good lad," he replied honestly.

"Well, just keep a good eye on him, you never can tell."

"Yes, sir!" John said, looking forward to getting back to work in the fresh air where the atmosphere was lighter.

Both men made their way quickly from the room before they were asked any more questions.

While John Williams was busy at the company's staff meeting, his new houseboy was making his way ever so slowly down the pathway towards *Uma* village. Stopping momentarily, he patiently waited for his small charge. Little Gwennie Williams happily tottered on behind him, listening to his every word.

He spoke a strange language, a mixture of his own native dialect with a few odd English words thrown in. Her little eyes lit up when he spoke as if she understood everything he was saying.

Stopping again to wait for her, he pointed to a palm tree where a giant coconut crab was scampering to the top. She watched, fascinated, drawing her tiny hand over her mouth while her new friend explained in detail the creature's important purpose in life. It did not seem to matter that she was so young, as Tetabo went about the serious business of passing on the same story he had been told as a young child.

On reaching his parent's *mwenga,* a house down in the village, Tetabo recognised the voice of his young aunt. She had come down from her village of Buakonikai up on the island's lush plateau to see his parents. Tetabo led Gwennie to a rattan mat spread out under the shade of the overhanging palm trees where the women and children were busy pounding pandanus leaves in preparation for weaving. Tetabo made the necessary greetings to his family that good Banaban manners decreed, while Gwennie, like all young children, was keen to play. She took an immediate liking to one young boy who was of a similar age. Even though she had no idea of what he was saying, she was captivated immediately when he began to show her pieces of broken coral he had gathered at his feet.

"Aunty, *Kona mauri*! It is good to see you," Tetabo greeted his mother's younger sister.

"*Kona mauri,* Tetabo!" She smiled, glad to see her nephew.

She had always been close to her sister's eldest boy because they were nearly the same age and had grown up together.

Tetabo noticed how well she looked. Childbearing had been kind to her, he thought.

"How is your new work with the *I-Matang* going?" she asked, noticing he had brought along a little *I-Matang* child with him.

"Oh, it is very good. Miti Wiriami is a grand I-*Matang* lady, and their little *tetei* is under my personal care," he boasted, indicating Gwennie.

His aunt giggled at her nephew's words. Tetabo's mother, who was nearby, nodded, feeling very proud of her son.

"You Tetabo, are a nurse-maid?" she teased.

Tetabo, feeling offended by his aunt's laughter, quickly retorted, "I am in charge of the Wiriami household, and that means caring for their daughter Gwennie until a suitable nurse-maid is found."

His aunt, realising she had offended him with her teasing, was eager to appease him. "Yes, you are a very important man now,

Tetabo. I will tell everyone in the village of your special work with the *I-Matang*."

Tetabo's chest swelled with pride at his aunt's words, and he glanced at Gwennie and young Ata crouched together.

"Look! Your Ata has made friends with Nei Gwennie," Tetabo stated, pointing to the two young children playing quietly together on the mat.

Tetabo's words seemed to fall heavily as everyone turned silently to look at the two children. No one made any comment, but the significance of the two children eagerly playing together was not lost on all of them. It was almost as if their kindred souls had been brought together; after all, they all knew that Ata was different.

* * *

Later that evening under cover of darkness, a lone figure made his way through the thick groves of coconut trees. Using only his night vision and heightened instincts, Captain Cozens deftly moved his large frame along the trail that meandered towards the lush plateau where the Banaban village of Buakonikai was situated.

He had made this trip many times before and knew exactly where he was going. Nearing the outskirts of the village he stopped, resting against the butt of a large palm, while he took the time to light his tobacco pipe. His blue eyes scanned the traditional houses while the dying embers of the night fires glowed weakly under the moonlit sky. Sucking deeply on his pipe, he made sure that no one was wandering around the village. The Banabans had a habit of going to bed rather early and rising with the sun. Assuring himself that he would not be seen, he quickly moved towards the *mwenga* on the far side of the village.

Quietly entering the darkened hut, he could smell the heady scent of coconut oil and fragrant blossoms. It was her smell; he knew she was here waiting for him as he made his way towards her pandanus-sleeping mat. Kneeling beside her, he started to undress, his eyes once again adjusting to the darkened interior. She had been waiting for him and, lifting herself up, she reached out to touch him. Consumed by desire, he silently pulled her into his arms, his large gentle hands stroking down the length of her lush black hair that fell past her naked buttocks.

She too was longing to have him, and her hands worked adeptly at removing his restricting garments while their mouths smothered each other in kisses, trying to silence the anticipating groans of passion that escaped their lips. When the last of Cozens's clothing fell to the floor, she pulled herself away from him and, gathering up a nearby coconut shell, poured her special love brew of coconut oil and flowers over his nakedness. With the potent exotic mix trickling over his rippling muscles, she expertly rubbed the oil into his white skin while his need for her was becoming unbearable.

He felt as if he was on fire as her fingers and hands teased him on. Sensing his hunger, she pushed him down onto her sleeping mat and mounted his large body, feeling his hardness pressing between her thighs. He could wait no longer; lifting her lithe frame with his strong arms, he pushed her down onto him.

The young woman let out a gasp as he thrust deep inside her. His thrusts only heightening the level of her arousal while her long tresses of wild black hair cascaded over him. Rocking her back and forth they were both lost now in a frenzy of wanton lust, thrashing about on the floor of the darkened *mwenga*.

Caught up in their passion, they did not notice the piercing blue eyes silently watching them through the darkness. A small boy lay on another sleeping mat across from the couple watching their every move.

3. John Williams (left) with Father Pujabet (right) and his work gang Ocean Island 1920s.

CHAPTER FOUR

WHEN THINGS GO WRONG

Company's Facilities Uma 1902

Six Weeks Later:

"Sir, we can't load the phosphate. It's still too wet," Cozens advised Ellis who stood beside him inspecting the loading facilities.

A muffled sound of disbelief escaped Ellis's lips before he turned to Cozens and spoke.

"Captain Cozens do I have to remind you this ship's been moored here trying to load phosphate for the past two weeks?"

"Yes sir, I am very aware of the problem, but I can't help the wet weather, sir," he answered, trying to keep his temper in check. What did Ellis expect him to be, a miracle worker?

Even though this was the second day running without rain, it had been such a wet year that the phosphate was full of water and the small dryer they had set up could not keep up with the backlog of wet phosphate.

"All right... all right Captain, I know it's not your fault, but we've got all this phosphate stacked here waiting to ship, and now it's too wet to load," Ellis lamented, lifting his hat to wipe the sweat from his brow with his white handkerchief.

Cozens could not help feeling sorry for him, realising that they had finally got over the immediate Banaban problems and the jetty was finished, but now their plans had been dashed once more, this time by the rain.

Ellis, almost as if talking to himself, said, "If the directors in London had let me build a tin roof over the mining area as I'd wanted to do from the very beginning, we wouldn't have this problem." Turning back to watch the loading gangs filling their large cane baskets with phosphate rocks, he continued, "all to do with money of course."

"Yes sir, it usually is," Cozens replied. Having worked for the company's directors for years in various guano-mining operations throughout the Pacific, he knew the problems Ellis was facing.

His last post had been supervising the Baker Island guano mine, and he had been given the orders to abandon the island and move all the company's plant to their new venture here on Ocean Island. His old friend John Williams had been working for the company on North West and Lady Elliot Islands off the Queensland coast of Australia, and he too had been given the orders to abandon the islands and move their plant here.

Ocean Island was a new type of mining operation. Previously, they had mined the guano or bird droppings by just scooping the residue built up on the surface ground, but here this phosphate was actually impacted within the rocks and care had to be taken not to let the limestone from the surrounding coral pinnacles mix in with the pure phosphate and contaminate the load.

It was not until Ellis had one of these strange looking rocks that had been lying around the Sydney office analysed, that the company's fortunes had changed. The word among the staff had been that the company was having major money problems. If it had not been for Ellis's discovery of this new phosphate of lime deposits here on Ocean Island and now on Nauru situated 180 miles to the north-west, Cozens knew he would probably be in some other far-flung corner of the world scratching around for God only knows what. He was also sure it would not be nearly as pleasant as this island and its inhabitants.

Cozens asked, trying to lighten Ellis's mood, "Sir, when is the new engineer arriving?"

"Shortly, I hope... but I can tell you now the only way to beat this water business is to roof the mining area."

Ellis became silent once again, lost in thought. After a moment, he continued, "All right, Captain, I'm off to inspect Williams's gang. See how he's getting on with the new track laying." He turned, look-ing up towards the eastern mining area.

"Very well, sir, I'll keep the loading going here as quickly as pos-sible under the conditions." He watched Ellis begin to make his way towards the flatcar that was waiting for him.

After stepping onto the flatcar, Ellis settled himself on the small timber seat while two Gilbertese boys took up a position standing behind him. They began to expertly push the flatcar along using their two long wooden poles. Ellis looked immaculate in his white suit and pith helmet. A pair of sensible canvas shoes adorned his feet, in what was now considered the ideal tropical garb by the prominent staff on the island.

Passing the grade behind Uma village, Ellis caught glimpses of everyday Banaban life as the people went about their daily routine.

Shaking his head, Ellis was annoyed at the thought of the Banabans and their growing attitude towards his company's presence. They had been such a likeable race of people during his original negotiations, but now nothing they did seemed to make them happy. Their demands were growing daily, and they were starting to insist on eating white man's food. Of course, Ellis had realised that with the mining operations destroying their food trees, they would have to be provided with food, and like all other native peoples, the Banabans had taken an immediate liking to the white man's sugar. So now the company had set up a trading store to trade food and provisions as part of their negotiated rations.

The Banabans were even insisting on drinking water being supplied to them. They were becoming so lazy that the women had stopped making the daily trip down into the *bangabanga;* water caves which had been the only supply of drinking water before the company's arrival.

Ellis's daydream was interrupted when he noticed the deep-golden skinned children up ahead playing dangerously close to the edge of the new track. Directing his men to stop the flatcar, he stood up from his seat and ordered the children in their native tongue to keep away from the tram line. The children quickly scurried away, fearing the *I-Matang's* words. Once at a safe distance they turned back cheekily to pull faces at the strange ghostly looking *I-Matang,* while the two Gilbertese men started the momentum of the small flatcar rolling again.

Yes, he would have to draft a memo when he got back to the office forbidding all children from playing on or along the tram tracks. That was all he needed at the moment, having to explain the unfortunate accidental death of one of the Banaban's beloved children. That was a problem he could well do without.

The flatcar moved faster, now building up speed as it glided along the freshly laid tracks, and the sounds of the children's laughter faded. Ellis felt more frustrated as he realised, he now had to contend with another new obstacle. A few of the men's wives and children had just arrived, joining his wife and daughter, Joan. He feared that the families, except for his own, of course, meant trouble.

As the flatcar neared the next curve in the line, his thoughts turned to another growing dilemma, this time among his own men; a problem he hoped would at least be solved somewhat by the presence of the wives and children who had just arrived.

Ellis had seriously considered a career as a Protestant preacher before joining the company years earlier. He still conformed to the Protestant beliefs and doctrines by shunning the sins of liquor and the flesh. Many of his men had no such leanings and had in fact taken a real liking to the beautiful over-friendly young Banaban women. Despite all Ellis's efforts to curb his men's immoral habits, he had heard the rumours of his men taking native women as concubines.

Florence, his wife, had already become a bit too friendly with the local minister and had heard some of the gossip from the Banabans. He did not know how much longer he could ignore the problem, but really, he had enough to contend with, without worrying about where his men were spending their evenings.

Breaking through the dense canopy of the jungle surrounding this part of the track, the flatcar suddenly came into a large cleared area where the sun's rays shone down unabated. Ellis, unprepared for the intense glare coming off the phosphate diggings around him, squinted as he made out the group of men working up ahead.

* * *

"Tetabo, where are you?" Ella called as she entered the house, her eyes not yet accustomed to the interior light.

"Here, Missy... me here in de eatin... room," Tetabo called from the kitchen.

"Oh, there you are!" She came through the door.

Tetabo smiled, his hands covered with slimy, moving octopus tentacles.

She was immediately taken aback, mesmerised, staring at the ugly thing in his hands.

"Oh my goodness, it's still alive. That thing is moving," Ella stammered, her eyes bulging in disbelief as the creature's bulbous head flopped to one side.

"Yes Missy... he gone eat," he replied, grinning, trying to break the grip of one of the long tentacles that was crawling up the length of his left arm.

"Tetabo do you have to do that in the house?" she asked him in disgust, "and please Tetabo, I'm a Madam, not a Missy! You must try and learn the correct English words now."

Tetabo, not easily dissuaded, smiled at her, showing a full set of healthy gleaming teeth.

"I okay Madam, me got *te geeka*, octopus for you and Miti Wiriami who ate... veree gone," he beamed lifting the tangled mass of withering suckers and quivering flesh up for her closer inspection.

She quickly backed away, realising it was useless trying to reason with him. After all, as John had pointed out, he was only trying to help.

"Please, Tetabo just get rid of that thing. Right now!" She turned her nose up at the idea of eating such a horrid looking creature. "Please, I do insist."

"But Madam, *te geeka* vere gone fish. Me catching jest fer you," he replied, making her feel suddenly guilty.

"Veree gone... you see!" To emphasise his words, he rubbed his belly with one free hand, covered in bright red rings where the octopus had been suctioned on.

Shaking her head, Ella knew she was beaten. How could she ever argue with such a happy smiling man with a terrible grasp of the English language and a liking for the strangest of sea creatures? Making her way back out the kitchen door, she paused, recalling why she had been looking for Tetabo in the first place. "Oh yes, Tetabo, we have an extra guest for dinner tonight. Captain Cozens will be joining us."

"Okay Missy, *te geeka* veree gone fish, he like veree much." His eyes lit up with excitement while he once again made his speech about his prized octopus and his free hand grasped a large sharp knife.

She escaped from the strong fishy smell permeating the room. She definitely did not feel hungry, knowing what was on the menu. *Veree gone* indeed!

Fleeing back out into the peace of her new back garden, she saw Gwennie was still happily playing with small pieces of coral under the shade of a large mango tree. Moving towards her daughter, Ella shaded her eyes and looked up, marvelling at the island's bright blue sky. The rain had finally stopped, and she was enjoying her first taste of island life without the annoying tropical downpours.

She had been here just on six weeks and still could not help feeling overawed by this strange place. Even in her backyard that had been carved out of the thick surrounding jungle, large razor-sharp pinnacles rose from the ground. John had told her they were made of limestone. The perimeter of the yard was ringed with a thick grove of tall swaying coconut palms, and the vibrant colour and the sweet scent of frangipanis and hibiscus wafted on the hot tropical air. Pretty yellow flowers grew wild in the full sun on the edge of the clearing and swayed gently with the light breeze drifting in through the breaks in the undergrowth.

Ella seated herself in the large garden chair next to her daughter's rug and picked up the letter she had been writing to her family back home. Yes, she could not leave Tetabo and what she had just witnessed out of the letter.

I've never seen anything like it... she began to write in her fancy scrawl.

She pondered her new life here and how very different it was to living back in Australia. Ella was determined to fit in, and she had to admit there was a certain charm about island life once you got used to it.

Tomorrow Tetabo is taking me on my first visit down to see his village at Uma... she quickly wrote, feeling the excitement rise at the thought of her trip and her meeting with the Banabans.

* * *

John Williams looked up and saw the small flatcar coming towards them through the heat haze rising from the bare, freshly cleared ground. The stiff upright figure of Albert Ellis was unmistakable in the middle of the vehicle's seat.

John turned to his work gang, eager to urge them on. "Hurry up lads, the big boss is coming," he warned them while they chipped away at the surrounding rocks. The boys bent their backs further into the task at hand, the sweat glistening off their bodies. John was a hard taskmaster, but he knew his gang of big strong Gilbertese boys was up to the job. He also knew that he was not in the good books with Ellis at the moment; not since he had suggested the idea of getting the Banabans to play sports.

Ellis, having fully backed the idea at first, set up the sports day as suggested using the company's resources and manpower, only to find that the Banabans were wholly opposed to any form of competition among their fellow men. The whole thing had ended up being a disaster and John had tried to keep a low profile since the fiasco. Anyway, how was he supposed to know? If the outcome had not been so serious, the whole day would have been looked upon as being totally hilarious with Banabans running in circles all over the sports field while they waited for their mates from the opposing village to catch up.

John watched from under the protective brim of his pith helmet as the flatcar stopped a short distance away. He lifted his arm to wave before moving forward to greet his boss.

"Good to see you, sir, we're nearly finished," John reported, shaking the manager's hand.

Ellis looked around to survey the men hard at work. "Good to see," he replied, stepping forward to get a better look at the operations. "I want you and your men to go down and try and give Captain Cozens a hand at the dryers."

John quickly fell in behind him, trying to keep up as he strode towards the work gang.

Before John got the chance to speak to him again, Ellis greeted the workmen in their Gilbertese dialect.

"Sir, we still have another day's work here before the entire line is fully operational," he tried to explain.

Ellis turned back to look at him. "Well, it will just have to wait! We have problems with loading; the phosphate's too wet."

"Yes, sir." John realised there was no point trying to reason with him.

"Just get down there with your men straight away and help them get that ship loaded."

"Yes, sir, straight away!" he replied, beckoning his men.

As they started to make their way down the track towards Uma, Ellis stayed behind to wander around the diggings.

God only knew what he and his men were supposed to do with the wet phosphate. What a shame Ellis was so uptight lately; he really was not his old self. He had always been such an easy-going, likeable sort of chap. Ah well, that was part of the responsibilities of being the island's manager. John wondered if he was also having troubles at home, adjusting to family life. Whatever the problem was, he hoped he would get it sorted out soon. Ellis was becoming quite unbearable.

4. Captain Cozens (Uncle Will) inspecting surfboats Ocean Island early 1900s.

CHAPTER FIVE

LEARNING THE CUSTOMS

Ocean Island 1902

Ella laughed at the humorous way Captain Cozens recounted the story of his first landing on the island. The evening meal of octopus that Tetabo had insisted on preparing had turned out very good indeed. It was just a shame, she thought, she had seen the poor ugly thing before it was cut up and cooked ready for their dinner guest.

The three of them had now retired for a sherry out on the veranda overlooking the beautiful full moon that was rising across Home Bay. While the Captain continued on with his comic story of trying to land in a half-swamped boat, Ella knew precisely how he must have felt at the time. Somehow, when he told the story, you could not help laughing, especially at his description of trying to communicate and give instructions to the locals who did not have a clue what he was talking about. From the moment she first met the big man when he lifted her from the surfboat, she had liked him. The Captain was not only a gentleman, but he also had a boyish sense of humour. No wonder he and John had become such good friends.

Suddenly, through the men's laughter, she heard the beautiful voices drifting up from Uma village below on the point. The harmonies and blend of sounds were lovely and melodic.

The men stopped talking, also taken by the singing.

"They definitely know how to sing," Cozens said, his mood softening. He seemed distracted, she thought, as though his mind was somewhere else.

"Beautiful voices," John said. "They never seem to tire of singing and dancing. They are at it every night. You can almost set your watch to them."

"Yes, it makes wonderful evening entertainment, being serenaded every night," she said, relaxing back in her cane chair to enjoy the sound.

"John tells me you're visiting Uma village tomorrow with Missus Ellis! I'm sure you'll enjoy it."

"Yes, I'm really looking forward to it. If the rest of the Banabans are anything like Tetabo, I'll be in for a real treat." Ella smiled, thinking of some of Tetabo's antics.

"I can assure you they are wonderful people with a very different culture to ours. Does take some getting used to though," Cozens replied. Ella noticed his fingers tapping in time with the steady beat of the music on the arm of his chair.

"Yes, I've already realised that. I'm wondering why those old men wear those horrible teeth necklaces?"

"Ah, yes, that's a fascinating story," Cozens replied. "The Banabans use them to recall their family history with each tooth representing an ancestor. They use them during their storytelling to remember the lives and skills of each relative going back over the generations.

"So, they are dead ancestors?" Ella innocently enquired.

"Yes." Cozens laughed. "The teeth are not removed until after their death. They are considered a precious and prized possession among the Banabans."

"I wasn't sure what they were when I first saw them," Ella replied, relieved to find out they were not some part of some savage torturous ritual or war trophy as she had first imagined.

John broke into the conversation. "Captain, will you tell Ella how she must belch if the Banabans give her some food? She won't believe me when I tell her it's a sign of good manners with them."

"John's right, Missus Williams, you make sure you give a good loud belch after you've finished eating if the Banabans ask you to share a meal with them, or you'll get the whole village offside." All humour was suddenly gone from his voice.

Ella at first believed the men were just having fun with her but Cozens was not joking.

"You are serious, aren't you?" she asked. "And how am I supposed to let out a loud belch, if I don't know how?"

"Well, I suggest, darling that you either learn quickly or don't eat any food down there," John suggested, smiling at his wife.

"John, she can't refuse to eat their food, or they'll be offended, thinking their food isn't good enough for her."

"How about I cancel the trip?" she suggested, realising her little planned visit was turning into more than she had bargained for.

"Now Ella, you've been here six weeks, and Tetabo's family have asked you personally to visit them and their village. Great honour, you know," John replied. "If you don't go, you'll insult his family terribly."

"Sounds as if I'm going to insult them whatever I do." Her previous enthusiasm for the trip had now vanished.

"Just go along and pretend to eat and belch if you have to. Missus Ellis will know the procedure. You'll have a wonderful time; just enjoy yourself," Cozens suggested, laughing at the look on Ella's face.

"Here, do you want me to give you a few belching lessons right now?" he asked, breaking into a real belly laugh.

"No, thank you, Captain," Ella announced, pulling a face at her dinner guest. "I'll try and pretend, thank you." She tried being solemn, but it was no use with the Captain and her husband carrying on.

Later as the night went on, the Williamses laughed and reminisced and spoke of home with their dinner guest. The night was once again quiet, with only the sound of their laughter and the pounding surf breaking down on the reef below carried on the evening breeze.

Down at Uma village, the evening dance had finished. Now the villagers, together with their children, gathered around one of the elders. They had spread their pandanus mats on the ground all around him and sat silently with legs crossed, listening to his every word. The embers from their cooking fires gave off a warm glow, lighting up the faces at the gathering.

Old Eri held them all captivated with his storytelling. The children's eyes were opened wide while they listened in awe at his incredible tale. Tonight's story was an important one that Eri knew very well; a story about not only his own survival but also the survival of the entire Banaban people.

"... it was before the arrival of the *I-Matang* and the arrival of the missionaries. It was the greatest drought this island has ever experienced. After many moons, even the water from the *bangabanga* was gone, and all our food trees had died. Only the ironwood scrub and saltbush by the sea and the large *Calophyllum* trees up near Buakonikai were still alive..." Eri's words seemed to echo through the silent night.

"... our people were living on the fluid they could suck from the eyes of the fish they caught. But after a time, people became ill. The fish, too, seemed to sense that the island was bad and stayed away from our shores. The men who were still able paddled out in their *te waa* to try and catch fish and collect rainwater that fell farther out to sea. Every day we would watch the big rain clouds come, and every day they would pass by or drop their precious load in the sea beyond our reach..." The sadness and despair were apparent in the old man's words.

"I was engaged to marry Nei Marawa from Buakonikai on the full of the fourth moon at the season of the Pleiades. But she and her family, like the rest of their villages, were too far away from the sea. Once they became too weak and sick, they could not make the journey down to the shore to fish. They died where they fell, and their surviving loved ones were too weak to prepare them for the death ritual, the 'Straightening of the Ways' and the special spell called, 'The Lifting of the Head'." He paused, now taking a deep breath before he continued. He could see the fear showing in their eyes.

"... those who survived grew weaker and very sick. Their gums rotted in their mouths, their teeth fell out, their bodies became covered in ulcers and sores. As more people collapsed and died, they lay where they had fallen, for everyone was too weak now. Here in Uma village, we were slightly better off because we were close to the sea, and my own mother would take my brother and me down to the water. She would sit us in the shallow ponds to let our skin take in the soothing moisture of the seawater, while our father used the last of his strength to paddle his *te waa* in search of rainwater. My own mother became so weak that one day as we sat soaking up the moisture in the shallow pools of the reef, she fell asleep and drowned as the tide rose over the reef ..." Eri wiped the single tear from the edge of his right eye.

"... all around us now there was death and great despair. Not one survived who had not lost most of his own family and loved ones..." The old man was building up to the main part of his tale, feeling the same familiar pangs of grief as if it had all only happened yesterday.

"... you see we realised, the ones who were still living, that we had brought the Curse of Nakaa down upon us and our island..." He paused now, hearing the usual gasps of shock and horror from his attentive listeners, at the mere mention of the curse.

"... For now, our dead ancestors were caught in the great pits of the evil spirit Nakaa in the land between the living and the dead. Because they had not received the proper burial rituals, their souls were damned for eternity to suffer in his pit and to haunt the island in search of salvation..."

The young ones huddled close to their parents for protection, a sudden chill filling the night air. They could feel the spirits of their tormented ancestors hovering nearby now.

"One day, when all was almost lost, and the people from our village numbered fewer than one hundred, a *te I-Matang* came in his great big *te waa* to our island. It was one of the blackbirding ships, but the captain took mercy on us and took my father and me and all the other survivors to Opah Island near Honolulu. Here we grew strong again, and after six years away from Banaba, my father died. Realising I owned no other land anywhere else but here on Banaba, I finally returned to my rightful home..." Eri swept his hands out across the island to emphasise his words before reaching the end of his story.

Now slowing his pace, he raised his voice to carry on the still night air accentuating his final words.

"... but we the Banaban people did survive. We returned here, and now we flourish..." His listeners seemed to sigh with relief while Old Eri continued, and the tone of his voice took on another edge. "But... the legend says that one day we must find a home for our children's children that is not haunted by the ghosts of our unburied dead."

Later that evening, while the full moon rose to its zenith in the balmy night sky, many of the villagers from Uma slept restlessly, tossing on their sleeping mats, sure that they could still hear the wails of their ancestors carrying on the wind.

The next day dawned with not a cloud in the sky. Ella wished it had rained and given her an excuse to call off her visit to the village with her new friend Missus Florence Ellis. Even though they were not on a first-name basis yet, they had already developed a bond since the welcoming party Florence and her husband had held in Ella's honour.

As they stood in the centre of Uma village, a large group of Banabans surrounded them, grinning and smiling, watching the women's every move and eager to draw their attention. They watched one of the men begin to scale the tall swaying coconut palm. One of the elders had sent him on the mission to get their honoured guests a refreshing drink. Ella had never tried fresh coconut juice straight from the tree before, but she knew there was no backing out now. Shading her eyes, she followed Florence's example and observed while the muscular dark body of the man quickly scampered higher up the trunk of the tree.

Ella suddenly blinked; thinking she was seeing things. Opening her eyes wider, she stared back at the man scaling the tree.

Oh, my goodness! She told herself, shocked and unbelieving. The man above them had no covering under his grass skirt. Even with his dark skin, Ella could clearly make out all the gentleman's private parts dangling freely from under him. Embarrassed, she turned to Florence, who had also looked away when she realised the spectacle overhead. They looked at each other, shocked, while everyone else around them showed no concern.

Florence quietly took her hand. "Just keep smiling, and don't say anything. We don't want to offend them," she whispered.

Tetabo must have thought she was looking a little sickly when he saw Missus Ellis holding her up and quickly moved in. "Missy... Madam you rite?" he asked.

Ella turned to look at him, a strange stare on her face.

"She's all right, thank you Tetabo; it's just the heat." Florence smiled at him. "A refreshing drink will help her. Do you mind if we just sit down a moment while we wait for our drink?" she asked, eager to get away herself without offending their hosts.

"Yes, Missy... Madam," he replied and quickly gave orders to the village women to put down the guest mats under the shade of the big breadfruit tree.

Florence was still quietly assuring a startled Ella that everything was all right while she escorted her to the mat. "I'm sorry, dear, I had no idea myself there was nothing under those grass skirts. Just assumed there would be of course. We both should have realised."

Thank goodness her Tetabo had been wearing white man's trousers since beginning work at their house, Ella thought. Now, as they waited for their drink, Ella's mind ran over the previous events of the day.

They had both survived the luncheon held in their honour in the big meeting house. Having to sit in front of the entire village while everyone watched them eat was only the beginning of the ordeal to come. There were about ten elders present with each one of them adorned with those scary teeth necklaces. Obviously, it was some type of status symbol among the village elders. The men had only begun to eat after Ella and Flo had been served first, while the women entertained them with singing and dancing.

Florence had just told her to pick at her food and appear eager with what she was eating. Ella could not believe it when she saw canned sardines sitting on her big banana leaf, liberally covered in what appeared to be strawberry jam.

She was about to protest to her new friend when Florence smiled and whispered, "Don't worry, it tastes better than it looks, so please just eat it."

Ella obediently did what she was told, trying to turn the grimace on her face into a smile. Her eager hosts watched her every move as the horrible mix of oily sardines and sweet jam assaulted her taste buds.

Before she had time to protest, her hosts were busy putting more food on her leaf. Now she had what appeared to be silvery slithers of raw fish in front of her. Hesitantly looking at Florence, she watched horrified as her friend eagerly scooped the raw fish into her mouth, enjoying it. Ella followed suit by gingerly placing one small strip on the end of her tongue and tentatively chewing on it. She was amazed at just how tender and tasty the fish was and noted the similarity to eating tinned salmon or tuna.

After more strange concoctions of fruit, fish and the white man's canned bully beef that the Banabans called *bullamacow* presented to them, they finally finished their meal to then witness the women of the village sitting down to eat the leftovers.

It was during that time that the first sounds of loud belching started as one after the other the men took turns to show their appreciation for the feast they had just eaten. Finally, as the last terrible sound reverberated across to where the ladies were sitting, Ella looked up, trying to keep her embarrassment in check, seeing all eyes eagerly on them. Florence next to her discreetly half-covered her open mouth with her hand and let out a sound that Ella thought resembled a deep moan, while all the audience smiled and nodded their appreciation. Even Florence turned to look at her, smiling profusely and urging Ella to follow her example.

Ella knew she was on her own now and moved her hand to her lips. Opening her mouth wide, trying to let out a similar deep groan, she was astounded when a loud belch rose up from her poor stomach, bringing a strong fishy taste of fish oil and sickly strawberries. She was so embarrassed!

Florence quickly congratulated her when she saw the Banabans' happy reactions.

"Well done, Missus Williams. You've made them all very happy," she said, patting her on the back.

Slowly looking up, Ella could see the approving nods and smiles of the Banabans. The elders were grinning and nodding from ear to ear, as she tried to regain her usual demeanour.

* * *

Now as the two of them sat in the shade of the large tree looking at the freshly gathered coconuts, Ella drank tentatively from the hole cut in the top of one of the fruit. The taste was sweet and warm, not unpleasant at all. She still was trying to wipe the terrible image of the man's naked nether regions from her mind.

Thank goodness their visit was nearly over. The people had indeed been wonderful, even overwhelming, in their friendliness towards them but, as George Cozens had told her, they were from a very different culture that did take a bit of getting used to.

"Missy... Madam... we go girlees white *mwenga*." Tetabo smiled, eagerly noticing the colour had returned to Ella's face.

After saying goodbye to the elders, the women escorted Ella and Florence, with Tetabo tagging along as their interpreter, away from the village where a large heavily covered thatched hut was situated. It looked different from the other ones back in the village. Not only was it set aside but also no men, including Tetabo, were permitted to enter the cleared grounds surrounding the hut.

The hut's walls were covered with thick palm matting. Before entering the area, Tetabo took the ladies aside and explained as best he could that they were entering the special house where all village girls went when they reached the knowing age. The girls must remain until they were full-fledged women, and they were ready for their wedding day. He also told them in his limited English, that they would greatly honour the girls by meeting with them. They were taken aback when he said the girls were not only forbidden from leaving the hut, but they must not let the sun's rays touch their skin. It was essential to do this, he told them, so they would become a good bride.

"Like Missy... Madam," he proudly stated, pointing at them.

Ella and Florence knew his English was not good, but he was not making any sense now, and they both felt more confused than ever.

Tetabo bade them farewell, saying he would wait for them back in the village so he could escort them back home.

The women lowered their parasols as they were led in through the slightly opened door. They were blinded by the darkened interior; the heady scent of sweet flowers and coconut was overpowering while the sound of nervous giggles erupted all around them. It took them both a few moments to adjust to their new surroundings and see the pretty pale smiling faces gathered together.

Now Ella realised what Tetabo was trying to tell them. The older girls had virtually gone fair, with skin paler than their own. It was amazing, something hard to believe. If they had not been half naked and dressed in short grass skirts with flowers in their hair, Ella thought some of them could have passed for their daughters.

Their escorts led them through to the centre of the hut where a large grass mat with intricate patterning was spread. After they were seated, one of their companions addressed the young girls who moved forward, eager to sit close to them. Ella could not understand a word they were saying, except she kept hearing the word *Matang*, which of course referred to them. While Ella and Florence smiled back at the admiring glances, the pretty friendly girls were oohing and aahing at their appearance.

Ella realised they must have never been so close to white women before; the young girls seemed very taken by their clothing. She felt at ease here among these friendly young women and moved forward to show the girls her long string of pearls. With her urging, small pale hands reached out to touch her strand of pearls. Amazed at the feel of these strange necklaces, the girls then started to touch the silk stockings adorning the women's legs. They all broke out in laughter at the various reactions by some of the young women who were eager to touch the fabric of their dresses. Ella and Florence were enjoying the innocent responses of the girls.

Some looked no more than mere children, Ella thought. They did not even take offence with some of the girls' inquisitive natures when they lifted their dresses to see what they looked like underneath. Luckily for Ella and Florence, the layers of petticoats and bloomers prevented them from any further embarrassment.

After the initial excitement of their arrival had calmed, the girls began to entertain them with singing and dancing.

"Isn't it wonderful to see such a primitive people as the Banabans with the moral understanding to shelter and protect their innocent young women like this?" Ella asked, turning to Florence.

"Yes, I suppose it solves the problem of them having children out of wedlock. You know they have arranged marriages?" Florence replied. "Their parents have already betrothed them to suitable partners at a very young age."

"Really!" Ella was truly amazed looking around at all the happy, grinning faces. She doubted if she would be this happy if her parents had organised a husband for her.

"Yes," Florence said, lowering her voice. "Of course, the good Reverend and his church are trying their best to curb this behaviour among the natives." She smiled.

"Really?" Ella responded.

No wonder Captain Cozens tried to warn her about their different culture; it would take some getting used to all right.

The singing had erupted all around them, and Florence turned to watch the young women now dancing provocatively in front of them, their hips twirling in rhythm with the music. Probably one of their mating dances she had also heard about from the good Reverend she thought, turning back to smile at Ella.

Ella sat mesmerised, watching the young women move gracefully, twisting and spinning their hips while their hands moved fluidly in strange patterns. Their young nubile breasts gleamed under the fine layer of coconut oil, highlighting their paler skin colour. She could not help picturing these beautiful young girls being delivered up like lambs to the slaughter.

Florence, realising Ella had probably had enough of Banaban culture to contend with for one day, did not tell her about the other bit of scandal the good Reverend had discussed with her. Especially now that she had heard Ella talk of Captain Cozens being her husband's good friend. The good Captain was gaining quite a reputation on the island, and his disgusting dalliances among the natives were now openly accepted among the Banabans.

5. Company man visiting Banaban woman in Buakonikai village Ocean Island early 1900s.

CHAPTER SIX

HARD LESSONS IN LIFE

Buakonikai Village 1908

"*Kona mauri,* Ata!" the big *Matang* man greeted him.

"*Kona mauri,* sir!" Ata replied, his eyes steadily fixed on the ground at his feet.

His upbringing, like that of all his fellow young Banabans, had been one of learning respect for his elders and because he had not yet reached the age of manhood, he was still living in the *mwenga* of his *tina,* or his mother, as the *I-Matang* put it.

As the white man made his way down the path leading away from the village, the boy slowly lifted his eyes, watching the *I-Matang* disappear. His beautiful piercing blue eyes that so belied his Banaban heritage were steadily following the man's every move. The boy's skin glowed a warm golden brown, but if one was to look closely where his grass skirt, known as a *riri,* slung low on his young loins a thin band of the purest of white skin could be seen. Ata was the name his *tina* had given him though he was not a pure-blooded Banaban.

He stood there just a while longer to make sure he had given Captain Cozens enough time to make his way back along the path that led to Uma village. He knew this man the *I-Matang* was his *tama*, or father, although for all of his ten years he had not known how to act in his presence. His mother, Nei Tebatete, had been this man's Banaban wife for as long as he could remember while their lives here in Buakonikai village were not that of a typical Banaban family. How could they be, when your father was an *I-Matang* living in one of those strange houses down at Uma settlement?

Ata and his *tina* lived alone in their *mwenga*. His mother's family clan lived in the surrounding *kainga*, or hamlet, consisting of a group of family houses as decreed by Banaban culture. Ata was loved and accepted by his family and community. But even at this tender age he knew he was different and missed the one thing all Banabans valued most - a *tama*.

"Ata, where are you?" came his mother's voice from inside their *mwenga*.

"*Kona mauri*, Mother," he obediently replied, making his way into the darkened hut where his mother still lay on her sleeping mat.

"*Kona mauri*, Ata," she greeted when he sat down beside her, her voice suddenly alarming him. He knew immediately that something was wrong.

"Mother, are you sad?" He leaned over to stroke her face.

"Ata, my little wise one, you are such a smart boy." She put her arms out and drew him into a loving embrace.

"Has he hurt you?" he asked.

"No my little one, your *tama* is a good man, and he loves us both very much, though you must understand that he is a very important *I-Matang* here on this island."

"I know, Mother. The elders say, he is a great man of the sea," he replied, trying to cheer her.

"Yes Ata, you also will be a very important man one day, just like your *tama*." The tears were beginning to well in her dark eyes.

"Mother, please, why are you so sad?" he asked, feeling her pain.

She slowly struggled to bring her emotions under control.

"Your father has taken an *I-Matang* wife. He will not be able to spend much time with us anymore." Again, she was overwhelmed with grief; her body racked with sobs and tears.

Ata rocked his mother in his arms and felt great sorrow for the father he had never really known and the heartbreak his mother was feeling. He knew of her love for this man and how she had given up so much for him. Her hurt welled up in him, adding even more pain to his already growing resentment of this important *I-Matang*.

After his mother had calmed herself, she asked him to go and leave her. He knew she wanted to be left alone with her grief. He turned and made his way from their *mwenga* with no emotion showing on his young face.

While Ata slowly ambled down the path towards Uma, he felt the anger growing within him just like the sun beating down on him every time he broke from under the protective palm treed canopy shading the pathway. Every morning he made this journey on his way down to the seashore. Swimming and bathing was a daily ritual, just as fishing would become part of his daily routine once he reached the age of manhood and he went to live on the *Anon te Tarine*, Buakonikai's village terrace, where the young males of the village were taught the ways of men.

On reaching the rugged coastline where the coral pinnacles rose from the edge of the shore, Ata did not even stop to think before he clambered down over the sharp edges of the pinnacles. He made his way out across the tiny fragments of coral, driftwood, pebbles and limestone that lay littering the shore.

"*Kona mauri*, Ata!" Gwennie happily called, waving her arm in greeting.

He had not even seen her standing there only a few feet from where he had been walking.

Turning back, he replied, "*Kona mauri, Nei* Gwennie!"

He did not feel like company this morning, but his upbringing could not let him show bad manners, and for all his mixed emotions towards the *I-Matang, Nei* Gwennie was his friend. Even though she was an *I-Matang*, she had grown up among his people. He felt they were kindred souls caught in the middle of two different cultures where their loneliness seemed to have drawn them together.

They had known each other for as long as he could remember, playing and swimming virtually every day. She had told him about the strange ways of the *I-Matang* and he, in turn, had told her about his people and their culture. She loved to hear his stories of Banaban Creation while she tried to explain the *I-Matang* God.

When he reached her, Gwennie immediately realised something was wrong. After her coaxing, he finally blurted out his sad tale. She had known the identity of Ata's father for a long time. Captain Cozens's nightly wanderings had not been made general knowledge, though Gwennie had told Ata that she had overheard her mother and father talking about the Captain and the scandal. She was soon to learn from other clandestine conversations around her home that the word scandal was something not to be spoken aloud or in public. Another word Gwennie had heard was *concubine*. So far, she had no idea of the meaning, only that it had something to do with Captain Cozens.

Gwennie discussed the matter with her good friend, Ata. She had also told him of her great liking for his father, whom she referred to as Uncle Will, and who, in her family's eyes, was just like an uncle. Now, as Ata poured out his sad tale, how could Gwennie tell him she already knew about Uncle Will's new wife? He had brought her to her parents' house for dinner only last evening. She had been shocked to hear that he had returned from a vacation in Australia with a new bride. It was the talk of the island.

She looked into his sad blue eyes, and with wisdom well beyond her years, she tried to search for the words that could soothe him. She loved Ata as much as she loved Uncle Will, and she knew that Ata's existence was not general knowledge among the white staff on the island. The words suddenly sprang from her lips in her flawless Banaban tongue.

"Ata, you know Captain Cozens is a very good man, and I'm sure he would never mean to hurt you or your *tina*. He is like an uncle to me, and he has a very kind heart. I know there must be some reason for his taking another wife. Your *tama* is one of the most important *I-Matang* on this island, and you know he is in charge of all the big *I-Matang te waa*, white men's canoes that come here," she quickly added, trying to think of all the good things she could say about Uncle Will.

Ata frowned in frustration. "But how can he love my mother and push her to the side while he lives with a new *I-Matang* wife? What he has done to my mother is very hurtful. I cannot understand why he does not want to be with her for life."

"I know, Ata, but you should realise by now just how different the *I-Matang* views these matters. Everything has to be *proper* as my mother calls it, something to do with morals. I must admit, Ata, that it doesn't make a lot of sense to me either but that is the way the *I-Matang* do things." Their carefree days would be over soon, she thought, with sadness in her heart.

"Well, I do not like the way *I-Matang* do things. They have no honour," he replied, the hurt apparent in his voice.

He bent down and picked up a heavy, smooth stone and flung it into the ocean in anger.

"Come on Ata, you must remember you also have the blood of the *I-Matang*, and whether we like it or not, it is the way of our world." She tried soothing him by placing her hand on his shoulder.

"I will never be an *I-Matang*. I'm a Banaban!" he said in defiance.

"Please Ata, you are my best and only friend, please do not hate all *I-Matangs*," Gwennie pleaded.

"I will never hate you, *Nei* Gwennie, because you are like me, a Banaban." Now he regretted his words as he could see the tears welling in her eyes. "I'm sorry, so sorry, I didn't mean to hurt you."

"Yes, Ata, I am like you! I may have *I-Matang* blood, but my spirit is Banaban, even Tetabo tells me so," she said.

"Well, I will never be an *I-Matang* who has no honour and lies and cheats against his brother," Ata quickly replied.

As a Banaban, Ata had been raised with a sense of honour and to respect his fellow man, and the colour of a man's skin made no difference. For Ata, a man's word should not be doubted, and the gift of sharing everything he owned was part of a Banaban's way of life. Just as the Banabans had welcomed the *I-Matang* and allowed him to take some of their land away in his big *te waa*, they had believed in their legend of the Land of Matang, the mystical homeland where the *I-Matang* dwelt, and so they must be honoured and welcomed to their island.

Now, eight years later, the Banabans had found to their sorrow that their honoured guests were not like them. They did not share or keep their word, but only took what they did not own. Of course, these things were often spoken of between Ata and Gwennie, for she was not like the rest of them. She understood the meaning of honour and just like Ata, she had a father who was also an important *I-Matang* here on the island.

Gwennie, unlike Ata, could not help having a deep love and affection for her father, even if he was destroying the island with his mining gangs and explosions.

"Come on, let's swim and forget these sad things!" Ata exclaimed, "and then we shall climb the largest coconut tree up near my village. The frigate birds will talk to us and tell me what to do."

"Oh, what a good idea, Ata. Why didn't I think of that?" Gwennie replied.

They both waded into the azure blue sea, swimming and jumping out of the water with such grace they seemed more like fish. The water became a natural place for them, the same as scaling the tallest coconut tree that reached so high up from the ground far below. They never thought of any of the associated dangers that accompanied such pursuits. Luckily Gwennie's parents knew nothing of her daring missions.

Later in the day, as *taai*, the sun reached its zenith, high up on the uppermost reaches of the island a tall, lean coconut tree swayed. Anyone coming in from the sea that day might have noticed the flock of frigate birds as they steadily circled above the island. There, under the heavily laden canopy, sat two children, both with light golden coloured skin and distinctive blue eyes. As they chattered in their Banaban tongue and talked to the birds, their faces lit up in unison as the birds happily squawked at their presence. Speaking to the birds always did lighten one's spirit.

6. Ella Williams (left) with friend visiting Banaban village early 1920s.

CHAPTER SEVEN

THE COMPANY'S NINE YEARS OF PARADISE

John 1909

With a hard day's work over, John Williams enjoyed the view from his favourite place out on the veranda. It had been a typical Ocean Island day, hot and sultry as a bank of thick black clouds was brewing and rolling in from the south. The afternoon sea breeze seemed to be almost gone. A lull before the storm, he thought.

This had always been John's favourite time of day, relaxing before dinner. His wife Ella made sure he was left in peace, with strict instructions to the household staff to see he was not disturbed. Sipping his tall glass of refreshing ginger beer, John looked down at the activity going on at the boat harbour. The Burns Philp vessel *Muniara* sat at the mooring buoys, and there was a scurry of surfboats going back and forth while she loaded, trying to beat the storm. He noticed the smoke rising from the thick grove of palms down near Uma Point. The village would be a hive of activity at this time of day as the women prepared the evening meal, making the best of the last hours of daylight. He could not help thinking about how much things were changing.

John was grateful for the company house that had been provided to accommodate his family. Their houseboy, Tetabo, had married recently and now had his wife, Meri, working beside him. She mostly did the cooking and was already pregnant. John sighed, taking another sip of his drink. Yes, the household staff was growing rapidly, and so were the bills down at the trade store. He wondered just how many children Tetabo was planning on having. With thoughts of babies, his mind turned to his wife.

From the moment Ella arrived, she enjoyed the island lifestyle, and so did Gwennie, while he was enjoying the challenges with his job. The company was continually improving the facilities together with a rapidly expanding workforce. John recalled constructing the original jetty which they had up and running within the first three months after their arrival.

The rattling noise momentarily drew his attention as the small steam train made its way back down the hill to the storage sheds. Yes, John thought, not a bad job when you consider the limited funds they had to get this new facility up and running. He laughed as he recalled just how difficult it had been. The first loading method proved such a slow process when they initially tried to get the Banabans motivated to work for them. The men were more interested in going fishing and usually returned to their huts for a rest around the middle of the day. As soon as the company realised they were wasting their time with the Banabans, they recruited outside workers from the surrounding islands, which proved successful.

He was now supervising different work gangs, except for one new group of recruits. In February, a force of over one hundred and forty

Japanese labourers was brought in together with some mechanics and cooks. They had been permitted to bring a supervisor, a Mister Watanabe, who seemed to be rather feared. John had heard the local gossip that part of the conditions of their employment was to have a Japanese doctor. Doctor Matsuoka had arrived with his wife and child and was already proving a real asset to the general island community, even though the rest of the Japanese kept mainly to themselves.

More staff accommodation had to be expanded to cope with the influx of workers. They had just completed electrifying the entire island, and new refrigeration plants provided the luxury of chilled food. The company's trading store supplied everything, which could be credited from staff wages. Ella had insisted Tetabo have the authorisation to buy anything they needed. From the size of the account, he must be buying top-shelf. John could not help pondering over his pay book and the amount that had to be credited every month.

A loud clap of thunder broke overhead, jolting John from his daydream as the wind suddenly increased. He reluctantly got up and walked over to close the shutters against the heavy downpour that was blowing in. Thank God, we need rain, he thought.

The island desperately needed its annual rainfall and water was strictly controlled. It had become the number one priority to build large concrete water cisterns. Unfortunately, as far as mining was concerned, the rain could be a dreaded curse; a frustrating situation, especially if they had a wet year. They could not ship the phosphate until it had been dried out and the dryers could not keep up with the amount they were mining. This was causing significant delays.

Now, with the veranda sealed off from the driving rain, John ambled back to his chair still with water on his mind.

Poor Harold Gaze, the Australian manager back in Melbourne, had become most concerned about the wet phosphate situation, and John thought of the endless stream of so-called experts he kept sending over. He thought Gaze was wasting the company's money, and it was not going down too well with the staff. The last so-called expert was Monsieur Nicaise, a Frenchman whose only experience was mining phosphate in Algeria. He had strutted around the island as though he owned the place. The man could not even speak English and expected them to take notice of him. Algeria was in the middle of a desert for goodness sake; what would he know about rain and wet phosphate?

Even Ellis had had enough, and it usually took a lot for him to lose his temper. John did not know what Ellis had told Gaze back in Melbourne, but poor old Nicaise ended up on the next boat home. The company did not even bother sending him over to Nauru. With the Australian and New Zealand staff on Ocean Island refusing to take any notice of him, Nicaise did not stand a chance with the Germans on Nauru.

The last John heard Ellis had finally persuaded Gaze to bring in Australian engineers, to supervise the technical side of the operations. At last, John thought, they would have some real experts that would know what they were doing and more importantly, the Australian way of doing things.

They now had up to forty ships calling each month to pick up phosphate, and this provided the company and residents with regular mail services and fresh supplies. The island's surrounding waters were rich in seafood, though, coming from a country of meat-eaters, John always appreciated the good old steak or lamb chops. His senses took in the rich smells of Meri's cooking wafting out of the kitchen. It must be nearly time for dinner. He wondered what was on tonight's menu.

Tinned foods made up the bulk of their daily diet, although Ella had taken it upon herself to remedy the situation. Together with Tetabo, she had built a vegetable garden in the backyard that was increasingly becoming a horticultural masterpiece. The chemist and engineers kept reminding Ella that nothing could grow in pure phosphate. Of course, Ella had to prove the experts wrong and took great pleasure in asking these gentlemen over for dinner so she could serve them some of her homegrown delights.

A deep voice interrupted John's reverie.

"Sorre to disturb you, sir, Madam asken me see..ee the shutters and if you or right?"

"It's all right Tetabo, I'm fine. How long will dinner be?"

"Oh... still a wee whirl sir. My Meri markin you a gud em tea. You have maw rest, sir, I leet you know em when cha reedy."

Tetabo disappeared through the doorway. John could not help smiling at Tetabo's use of the Ingerlish language, as he called it. He seemed to be getting decidedly worse. It must be all the talking he did with Gwennie.

John's thoughts returned to their achievements and the price of progress. Every second year when they returned to Ocean Island from vacations abroad, he could see just how much the place had changed. The haze of white dust that rose from the crushers was visible offshore. Since they blasted the outer reef, the ships could anchor much closer. The flatcar ran along the top of the jetty and provided transport right to their residence. No more climbing the steep incline to the house—a nuisance now ended.

He knew Ella was not impressed with all the progress; she did not understand the business side of things. He thought she was more in love with the romance of being on a tropical island. John was still immensely proud of his accomplishments. The Banabans and their island, once so isolated from the rest of the world, were now being introduced to modern civilisation.

Of course, the other worldwide benefits of the phosphate they were mining made the smaller issue of Ocean Island and its native people pale into insignificance. The island's phosphate was one of the most significant agricultural developments to benefit Australia, New Zealand and millions of people throughout the world. Food was being produced at a much higher rate due to the improved pastures, all because of the phosphate Ocean Island was providing.

On the other hand, the Banabans believed that the *I-Matangs* were only interested in destroying their island, and they had no understanding of the world's agricultural needs. It was still challenging to try and get them to understand the concept of money. They were nevertheless very law-abiding people with strong family and community values. John believed they could have taught western civilisation a few things in this regard.

The Colonial Office had already utilised the local Banaban court system, *kabowi*, to control law and order. They had also established a police force as the number of outside labourers grew. With such a potpourri of races and cultures, problems were increasing. The majority of John's workers were Gilbertese, who also had a casual attitude to work. They were very jovial people and extremely fit. Part of their contract permitted one-third of the group to bring their families.

Chinese skilled artisans and labourers commonly referred to as Coolies, now made up a significant part of the workforce. Due to the Chinese class system, John had his hands full, just keeping an eye on the two separate groups as they did not mix well with each other.

This only added to the tension, making his job more difficult. He massaged his brow; easing the pressure he felt just thinking about it.

The rest of the workforce was now made up of the new Japanese workers and Ellice Islanders. The Gilbertese, for some reason, took an instant dislike to the Chinese, and seeing they had to work side by side, the Gilbertese loved to play practical jokes on them. The Chinese were not able to laugh things off. One common problem among all the workers was their lack of understanding of English, or any language other than their own. He was in the middle of them all trying to communicate and mediate through various interpreters, whose own grasp of English was minimal. With just a handful of Australian staff, he had to try and get everyone to work and keep things running smoothly. John was finding it harder and harder to suffer fools.

He loved his job, and he believed the pressure and stress were just part of the challenges. He made a point of keeping his own counsel, especially when it came to company matters in his home. Ella was very friendly with their household staff, and Gwennie seemed to become more like a native than a white child. He had even brought up the idea of sending her to boarding school back in Australia, but there was no way Ella was going to part with her. He did not know whether the tragic loss of Bertie, their firstborn son when he was just five years of age, had contributed to this; he just knew it was pointless to pursue it. When Ella put her mind to something, there was no point trying to argue. She could be one very headstrong woman.

In those first few years, Ella and John would sit over dinner and discuss work matters, but now he discouraged such conversations. The company was still having trouble with the Banabans over buying more land and even though he was not involved, he knew how sensitive the subject was.

They had to call in the Resident Commissioner who resided on Tarawa Island over two-hundred-and-forty miles away for help. John knew it was general knowledge that Ellis was becoming more annoyed with the attitude of the Resident Commissioners, who seemed to worry more about the welfare of the Banabans. Now the company was in a complete deadlock with the Banabans. They had already mined two-hundred-and-forty acres, which had yielded over two million tons of phosphate.

Ocean Island had a total area of just under fifteen hundred acres, with more than two hundred acres covered in coral pinnacles where the natives were unable to plant any of their fruit trees. The argument was that with the addition of such a large workforce, the four hundred and seventy Banabans could not survive on what was left.

The company was also in dispute over not replacing the Banabans' fruit and coconut trees they destroyed during mining. John could not see how they expected to grow trees in a mined-out area of bare limestone rocks with no proper soil or water. The heat that came off these areas was almost unbearable. John was suddenly aware that the sound of the rain had eased, and he was beginning to feel the stuffiness of the enclosed veranda.

Lifting himself once again, he walked back over to the shutters and began swinging them outwards to catch the breeze. The steam from the heat of the day together with the smoke from the dampened village fires rose to form a veil of fine mist. John's thoughts once again returned to company matters.

The word around the office after they got rid of the last Resident Commissioner was that his predecessor, Captain Quayle Dickson, was the best man to resolve the land deadlock. Instead of that occurring, he proceeded to formulate a plan that further slowed down the operations. He also introduced a scheme to get the company to make annual contributions into a fund that would enable the Banabans to purchase another island, should Ocean Island become uninhabitable. The company opposed both items, and Ellis, who usually was a good man for diplomacy and tact, finally lost his temper.

With Dickson backing the Banabans in their fight not to sell any more of their land, he had created an even bigger deadlock. The company once again was bombarding the Colonial Office in London, demanding to have the Captain replaced. John personally thought that the new Resident Commissioner had strong principles regarding the Banabans, and it might take all the influence of the old powers that be back in London to get rid of this one. John had to admit he admired the man's tenacity, even if he did not share the same views. It took some man to take on the full strength of the company's influential directors, together with the wrath of the Colonial Office back in London.

John, of course, kept his thoughts to himself, since the mere mention of Dickson's name was enough to bring a tirade of invectives from any of his colleagues. Yes, times were changing.

He slowly breathed in the fresh air after the cleansing rain. The politics regarding the Banabans seemed to overshadow everything. He noticed the last of the mist join the wisps of clouds moving away to the north.

He just tried to keep his head down and avoid as much of the ongoing dispute as he could. It was not always an easy task, especially when you had a wife at home that treated the Banabans as long lost relatives and a daughter that sounded like one. John did like them, but he had to keep reminding himself he must stay as impartial as possible. His position was riding on it and his loyalty, in the end, must lie with the company. They were the ones who had employed him and also paid and cared for not only him but also for his family's welfare.

"Darling, dinner's ready!" Ella called from the doorway.

He turned around, making his way towards her.

"Darling, you're looking awfully tired, I hope you're not worrying about work again? You're supposed to be resting," she scolded.

"I'm fine, dear. You know I don't bring work home. Now, what's for dinner? I'm famished!"

7. Uma (left) and Gwennie Williams Ocean Island c.1917.

CHAPTER EIGHT

DISCOVERING THE LAND OF MATANG

Gwennie 1910

Gwennie Williams would be celebrating her tenth birthday in September. Her parents had always called her Gwennie although her real name was Gwendoline Hazellette Williams. The only time she was called Gwendoline was when she was in trouble. She did not know if that was the reason she disliked her name, but whatever it was, she much preferred Hazel.

Since the age of two, she had been living and enjoying island life, believing that the rest of the world must be like Ocean Island. It was not until more recently, while on trips abroad to what her mother referred to as their homeland, Australia, that she realised just how different Ocean Island was.

It was a startling experience the first time she disembarked from the ship in Sydney. There were people everywhere, reminding her of thousands of crabs scurrying to and fro. The cars, trams and buses were all new to her. Back on the island, they had a train, but nothing like the large ones in Sydney. Their island train had a small open platform on wheels and other fancy steam ones they used to pull the buckets of phosphate. She always thought they travelled fast until she saw the ones in Australia.

In some ways, it was exciting to see Sydney, but it was also very frightening. Gwennie did not leave her parents' side for fear of being lost forever in the maze of those enormous buildings that rose right up into the sky.

On her way to visit the zoological gardens overlooking the harbour and other strange places, she did not see any native people. Her parents had told her there were Australian aboriginals that were like her Tea Tup, but all the faces seemed white in the big city.

Another very strange thing was that wherever they went, no one had any servants, except for the boarding houses and hotels. It was the first time in her life that she had ever seen a white woman doing household chores. Once at the home of family friends, she could not help asking the lady why she was making them a cup of tea.

The lady looked at her, puzzled, while her mother had coughed and spluttered and apologised for her rudeness. To Gwennie, it was just a simple, innocent question.

Later that night, her mother explained why young girls did not ask those questions and told her that most people in Australia did not have servants.

She replied, "Why ever not?"

"Because they just don't!" her mother answered.

Well, she still could not understand what all the fuss was about and was sure her mother didn't know why. It was just the start of many questions she would ask which all seemed to receive the same reply. By the time she boarded the ship to return to the island, she was more confused than ever.

While she enjoyed the family's trips abroad and the accompanying sea voyages, Gwennie also looked forward to returning home. That first sight of their island was always an exciting moment for her, and she would stay up on the deck so as not to miss the event. Sometimes, depending on the weather and the direction of the wind, she could hear the island before she sighted it. The roar of the surf breaking on the many surrounding reefs was like familiar music to her ears. The only better sound was the Banabans singing down by their village at dusk. Unquestionably Gwennie believed her Tea Tup was the best singer of them all. No one could sing as good as him. Tea Tup had taught her all of his songs over the years, and she could now sing them in his native tongue or English. For some reason, his native language made the songs sound even better.

Gwennie could not remember when Tea Tup had taught her his language, but she was as fluent in Banaban as she was in English, and now her parents were starting to object.

Her mother would often say, "Gwennie, how are we going to make a lady of you, if you do not learn to speak correct King's English?"

She could not understand what the fuss was all about. She just happened to be the only white child of her age on the island, and the adults kept reminding her she had been one of the first European children to grow up there. Until now, her life revolved around her parents, Tea Tup and Meri, and their baby son, Nete. She also had a special friend called Ata, who was the Banaban son of Uncle Will. He had been sent off to the terrace at *Anon te Tarine* where he was learning the ways of men. She was missing her good friend, who was not allowed to see women while he lived there.

All of the other adults Gwennie's parents knew seemed very nice but not very interested in having a conversation with her, Miss Williams, all of ten years old. She was usually told to go out and play once the adults got together. She had started taking lessons from the holy brother who ran the school at the Sacred Heart Mission in Tabwewa on the other side of the island. Gwennie enjoyed school even though there was only a handful of younger *I-Matang* children in the class. It gave her something to do during the day while Ata was away. Gwennie had lots of native friends, but she knew her parents did not like her mixing too much with them, and she was beginning to feel like the odd one out.

Gwennie could not remember when it started, but with her strong belief in God and the culture she had acquired from the Banabans, she began to communicate with God and the Banaban ancestral spirits. Gwennie would scale a coconut tree near the seashore, and on reaching the top, perched close under the fronds, she would talk to God. On other occasions, she would speak to the spirit of the frigate birds, watching them soar out over the ocean. She would feel herself flying along with them as part of their flock before they returned. Before he went away, Ata had often gone with her on these missions

Her loneliness was becoming all-consuming except for her secret times talking to God, the birds, and the spirits of the sun. One day when she arrived home for lunch, Tetabo was waiting for her.

"Missy Gwennie, are you okay? What have you been doing?" he asked, speaking to her in his language.

"Yes, I'm fine, just playing and watching the frigate birds down at the terrace."

"Did you talk to the birds too?"

Gwennie frowned. "Ha, ha, birds don't talk, Tetabo. Do you think I could get my own frigate bird to train?" she asked, trying to deflect Tetabo from asking more questions.

It was so hard to hide anything from him. He was like a mind reader. As Mother always said, he had that typical Banaban instinct, which she called, 'the knowing'.

"Well, we will have to ask your parents, but I am happy to help you look after it."

Gwennie was so excited; she hugged him. "Oh thank you Tetabo, I will make sure my father's in a good mood before we ask."

Later, when her father arrived home, Gwennie was all over him, making sure she had a drink ready and asking if he had a good day at work.

John was taken aback, as this was not her usual behaviour. He wondered what was coming next.

"Fah, can I ask you something?"

John thought, here we go. "Yes, what is it?"

Before Gwennie answered, she called for Tetabo to join them.

"Tetabo and I need to ask you something," she said, as he appeared in the doorway.

"Oh, I see, so what do you and Tetabo have on your mind?"

"Go on, Tetabo, tell Daddy what we want to do!" she prompted.

"Well sir, Gwennie been talking to birds. Sir, she wants one them birds."

"Thank you, Tetabo. Gwennie, can you explain? What talking birds?"

Gwennie had no idea how Tetabo knew about her talking to the birds and tried to explain to her father.

"Fah, Tetabo means one of the frigate birds they have down on the terrace. If I can have one, he will help me look after it."

"Those frigate birds are serious business, Gwennie, isn't that right Tetabo?" John asked.

"Yes, sir, vereee right."

"In that case, before I agree, I will have to speak with Old Man Eri and see what he says."

As the two of them left him alone, John thought it would be interesting to see what Eri and the other elders would think of this. The frigate birds were their prized possessions and taken very seriously within the culture, not just a white child's pet. He would have thought a request for a bicycle would have been appropriate, but a bird?

Gwennie was happy about her father's decision. He didn't know she was already well aware of the cultural importance of the birds as part of her learning from Tetabo.

"What time is it, Tetabo? Don't forget we have to go to the picture show," Gwennie reminded him.

Her father's workmate, Mister Miller, had recently opened a new picture theatre. She was fascinated by his new invention and had persuaded him to let her help. He had a bicycle set up behind a very large camera. It had to be pedalled vigorously so you could watch the pictures. Mister Miller said it was not appropriate for a young lady to pedal a bike like that, so he had one of the native boys do it. He did allow her, however, to collect the tickets, and she thought it was wonderful.

She had even let Ata sneak in a few times to watch before he went away. The natives thought it was a new type of *I-Matang kouti*, or magic, and they took an instant liking to the American cowboy movies. However, like all Banabans, they did not like violence and killing, and it took quite a while for Mister Miller to convince them that he personally had not killed anyone. Gwennie noticed he was becoming a lot more selective with what he was screening lately. He obviously did not like the idea of being known on the island as a murderer.

One day, on returning home, her mother called her into the parlour.

"Sweetheart, I have some wonderful news for you." She sounded excited. "You're going to have a new brother or sister to play with!"

"What do you mean, Mummy?"

"I'm going to have a baby."

"Oh, when can I see him?" Gwennie asked excitedly.

"Well, you can't have him or her until around Christmas, God willing."

"I just can't wait. I'll be getting two presents this Christmas. I'm the luckiest girl in the world." She felt so positive the baby being a boy, not that she did not want a sister; she just assumed it would be a boy.

Gwennie's life was definitely looking brighter as the days passed. She received the good news from her father that *unimane* Eri had given his permission for her to have a bird.

She could not believe her good luck. Not only was she getting a bird but *unimane* Eri had arranged to have Ata assist her with the training. He had just finished his initiation in the ways of men, and, because he had *te I-Matang* blood, the elders decided that he was the best person. Gwennie was wondering if it was just the fact she was now blessed. All the talking to God and the birds had finally paid off.

8. Tetabo (Tea Tup) Williams houseboy Ocean Island early 1900s.

CHAPTER NINE

GIFT OF THE FRIGATE BIRD

Tetabo 1910

Ata had been summoned to attend a meeting with three village elders and was not sure why. He had recently returned from the terrace and thought it might have to do with that.

Unimane Eri and his fellow elders had a serious matter to resolve in regard to Nei Gwennie's request to own a frigate bird. The main issue was the fact that a woman could not be involved in the *kauti*, or magic rituals, and secondly, she was a foreigner who had no Banaban blood and was only a child.

Eri said, "Ata, we have asked you here today to address a problem we have. Young Nei Gwennie has asked to own one of our frigate birds. As you know, this is a very serious matter." He added, "firstly, whenever there is a *kauti* ritual you will attend on behalf of the girl. Secondly, you will have to tell her what is required, but you cannot tell her any of the secrets regarding the rituals for her own safety."

He went on, "as you know, you will have to ensure that you follow the procedures accordingly, or the young one can end up in trouble."

Ata was fully aware of how serious the situation was and the curse that could befall Gwennie if the rites were not upheld or done correctly. He would make sure that she knew that this was not child's play. Ata also realised the gravity of his elder's request. A man could own only one bird and undertake the rituals as part of his manly duties within Banaban society. With the elders granting Gwennie her request, his bird would now become hers.

Eri further instructed, "tomorrow you will meet us at *Aon te Tarine* terrace at dawn. Nei Gwennie needs to attend, and we will allocate her area to keep and train her bird."

The elders had already decided they had to tread carefully with the child's father being an important *te I-Matang*. They were depending on Ata to provide the solution.

The next morning at the Williams residence, two hours before the sunrise, Tetabo was already awake. His daily dawn fishing had been cancelled due to the exciting event happening today. He quietly woke Gwennie and told her to get dressed while he prepared a quick breakfast.

"Tetabo, who will be there today?" she asked.

"Some of the elders, *unimane* Eri and Ata will all be there," he replied. "There is something else you should know."

"What is that?"

"I have not mentioned it before, but Ata is my nephew."

Gwennie was shocked. "Ata! Your nephew… why didn't you tell me?"

"I didn't tell you because I know he is your special friend. I do not want you to think I will interfere, especially seeing I am his uncle."

"But that is good news, I am glad I finally know. It looks as if we are more family now than just friends." She laughed. She had always been so close to both of them. It explained a lot. Maybe it was not all just the Banaban 'knowing' after all.

"I just want to make sure to remind you that this is very serious business today and a great honour. So please listen carefully to the elders' instructions."

Tetabo had trained her well over the years, but today was a very crucial step in the Banaban side of her life. "Come on Nei Gwennie, we have to go!"

They made their way down the darkened path in the last of the moonlight. The chill of the morning air was starting to affect her, and she could feel the goose bumps coming up on her arms. Tetabo was also feeling the same.

"The ancestors are here with us," he calmly assured her.

John woke to hear Tetabo and Gwennie chatting away in the kitchen in their usual native talk he could not understand. He knew they were going off to get her bird this morning but had never realised they had to get up this early. Must have to do with catching them while it was dark and before they flew off. He was glad she was so excited over a darn bird, and while he knew the Banabans considered it serious business, he had no idea his ten-year-old daughter was getting involved in Banaban magic rituals. Being a good, God-abiding man, he found it hard to believe in all the Banabans hocus pocus.

He heard them leave and got out of bed. By the time he came back in from the washroom, Meri was already in the kitchen preparing his breakfast.

"Mauri Meri, Tetabo and Gwennie were up early today," he said. "She's so excited about her bird."

"Yes, sir, big day today. Her bird day," Meri replied.

A bird day, well, that was an interesting term. Now, John focused on important things happening at work today. He had heard enough talk about birds over the past weeks and wondered if the bicycle would be the next thing on his daughter's mind.

The elders were already at the terrace and had everything ready for the ritual. They had built a small perch in an area they specifically allocated for her. After their arrival, Tetabo stood back while Eri solemnly directed Ata *an*d Gwennie to sit facing the rising sun. The elders began chanting to evoke the spirits of the frigate birds to safeguard and bless Nei Gwennie and to recognise Ata as her protector.

As the first rays of the sun broke in the eastern sky, their chanting came to an end. Eri walked over to them and anointed them both with oil before garlanding them with a *buna,* or ceremonial lei. All of a sudden, they started to hear fluttering sounds around them and seemingly out of nowhere, a bird landed on the small perch near them. Eri began to talk to the bird in a language that even Gwennie could not understand.

He turned to her and said, "your request has been granted and therefore, from now onwards, Ata will do everything necessary."

From that point on, the mood seemed to lighten, and all the elders and Tetabo moved forward to look at the bird. Eri had a small coloured green ribbon that he attached to the bird's leg, marking him as Gwennie's.

She was excited. To think that her bird had arrived from the Banaban magic. She could not believe it, and she wanted to give it a name, but this did not seem to be part of the ceremony.

Tetabo tried to hide the tears in his eyes. She was so special. Not only was she a young *te I-Matang* girl, but to be given such an honour! He was as proud of her as if she was his own daughter.

They all enjoyed the rest of the morning, and Gwennie was amazed at how fast her bird was learning. He seemed so special, she thought. Tetabo did not have the heart to tell her that it had been a gift from one of the elders.

9. Young Banaban boy feeding the family's tame frigate birds on the terrace Ocean Island c1903.

10. Young Banaban friends of Gwennie Williams visiting their home Ocean Island early 1900s.

CHAPTER TEN

CHILD OF GOD AND MATANG

Gwennie 1911

With all the excitement of her mother's growing tummy, Gwennie's life was becoming much brighter. Every time she asked her mother about who had made her brother, she would always reply in one of her hushed tones.

"God has blessed us by planting a little seed in Mummy's tummy."

But for Gwennie, God planting the seed was more like God heeding her prayers or little talks, and she was convinced of a miracle.

She was not privy to a lot of the conversation regarding where and when the baby was going to be born. She knew her mother was having long talks with Nei Meri. Of course, she tried to eavesdrop, but from the muted discussions going on in the parlour, Gwennie could not understand much of what was said.

Her mother just kept telling her, "talking about babies is not for children's ears."

Gwennie was starting to feel a little shut out as far as her parents were concerned. She was glad she had her own frigate bird to keep her company and enjoyed spending time down the terrace each day looking after him with Ata helping.

She also had gathered from a scattering of talk that it was decided her mother would have the baby on the island.

She had overheard her father talking. "Well my darling, it really is your decision, but I must admit I am most concerned; no European woman has ever had a baby on Ocean Island before."

"Don't worry, dear, there's always a first time, and I've never had any trouble having my other two babies. Besides, Meri has delivered a few babies in her time. I'm sure she will be a big help."

Gwennie had also overheard her father lowering his voice as he softly referred to her brother Bertie. They always lowered their voices when they spoke of him, and her mother usually cried. Gwennie had never met him, but she sometimes talked to him too, when she was perched high on the palm tree. She thought in some ways that she did know him, if only in her vivid imagination and she knew positively that he was up there in the sky with God and the birds.

The big day finally arrived on the 15th of January. Not exactly Christmas, Gwennie thought. As usual, she was told, to go off and play. Apparently, it is not a place for children when a lady is about to have a baby. She wandered out into the back yard, knowing this would be the last time she would have to play on her own. It would be worth the wait.

Meanwhile, she could hear her mother moaning back inside the house. She started to become a little alarmed as her cries grew into louder shrieks. Gwennie thought surely she was dying. No one could make that much noise and live. It seemed to go on forever, and she became transfixed on the sounds emanating from their house.

Suddenly one loud scream pierced the still air around her, and she could hear Meri squealing.

Gwennie yelled out to ask Meri if her mother was still alive.

"My little one, thou art blessed!"

Gwennie again yelled from outside, this time nearer the bedroom window, "Nei Meri thou art blessed, have I got my little brother? Can I come in and see him?"

"Yes, come on in, you are truly blessed!" she shouted back.

Gwennie ran up the back steps two at a time and sped through the house to her parents' bedroom. Arriving at the door, Meri opened it to let her through. All she could see was her poor mother exhausted, and eyes closed, propped up on the pillows in her bed. Her mother's long hair was all tangled up, not like her at all. Nei Meri stood with a big bundle of rolled-up sheets in her arms and a terrifying large butcher's knife in her hand. Gwennie could not see the baby and wondered what was going on.

"Where's my brother? Please tell me what has happened," Gwennie asked, thinking he might have already gone to be with poor Bertie. Concern suddenly overcame her while she stood waiting anxiously for an answer.

"Here Gwennie," her mother replied weakly.

Tucked in the crook of her arm, lost among all those white sheets, was her brother. She moved closer to see and touch.

"Gwennie, your brother is a little girl."

Gwennie frowned, "A girl... it can't be?"

"I'm sorry, but she is." Her mother sighed, not knowing how to console her daughter.

"Well, she looks like a boy," she protested, looking at the puckered little red face.

"No she doesn't, it's just because she hasn't got a lot of hair yet. Just wait until she grows a little older, she'll look prettier then." With that, the little thing opened its deep blue eyes and let out a yawn. Gwennie fell in love with her from that moment.

Someone must have let her father know down at the office, and he suddenly came rushing in.

"Oh, darling are you, all right? You look so tired." He was concerned when he saw his wife's state. "I'm so glad that it's over and done with," he continued.

Her mother still did not get a chance to answer him. His excitement was overwhelming.

"Well, is it a he or a she?" he asked, his eyes lighting up.

"I'm fine darling; here… meet your new daughter!" With that, her mother lifted Gwennie's new little sister up for her father to take a closer look.

"Oh, she's beautiful and looks so healthy and a good size too. You're truly a marvel." Her father leaned across to kiss her and seemed to have noticed the dark circles of exhaustion under her eyes.

"Now, are you sure you are all right? Would you like me to get you anything?" he asked in a worried voice.

"Please, John, stop all the fussing. I'm fine, maybe just a little worn out, I'll be back on my feet within the week," her mother scolded mildly.

Her mother did not take kindly to people fussing about, even her husband.

"All right, but I have to get back down to the office and tell the lads the good news, everyone's so concerned. Don't you think she's beautiful, Gwennie?" he asked as he hesitantly placed his large finger under the baby's little chin.

"Yes, she's kind of funny looking but really cute, even if she's not a boy," she finally admitted. Her parents already seemed to think her new sister was the most beautiful creation God had ever made.

With that, her father ruffled her hair and hurried through the doorway. "I'll be back as soon as I can, darling, you just have a good rest."

Her mother lay back and laughed when he bumped into something in the hallway. Gwennie could hear him muttering something to Nei Meri before he rushed back out of the house. No doubt, he was asking her to keep an eye on her mother.

Gwennie could never remember seeing her father so excited. It was so out of character for him to be jumping all over the place as he was usually so calm and collected.

She knew he had a very responsible position with the company and was the man who looked after the running of the entire mining staff here on the island. The number of people employed by the company seemed to increase daily, which, from what she had overheard, made it more difficult for her father to supervise things. Gwennie did not know whether it was really his job or just his calm nature, but he was a very dominant figure in her life. He was someone she loved dearly.

Her father finally arrived home later that day with a half-smoked cigar and looking a little seedy. She heard him say to her mother that the chaps at the company had laid on a bit of celebration.

"John, surely you haven't been drinking?"

"Well darling just a little brandy to steady the nerves, I couldn't be rude. Medicinal, of course!"

Gwennie thought this conversation sounded rather promising, so she put her head around the bedroom door to hear more clearly, just in time to see her father pulling the half-smoked cigar from his shirt pocket.

"Oh John, no wonder you look so bad… smoking one of those hideous things when you don't even smoke?"

"Well Ella, I couldn't insult the lads after they had gone to the trouble of giving me this gift; anyway, it's not every day you get to celebrate the first little European to be born here. I suppose this makes her a Banaban as well?" he laughed, bending down to kiss her.

"All right, but I suggest you go and lie down for a while before you fall down and throw the rest of that filthy thing out of this house at once! It's making me nauseous," her mother said, turning her head away in disgust to avoid the smell of the cigar.

"Yes my darling," her father said meekly.

Gwennie watched as her poor father staggered from the bedroom and made his way towards the guest room, which would be his new quarters for the next few weeks.

Over this period the household routine practically returned to normal. Gwennie's bird was becoming her only companion. She tended to him every morning and let him fly far out to sea with his coloured ribbon trailing behind him before he faithfully returned to her. Ata was becoming busy with the other young men living down at the terrace, and while he never missed their morning ritual, he would quickly have to leave to catch up with his other duties. She had told him about her new baby sister and could not wait to introduce them. Mother insisted she was too young to leave the house yet. They were all so busy with the new baby. Gwennie did not know why, especially with all the excitement they had going on at home, but she now felt more alone than ever. Everyone was referring to her new sister as *the baby*, and her mother said that a name would be given to her at the baptism ceremony.

The baptism finally arrived with nearly everyone attending including a lot of the villagers from Uma. Her mother had made the most exquisite christening gown and a pretty dress just for her as well. During the ceremony, Father Quoirer finally announced her sister's name as Lillian; after Lillian Point, Francis; after her father, Uma; after Uma village, Williams. Gwennie was impressed with her parents' decision and understood now why there seemed to be so many discussions regarding the baby's name with Tea Tup and his family. The name Uma was a gift to the people from his village in honour of the fact that she had been born there.

This indeed became a very memorable day for not only Gwennie but for all the family's Banaban friends. The Banabans felt that they had been greatly honoured by the *I-Matang* and from that day, her new sister was always known as Uma.

11. The Banabans refused to negotiate any more of their land for mining Ocean Island 1913.

CHAPTER ELEVEN

CHANGING TIDES OF PARADISE

Ella 1913

"Darling, how much longer are you going to take?"

"I'm almost done," Ella quickly replied, calling out through the closed bedroom door.

"Well if you don't get a move on, we'll be late, and we can't afford to give the wrong impression." She knew her husband was becoming impatient.

"You'd think we were having dinner with the King the way you're carrying on. Anyway, he's the third Commissioner we've had since we've been here. I really can't understand all the fuss," she called out as she fastened the hooks on her bodice.

"It's all right for you, but with this deadlock in place, the government has finally decided to send someone out here who can sort things out for us."

Ella thought he really was not acting his usual calm self, tonight.

"I thought that's what they said with the last two Commissioners they sent?" She couldn't help tossing back that little quip.

"Yes well, believe it, my dear, he's going to set up the government's headquarters right here, and I don't need to get on the wrong side of him at our very first meeting," he called back.

Ella noticed the slight edge of his voice and decided she'd better hurry with her dressing. He was indeed suffering from a case of nerves, and she felt it was better not to add to it.

As she sped out of the bedroom door, she ran straight into him. Realising he was not in the best of moods, Ella flung her arms around his neck and kissed him. She had learned over the years that a slight distraction was the best way of taking a man's mind off work, and John had his mind more on work than on her these past few years.

She knew why. It all had to do with the deadlock over the land resumption with the Banabans. Of course, John did not call it resumption, but more the purchase of Banaban land for the company's mining operation. Whatever you wanted to call it, Ella was on the Banabans' side. John was definitely on the company's team and refused to have the matter discussed in the house. Therefore, she kept her thoughts to herself; she was not foolish enough to air her views in public. The only person Ella could discuss her concerns with, in complete confidence, was Tetabo. He kept her informed on all the latest news from the village while she tried to keep her ears open when they attended company dinners and functions.

This dispute had been going on for four years. The pressure was starting to show on John. He had to keep the mining going as best he could while the deadlock strengthened. Ella knew he had always tried to stay out of the politics, but she felt he was now being drawn more into the company's dealings than ever before.

Her love and loyalty for her husband only made matters harder. That first day they had landed on this magical place was still fresh in her mind, and the beauty of the island and its people had made a lasting impression. Not only was there a conflict about the way she felt about John and the preservation of this place, but also the way the company had treated her husband. They had provided them with everything they needed. The best accommodation, the best food and provisions, staff to run the household, which was her dear friend Tetabo and his family, and a good salary. Ella felt she was being pulled in three different directions.

When her husband accepted this job, they had been fortunate indeed to experience and to live in this beautiful part of the world. She knew now after living here for over ten years that they would be the ones responsible in the end for destroying the place. Living with that underlying guilt was hard for her to endure. She usually went on with her life and tried to push all those darker thoughts to the background.

Ella turned her mind back to the moment, with John still in her arms. He squeezed her tightly and kissed her.

"I truly love and admire you!"

"I love you too. I'm sorry I raised my voice. I really didn't mean it. I've been feeling a bit tense lately. I don't mean to take it out on you." John's voice had lost its sharp edge.

He held her in his arms, suddenly remembering the lateness of the hour. "Now let's go and enjoy ourselves, and by the way, have I told you lately how beautiful you look?" His hand lovingly swept a lock of hair from her face.

"Thank you, darling, don't worry, you'll be proud of me tonight."

"I'm always proud of you." He kissed and hugged her again.

This was more like the old John she knew and loved.

As they entered the company manager's residence, Ella felt the tension return again as he gripped her hand. This really must be a significant evening for she had never known him to be so tense. She squeezed his hand a little just to offer him her support as they were both ushered into the main reception room full of the company's officials and their wives. The formal introductions were already taking place.

Cleeve Edwards, the company's manager, stepped out of the official party to greet them first.

"Good evening Mister and Missus Williams, so glad to see you could join us."

He had been promoted from his previous position as a head civil engineer to replace Albert Ellis when he left the island two years ago.

"Thank you, sir, we are honoured to be here." John shook his hand.

"I'd like you both to meet our new Resident Commissioner, Mister Eliot and his lovely wife, Missus Eliot," he said as he turned towards the small gentleman with the large handlebar moustache standing beside him. His white Resident Commissioner's hat helped to add quite a few more inches to his short stature.

"Sir and Missus Eliot, I'd like you to meet Mister and Missus John Williams. Mister Williams has been with us from the beginning and is the company's overseer."

With their introductions, John and Eliot shook hands, while Ella greeted Missus Eliot.

"Welcome to our island, Missus Eliot, I do hope you like it here." Ella noticed her ruddy red complexion and thought how she must have once had that beautiful pale English skin that was so prone to sunburn. The years spent in colonial outposts obviously had not been kind to the poor woman.

As she finished her greeting, she heard John saying to Eliot, "I hope you and your wife both had a good journey out here, sir?"

"Yes, thank you, Mister Williams, although I must say it seemed a rather long-winded trip."

Ella noticed his strong British accent.

"Did you run into some bad weather, sir?" John asked.

"Not really, just the usual run of weather; it was more the way we arrived here," Eliot replied. "I had the cause to return to London first, after leaving my previous position in Tobago, then on to New York, Vancouver and finally Fiji, where we were picked up by the company vessel. I can't tell you how glad we were to finally set foot on solid ground," he proclaimed, the gold braid sparkling off the white colour of his uniform.

Cleeve Edwards, not wanting to be left out of the conversation, abruptly interrupted John's reply to say, "well, I must say, Commissioner, on behalf of the company and my colleagues, we're delighted you're finally here."

Ella had always thought the island's new manager was rather pompous.

"Thank you, gentlemen, and I will say how impressed I am with the standard of living you have here on the island. Definitely not what I expected in this far-flung corner of the world." His cultured voice was the epitome of everything Ella thought of as British.

"Yes, Commissioner, we are very proud of our achievements to date, and we hope that when we have this latest little problem sorted out, you will really see some progress."

These words sounded so profound coming from the lips of their industrious manager. A little problem, indeed! It had taken five years, only to compound the issue more, Ella thought. She saw John just standing there smiling, while it took her all her efforts to keep her mouth closed.

"Now ladies and gentlemen, would you all please follow me into the dining room so we can commence dinner? Your names are all clearly marked on the place cards," Edwards said to the assembled guests.

John must have noticed the strained look on her face, for he squeezed her hand. "Come now, darling, let me help you find your place at the dining table."

"Of course, dear!" she replied, emphasising the words.

She noticed her husband give a strained grin, and she returned the smile. She knew she probably was not helping to ease his tension, but the devil inside her could not help it.

Dinner, as usual, was excellent. No one would ever guess that they lived in a far-flung corner of the world, as Eliot had put it when it came to food.

Eliot also commented on the meal. "That was the best meal I've had since I don't know when." The Commissioner patted his stomach, satisfied.

Ella noted the happy look on Cleeve Edwards' face. She wondered how much longer he could contain himself.

After dinner, the ladies were sent off to the parlour as usual, while the men adjourned to the veranda for port and cigars. She knew what the gentlemen were going to discuss. The dinner conversation had been somewhat stifled and knowing how John felt about discussing company business around her, she supposed the others were all the same. You could tell they were anxious to feel out Eliot on what he was going to do to resolve the company's current little problem.

Ella suddenly had an idea. "Excuse me, ladies, I seemed to have misplaced my handkerchief. I'll just go back to the dining room and see if I can find it," she announced to the happy little gathering of wives, as they made themselves comfortable before the tea was served.

"Oh, Missus Williams, our boy can go and look for it for you," Cleeve Edward's wife replied.

Ella thought, she seems almost as pompous as her husband. She supposed it came with being in the top job.

"Thank you, Missus Edwards, but it's really no problem, it will only take me a minute, and I'm sure I know where I dropped it." Ella was already walking towards the direction of the dining room, not waiting for her reply.

She heard their raised voices drifting through the opened doors on the veranda. It amazed her, how men seemed to raise their voices with each drink. Drawing closer, she could hear every word.

"A handful of pagans here seem to think they can hold the rest of the world to ransom with their silly land demands," a voice boomed, drowning the other men.

"Mister Eliot, sir, when will you be intervening with this senseless deadlock over land?" another voice asked.

"Now gentlemen, I'm here to represent the King of England and to assist in the administration of these islands on behalf of the British Empire, and that also means doing what's best for the native people." Obviously, Eliot was non-committal, Ella thought. "Don't forget, please, gentleman, that the Banabans are also part of the British Empire and should be treated as such."

She laughed to herself. She could hear a few coughs and quite a bit of grumbling going on after that statement. Eliot obviously had not said what they had expected or wanted to hear. He sounded like a man of principle.

"Can I help you with anything Missus Williams? Why aren't you with the ladies?" a familiar voice came from behind her. Ella quickly turned around to see Cleeve Edwards, looking annoyed.

What a sneak, she thought as she quickly brought forth her excuse. "No, I'm fine, thank you. I'm just trying to find my handkerchief I misplaced earlier. Should be around here somewhere," she said, smiling profusely, and looking down behind the chairs. Her face felt flushed.

"I'll send in one of the house boys to give you a hand to look for it, and then, if you don't mind, I'd prefer if you stayed out with the other ladies."

"Er... thank you, that's very kind of you." She was embarrassed at his brusque manner.

She was not in a position to stand there and decline his offer as he turned and left the dining room. Meanwhile, she hurriedly dropped her handkerchief behind the chair on the other side of the table and waited until she saw him returning with his head houseboy in tow before bending down and picking up the handkerchief as they walked in.

"Oh here it is!" she said, turning to face Cleeve Edwards. "I'm sorry I bothered you."

Before he had the chance to reply, Ella sped past them, and out through the door and back to the ladies in the parlour.

She was glad when John came in to enquire if she was ready to leave. She hoped he had not heard about her little mishap in the dining room. Ella certainly did not want him upsetting himself. His colour was not looking too good as it was.

Her mishap was not going to make any difference. John was in a terrible mood all the way home. She thought part of what she had overheard was the reason. Of course, he was not about to discuss it with her.

She waited until they finally retired for the evening and tried to see if she could turn his mind to other things. Ella had learned from experience the best way to get a man's full attention was sex, even if she did not particularly enjoy the act itself. It was always better than being ignored, and she still liked her husband's affection and undivided attention when they were at home. But all she got for her troubles was a kiss and a curt goodnight. That lovely little interlude earlier this evening looked as if it could become more infrequent, at least until whatever it was that had John so worked up was remedied.

"Goodnight darling, I love you!" she said, as she turned away and extinguished their bedside lamp.

John's back was her answer, together with his cold silence.

Eventually, Eliot did sort out the mess. Eliot had told the younger Banabans they could be a very rich community in future years if they sold off more of their land. The older Banaban diehards refused point-blank to compromise. To them, money still held no great value, but with quite a few of the younger ones selling it allowed the company a few more years of unhindered mining before the issue of land ownership would rear its ugly head again.

John had, at long last, returned his attention in Ella's direction. He even relaxed enough to take holidays with the family at their holiday cottage, known as Williams's Camp, located on the beach on the other side of Sydney Point. For Ella to see him relax and take such pleasure in just spending time with her and the girls was wonderful. That little beach cottage, perched high on the edge of the water, was like another world and would always retain a special place in her heart, along with the happy times they all shared.

But all good things had to come to an end, and John had to return to work. Whether it had been part of an omen, Ella did not know, but before they knew it, World War One had broken out.

12. Banaban with his *te waa* in front of his canoe shed (*bareaka*) early 1900s Ocean Island.

CHAPTER TWELVE

LIVING WITH THE MAN OF MATANG

Tetabo 1914

As Tetabo opened his eyes, the darkness surrounded him. He could hear Meri breathing beside him, still deep in sleep. Without thinking, he made his way silently across the darkened room, his body going through its daily ritual. On reaching the door, he made his way from their small quarters at the back of Williams's house, moving effortlessly through the darkness to the path that would take him down to the island's shore.

Looking up, he could still see the twinkling of the stars in the dark night sky. He knew he must hurry as Nei Tengaina; the Virgin Spirit of the Dawn, would soon be upon them. Here on Banaba, Bue, the sun-hero, would rise so suddenly from the east. Tetabo always followed the same ritual that had been passed down from his ancestors. Every morning, without fail, he would make his way down to the sea to fish and worship Nei Tengaina as she came upon the island. She had always blessed his family's clan with abundance and happiness. He did not want to upset her now by being late.

On reaching his *bareaka*, the thatched roof shelter where his *te waa* was housed, he removed his ancestor's skull from its perch on the rafter and lashed it to the side of his outrigger as part of his daily ritual. His ancestor was known for his skills at seafaring and Tetabo always took the skull to sea with him. As he started to place the other essential items he needed into his canoe, he recited his daily chant to his ancestor, evoking his powers asking for his blessing of protection.

He dragged his *te waa* down to the water's edge with ease. Jumping aboard, he paddled out through the reef. There was no hoisting of a sail since the use of sails had long been taboo. Once outside the protection of the reef with the winds and currents running, a canoe could be easily set adrift and never seen again. Today, however, the sea inside the reef was calm, and only the sound of the pounding waves breaking nearby broke the quiet that surrounded him.

When he neared the edge of the reef, he saw the white-water glistening under a now dying night sky. He heard the sound of the flying fish splashing through the water around him. Ah, soon Nei Tengaina would grace him with her presence; she would bless him with a great catch. He stopped paddling and let his canoe drift over the reef, dropping his lines into the sea as the Virgin Spirit of the Dawn suddenly began to rise up from the vast ocean beyond. She came as quickly as she would leave when the day was over, a truly special time for him when he became one with the sea.

Here in this place away from the island and its people, he felt he was in a different world. This was his thinking time. A time to recollect what was happening in his life and all around him. He knew he had been blessed by the arrival of the *Wiriami,* but the *kambana* he worked for was an unpleasant element for the islanders.

The *kambana* wanted to take their beloved land and chew it up with their machines. He had heard them say how important their grey dust was for the big farmlands of the *bullamacow* in Australia and New Zealand. To think that all these people had come to their island just to take the dust and rocks. The great King George had said these *I-Matang* could have their land for the grey dust if they did not harm their food trees.

Now, after years of argument with the *kambana,* it had been agreed that they must replace the fruit trees it had taken for the mining land and justly compensate the people. He did not know what would happen anymore now; they knew that the *I-Matang* did not keep their word.

Sir and Madam Williams had always kept their word and were very good to him and his family. Madam Williams does not like what the *kambana* was doing to Banaba, but her man is with the *kambana,* Tetabo thought as he tossed over another fishing line. He knew Williams was a good man, but it had been said down in the village that he was the one who made the men and their machines chew up more of the land.

Madam had told him that Miti Wiriami did not mean to hurt his people; he was just doing as the *kambana* told him. Wiriami and Madam were like his family, and at times, he did not know where his true loyalties should lie. Now Germany, the country that ruled their sister island called Nauru, was making war with their good King George. The Banaban people had already contributed one thousand pounds worth of their coconuts to the War Fund to help their good King in his battle. These were indeed troubled times. Maybe as he sat there and fished, Nei Tengaina would help him with the conflicts he felt. She brought new life to the land every day and perhaps today she would bathe him with her wisdom.

His catch this morning was indeed proving good. Twelve *te eti* or bonito as they were also called, two *te baara*, which were a large mackerel with powerful jaws and teeth and three *teonauti*, or flying fish. He had to use his noose to catch the *te baara;* otherwise, they would bite straight through his line. Each time he hooked another *te eti,* he would toss the fish onto the floor of his *te waa*. Now, as Bue grew stronger, and brought the heat down upon them, it was time for him to be getting back to his home. Meri would be waiting for his catch to make the household breakfast.

Arriving back onshore, he put his *te waa* back in the canoe shed and hurriedly made his way back up the path, stopping for a short time at the *mwenga* of his family in Uma village. They were waiting eagerly to see what he had caught. Now his parents were getting older; it was up to him to help provide them with food and the comforts in life. After leaving most of his catch with them, he continued his journey up to the house. Walking through the kitchen door, he gave Meri his catch and hurried off to Wiriami's bedroom and rapped loudly on the door.

"Sir, Madam, thou shall be blessed, Bue is upon us!" Tetabo being a man of habit had used this same expression every morning since he had begun working for the Williams.

"Thank you, Tetabo," Wiriami called out through the closed bedroom door.

He then went down the hallway to Missy Gwennie's room to organise her for breakfast. When he walked into her room, she was already out of bed and playing with baby Uma.

"Ah Missy Gwennie *Kona mauri*," he greeted eagerly. They had always used the traditional welcome between them.

"*Kona mauri* Tea Tup," she replied with a perfect accent.

"Breakfast will be ready shortly Missy. Here, I will take our little one."

He gathered little Uma in his arms, and the three of them made their way to the veranda where Madam liked to have the breakfast meal served.

Madam and Sir were already dressed and sitting at the table when they arrived.

"How did your fishing go this morning, Tetabo?" Wiriami asked as he did every morning.

"Oh, very well, sir, many *te eti* this breakfast."

"How was the swell this morning?"

"Oh very good inside, but big waves pounding on da reef tis morning, I think te winds will soon be upon us."

"Let's hope they don't arrive yet; we have the *Messina* arriving from Australia with army troops on board today."

"How long will she be here?" Missus Wiriami asked.

"Well, now that *HMAS Melbourne* has landed on Nauru and taken out the wireless station, she is supposed to pick up all the deported Nauru staff and return them back."

"Oh it good news, Sir, our good King George tis winning te war." Tetabo smiled at Madam, who was obviously glad to hear some happy news too.

"Well Tetabo we haven't won the war in Europe yet, but King George has won Nauru, and that's indeed a good sign." Wiriami sipped his tea, trying to hide his amusement.

"Yes Sir, Nei Tengaina trulee blessed us te dae." Tetabo was beaming.

"Yes indeed, she has, Tetabo; let's hope she keeps blessing us before too many good men are lost," Wiriami replied.

"That's wonderful news, darling." Madam smiled at her husband.

Tetabo smiled with them both and then grew silent; deep in thought.

"Yesss siree!" he proclaimed, making his way off towards the kitchen to fetch breakfast.

"Why are you so happy today?" Meri inquired when he entered the kitchen.

"Ah, we are truly blessed, good King George has taken back Nauru."

"Oh, what wonderful news. You must go down after breakfast and tell the village."

"Yes, I'm sure everyone will want to know, especially Eri; now hurry up and give me the breakfast tray." He was eager to get away as soon as breakfast was over.

Meri handed her husband the heavily laden tray, and he quickly made his way back out to the veranda. Breakfast had indeed been good this morning, and an air of happiness seemed to permeate the household. Wiriami again thanked him for providing excellent fish before he left the table. He seemed eager to go to work this morning to see if there was any fresh news regarding the war. Madam always enjoyed her time at breakfast, Tetabo thought. It was the only time the whole family could be together before the long day began.

As he began to clear the empty dishes from the table, Missus Wiriami asked, "How are your parents today, Tetabo?"

"God has blessed them, Madam."

"Oh, that is good to hear. Has your father recovered from the fever?"

"Yes Madam, he is indeed well, but of course he is now a *te unimane*."

Madam let out a loud laugh. "Tetabo, your father would be no older than Mister Williams, and I'm sure he doesn't consider himself old."

"But Madam, Father's hair is turning white, a sign he is *te unimane* now."

"Well maybe in Banaban eyes, but definitely not in the *I-Matang* eyes. Anyway, your father is now a member of the village *kaboui*, a very privileged position I would think."

"Oh yes Madam, now he *te unimane* he has much wisdom needed for *kaboui*. He does no fish anymore," he said with some regret.

"But knowing you, Tetabo, I'm sure you give him most of your catch?" she quickly replied.

"Oh yes, Madam, my parents trade phosphate money for *kai* at *kambana* store. I see *te* tin food when I visit their *mwenga*. It make me wor… rry."

"I must admit, things are changing from when we first arrived here. The people do not seem to tend their fruit trees the way they used to or worry about the fishing so much."

Madam Wiriami could also see the changes that were happening to his people. He knew she felt strongly about the company's interference with their everyday lives.

"Well, Madam, still many many fish every day like our ancestors, but more my people want to sleep." He added, "they open the *bullamacow* and *te* tin fruit than go get fish or look upon *te* trees."

Fortunately, some of them still realised the importance of maintaining their daily rituals and traditions.

"And what about your father; how does he feel about the changes?"

"Ahhh, alas, he now go want to sleep. He says now he da *te unimane* he no need to. He want to eat *I-Matang* food too because I work here," he answered with regret.

"You know Mister Williams and I are only too happy to give you and your family any food you need, but it worries me that your people are losing their old ways. You know Tetabo, the *I-Matang* won't be here forever and then what will your people eat?"

"*Aia*, yes, Madam. Everyone have money for *kambana* store, now easy buy food and da water. My friend Terara, he agree, but we only young men, *unimane* do not listen to us."

"Well the *unimane* are very honourable men and the trouble is they think everyone else in the world is as honourable. I only wish it were true."

"*Aia*, Madam very honourable," he replied, deep in thought. Madam seemed to be able to understand their situation.

"Now, let's get ourselves moving and keep our day on a happy note with the *Messina* arriving. All those Australian troops on board so far from home…it makes me feel a little homesick."

He suddenly felt alarmed, concerned at her words.

"Madam, how be your home is sick, I take good care of it?"

Madam laughed. "No Tetabo, not this actual house. What I meant was feeling sad about being so far away from one's homeland. You know, like being away from Banaba where your heart must lie?" Her hand moved across her chest to cover her own heart.

"My heart always on Banaba because it is me," he solemnly answered, placing his hand over his heart in the same manner.

"Well, that is what one means by being homesick, missing your homeland," Ella tried to explain.

"Oh Madam, please *no* be homesick. Here I make you happy," he said, concerned now that he had upset her.

Again, her laughter returned. "Tetabo you always make me happy; now hurry up and let's get going, there's so much to do."

"*Aia*, Madam," he said with relief, making his way back to the kitchen.

Meri was getting the girls dressed. Missy Gwennie had to get ready, so Madam could accompany her on the flatcar to the Sacred Heart Mission School at Tabwewa village on the other side of the island. Madam Wiriami liked to ride on the flatcar and rarely missed the opportunity to accompany her daughter on these daily trips. Tetabo would accompany her if Madam had another engagement.

Missy Gwennie was becoming quite a lady and Missy was now the only *I-Matang* girl of her age on the island. The other younger *I-Matang* children had all been sent away to school back in their homelands when they had reached the age of nine or ten. But he knew Madam would not send her Missy away. He had heard the many arguments she had with Wiriami, and Madam always got her way.

He had also overheard Madam saying that she would ensure that Missy Gwennie was chaperoned at all times. She had even called him into the parlour a few days later to explain the responsibility she was giving him in ensuring that Missy Gwennie was always correctly escorted. It had taken him quite a while to understand the ways of the *I-Matang*, especially chaperoning. When the Banaban girls were nearing maturity, they were sent away so they could be kept out of the sun. There they would stay for many days until they were fully-grown and ready for marriage. Their fair skins made them much sought after brides. The *I-Matang* liked their brides very old, nearly *kaka te aine*, grandmother-age, by the time they had their babies.

That morning, after he returned with Missy Gwennie on her daily trip to tend her bird, he had accompanied Madam and Missy Gwennie to the flatcar before he made his way back down to the village.

The village, as usual, was full of activity with women busy weaving pandanus mats and children gathered around playing and laughing. His own child, Nete, was still only a baby and stayed up at the Wiriami's house with them. He walked up to the *maneaba* standing in the centre of the village. The *kabowi* was already in progress, and his father was sitting at his *boti*, the ancestors' place inside the *maneaba*. He lowered his head and stooped low, making his way to sit next to his father. He quietly told him of the news about Nauru so as not to disturb the discussion that was in progress.

When it came his father's time to speak, he told the gathering about the taking of Nauru by their good King George. While much excitement broke out among the gathered men of the *kabowi,* a motion was put forward for the people of Uma village to give more of their coconuts for the war fund to help their King in his victories. A vote was taken, and all agreed. When the war had first begun the elders of every village had wanted to send their young men off to fight. But Eliot, the Resident Commissioner, said he could not let their young men enlist, so it had been decided throughout the island to supply the war with coconuts.

By the time World War One would be over, the Banabans had given copra alone worth about 10,000 pounds.

After the meeting was over and the men were leaving the *maneaba,* he saw young Rotan with his father Tito, who was the local church minister of Buakonikai village.

"*Kona mauri,* Tito!" he greeted the old man as a show of respect

"*Kona mauri,* Tetabo!"

"*Kona mauri,* Rotan," Tetabo now greeted Tito's son.

"*Kona mauri,* Tetabo!" he replied.

After their greetings and exchange of courtesies, the older man Tito moved on to talk to some of the *unimane* that were still gathered.

Tetabo took the opportunity to speak with Rotan and find out what was happening in the different villages. Rotan was a fine young man who had just married after his training according to Banaban custom. His father had plans to send his son to the Mission school in Tarawa so he could also follow him and become a Christian minister.

Rotan was an intelligent boy who had met Miti Ariti, the old man Mister Albert Ellis, many times while accompanying his father on trips to discuss the various land problems the Banaban people were having with the *kambana*. His father, Tito, had always got on reasonably well with Miti Ariti, but now over the years, even Tito had grown very wary of old man's real intentions for the Banaban people. Since his suspicions had grown and the land problems had finally come to a complete deadlock, their personal relationship had also deteriorated.

The old man, Miti Ariti, had now left Banaba and even though the matter had been resolved for the immediate future, as far as Tito was concerned the *kambana* would never buy any more land from him. A lot of the *unimane* felt the same way. While the younger people were being persuaded to part with their landholdings, the *kambana* was busy chewing up more of Banaba's dust and rocks.

After he and Rotan said their *tia kabo* on that fateful day, he watched the impressive young man make his way to the path that led down to the canoe sheds. No one could have foreseen then what would happen in the years to come when Rotan's son would become one of the key figures in the survival of his people.

13. Uma village near Sydney Point, Ocean Island early 1900s.

CHAPTER THIRTEEN

CHILDREN NO MORE

Off Sydney Point 1915

"Ata, I'm frightened!" Gwennie called over the roar of the waves.

"Sit still, Nei Gwennie, I know what I am doing." She could hear his voice distinctly over the noise of the surf. It had deepened lately, a sign of his new maturity.

Ata proudly paddled his new *te waa* out through the reef and headed straight into the incoming waves. His small, slender craft looked no match for the might of the giant surf that seemed to break with all its fury upon the shallow reef below. The dawn was not far away, and like all Banabans, Ata considered that this was a perfect time to put to sea. It also helped that most of the *I-Matang* staff were still in bed, including Gwennie's parents.

The pair was on one of their clandestine meetings, but this time it was different. Ata had been away for many months, and this was their first time together since he had returned from the terraces. Ata was eager to show her his *te waa* he had made, another sign of his impending manhood.

Gwennie tried to hide her fear at being out here on such a wild sea, while her thoughts turned to her own father and his explanation of why the island was known for its vicious surrounding waters. He had told her how the island rose like a giant mountain from under the sea in a place where the Pacific Ocean sank to a vast depth. The waves would build up under the water when they came in contact with the steep landfall of the submerged part of the island far under the sea. Most people thought the waves just appeared from nowhere, but her father had said there was so much activity in the vast depths below that caused the swell to rise as if by magic.

Some days the surrounding sea was almost like a millpond. Uncle Will had told her that when this occasionally happened, the sea was at its most dangerous. When the sailors and seamen attempted to use the waves to guide their large ships into the bay none of the razor-sharp reefs could be seen until the ships were right on top of them, sometimes with fatal consequences.

Ata's solidly muscled body glistened with sweat as he increased his powerful strokes with the paddle while the *te waa* silently pierced its way farther through the breakers. She was sitting in front of him, now, reciting one of her favourite psalms, in an effort to forget her fears. This always seemed to calm her and gave her the confidence that should anything untoward happen; she would at least be ready to meet her maker.

Fear was something that usually never came into her way of thinking, but since Ata had become a man and had built his own *te waa,* he suddenly seemed different. She could not help noticing the shape of his body and the new strength in his arms and shoulders. His voice was now much deeper, and he was beaming with confidence. His hair, like that of all Banaban men, was black and glistening with coconut oil, kept short by his mother's constant trimming with a treasured piece of glass. The brilliance of his blue eyes had not changed, but the features of his face were now more prominent with the jut of his square jaw. Except for his striking eyes, he looked like a Banaban, although there was also no mistaking the strong resemblance to his *I-Matang* father.

Suddenly, on reaching the crest of the next wave, the *te waa* came crashing down into a trough of calm dark water, and they quickly raced ahead of the waves' powerful white water into the gently rolling swell. Gwennie gave a happy sigh and for the first time, released her grip on the sides of his canoe.

Ata was anxious for Gwennie to give approval of his seamanship.

"See Gwennie? I told you this was a beautiful place out here beyond the breakers and looking back towards our island."

It was just before dawn, and the silhouette of the island could be clearly seen in the dying night sky. It was, indeed, a beautiful sight.

"Yes, it is beautiful, Ata, but now I know why it is forbidden for us *I-Matang* to venture out past the reef. It is very dangerous, and I was frightened at times."

She knew in her heart that Ata was competent enough to guide his *te waa*, but she had been afraid and felt guilty for openly disobeying her father's orders. She suddenly remembered another story her father had told her; just realising she could end up in the same position.

"Father has already lost two of his best men out here on a fishing trip with one of your people," she said, hoping he would take notice of her fears.

"Nei Gwennie, you know you can trust me. I've been initiated into the ways of the sea now," he boasted.

"Well, that did not save Mister Greenway and Doctor Hills, and Tamanwewa, from the Gates of Nakaa," she retorted. The Banabans feared the guardian of the gate between the worlds of the living and the dead. Her breathing was still quick; the fear had not entirely left her.

"Do not be afraid, Nei Gwennie, Nakaa will not catch us in his nets." He was referring to the legend where all of the dead must escape the nets of Nakaa before entering the Land of *Matang*. "My mother says I am destined to be an important man. Do you agree, Gwennie?" He laughed.

She could not resist his laughter and turned around quickly to face him. The aura of the waning moon suddenly seemed to accentuate his lean muscled body, glistening from a film of moisture that covered his chest. The intensity of his piercing blue eyes made her gasp. She clasped her hands tightly and drew back, throwing herself off balance. Ata's expression suddenly changed as he quickly shifted his weight to correct her mistake, then the craft settled back safely in the water.

They sat there in silence, pretending not to notice the change in their feelings.

Ata had observed the changes happening to his good friend as she sat up there in the bow of his *te waa*. His eyes took in a glimpse of her bare flesh just showing through the gap at the back of her bodice. He wanted to touch the silky paleness of her skin. He had also noticed that she now was a *neiko*, a woman, with shapely breasts that were always hidden underneath bulky coverings. Why would such a beautiful girl hide her body so? Ata pondered. She should be proud of being a woman.

"Missy Gwennie, will your *tama* wish to marry you off soon?" He suddenly realised she was now of the marrying age.

"Oh, Ata, you are so funny. Of course not, my father thinks I am still a *tetei*," she said, laughing at his question.

"You are no *tetei*!" His voice sounded deeper than usual.

As the laugh began to die on her lips, she realised for the first time that he was serious. She had known him for all of her life and had just noticed the changes happening to her friend. She now understood why she had been so concerned about him seeming so different. He had become a man and the boy she had known all her life was gone. Luckily, she had her baby sister Uma to keep her company now because she was missing these special times she spent with him.

With all these thoughts running through her head, she suddenly heard her voice break the silence of the sea all around them.

"Do you love me, Ata?"

Why did she say that? She couldn't believe what she had just said, and now she realised, as her mother would say, 'Words once said can never be taken back!' She really did not want to hear his answer.

Over the sudden pounding of her heart, she heard him say, "Yes... and I will marry you; we will be together always."

She sat motionless with her back to him, not daring to turn around and look at him again, still hearing his words.

Ata waited until she recovered her composure, resisting the strong urge he felt again to touch her. He would have to wait until they were married, he told himself, trying to control the sudden flood of hormones rushing through his body.

"We have always been together; I cannot lose you." His voice was husky with emotion.

Gwennie had not given serious thought of how this situation had happened. With her *I-Matang* background, she knew any further relationship with Ata would be unacceptable. A scandal, as her mother would call it. She had known from such an early age that she would have to keep their friendship secret, so why now was she saying these things?

While these thoughts churned within her, she could deny the growing feeling of warmth that consumed her whole being. Ata really did love her! She had always known he did and she, in turn, had loved him for a long time. Their silence grew as they both became lost in their thoughts.

Ata realised that he must take her back before the *taai* was too high in the sky and the *I-Matang* were up and about; otherwise, they would be at risk of being seen out here together. Slowly, he began to turn his *te waa* back towards the shore, his mind awash with the idea of the two of them being together. He knew he would be an important man one day, just as his mother had always said, and when that came about, he would have Gwennie by his side. He knew Gwennie could live among his people. She would not need the ways of the *I-Matang,* and he would be a very proud man. Quickening his strokes, he made their way back to the point where the surf began to boil up out of the depths, and without a moment's hesitation, he ploughed his way through the hostile waves. He did not notice Gwennie taking up her vice-like grip again, for his mind was far away. His lips held a smile that would not leave his face.

The resentment he felt towards rarely seeing his *tama* had been directed towards all the *I-Matang* when he watched their thirst grow each year for more of his people's precious land. Ata realised he could change all these things because suddenly he was now a man of strength and one day Ata knew he would be a man of influence.

On nearing the shore, Gwennie noticed a lone figure standing near Ata's *te waa* shed. Taai had just begun to light up the sky. Drawing closer, they both realised with regret that their trip had been discovered and there, waiting to meet them, was Captain Cozen, Ata's father. Before they even had a chance to jump ashore and Ata could drag his *te waa* from the water, Uncle Will had grabbed Gwennie and lifted her clear out of the canoe and straight onto the shore. They could both tell by the look on his face; he was not a happy man.

"Hello, Uncle Will, I've just had a little trip in Ata's *te waa*," she said.

"Well, have you now!" His voice was gruff as he turned to face Ata. "And you, son, should know better than to take Miss Gwennie out on that ocean."

They kept silent in embarrassment at being discovered. Gwennie was trying to hide behind Ata.

"You both could have got yourselves killed!"

Even before Cozens had a chance to add to his tirade, Ata swiftly walked up to his father and looked him straight in the eyes. "Nei Gwennie and I are going to marry," he said defiantly, in spite of his father's anger.

"Don't talk rot, Arthur, you know that's not possible," his father replied, taken aback by his son's statement.

It was at that moment he realised his son was serious. "You are both just children and from two completely different worlds." His face turned a brighter shade of red.

It was not until he had calmed down later that he had realised what he had just said to his son. It had been the same advice that he had been given and disobeyed, but now, his love and protection of his son was one of the strongest instincts he possessed. Unfortunately for Ata, he was not to know this, for the *I-Matang* did not allow a person to know their innermost thoughts for fear of showing weakness. Ata was now even more agitated by his father's use of his *te I-Matang* name and stepped closer.

"I will marry her, and no one will stop us! She will be my wife!"

Gwennie, now realising the severity of the situation where the father was pitted against son, saw Ata clenching his fists and the anger of his father, who was one of the largest men on the island. She could see him physically shaking with rage at his son's defiance, and she suddenly burst into tears. She could not bear to see them fight, knowing how Ata really felt about his father.

Cozens suddenly realised that he had a near-hysterical young woman to contend with, as well as the prospect of the wrath of her father, who was one of his closest friends. He turned to her.

"Come now, Gwennie, you're overwrought. I had no knowledge of you and Ata," he explained, trying to calm her. "It's all right, I'm not going to mention any of this to your parents, I think the less they know about what's obviously been going on between the two of you the better!"

Gwennie continued her uncontrollable sobbing, making Cozens feel even more ill at ease.

"Please Gwennie, don't be upset. I apologise for my bad temper."

Her body was racked with more tears and, being a practical man, Cozens felt at a loss how to console the poor little thing.

"Come on, Gwennie, we must get you home before your parents begin looking for you, or before someone else sees us all down here. Come on, please! Please, Arthur, tell her she must go now," he pleaded with his son, forgetting his anger for the moment.

Ata realised that his father was really concerned with Gwennie's state.

"Go with him, Gwennie. He is right, we will be together soon," he said, reaching for her hand, her tear-filled eyes looking into his.

With his final words, Cozens took her other hand and slowly moved her away from Ata. She reluctantly left him and made her way up to the pathway with his father, looking back to catch a final glimpse of Ata. He stood there watching them both go, his mind going back to the last time his *tama* had hurt him so badly. It also involved the only other woman in his life he loved, his *tina*. Why did this man take such pleasure in hurting them? He was more convinced than ever that at times, this man had a heart made of pure stone. He would one day show this man that he was a man of honour. That even though he had his father's blood running in his veins, he was a man of his word, and he would marry Gwennie.

14. John Williams (white pith helmet) with Father Pujabet and his work gang top-side on Ocean Island 1920s.

CHAPTER FOURTEEN

LIVING WITH WAR

John 1917

John Williams walked along the exposed track towards the diggings up on the central field, commonly known as topside. A fine trickle of sweat ran down the side of his face. It was turning into another one of those rather trying days, and he was glad to try and get a break, even if it meant walking up here in the heat of the day to inspect the cableways.

Stopping to reach for his handkerchief in his trouser pocket, John looked up into the bright blue sky. There was not a cloud to be seen anywhere; another hot day with no rain in sight and another day added to this hideous drought. He slowly lifted his white pith helmet to mop his damp brow. It was still too early in the day for the daily afternoon breeze that usually brought some welcome relief from the heat. Replacing his hat, he started his slow ascent back on up the path, wishing at least to find some shade farther along.

It seems strange how life has its ups and downs, John thought, while he silently ambled on. He was thinking of how he just seemed to get one problem straightened out and believe he would sail through the rest of his life enjoying the good times when all of a sudden something came along again to change it all. A World War or *der tag,* as the Germans so kindly called it, was something over which he did not have any control.

After years of problems with the Banabans and their land, and Resident Commissioners who all wanted to stand by and hold the natives' hands, they had finally got things sorted out just in time for war. The same company also mined Nauru, the German-owned island to the north-west, for phosphate. It had become a tricky situation with the Resident Commissioner on Nauru being a German and the company's manager being British. As soon as the war had been officially declared, the company staff were all deported and sent to Ocean Island. Luckily, all of them were unharmed, probably because they had all been friends with their German workmates.

With each step that John Williams took along the trail, his feet kicked up fine white dust. The dust was in fact pure phosphate, and because of the continuing drought conditions, the island was becoming a real dust bowl. John glanced at his feet and was thankful for his canvas shoes that looked almost white. God, he hated droughts.

Turning his gaze towards the expanse of the ocean, John noticed a small speck out on the northern horizon. He wondered if it was friendly or one of those German raiders they had all been talking about.

Yes, he thought, to make matters worse they now had reports of three German battleships cruising near the island. The threat of warships and German raiders on the prowl had made it difficult for them to have the phosphate shipped out. John tried to keep his mind on his job, which was the overseeing of the mining. As long as he kept production going at its usual rate, his job was done, but for his old mate Captain Cozens, it was a different story.

They had to close down the Tabwewa settlement due to reduced staff. Thirty-five of the men had returned to Australia and New Zealand to enlist for service at the front, and phosphate shipments had been reduced. Because of the restrictions imposed on them, they were making some outstanding developments in other areas, especially when it came to the plant and equipment. These developments, John believed, would significantly improve the way the mining operations were carried out in the years to come. Just the difference the cableway had made already! He noticed the top of one of the tall narrow towers sticking up from the crest of the hill up ahead.

Everyone had been kept at the ready in case they had to evacuate the women and children. John grinned to himself at the thought of them trying to evacuate his wife. It would be something worth watching. She had already told him that she would stay as long as he stayed, and she would not leave without him... 'and do not bother arguing', to quote her words. He had no intention of trying to take her on, and he would appreciate seeing any man who could. He would be a man indeed, he mused, who would earn his respect.

To Eliot's credit, he had made them ready in case the island was attacked. The Resident Commissioner had the company's vast stores of oil and coal, together with tins of kerosene, stacked so that the lot could be fired at short notice. He had also formed a volunteer force comprising some of the European staff and the native constabulary, who would put up a defence should they be invaded. Luckily, they had not had to use the precautions yet, but if the Germans did decide to land here, the lads were ready and waiting to put on a decent welcome for them.

"*Kona mauri,* Miti Wiriami, sir !"

John looked up. Two Gilbertese lads were coming towards him on the trail.

"*Kona mauri*! Where are you two off to?" he asked, wondering what they were doing here, away from the work gangs on topside.

"Oh, sir, we both very sick. Must go down to hospital," one of the lads said.

"What's wrong with you?" he quickly asked, noting they both looked fit and well.

"The runny belly sir, very bad." The same boy spoke again.

"Oh! Well, you better hurry along and get something for it. Quick now, on your way!" John was not going to stand and argue with him over the dreaded runny belly. Diarrhoea and gastric upset was every man's dread on the island.

"Yes, sir!" the boys answered in unison.

John quickly moved on, hoping he had not got too close to the two lads. It was usually highly contagious. He started to settle back into a more leisurely pace, and his mind once again returned to war.

Only four days after the deportations on Nauru, an Australian navy vessel had landed an armed party back on the island, destroying their wireless station. The Germans had then surrendered into Allied hands... if one could call it that. It was rumoured that it had been more as if the Germans were glad to see them. John laughed, thinking of the mates he had befriended over the years on his many trips to Nauru. All the Germans he knew had grown extremely fond of Australian beer and probably if the truth was known, they had all been away from their homelands for too long to become involved in such unsavoury business, especially when their supposed enemy turned out to be their friends and fellow workmates.

The company in the meantime had chartered an Australian cargo vessel, and a combined group of four hundred Australian Army and Naval officers and men had picked up the deported Nauru staff before continuing on to Nauru, where they formally hoisted the British flag. Nauru was now officially under Australian Military occupation.

John spotted a small strand of coconut palms up ahead and thought that even out here in no man's land in the middle of the Pacific, the cruel tentacles of war could still be such a threat. He supposed it probably had more to do with the enemy wanting to get their hands on the phosphate than anything else. But in his view, it did not matter that the world was in the grip of war; politics always seemed to be lurking its ugly head somewhere in the background.

Just before the war had started, Eliot, as the Resident Commissioner, had decided, in his imperial wisdom, to change the protectorate of the Gilbert and Ellice Islands into a colony. His reasoning behind this move was to offer the Banabans some protection from the company, but in fact, as a colony, Ocean Island was now no longer a separate entity. Therefore, more phosphate revenue would be siphoned off to the British Empire; which really meant that the company could now legally distribute the phosphate royalty money paid to the Banaban landowners to the new colony.

Crafty people those Poms, John mused. They not only had taken over the island and given the poor local buggers a contract to tie them up for a pittance for the next 999 years but now they even wanted to take their pittance from them as well. He wondered if the poor old Banabans knew they were now going to be supporting the whole British colony of the Gilbert and Ellice Islands? Yes, the old Poms were greedy buggers. They wanted it all, and he supposed the old Krauts were not angels either.

While the rest of the world was busy killing each other, this significant transformation was quietly taking place. Ah well, John mumbled to himself, as the Poms would say, 'never pass up a good opportunity!' God, he hated droughts and wars and politics. He was starting to wonder if walking up here in the middle of the day was such a good idea. It was not really improving his frame of mind.

John's thoughts had only touched on the idea of things to come, on that day as he made his way up the path to the topside. Just how significant these implications would be to the future generations of Banaban people he could never have imagined. History would state that Eliot had only the best of intentions when it came to protecting the Banabans and he never intended to hurt them. If anything, Commissioner Eliot was proving to be another thorn in the side of the company, and that had been the general opinion around company circles from the very first moment Eliot had set foot on the island.

Once Nauru had been captured, John reflected, things had started to return to reasonably normal back here on Ocean Island while the battles still raged on the continent. All news of the war was eagerly awaited, while his attention was now returning more to island matters. It was better to take one's mind off all these depressing thoughts of war he told himself, with its death and destruction.

Trying to brighten his mood, he turned his mind to the latest amusement on the local scene. They had a young cadet called Arthur Grimble who had arrived from England just before the start of the war to serve his time under Eliot. Old Eliot had made it plain to everyone from the beginning that the new cadet was not welcome. This little saga was turning into one of the best sources of entertainment as this young protégé walked around and never seemed to be able to put a foot right.

Eliot kept giving him these silly jobs to do, obviously trying to keep him out of his hair. Unfortunately, all this poor Grimble fellow could do was keep making an even bigger hash of things. It got to the stage where they were all wondering what he would do next, especially after the Christmas fiasco.

Grimble had been told to go out to the ship moored in the boat harbour and return with the government's ration of Christmas good cheer, however, in true Grimble fashion, he let the ship sail away with all the government's Christmas provisions still on board. Everyone thought old Eliot would have heart failure over that one and the word was Grimble had kept a low profile at the official, and lean, Christmas dinner.

But the icing on the cake was to come. Eliot had put him to work helping the works department build more water cisterns the government needed to try and preserve water for these droughts. Now the government's headquarters were stationed on the island, they were officially responsible for the Police, Main Roads (more like pathways as there were still no vehicles on the island), Public Works, Education, Plumbing and Sewage Works, Justice and the list went on.

Seeing Grimble was so eager to try and please after making such a hash of things, he obviously thought he would try and make amends. He started on a water cistern in his own back yard, which just happened to be right next to Old Eliot's residence. John grinned to himself at just recalling the incident. There was no doubting the useless young Grimble's enthusiasm, he mused. Grimble had apparently started to dig and found the ground so hard that he decided that explosives would be needed to do the job.

John, being an overseer himself and in charge of all explosives used in mining operations, knew just how dangerous explosives could be. Well, Grimble, being a government man and not answerable to the company, had gone off on his own and organised what he needed. He did not realise you needed only half a stick of explosives to blow a hole big enough for a water cistern and instead for some reason known only to himself, he put two full sticks down the sinkhole.

He not only blew an enormous crater in his own back yard, but most of the blast ended up landing on Eliot's house. Word was that Old Eliot was in the bathtub at the time and was nearly blown clean out of the tub. John pictured the scene again in his mind and thought just how much he would have loved to have seen the expression on Grimble's face when old man Eliot came after him.

Yes, he chuckled to himself; the Australian lads love a good laugh, though these British chaps took some beating. He had heard that things around the government offices were a little strained at the moment. The continuing Grimble - Eliot saga definitely helped him take his mind off the horrors of war.

On reaching a strand of sad-looking coconut palms, he decided to rest. Making himself comfortable on his handkerchief which he had placed on the ground, he sat down and looked up at the twisted, distorted tops of the trees. The shade itself was barely a relief from the scorching sun, but at least it was something. He studied the trunks of the coconut palms, realising they could tell the whole history of the droughts and good years here on the island with the rings of growth around their trunks.

Leaning back against the notched trunk of the tree after taking his hat off to cool down, he carefully inspected the canopies overhead. The trees had really suffered this time from the drought. Most of them were down to only one or two fronds shooting straight up from the top of their long gnarled trunks. Nothing was sadder, he thought than a usually lush coconut tree with healthy graceful fronds arching from the bow to something that looked like this. It was hard to believe they were one and the same. Shutting his eyes just for a moment, he felt his mood once again turning somewhat melancholy.

He was thinking of his old workmates that would not be coming back to work on the island. They had received news that four of their men had paid the ultimate price from the war in Europe. Now they had things sorted out on Nauru, the war seemed to leave them otherwise untouched, although the news of their former workmates had brought the realities back home to all of them.

Meanwhile, they had all heard that the London board of the company had taken the necessary legal steps against the shares held by enemy subjects. The Public Trustee in Britain had ordered the shares to be auctioned off and sold them to a large British shipping company. Not before time! John thought.

Opening his eyes, he sighted the central field up ahead. The tall cableway structures were clearly visible, and the mast of the new wireless station was reflecting the bright sunlight. The wireless had been one of the benefits they had gained during the war. After the wireless station had been repaired on Nauru, it was decided to build one here. Now, at last, they would finally have communications with the outside world and not have to rely on the ships to relay the current events happening in the rest of the world or the months it took to try and organise just the movements of shipping around the two islands. His mate George Cozens had been delighted at this prospect, as most of the vessels called between here and Nauru, and now he would have the luxury of radioing ahead.

John got to his feet, dusting off his trousers, and picked up his handkerchief. He placed his hat back on his head and started the last leg of his trip to the top. Up here on the crest of the island, all the sounds carried up from the activity going on down below. It was a strange assortment of children's laughter, clanging machinery and a mixture of voices. All of these, if you listened carefully, spoke a different language.

Now pacing himself and eager to get to his destination, he thought, where else in the world would a person find so much going on in such a small area? Over two thousand people of so many different cultures living and working side by side all crammed together on this tiny speck in the middle of nowhere… No, he told himself, they're probably just all mad like the rest of us. He laughed, feeling a little more refreshed after his short rest.

After finally reaching topside, he carried out his inspection and was rather pleased with what he saw. The whole central area was really moving along now they had the cableway in. With the two towers mounted at each end of the diggings, the large bucket could be suspended all the way along the line of overhead cables. This saved a lot of time lifting the phosphate over the ever-growing mountain of coral pinnacles that were left after mining was completed. It was one of the biggest pitfalls they had to overcome. The more phosphate they removed, the more mined out areas they had to try and get through. The only way they had been able to do it in the past was by building planked walkways over the top and wheeling barrows through.

John finished his business on topside and enjoyed a chat with the other overseers in charge of the different work gangs, and then once again found himself rewinding his way down the track that would take him down to the company office at Uma. This time he had decided to walk around via the government residency and loop his way back past the Chinese quarters. John felt in a better frame of mind now with a bit more shelter here along the trail and the afternoon sea breeze springing up. His thoughts turned to another problem he had on his mind. This one seemed to keep nagging at him and just would not go away.

While all these new developments and world conflicts had been taking place, John had begun to notice another struggle looming on the horizon that was not associated with the war or politics. This one was happening right in his back yard. They had now been living and working on Ocean Island for nearly sixteen years. This gave them the title of being the Old Timers. Ella especially had turned into a real matriarch figure. While the young single men were living so far from home and families, they really enjoyed the hospitality she showed them. Similarly, the wives of the younger married couples that arrived over the years sought her guidance.

Rounding the bend at the government residency, John turned at the fork in the path and took the one running past the sports oval. Even though he was deep in thought, he suddenly stopped, shocked at the poor state of the oval. The Residency was set in a picturesque place, in a clearing among a thick grove of coconut trees. Even though the oval itself had no actual topsoil on it, as, like the rest of the island, it was covered in phosphate, it still usually had a covering of some grass.

Now, in the grip of a drought, it had turned into an expanse of grey dust. As the wind gusted through the clearing, John picked up the loose chalky powder in his hand and watched the wind blow it back towards the grove of trees that ringed the area. The sickly trees were not only looking in need of a good drink but, like John's shoes, were also covered in a fine white film of dust. Darn drought, he told himself, now a man will be flat out playing a decent game of cricket.

He picked up a small, dusty-looking pebble that he knew if analysed would come out as pure grade phosphate. In frustration, he hurled it towards the side of the stands. Turning back to the trail, he heard the small ping on the tin sheeting as his projectile reached its target. Smiling to himself, his mind once again turned to family matters.

His Ella, with her years of experience living in these remote parts, was often called upon to help out and lend an ear to homesick expatriates. One of the main reasons she had stolen his heart in the first place, other than her beautiful looks, was her kindness. Ella was nearly as bad as the natives when it came to giving things away, though he would never let it be said that she did not possess a mind of her own. He knew a lot of people thought she was such a sweet little abiding wife and he knew she did everything in her power to make his life as easy as possible, but after twenty years of marriage, he also knew the determination this kindly little woman possessed.

Due to all these happenings, there was constant activity on the home front. Their social life was busy. No one could complain of never having anything to do. In between the busy schedule Ella had mapped out for them, their house was continually full of guests, usually visitors or family of the single men. As the company's single accommodation consisted of barrack-style bungalows and proved unsuitable for visitors, especially the female variety, they happily obliged by inviting them to stay in their large house. The company also had excellent guest accommodation, which was mainly used for visiting management or officials.

Over the past years, their household staff had increased. At first, it was just Tetabo's wife and then their baby son, Nete had come along. Next, it was Meri's sister, who now did the laundry and was known as Jane, like all the other native laundry girls. She was about to marry a young Tabiteuean lad who was here working for the company. He knew what was coming; he would be asked if the new husband could also move in out the back of the house as well. He would have to say no. No more! He may as well be working for nothing the way it was going. He worked just to pay the bill at the trade store.

Seeing the company paid only for Tetabo, he had to support the rest of the household from his own funds. Ella believed they had an obligation to do all they could for the natives, and she argued that Tetabo and his growing clan did a decent job of looking after the household. He was sure she would have loved to move the whole village into their back yard if she could have got away with it.

Luckily for him, the company and its policies were the one thing that she did not argue with. No, he would have to be firm with her. She would have to realise that they just could not help everyone. He would speak to her tonight. Clear the air and sort things out about Gwennie too. They had a responsibility to look after their own first and Gwennie was more important.

Over the last few months, John had noticed the younger men had taken to referring to how beautiful his young Gwennie was. At first, he regarded these comments as just being polite until some of the young fellows had even gone as far as to ask his permission to court her. John was so taken aback that he quickly advised them all that she was only a child and would not require their company for a few years yet. He was beginning to wonder if these young lads were turning up at the house for his and Ella's company or trying to get a chance to see their daughter.

Now, walking past the myriad of shanty style buildings that housed the Chinese quarters, John turned at the next fork in the path leading to his office back in Uma. He had been so preoccupied with his thoughts that he had failed to hear or see the people who had called out greetings along the way.

No, he would talk to Ella tonight. Bring all this to her attention. A man's responsibility was to look after his own first, and they would not be taking in any more household staff. N… O!

That evening, after the children had retired, John took his wife aside. "Ella dearest!"

He had observed that she was in a pleasant mood. The dinner had been a success, and she had already mentioned what a lovely day she had at her Bridge Club.

"I have something I wish to discuss with you," he said, trying to make his voice sound authoritative. Better to let her know straight away that he was in control.

"Yes dear, what's wrong? Are you having problems at work?" She frowned, looking concerned.

"No, not with work really." He cleared his throat. "More like a personal problem," he said, trying to ready himself.

He had already decided to confront Ella about Gwennie first, and that would set the mood to discuss the household staff issue.

"Well, what personal problems could you have, dear?"

Goodness, she is in a good mood, he thought. "Well it's not a problem yet but, if we don't take the situation in hand, we could have a problem." He watched her eyes start to cloud over.

She was cautious at his mention of the word 'we'. "What situation are you talking about?"

He noted the slight change in her voice. "Well, the young lads at work have been carrying on about how beautiful our Gwennie is lately."

After a brief moment's silence, she smiled. "Well they're right, she is turning into a beautiful young woman." She sounded pleased with herself, walking over to where she kept her sewing basket.

"But that's the problem, Ella, she's still only a child, and I don't like all these young men looking at her." He watched as she returned to her chair and placed the basket in her lap. "And especially with bad intentions in mind," he continued, trying to emphasise how serious the problem with Gwennie was.

Ella casually looked up if seeing him for the first time. "My poor darling, I know it must be hard on you, but you must realise, our Gwennie's no longer a child. She's a lovely young woman," she asserted, "and whether we like it or not, she'll be taking an interest in gentlemen herself shortly."

He could not believe it, hearing her talk like this. "But Ella, don't you realise she's becoming the talking point of the men on the island?"

"Yes, that is unfortunate, but she can't help being a woman and a beautiful one at that and don't forget; the only unmarried woman on the island," she calmly replied. She was apparently enjoying the situation.

He was annoyed. "Well if you had allowed me to send her off to boarding school we wouldn't be having these problems!"

By the expression on her face, John knew he had finally got her full attention.

"Now please let's not start that argument again. You know why I won't send my girls away, and besides, even if she had gone to boarding school, she still would have had to come back here for vacations." He noticed her voice slightly raised; a sure warning sign that he had hit a raw nerve.

"I know, Ella, but..." He had not even got the rest of the words out before she interrupted.

"But nothing, dear! You know I'm right, and I can assure you. I keep a lot better eye on my daughters than what they would have done at boarding school. Between Tetabo and me she never goes anywhere on the island unchaperoned." Now looking at John, her eyes were defiant.

This was not going the way he had planned. "Well, what do you expect me to say to all these young lads at work? They are even getting bold enough to ask my permission to escort her out," he challenged.

"And what did you tell them?"

"What do you think I told them?" he asked, his temper beginning to rise. "Ask me in ten years!"

"For goodness sakes, how are we going to keep her under wraps for another ten years? Anyway, have you forgotten I married you at the age Gwennie is now?"

"Ella, you did not!"

"I had just turned eighteen on my wedding day, nearly the same age as Gwennie," she said triumphantly.

"Well, that's you, not my Gwennie," he replied. He had never heard such nonsense.

"I seriously believe we will have to look for a suitable husband for her," she stated.

"A husband? My poor child!" he yelled, feeling his blood boil.

"Now John, calm down, it's no good trying to talk to you while you are all upset. Just try and think about what I have said. It would be for the best," she replied in that sweet voice of hers, once again closing off any further discussion on the matter.

She rose from her chair, placed her basket back on the sideboard and walked over to take his hand.

"Come on, enough talk," she said, bending down to kiss him. "I think we should both get an early night, don't you?"

He rose from his seat and followed her into the bedroom, his mind suddenly on other things.

Later that night, as John tried to drift off to sleep, he realised that he had let Ella do it again. He could not believe it, and he had not even got around to telling her about his decision on the household staff. That night he finally drifted in and out of a restless sleep tossing and turning all night, visualising terrifying images of horrible ugly old men chasing after his sweet, innocent, gentle Gwennie. All he could do was try and catch up with her while she screamed endlessly for him to help.

He tried to get on with things at work and home as usual, though his mind was never far from what would become of his elder child. Ella, the reliable trooper she was, sensed his unease and to her credit had the watch on their daughter tightened. Tetabo was also given new instructions; not to let her out of his sight even when she made her daily trip down to the terrace where she kept her frigate bird. Now when young men came to visit nothing was left to chance. He could tell Ella was sizing them up over dinner, throwing questions at the lads all about their backgrounds and what kind of homes they came from. He was not having any part of her games. Gwennie was far too young for marriage, and this time he would stand his ground!

* * *

Over the next year, John tried to keep himself busy with work. He had never got around to having that chat to Ella about the household staff, and they now had a gardener at home in the form of Jane's new husband. Seeing they were still in the grip of a drought and they were all on strict water rations they had no garden left anyway. Never mind, the lad was not bad at raking up leaves and dust.

He did not know whether it was the distractions going on at home because he usually never mixed business and pleasure, but the breakthroughs at work with all the new improvements that were going on seemed to be like water off a duck's back. He knew that the natives now believed the white man could do anything. He remembered how they had reacted after seeing how they could turn the seawater into freshwater, make cold ice out of it and then cut it up into solid blocks with a saw. To top it off, 'make lightning', which was their term for the electric lighting system the company had built, had them totally amazed. As far as the Banabans were concerned, the white men could make good *kouti*, or magic.

He was not nearly as excited about things at work as he knew he should have been. These were significant events, he told himself. Just imagine it, an island covering less than fifteen hundred acres surrounded by such an expanse of ocean, with approximately fifteen hundred people of all different races living and working together, carrying out an industry under some of the most challenging conditions found anywhere! All these difficulties were slowly being turned around, and they could now boast some of the best plant and machinery found anywhere in the world. Not only had they built more staff houses, but now had improved on all the other facilities, including the hospital.

The only two problems that did not look like being solved in the foreseeable future were the loading facilities and his elder daughter. The ships still had to sit out off the reef to be loaded. The way the stevedores handled the loading of the surfboats under such conditions was remarkable. When the bad westerly weather came in these men deserved a medal for their bravery.

They would still continually break their loading records, and the management would boast that the system of loading they employed here on the island produced one of the highest loading rates found at any seaport around the world. There was constant competition between Uma and Tabwewa jetties, and the company facility on Nauru, to see who could break the loading record.

While all these developments were happening here on the island, there were other changes about to take place.

Apparently, while the war had been going on, another crucial decision had been decided by the powers that be back in London; the forming of a new multinational consortium of no fewer than three governments; Great Britain, Australia and New Zealand.

What it all meant for John, was that he would end up working for the government. Not just one, but three of them. It would be the start of what would be commonly known as the BPC or British Phosphate Commission. The old company would be gone forever, and he knew everyone felt uneasy at this new talk. There would be three new groups of employers to please who would all have cultural differences— not to mention their political differences.

Being an Australian, he knew how the British still referred to the Australians as being no more than convicts, and it would only be a matter of time before the sparks would fly.

15. Buakonikai village Ocean Island early 1920s.

CHAPTER FIFTEEN

ENTERING THE WORLD OF TE I-MATANGS

Buakonikai Village 1917

The sea breeze lifted up over the edge of the steep sea wall and past the seven ancient stone monuments that were the main feature of the Aon te Tarine terrace. This particular terrace had seen the passing of many young Banaban youths from Buakonikai village. On reaching the age of manhood until the time he became a *roro buaka*, a warrior, and could marry, a youth would spend a considerable amount of his time between the *uma n roronga*, the young men's house, or living on the terrace preparing for manhood.

Once at the terrace, he would be guided by his *utu*, his kindred who would instruct him in the *kouti*, the family's traditions. Many years earlier, part of these instructions had been the actual construction of these sea walls. At first, stones of coral would be gathered and then stacked along the edge of the bedrock to the required height.

Next, the young men would place fill behind the new existing wall and continue to fill until the whole area behind the wall was brought level with the tops of the stacked rocks. This large smooth level platform was then covered with a few inches of white coral shingle, resulting in a terrace.

Up until the arrival of the *I-Matang*, seventeen of these types of terraces were scattered around the island. Those in the village of Uma were destroyed in the process of building a government cemetery and three belonging to Tabwewa were being utilised for the company's harbour works. Some of those still remaining were no larger than a single large slab of rock where a lone man could practise his early morning *kouti*. This ceremony was mostly performed at sunrise facing east and consisted of a ritual washing with saltwater from a special coconut shell followed by the massaging of the arms with smooth pebbles from the beach. During this rite, a man could capture the essentials of life, health and strength.

At the back of this particular terrace was a line of open-sided houses or *mwenga* with a central *maneaba*. These buildings would offer accommodation for the young men while they lived away from the main village until they were of the marrying age. Buakonikai was the island's only village not situated right on the coastline and was reached by a pathway leading up to the central plateau. It was so named as 'the place among the trees', and there is no doubt it was considered among Banabans and *I-Matang*s alike, to be the most beautiful place on the entire island. Here, the lushness of the jungle was most apparent. Extremely tall coconut trees grew there atop of this tiny isle as if in salute to the rest of the unseeing world far away.

While the clouds rolled in from the eastern sky, the accompanying breeze and thick jungle canopy gave relief from the scorching heat of the fierce equatorial sun. The village was unusually quiet for this time of day, due to an unexpected meeting of elders that was in process at the main *maneaba*. Another important event was also taking place on this day.

Each male elder of the family or different clans of the village was in attendance, and because of the formalities of this specific meeting, each man sat in his clan's designated sitting place.

One of these men was young Ata, who now, as a man of age, could represent his mother's clan in official proceedings. After the usual lengthy extended formalities were over, a foreign voice boomed out, speaking in their native tongue from under the eaves of the overhanging pandanus roof. Formalities insisted this new man stand there with his hand laid on the edge of the supporting frame, while he begged admission to the meeting.

"*Kam na mauri* and bless this *maneaba* and everyone within!" called the large *I-Matang* man.

"*Kona mauri,* Kaben Kurte!" the elder spokesman replied. "Enter! Enter!" he commanded.

As Captain Cozens made his way to the guest mat at the front of the meeting, Ata felt as if his innards had been suddenly dealt a sickly blow. His mother had told him of his father's request to speak to the elders. It still did not make it any easier for him sitting here under the same roof with the man.

Over the past eighteen months, the relationship with his father had only become more estranged. Since the day when he stood on Uma beach and confronted his father with his defiance, he felt he had closed his heart permanently to this *I-Matang*. Ata had been raised a Banaban by his mother and had learned the family's traditions down on the terraces. His only knowledge of his father's family traditions came from what he had learned from Gwennie.

One Banaban tradition he had learned was respect for his elders, and up until that fateful day on the beach at Uma, he had always held to this. He felt ashamed of himself, not only for losing honour but the honour of his mother, for she was after all this *I-Matang*'s first wife. He had up until now mostly avoided seeing him, finding any excuse he could find to escape his company. With all these mixed emotions of resentment, shame, and loss of face going on within him, he heard his father's words suddenly sound as he addressed the meeting. All he could do was sit there with his head bowed and listen.

"I have come here today to ask the elders of Buakonikai to give their permission for me to take my son Ata, Arthur, and adopt him into the ways of my people *te I-Matang*."

His words fell heavily over the *maneaba,* the elders taking in what he had just said. Ata felt numb, and, realising that a sudden outburst would be shameful, he sat there in stunned silence. Each elder took his turn to stand and address the gathering, asking questions and offering his views on the matter.

Captain Cozens stood next to the visitor's mat, addressing each question and adding more argument to the debate. After what seemed like an afternoon of discussion, someone finally suggested that Ata should address this question and offer his view on the matter.

Ata by this time was so lost in his thoughts that when he slowly stood up to address them, he didn't really know what to say. Ata now stood over a height of six feet, towering over his fellow Banabans. He showed the full signs of manhood, and his muscled limbs glistened under the layer of coconut oil he had applied as tradition stated for such special occasions. He was indeed his father's son and to deny it was now impossible, especially as they stood facing each other in this formal way.

"*Kam na mauri, ao kam raba*, greetings and thank you!" he slowly said, his deep voice so similar to that of his father. "I may be of the blood of the *I-Matang*, but my heart and spirit will always dwell in my homeland of Banaba." His emotional words summed up his predicament.

The elders seemed to understand his desperation, his agony of being caught between two worlds.

But his words added more fire to the already vigorous debate as the elders' spokesman finally stood to address the meeting.

"I have listened to our important guest, Kaben Kurte and my fellow elders," he began, "and as we do not seem to be able to come to an agreement on this question, it is my responsibility to decide the answer."

Ata felt his innards knotting inside him again.

"Yes Ata, I know your heart dwells here in Banaba, but a man must not deny his ancestors." The elder's spokesman solemnly emphasised every word. "A man must also show respect for his elders, especially his own *tama*, his father, his blood, regardless of all other issues." His voice rose in strength while his audience nodded in agreement. "Furthermore, this request from Kaben Kurte allows us to have one of our own educated in the way of *te I-Matangs* world and a chance for you to become a very important man in the eyes of the Great King George."

Ata could hear them all agreeing with the elderly spokesman, including his father. It was then at that moment he realised that this was his fate. Why all these years his mother had so often spoken of him one day becoming an important man. She had always known that this day would come. Now, here in front of all the elders of his village, he had been propelled into an awkward position. He knew there was no way out. He would go with his father, and yes, he would become an important man, but he too would return to where his heart would always remain, and that was with his homeland and his people. Yes, he thought, one day he would be in a position to change things with the Great King George.

Suddenly another question came to his mind. What about Gwennie?

A week later, George Cozens had actually arranged a meeting with Ata and Gwennie. He had realised how increasingly difficult it had been for the young couple to try and be together, and both of them were still single-minded in their secret plans to one day get married. He was also feeling the pangs of guilt, as his plan to send his son away was now becoming a reality.

Gwennie Williams had grown into a beautiful young woman and so had the interest from every young, healthy male on the island. Cozens knew that her father, John, who was one of his oldest friends, had already been at his wit's end with his daughter's sudden status. He had often discussed the subject at length with him, while all the time Cozens kept his mouth shut about the ever-increasing problem of Gwennie and his own son.

John Williams had always been privy to the existence of Arthur and like the good friend he was, did not discuss the matter further, even when his wife Ella had heard the story through island gossip. John never passed judgement on his morals, especially when beautiful, over-friendly, naked women on a tropical island were concerned. It had always been a problem with the European men when they first started landing on these places and men were men. There was no denying it.

Cozens also knew John's attitude towards his daughter. She was untouchable, and he did not see him changing his mind for a long time yet. He would not even be surprised if he told him in years to come that Gwennie had never married. If only John had seen Gwennie with Ata, he would have realised that his daughter was in love. It was just a shame she had chosen the wrong person. He felt it was now his duty to not only put into effect the plan he had mapped out for his son many years ago but also to protect these two young people from what could never be.

Agnes, his Australian wife, also knew of Arthur's existence, which had been kindly pointed out by some supposed lady friend when she first arrived after her wedding to him. It had taken him many years to mend the damage. Fortunately, Agnes loved him enough to stand by him and seeing she was unable to bear children of her own, it was agreed that they, as a couple, should legally adopt the boy. It was also decided that Ata should be educated at the best Australian institutes possible.

Now with everything decided with Arthur's mother and the village elders, it was only a matter of him finding him a job on the next voyage he had to make to Australia as his personal assistant. There was no need to make Arthur's relationship general knowledge among the company staff because this would only make it more difficult for all of them, especially on such a tight-knit island community.

Now he must see to the unfinished business of Ata and Gwennie. With his influence, he had organised a secret meeting for the two sweethearts where he hoped no one would find them, in his own home.

Agnes had seen to the staff being absent for that particular afternoon while he sat quietly out on the front porch to keep watch over anyone walking up the path towards his home. Agnes, being the lady she was, had also taken herself off for a game of Mahjong with

Gwennie's mother. He knew John Williams was busy up at the new diggings at the central mining area. To dampen any suspicion, Ata had secretly come in through the back path and had been there for quite a while, pacing back and forth in the parlour.

Gwennie made her way towards the Cozens's house with her faithful Tea Tup in tow; even Uncle Will was not able to alter Tea Tup's ever-watchful surveillance, but she knew by the nature of this meeting that something was amiss.

Uncle Will would say nothing more than, "It is important you meet with Arthur; he has some news that concerns you!"

Now, as Uncle Will stood to greet her and made small talk, he asked Tea Tup if he could go down to the main office and pick up some new shipping schedules he needed. Tea Tup happily made his way off down the red path.

After ensuring that they were alone, Cozens whispered to her, "Quick! While no one is about. He's in the parlour." Before she had a chance to ask, he quickly added, "Don't worry, those charts Tetabo's collecting will not be ready for at least another half hour, so quickly, go in!"

Running in through the front door and into the cool interior of the house, she could see him standing at the end of the hall.

They rushed towards each other and Ata uttered, "Gwennie!"

"Ata, I've been so lonely without you," she replied as she placed her hands on his; eager to feel his warmth.

Tears were already welling in her eyes as he looked at her and led her to the couch. She seated herself on the settee as he took up a position on the floor sitting at her feet. As for all Banabans, the *I-Matang*'s furniture held no charm for him. He placed his hands over her clasped hands resting on her lap as he began to speak.

"I don't want to hear bad news," she said before he could talk.

He began to speak quickly in his native Banaban tongue, telling her what had happened. Gwennie, expecting the worst, sat there stunned and tried to gather strength from the pressure of his rough hands and the soothing flow of his deep voice. On completing his sad tidings, he rose up on his knees.

"I love you, Gwennie, and I will be back one day," he reassured her through the cascade of tears and sobs.

Ata felt helpless in easing her pain.

"Please Gwennie! It hurts me whenever I see your sadness. The time will pass by. We have to live for tomorrow and think of our future together."

When she regained her composure, she spoke. "You know Ata, I have scarcely seen you at all these past months," she sobbed, "but even though I was lonely and missed you, I knew that you were with me here in spirit." She smiled through the tears, placing one hand over her heart while Ata gently brushed a stray tress of hair from her face.

"I will be back here where we both belong as soon as possible." He sounded confident. "And when I return to you and my people I will be an important man and your parents will welcome me as your husband. You will see!"

"I will wait for you Ata, for as long as it takes," she sobbed.

He lifted his hand to wipe away her tears.

"When do you have to go?"

"Tomorrow on the high tide at first light," he replied.

"Oh no! Why so soon?" she sobbed again.

While their grief began to overwhelm them, Captain Cozens quietly appeared in the parlour door. He did not have time to worry about the young couple's current state as he tried to get their attention.

"Ata! Ata! Quick you must go; someone's coming!" he said, moving towards them.

Repeating his words again, he took a firm hold of Ata's arm and started to lead him toward the hallway and back door.

"Quick Ata, quick!" He virtually had to throw the lad in the direction of the stairs and quickly pulled the door shut behind him as he spoke.

On returning to the parlour, he saw Gwennie slumped in the chair, in a state of confusion.

"Come, Gwennie, straighten yourself up, Welsh is on his way up the path," he pleaded.

Now coming to her senses and realising the risk they all were taking, she quickly fled to the bathroom to tidy her appearance while Uncle Will returned to sitting on the veranda, trying to gather himself for the new arrival.

Warren Welsh had been a stevedore under Captain Cozens for the past six months since arriving on the island from Australia. Even though he had been accepted by the Melbourne office as very suitable for the position, not a lot of information was known about the man's personal background, except that he had a wife and three children still back at home. This was not unusual as it was not always possible to arrange for the applicant's family to journey straight over until it was seen if he could adjust to the island lifestyle. Many of the men's wives chose to stay back in what they called civilisation, so their children could get a proper education.

As Welsh approached the front steps, he suddenly noticed a quick flash of movement out of the corner of his eye.

"Good afternoon Welsh, to what do I owe the pleasure of this visit?" Cozens called down from the veranda, noticing that Welsh was busy staring at something up the hill.

"How are you sir, I hope I didn't disturb you?" he replied, removing his hat and turning his attention to Cozens sitting on the veranda before him.

"Of course not!" Cozens replied as Welsh made the final few steps to where he was seated.

"Sir, Mister Daniels has asked me to drop in these new charts to you," he said, giving him a bundle of rolled maps he held in his hand.

"Thank you, but he really shouldn't have bothered. I had already sent someone down to the office to collect them," he replied when he suddenly realised Welsh was standing there with his mouth open and his eyes focused on the doorway behind him.

"Good afternoon Miss Williams, I—"

"Good afternoon Mister Welsh, how are you today?" she replied as she made her way from the front door to the seat next to Cozens.

"I'm so sorry, sir, er, Miss Williams, I didn't mean to intrude I..." he again stammered.

"You didn't intrude, young man, Miss Williams has just dropped in to see Missus Cozens. Now if you have finished your business, I suggest you'd better get back to work before someone thinks you've gone missing," he said coldly.

"Yes sir, right away sir, good day Miss Williams!" Welsh said as he turned and made his way back the way he had come.

"Good day Mister Welsh!" Gwennie called, watching him leave.

Both of them failed to see the knowing smirk that had formed on Welsh's face when he placed his hat back on his head and quickly made his way back down the path.

"You don't think he saw Ata, do you, Uncle Will?"

"I hope not, and if he did, he wouldn't know Ata was coming from here," he assured her.

What he did not tell her was that there was something about that man Welsh that he just did not like. Nothing he could put his finger on, just a feeling. It would pay to keep an eye on him.

* * *

Just on dusk, Ata slowly made his way up to his family's *bangota*, their ancestral shrine, situated in the sacred area behind his village. He savoured every aspect of his surroundings and the natural aromas wafting on the light breeze. His island, his home, was so alive all around him and his emotions felt raw. It had already been a harrowing day, what with saying goodbye to *Nei* Gwennie, and now he had an important mission to visit the spirit of his ancestors. He needed to make sure they would give their protection and would go with him on his important journey to the Land of Matang. Suddenly, as he drew closer, the birds appeared and starting circling above him. He knew the spirits of his ancestors were near.

Ata entered the clearing and began to chant, announcing his entry to the sacred ground. He went over to one of the old stone cairns, or *bangota*, and sat down cross-legged in front of the structure. He removed three items that his mother had prepared for him from his plaited sinnet bag; magic coconut oil, a small parcel of food, and a coconut shell filled with water taken from the *bangabanga*. He placed the items on the small ceremonial mat. These were the essential items to offer up for his coming journey.

Ata carefully removed the skull from the shrine, placed it on the mat and began anointing it with the oil. Next, he sprinkled the water around the outer edge of the mat before spreading the food out in front of the skull as his chanting intensified. He was momentarily aware of a fluttering sound of bird wings and he sensed the presence of his ancestors all around him. Ata started to tremble as he felt the energy entering his body and tears of relief flowed, knowing that the spirits were there with him. He knew he had their support, guidance and protection.

After placing the skull and the offerings back under the shrine, he made his way toward the edge of the clearing to return home. The moment he stepped away from the sacred grounds rain began to fall, as if cleansing his soul in preparation for what lay ahead.

* * *

After returning home with Tea Tup and what seemed the worst night of her life, Gwennie quietly rose from her bed just before dawn. She had heard Tea Tup softly close the door of his cabin out the back when he went off for his daily fishing trip a few moments earlier. It would be safe now for her to go down to the point and try to say farewell to Ata.

She quickly made her way down the path in the dark, stepping confidently as she, like Tea Tup, felt at home here in the darkness. On reaching the back of Tea Tup's canoe shed, she waited until after she was sure Tea Tup had gone. Then quickly she crossed over the headland known as Sydney Point to Home Bay, where the large mooring buoys lay close to shore. This part of the island was also the main area for the company's buildings, and with all the activity going on while the ship was being made ready for sea, she made sure to keep herself hidden back in behind the natural vegetation covering the point.

The sky was beginning to suddenly lighten as her eyes scanned the large ship tied at the moorings looking for a glimpse of Ata. A loud shrill from the ship suddenly filled the air. The sound gave her such a fright when she realised the finality of its meaning. The familiar clamour and rattle of the anchor chains being pulled up together with the cloud of thickening black smoke spewing from the ship's stack sent a further shiver down her spine.

The ship was turning and moving away from the moorings so quickly that Gwennie had forgotten just how pulling away from the island in such dangerous waters happened so fast. Realising that this was her last chance to try and see Ata, she ran straight down onto the beach to the edge of the sharp fringing reef that covered this area, waving her arms frantically.

The sudden movement on the forward deck caught her eye, and she realised it was Ata. When he waved back to her, she was so overcome she forgot the situation she was in, being out in the open, and called out in Banaban.

"*Tia kabo,* Ata, my heart is with you!"

She heard his deep voice for one last time boom out across the ever-increasing expanse of sea.

"*Tia kabo,* my Gwennie, my heart dwells with you always, I..." As his voice faded on the wind and the sound of the buffeting surf nearby blocked out all other sounds, she knew he was gone.

Realising where she was and the risk she had placed herself in, she turned and scurried back up through the undergrowth.

With her sadness and sense of loss so all-consuming, she didn't realise that she had been seen.

Standing back on the jetty just behind the large phosphate bucket that ran down to the ships was the stevedore Warren Welsh on early morning duty. He had seen her in a state of excitement and then running down to the sea and calling out loudly in that strange native talk. Then more unbelievably he had heard a man's voice return her calls from the ship. Obviously, someone on board had heard them also because they did not seem to be too worried about people knowing about this latest scandal. He only wished he had been here long enough to pick up that native talk. But as far as he was concerned it did not really matter, there was no mistaking that deep voice. It was the distinctive voice of Captain Cozens.

* * *

Tetabo tried to keep up with the ship, paddling quickly as the bow waves of the large vessel lifted his frail *te waa*. Ata was still at the bow rail calling down to him and waving wildly.

"*Tia kabo* uncle, *tia kabo*!"

Tetabo stopped paddling and lifted his oar in the air to acknowledge his nephew, "*Tia kabo* my special boy, your family will always be with you!"

The hulk of the ship moved past him and Tetabo knew he had to move away from the churning waters generated from the powerful engines at the rear of the vessel. As he turned his back and began to paddle out to a safer distance, the tears flowed down his cheeks.

Upon his return to Wiriami's house, he quietly tapped on Missy Gwennie's bedroom door with his usual morning greeting. There was no reply. He slowly opened her door to find her bed empty. He knew he had to hurry and find her before her parents discovered she had gone off on her own.

He made his way along the path heading towards the terrace. His instincts told him she would be there with her bird and probably trying to catch a final glimpse of Ata's leaving.

As he arrived at the clearing on the edge of the terrace, he saw her sitting there alone watching the sunrise and quietly walked up behind her. He noticed the bird's perch was empty.

"Missy Gwennie you should have waited for me," he scolded, "Your parents will be very unhappy with me."

She turned to look at him, and he knew she had been crying.

"Are you okay, Missy Gwennie… it's okay, I am here."

"He's gone, Tetabo!"

"Yes, I know, but he will come back, do not be so sad," he said, sitting down next to her.

"No, Tetabo, he won't be coming back!"

Tetabo was taken aback with the sincerity and conviction in her words.

"Of course, he will be back, he is a special boy; his destiny is already foretold," he assured her.

She slowly lifted her right arm adorned with the small matted armband where her frigate bird would perch. Her bird was missing.

"He's gone too," she sobbed, "My bird has gone with him… he knows he has gone and both of them won't be coming back."

Her statement and the look in her eyes surprised him. He suddenly was lost for words as he felt the emptiness of her broken heart.

CHAPTER SIXTEEN

LOSS OF INNOCENCE

Ella 1918

Sixteen years spent living in Paradise. Yes, there had been a lot of changes, Ella thought. Some for the better, a lot not so good, and she was sure if somebody asked the Banaban people, except for the constant complaint regarding land issues, they would probably receive the same reply.

People were so busy enjoying the benefits of what progress brings that they never stopped long enough to see what really was happening until it was all too late. Yes, Ella reflected, people were too busy living for today. As far as she was concerned, the only thing the company was interested in was mining the phosphate as fast and as cheaply as possible.

To do this, the company was forever updating plant and machinery to achieve their ends. Of course, the families of staff reaped the benefits; electricity, imported foods, including fresh vegetables and dairy products, refrigeration, a company store that supplied your heart's desire, a mail service and education for your children. To top all this off, everyone who lived here lived in a cashless society. All additional purchases and expenses were placed on employees' accounts and traded off against their wages. The only time people needed cash was when they went on vacations abroad.

The social life on the island was second to none. If someone came to her complaining of boredom, she suggested they would be more suited back at home. She believed there was no excuse for boredom, and she made sure troublemakers were not welcomed into the fold.

The Banabans were also reaping some of the benefits that came with the company's progress. But unlike the company people, they were really affected by the white man's ways. In fact, so much so, that their actions would nearly threaten the extinction of their whole civilisation. They had lived off this island for thousands and thousands of years. The only problems they suffered were droughts, which always seemed to come in seven to eight-year cycles.

When the white man arrived, he promised to solve the island's water problems. The Banabans were so impressed with this claim; they indeed thought the *Men of Matang* came with great magic, *te kouti* as they called it. But Ella had always believed the most significant asset a Banaban had was his ability to catch fish. He was a master of the ocean. He could make one of the finest ocean-going canoes found among the Pacific Islanders. Their primary method of catching fish was the use of a line made of fibres from the coconut husk entwined with the long black strands of hair taken from their womenfolk. A unique hook was carved from the stalactites taken from their sacred *bangabanga* caves and human bones retained from their beloved ancestors. Diving for fish was another great skill of the Banabans. The diver attached crude floats to his arms and either speared or lassoed his catch. The greatly prized octopus was caught by wrestling the creature to the surface while at the same time, the diver would bite his prey to release its deadly grip.

They also fished with nets made of supple wood and coconut sinnet. In the case of flying fish, lit torches were used to attract them to their canoes at night. Many Europeans had watched with amazement as a native paddled into shore with a large shark precariously balanced across his small canoe. They not only were expert fisherman and sailors but also great swimmers. They were a people of the sea indeed, and the surrounding waters played an integral part in their culture. But all this was beginning to change, so much so that many of these outstanding skills were being replaced with a liking for white man's canned food.

Since the introduction of the company's trade store, the Banabans were receiving royalties for the rights to mine phosphate. In actual fact, no money was handed to the Banabans, but trade was set up at the store. They soon found it easier to go to the store and buy the white man's food than spend time out fishing or tending their fruit trees.

Some of the delicacies they developed a taste for never failed to amaze Ella. Things such as tinned sardines mashed with strawberry jam and fish heads in molasses, in their eyes a delicacy and served only at special occasions. They developed a taste for sugary foods such as mixing raw sugar with water, enjoying it as a drink and also eating sweet lollies. A large part of their staple diet was now made up with tins of bully beef.

Over the years, the Banabans would have the unenviable title of being known as 'the best can openers in the Pacific'. This would be one of the saddest indictments for such a beautiful and noble people. Both she and John had always encouraged Tetabo to keep up his daily fishing routine even though he had the run of the company store. They always looked forward to his regular accounts over breakfast.

As Gwennie had become older, she had wanted to go fishing with him but was never permitted. The company had even brought in a ruling forbidding Europeans from going out sailing in canoes with natives. They had already lost a few men to earlier mishaps; their bodies were never found. Relating how they disappeared was not an easy story for her John, who had to inform their loved ones waiting back home.

Now, after the first eighteen years of mining, the landscape and look of the island had changed. When ships brought new arrivals into Home Bay, the first thing they caught sight of was a large cloud of dust that rose up high over the island and covered the whole hillside in a sickly grey film. The harbourside of the island was now covered with massive buildings and machinery installations, standing out at odds with the surrounding tropical vista.

Uma village was like an oasis surrounded by progress. Over on the eastern side, farther behind the European settlement and village, large tracts of land were being left bare, with only the twisting tall monoliths of limestone left where the phosphate had been extracted down deep between them. Ella remembered the time the company had tried to bring in a herd of cattle to breed on the island. They did not realise that the animals would be a little taken aback on the precarious landing arrangements. It was something she could have told them if someone had bothered to ask her. When they hoisted the poor cattle one by one over the edge of the ship and finally got the terrified beasts to the land, they ran off in a stampede of fright.

They were in fact so frightened that all attempts to capture them drove them on even more until, in the end, they ended up trapped in among the razor-sharp pinnacles. All efforts to rescue them were fruitless, and in the end, they wedged themselves so deeply into the maze of limestone formations that they had to be destroyed and actually cut up on-site to remove the carcasses. It was a sad end to a good idea, which was never attempted again. The only positive thing to come out of the fiasco was an abundance of fresh beef steaks.

The mining operations were also underway on the other side of the island near Tabwewa. A site on the plateau near Buakonikai village known as topside was now proving the most fruitful. All these areas were left the same when mining was finished with just pinnacles and no vegetation growing there. The other problem was the heat generated from these areas meant it was like walking into a large baking oven. As the land was mined, the actual liveable areas on the island became less.

The Banabans' fruit trees also diminished, and the compensation came in the form of the natives eating more of the white man's food.

The other thing Ella believed was a great injustice to the Banaban people was the fact that they had to pay for anything and everything they got from the company. The Banaban women just went to the store and bought or traded water. The company had given them the water they promised all right, though they would have to pay for it. Every item of clothing, food or provisions they obtained at the store would cost them dearly.

Ella realised it cost the company money to operate the store and provide goods, but the real problem or injustice she felt was the fact that the Banabans were charged double the white man's rate for everything. She was so angry in this regard that she had insisted Tetabo buy everything his family needed through John. Regardless of how the company came about the rights to mine phosphate on this island, it did not justify the natives paying double for goods on their own island.

Seeing the Banabans had no concept of money, only trading a few simple items mainly for food, they too had no idea of the ramifications of living in an *I-Matang*s world. Ella had heard the men often argue over the fact many times, justifying the company's actions and in all truth, their own efforts in teaching the Banabans and the other islanders employed here the white man's way. They believed the inhabitants needed to know how to survive in a civilised world.

They honestly thought they had done the islanders a favour by bringing them progress. She believed that their intentions were probably genuine. But did they, the *I-Matang*, have all the answers? Surely the white man did have things to offer them, but they would also give them things that would help destroy them as a people. The Banabans had survived for thousands and thousands of years without the white man through such adversities, yet still, they could survive. Now, bit-by-bit, the white man would slowly destroy this beautiful place and a way of life that had taken a millennium to evolve and Ella knew in her heart that she would be one of the people responsible.

She looked back over her life and wondered in some way if her family really would pay the price for being part of all this. They had a good life, but it was the same as looking at a beautiful butterfly and knowing it would last only a short time before it died.

A disturbing episode came to light around this period that made her question their very existence here in Paradise and leave her with a nagging question that would haunt her for the rest of her days. Could she have prevented events that would unfold from happening?

After the first six years of married life spent mostly on her own with John away working, Ella had become very independent, and she knew she had toughened considerably. She had to face the birth of two babies, both of whom she had delivered on her own, with no one around to help and the hardest time of all was coping with the death of her baby Bertie. To nurse him and watch him fade away before her eyes had been so hard. Then to deal with his burial all while her husband was away was not easy. But she survived and got on with life.

When the opportunity came for them to be together at last here on this magical place, a significant change had come over her and her life. She could never have foreseen the gift she would be given with a beautiful baby Uma, born later on in her life at thirty-three years of age. God had truly blessed them in their later years. Their Gwennie was also a beautiful girl who had spent all her life here on the island with them.

Ella knew she was very protective of her girls; her whole life revolved around them. She had withstood the company's pressure and John's also, regarding the practice of sending them away to boarding school in Australia. The thought was just too much for her to bear, even though the company's managers and John also, had clearly explained the difficulties of having two young women on the island. She would never let them go.

They were her responsibility, and she alone would look after their welfare. She had recruited the help over the years from Tetabo, whom they considered as part of their family. He certainly kept an eye on them and made sure, especially as they grew older, that they never went anywhere unescorted. Everything had gone well to date, and except for problems with Gwennie and her bouts with loneliness over the years, they were both good girls.

Now John was being confronted at work about his beautiful daughter. Gwennie was eighteen years old and starting to turn into an attractive woman. She had led such a sheltered life here that she had no knowledge of what men and the responsibilities of an adult life entailed. Ella had decided they would have to marry her off as soon as possible.

John was aghast at the idea of his little girl being married though Ella knew she would have to persuade him otherwise. Meantime, she had begun to invite suitable young men around to the house for dinner in the hope that an appropriate suitor could be found. She quite liked the look of at least three of the young chaps, but Gwennie showed no interest at all. All the young men were keen at a chance to dine with their daughter.

It all seemed to be going over Gwennie's head. John was aware of her plans and was acting in a very brusque manner during her dinners. Ella thought it was a miracle that any of the poor lads were brave enough to set a foot back in their house. God only knew how John was treating them at work. She really dreaded to think. Nonetheless, it did not stop them from coming.

One night, they were invited to attend a fancy-dress ball over at the mess rooms at Tabwewa, or as the company, people called it, Tapiwa. Knowing that it was on the other side of the island, plans were made to take over the Uma village guests via the open flatcars, a nice trip at night with the surf pounding off in the distance and the moon shining through the palm trees. They all went, including their little Uma, who was all of seven years of age.

Ella had taken great efforts in the making of their costumes. Uma went as a fairy, John as King Neptune, while she dressed as the Fairy Godmother and Gwennie looked stunning as the Archangel Gabriel. Her long flowing wavy hair swept down to her waist and her gown all in white made her almost look like a bride, except for the wings and halo which she had attached.

That night as all the men hurried to mark Gwennie's card for a dance, John seemed to realise just how beautiful his daughter had become. Yes, Ella thought, she resembled a true innocent angel. It was a lovely night for all of the family, but a few hours after arriving, Gwennie insisted on wanting to go home. Seeing she and John were part of the organising committee for the evening, Ella told Gwennie they could not leave yet as supper had not even been served. Gwennie seemed most insistent about leaving, saying she felt unwell. Ella assumed she had the usual ladies' complaint, so she agreed to let her go as long as she was chaperoned home.

John arranged for one of the older staff, a Mister Douglas who worked in the office, to escort her back to the house. Ella had no idea of the trouble her poor daughter would be in.

When John and Ella arriving back home around midnight, they discovered the house lit up like a Christmas tree. This seemed most unusual. On entering the house, they wandered through their silent home with trepidation. John heard a noise coming from the parlour, and they quickly made their way to the room only to find Gwennie looking dishevelled, sitting on the sofa in an apparent state of shock, and rocking back and forth. She kept uttering the words, "No! No!" to herself, not comprehending that they were there.

Ella immediately panicked and started to scream at her, "Gwennie, what's happened?"

The more she screamed, the more her daughter sat there staring wildly into space. Her husband tried to calm her down, but she knew someone had hurt her daughter.

"Gwennie, who's been here?" she screamed, her mind flooded with all types of terrible images.

Finally, she slapped her daughter's face in an effort to make her speak and explain matters. All Gwennie did was to sit there blankly in silence rocking slowly, with tears streaking down her face.

While Ella was in still in her state of panic, John went searching through the house, trying to find out who had been here. Tetabo and his family were not in their little room out the back. They had gone down to the village to spend the night with their relatives because they knew the family would be absent for the evening.

John raced back into the parlour and sat down next to Gwennie, putting his arms around her. He rocked her gently in his arms, speaking softly. "Who hurt my little girl? It's all right Gwennie, your daddy is here!" he cooed while she cuddled into his arms.

John's paternal manner completely took Ella by surprise, and now she too sank down on the sofa next to them.

Poor little Uma did not know what was going on when Ella began to weep uncontrollably. They all sat there on the sofa, sharing Gwennie's pain. All Gwennie could manage to say coherently that night was something about the window. She kept pointing to it and crying, too overwrought to continue. John and Ella had gathered that someone had come through the window.

John tried to soothe her sufficiently enough to call in Methven, the officer in charge of the island's police. He also wanted to speak to Douglas, the man he had arranged to accompany Gwennie home.

Ella could see the anger in his eyes, but every time he tried to leave her, Gwennie would become hysterical and cling to him.

After Ella had calmed down enough to put poor little Uma to bed, she returned to the parlour, and that was where the three of them stayed. Still dressed in their costumes, they made a strange sight as John held his daughter in his arms while Gwennie drifted in and out of fitful sleep.

Next morning just after dawn, Tetabo came in with his usual morning's catch to find them still huddled together on the sofa. He got such a shock to see them that he immediately rushed over to wake them up and find out what was wrong.

Gwennie was so exhausted and still somewhat disorientated that John told Tetabo to quickly fetch the doctor and Mister Methven. He then picked his daughter up in his arms and carried her into their bedroom where Ella had pulled down the bed covers.

The doctor was the first to arrive and then Methven.

After John had explained the situation, Methven went off to interview Douglas, not allowing John to accompany him. He probably realised that he was not in a fit state to be objective. Ella stayed behind with Gwennie while the doctor examined her. On finishing his examination, he gave her a sedative to allow her to get some rest.

The doctor gathered them both together in the parlour and told them that he was not sure if she had been physically interfered with, but she had definitely been attacked and was suffering some type of nervous exhaustion as a result. They asked the doctor what they could do to help her recover. He could only suggest plenty of rest, as there was not much anyone could do besides give her some time to get over it and medication to help relax her.

As word broke out on the island about the attack on Gwennie, immediate suspicion was cast over the native population and workforce. An even darker cloud of suspicion was cast in the direction of the Chinese. To Methven's credit, after nearly a week of investigations, the culprit was tracked down and proved a shock to the entire European staff on the island.

Methven had interviewed Douglas thoroughly and discovered he had indeed escorted Gwennie home to the door and then returned to the dance at Tabwewa. Apparently, after Douglas was seen leaving the dance with Gwennie, a young man also left not long after. He was not one of the native or Chinese staff as initially suspected, but one of the company's own men. He was a married man who had come to the island on a two-year contract and left his wife and children home in Australia. Warren Welsh was well known to the family and had been invited to various functions at their home. Ella had always thought him such a decent chap and from an apparently good background. His scandalous violation came as a real shock to the entire community.

Gwennie herself would not talk about the attack at all and remained very withdrawn. Methven obtained a story from the loathsome creature, as John and Ella now referred to him. Welsh confessed, though the story had been twisted with Welsh saying that Gwennie had invited him to come back to the house for a liaison and had changed her mind halfway through proceedings, becoming hysterical. This story was unbelievable in their eyes, and Gwennie refused to discuss it.

Methven also doubted his story, which was probably fabricated by the villain. So instead of charging him with assault and bringing him to trial here on the island, he took the delicate matter into serious consideration before acting hastily. Methven realised that a trial would entail dragging poor Gwennie through more distress and scandal here in this small community. He made arrangements with the company to dismiss Welsh immediately and have him removed from the island as soon as possible.

John was a tower of strength to them during all these horrendous circumstances. He arranged for Ella and the girls to take a trip over to Nauru and stay with the Cozens family, who were the family's old and trusted friends from their early years here on the island. The

Cozens had been transferred to Nauru a year earlier, and George was currently the harbour master there.

John could not come with them because he had no leave due and insisted on getting Gwennie away from the island long enough to allow her to get well again. The company was helpful and supportive during this most unpleasant and trying time and helped John with their travel arrangements by organising a passage on the company's vessel. Their trip to Nauru would take them away for a month and indeed give Gwennie some breathing space to aid her recovery.

They all enjoyed their time spent with their old friends George and Agnes Cozens who were sympathetic and understanding of the family's current dilemma.

Over the next three years, Ella would take the girls abroad as often as possible. During that period, Gwennie had nearly returned to her old self except that she was still unable to sleep. She was terrified of going to bed at night, and the dark made her afraid to be alone. Her lamp always had to be left on. Even Tetabo had tried to talk to her about her fear of the darkness, but to no avail, and the doctor had duly prescribed more sleeping pills. Gwennie now relied on her nightly pills to allow her to get to sleep, a legacy that would sadly remain with her for the rest of her life.

John's annual leave fell due in the latter part of 1920, and a trip home to Australia was arranged for all of them. It was a wonderful vacation spent in Victoria, and mostly in Melbourne. John had to return to work, but the family was having such a good time that Ella decided to stay on with the girls for an extra two weeks. Their time was spent visiting the art gallery, museum, zoological gardens and the various ballets and opera performances that were in town at the time. Melbourne was a town bred on culture, and she wanted her girls to experience as much of its influence as possible. Gwennie was becoming less timid, every day regaining some of her old confidence.

Uma was the complete opposite, a mature child with a great sense of confidence.

After experiencing what was happening back in Australia, Gwennie wanted to get her hair cut into a modern short style. Ella insisted on her keeping it long and assured her that her father would not permit her to cut her beautiful hair. Gwennie argued that it was too old fashioned, and she wanted to wear her hair like the rest of the young ladies. Ella was not about to permit such silly nonsense and was utterly shocked when Gwennie walked out from her bedroom at the boarding house one morning with all her lovely hair hacked off. Ella almost swooned on the spot and began to berate her severely.

Gwennie had turned on her. "Mother, I am not a child any longer. I'm a young woman and should dress as such," she stated calmly, turning away and walking off. No argument, just a statement and the subject was seemingly closed.

Ella sat there, feeling annoyed while she also realised that her daughter was right. Gwennie was now twenty years old and did not even have a beau seriously courting her. If she did not find her a husband shortly, her Gwennie would become a spinster.

She had no idea that things would shortly change, and the changes that would occur would not really be what Ella and John Williams had in mind for their elder daughter. Matters would be taken out of their hands, and one of their worst fears realised.

ALL MEN EQUAL UNDER THE SUN

The Residency - Ocean Island 1920

"All right gentlemen, please, we have quite a lot of business to discuss today, so could we please get on with it!" announced Arthur Grimble. He had initially begun as a cadet with the colonial service on Ocean Island and now chaired his first government staff meeting.

He had been appointed Acting Resident Commissioner to cover while Resident Commissioner Eliot was away on leave back in London and he was quite enjoying his new rise in status.

"Now the next point of business we have to discuss is the appointment of a new Police NCO to be put in charge of the Chinese quarters. Who do you suggest, Methven?" he asked.

"Well sir, I feel the most suitable man for the job is Teakai, who has eight years of good service," Methven replied.

"But isn't he a Gilbertese?" Grimble was puzzled why Methven would even suggest such an idea.

"Yes, sir!" the head of Police answered.

"Well, do you think it is wise to appoint a Gilbertese to oversee the Chinese? You know they hate each other as it is." Grimble looked dubious, his eyebrows raised.

"Yes, sir, I realise there is animosity between the two groups, but Teakai has a very calm and level head on his shoulders," Methven replied confidently.

"Well, I'm not too sure about putting a Gilbertese in charge of some four hundred Chinese."

"Sir, I can assure you he is the best man I have for the job and if anything, appointing Teakai to the position could work to our advantage when the Chinese realise how understanding a man he is." Methven was feeling resentful towards Grimble. This relieving position of his had already gone to his head. "I'm sure, sir, a heavy hand is the last thing we need at the moment."

"Yes, yes, all right, but I'm making it your personal responsibility to keep an eye on the situation. We don't want anything getting out of hand, do we gentlemen?" Grimble set his papers in order and waited.

The other men gathered in front of his desk answered, "No, sir!" their voices sounding almost in unison.

"Now our next subject is the dispensing of the Japanese labour force here on the island." He moved on, changing the subject, to Methven's relief.

"As I'm sure you're all aware, gentlemen, due to the current problems between England and Japan we have to dispense with our large contingent of Japanese labourers." He paused to look up at the men gathered in his office. "I'm also sure I don't have to tell you all that our friends over in the company offices are not too pleased with the government's decision, so I trust that you will all tread carefully. I would prefer that you try not to discuss the government's policy in this matter over a few cool ales at the next cricket match, thank you!"

He paused before continuing. "Now the last matter for today's meeting is the retirement of the present company manager, Mister Stevens, and our Catholic priest, Father Berclaz. As you all know, Father Berclaz has been recalled to France, and I have just received the name of his replacement, a Father Pujabet." Again, looking up from his papers, he continued, "A strange name somewhat, obviously French, and I have been told he has been working with the Sacred Heart Mission in Fiji.

"As for Mister Stephens, I have been advised that his replacement will be Captain MacFarlane who as you all know has headed the Marine Department here for the last few years."

He paused from reading the report for a moment and added less formally, "Of course there will be the usual farewell and welcoming formalities and formal dinners thrown for the men in question, and regardless of your persuasion, gentlemen, I ask you all to show the necessary courtesies towards Father Pujabet." He nodded briefly.

"Now gentlemen, if that is all and there is no further business I'd like to bring this meeting to a close." He straightened the papers once again.

Noting there was no further discussion from his men, Grimble rose from his chair, anxious to carry on with his other duties.

"Thank you, gentlemen!"

Over the next week, Methven, having advised Teakai of his promotion to corporal, was busy as usual in his many roles of official capacity on the island. He was not only in charge of Police and

Prisons but also Superintendent of Public Works and Public Prosecutions, which necessitated his weekly appearance in the Magistrates' Court.

Corporal Teakai took on his new position with gusto, spending as much of his time within and around the Chinese quarters as possible. Being the first-rate policeman he was and with the honour of being the only Gilbertese appointed to the position of NCO, as the Ocean Island Constabulary was made up mostly of Fijian and Ellice Islanders, he made it his duty to find out as soon as possible what was going on under his jurisdiction.

He took it upon himself to personally patrol his sector and to meet and be seen by as many Chinese as possible. The Chinese soon referred to him as The Shadow as he stealthily moved in and out of the different company's work sheds and the Chinese living quarters at night. He came to know which men worked on different work gangs and in which mining field they should be working. He also discovered things about the Chinese that he had never known before.

There were things like the secret society they seemed to have here on the island. It was this same secret society that seemed to manage all the mah-jong and fantan games in the Chinese quarter with the sanctioning of the company. He had also started to suspect that the same anonymous men might have something to do with the food and clothing stalls that the Chinese had set up after hours in their compound.

The other thing he had learned to appreciate was the Chinese Theatre. It was certainly different from the Alexander Theatre run by the European staff, and seeing the Chinese were not permitted to bring their women with them, all the female roles were played by men dressed as women. This, they seemed to take very seriously, and he found it amusing.

Because of the special diet of the Chinese, all their food had to be imported from Hong Kong. He was even beginning to get a taste for their exotic food. One day, while on his usual rounds, he found himself nearing the company's work sheds down by number four jetty. The shed was used for the repairing and making of the big cane baskets that were used on the surfboats to transport the phosphate rock out to the ships. It needed special skills to make such large, sturdy baskets, and the Chinese were expert at it.

He always liked to pass by and have a look in as it fascinated him to see such a small man standing in the beginnings of a new basket as he wove the cane around him. His fellow Gilbertese also worked in the same shed doing the heavy work of lifting the towering stacks of bamboo and handling the finished products. As he neared the shed, intending to drop in, he heard screaming and yelling. Realising that a fight or argument was in progress, he quickly made his way into the shed to find a bulky Gilbertese labourer with both large hands firmly planted around the throat of a poor weedy little Chinese Coolie.

He yelled, "Hey you! Let him go, let him go now before you kill him!"

After repeatedly barking these orders at his fellow countryman and with some physical brute force on his own part, he finally was successful in getting the large man's attention. The poor old Coolie, on the other hand, was beginning to turn a shade of blue. On finally breaking them apart, he placed the half-conscious Coolie into the care of his fellow workers and ordered that he be taken up to the Chinese infirmary. When this had been done, he ordered the other men back to work while he had the offending Gilbertese worker follow him outside.

When they were alone, he demanded a full explanation of why he had tried to kill his fellow worker.

"He is an evil man with the heart of Nakaa!" he replied.

"But why is he evil?" demanded Teakai.

"He is giving our children bad tobacco, makes them see *anti*, ghosts and Nei Terang, the Spirit of Madness."

Teakai, being a Gilbertese himself, believed in the superstitions of his people, but with his newly acquired position, his role as a policeman must come first.

"Well, this is a serious matter, I will have to arrest you and take you back to the police lock-up, and you can explain your story to Mister Methven." He took him by the arm, grasping it firmly.

The story was taken up with Mister Methven back at the office. He in turn called in the Chinese interpreter to help him interview the victim who had just been released from the infirmary. The Chinese labour managers attended the meeting, and in the end, it was decided that the fight had been over an ongoing dispute between the two men concerned. This argument had been started by the Gilbertese man's love for a good practical joke and belly laugh, while the Chinamen's more severe nature had been offended.

Teakai did not see how this would have led to the fight he had witnessed, and the unusual statement made by the perpetrator about tobacco making madness. On telling Methven his doubts a few days later and requesting permission to reinterview the offending Gilbertese worker, he was informed that the offender and his family had already been repatriated back to his island homeland so as not to cause any further trouble among the two factions.

He thought this was most unusual, as the man had not even made an appearance in the local *kaboui*. Furthermore, he had this nagging feeling that Methven, who was a very honourable man, was not telling him the whole story.

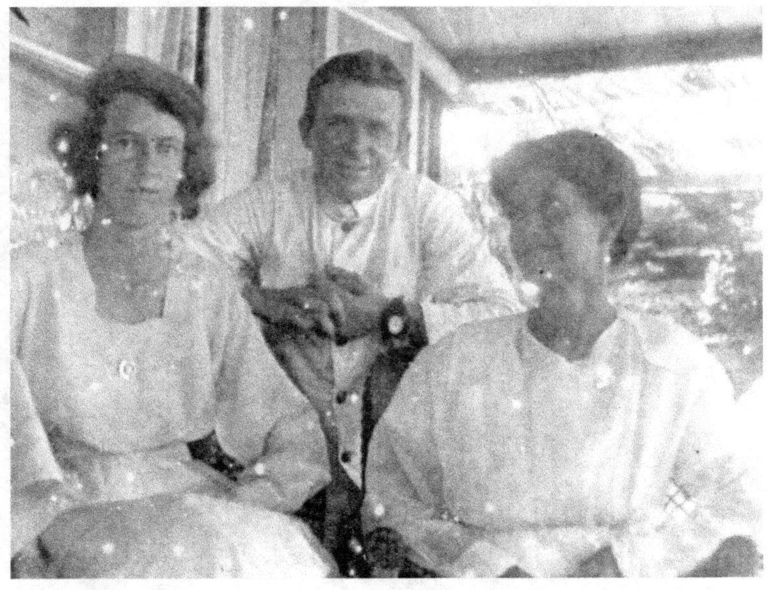

16. Gwennie Williams (left) after cutting her long hair with her mother Ella and one of many suitors at their home Ocean Island.

17. Ella Williams (right) and friend riding the flat car on Ocean Island early 1920s.

CHAPTER EIGHTEEN

TOM

Gwennie 1921

The family's last day in Melbourne was the end of a perfect holiday. They had been here for ten weeks, and as Gwennie rushed to pack her belongings for the long sea voyage home, she realised how much better she was feeling. It had been a trying time over the past couple of years when at times she thought she just could not go on, but now she was starting to feel differently, realising just how much there was to live for.

She loved her home on Ocean Island; though unfortunately because of the distressing events that had happened to her there, she now felt a slight unease and nervousness on returning. Melbourne had been such an exciting place this trip, and she had really enjoyed the atmosphere. To see automobiles driving down the streets and to be able to ride in the taxi cabs was exhilarating compared to the quiet of the almost traffic-free pace of the island. The trams running down the middle of the streets and such tall buildings were just incredible.

The city people dressed differently here; they looked sophisticated. The shorter dresses that now showed more of a lady's legs and the beautiful hats and hairstyles, which they wore with such casual elegance, were delightful. Her mother called them stylish city-dwellers. She wanted to take this new sophisticated fashion back to the island with her.

It had been marvellous spending so much time together with the whole family and these last two extra weeks after her father had left. It had been full of fun and frivolity. Her mother and her sister Uma were also enjoying the additional stay. Over recent years, they had never discussed or referred to her previous predicament. Her mother knew it always upset her to talk or think about it, and her parents had been supportive. How could she ever try and explain to them her relationship with her first and only love, Ata? It had all seemed so long ago in a time and place that was so ideal, a love that could only be forbidden. She now realised she lived in a world where people were judged by the colour of their skin and the status they held in life.

Yes, how could she ever break her father's heart and tell him what had really happened? He had always thought of her as his little girl. Her mother, on the other hand, was more realistic, and she knew her mother wanted her to be married as soon as possible. When she tried to look back and think of Ata and those wonderful innocent childhood days they had shared and the love that they felt for each other, everything would become clouded over by that horrible man. The man who they all believed was a fine upstanding white man was married with his own children living back here in Australia. Society would decree him to be an acceptable gentleman, but she could tell them otherwise.

She knew that the company had got rid of him after what had happened to her, but she would never be able to bring herself to tell another living soul of what he had done to her. Time had undoubtedly helped heal some of those memories. In Ata's case, it all seemed too hard, as if it was the end of the old naive Gwennie. Now the only time it would all come back to haunt her was in her dreams.

Her mother honestly thought she was not interested in boys. She felt painfully shy and very self-conscious of how she looked. She hated it when all the men on the island used to stare at her. It always upset her and made her feel out of sorts.

She did not know if being away from home in such a lively town like Melbourne was the reason, but she was feeling so much better about herself. She had even spoken to a few men she had met on several outings to the theatre and on various occasions around town. The men seemed different here. They appeared to be more refined and gentlemanly, and they did not make a habit of staring at you.

For once, she could stand there and talk to a complete stranger and not feel as if she was going to be ill. She had not spoken to a man for years for fear of the consequences. Gwennie did not dare tell her mother how much better she was feeling about men for fear of her mother wanting to pounce on the first bachelor she could find. She would decide who she would marry and no one else. She was not going to have some slimy creature having his way with her. Her mother had always told her it was a wife's duty to please her husband. Well, when the time came, she would have a say in who her husband would be, duty or no duty.

As she was pulling the last strap tight on her suitcase, her mother came rushing into her room, "Are you ready, dear? I don't want to miss our ship," she announced, before helping her with her bag. She then retied the ribbon on her blouse and finally pushed her towards the door.

Her mother never failed to have a last-minute fluster when it came to catching ships. She seemed to have a fear of missing them, and for that reason, they always arrived at least an hour before departure time. As soon as they boarded the ship, her mother would turn back to her old self. She was usually so under control and confident that you would never believe only minutes earlier she had been frantic with worry.

The three of them rushed downstairs to the taxicab waiting to take them to the docks. Uma, who was now a very grown-up child of nine, took her mother's panic with her usual ease. She was such a happy child, and it took a lot to upset her. Turning to Gwennie with a small grin, Uma slowly made her way into the cab. Gwennie could not help laughing, knowing she had seen this story repeated so many times over the years.

Just when the poor driver was about to leave, their mother went off again upstairs for her usual last-minute check to make sure they had not left anything. When they finally pulled away from the boarding house, their mother told the driver to hurry because she was worried they would miss their ship. He, like the gentleman he was, increased the speed. Gwennie did not have the heart to tell him their ship was not departing for at least another two hours yet.

There was something about a bon voyage, the moment when a ship hauled up the anchor and pulled away from land. It was a very emotional time, and sometimes she believed she could still hear Ata's voice calling to her, but she knew it was over. Gone forever, gone with the old Gwennie. The Williams family had travelled on ships all their lives and were hardened seafarers, but they still felt those old familiar stirrings when it came time to take to the sea. On their voyages back to their island they usually did not have the bands playing, and the coloured streamers and paper with masses of people gathered around. It was because they travelled on cargo steamships that carried only a few passengers while transporting the phosphate between the island, Australia and the rest of the world. They had much quieter farewells. People gathered to say their goodbyes, some with nervous laughter, while others could not refrain from crying and kissing goodbye.

Gwennie would always look back to that fateful day and wonder if that was the reason why things happened the way they did. It was the day she fell in love again, this time with a total stranger. It was something she never dreamed could be possible.

The ship's siren was sounding, and the steward with his megaphone was calling, "Would all visitors not travelling on this voyage please go ashore."

Leaning out over the side of the ship, the steward called down to the people gathered on the wharf.

"Ahoy, ahoy, all passengers aboard. Leaving in fifteen minutes!"

Over the next few minutes, a rush of people was gathering around the gangway while people made their way off the vessel, and a few more of the last-minute passengers made their way on board. Their ship, the *SS Bulga,* would be returning them home, stopping at a few other ports of call along the way. For this reason, there seemed more passengers than usual.

Gwennie stood up on the deck with Uma at her side, observing the goings-on down on the wharf below. Even though no one was there to see them off this time, they both waved regardless. It seemed as if all of the people down on the wharf had suddenly become their friends.

The siren sounded again as more messages were called across the decks and wharf below, while the ship made ready to pull away from shore. She noticed four men starting to make their way towards the gangway, and the hum of the steam engines could clearly be heard over the surrounding din. While all this last-minute activity was in progress, she suddenly noticed a commotion down among the crowd. The people at the wharf had been forced to move farther back behind the barriers to allow the men to work on the ship's mooring lines. Suddenly, a man broke through the barricades and ran towards the gangway, yelling.

"Stop, stop, wait for me, I'm boarding that ship! Wait! Please Wait!"

The men heard him and stopped removing the gangway, which had already been moved away from the edge of the wharf. They stood by for further instructions from the purser of the ship.

Gwennie thought he was one of the most handsome men she had ever seen; tall and slim, with a shock of jet-black hair, his suit jacket thrown carelessly over one shoulder and his tie hanging loosely knotted around his neck. He carried a battered leather suitcase that seemed to be bulging, with what appeared to be half of his clothes protruding from the seams. While he looked slightly dishevelled, he seemed a real character, not just in his appearance, but also in the way he moved. He looked like a man in a total panic; though his face told another tale as his smile made him look as if he was enjoying the situation.

When this dark stranger finally reached the edge of the wharf, he suddenly leapt up on to the suspended gangway. After realising he had made it, he looked up almost with happy relief to where she was standing on the deck above. It was at that moment their eyes met. Nodding, he tipped his hat in acknowledgment and gave her a quick grin. She felt her face redden and swiftly turned her head away to save embarrassment.

Not knowing what had come over her, she made her way to where the passengers' names were posted on the notice board, with Uma in pursuit. The majority of the names she knew and the ones she did not know were all listed as Mister and Missus. On previous trips, Uma would make a game out of scanning the passenger lists in search of a lone man, but this time Gwennie was with her.

"Look, Gwennie, there's a single man for you on this trip," Uma called in an excited voice, pointing to the passenger list.

Even at nine, Uma knew the importance of trying to find her sister a husband. She had obviously listened in to all the conversations around home regarding Gwennie's marital status. Hence, every new bachelor that arrived on Ocean Island was a prospective husband. This time there was only one man's name that stood out.

"Thomas... O... Sulli... van," Uma carefully read aloud to her sister's embarrassment.

She knew this was silly, but from the moment she first saw that dark-haired man at the wharf, she knew right then that she liked him. She felt smitten by this stranger, and she had not even had the honour of meeting him yet. She had never felt such excitement before. Rushing down to her cabin, she made special preparations for dinner that evening, wanting to look her very best.

When the time arrived for dinner, she made her way up to the dining salon with her mother and Uma. They always dressed in their best for dinner, but tonight she had paid even more attention to her appearance. On finding their table, she saw that there was already another couple sitting there. The table seated six, and one place remained empty. Could it be for him? She hoped so, fervently. While the dining saloon filled up, she could not see the young man she thought was called Thomas O'Sullivan anywhere. Doubts began to cloud her mind, wondering if she had made a mistake. Maybe he was one of the ship's crew? She shrugged her shoulders in disappointment.

They were just beginning on their first course when suddenly he came rushing into the dining saloon. After looking around, he finally arrived at their table.

Smiling at them, he let out a sigh of relief. "Number three; this must be it!"

Gwennie noticed his smile as he seated himself at their table.

Her heart thumped wildly as she felt the blush rise on her face. She quickly put her head down.

"I'm Tom O'Sullivan, glad to meet you! I'm sorry I'm a little late. Been one of those days!"

After everyone at the table introduced themselves and made pleasantries, she noticed her mother seemed somewhat affronted. She did not look terribly impressed with the young Mister O'Sullivan sitting next to her. She could see her mother was looking at his attire with thinly disguised distaste. The handsome young man did not look much better than when Gwennie had seen him running down the wharf earlier. His tie was still hanging loosely around his neck, and though he now had his jacket on, it needed ironing. She knew how particular her mother was when it came to a person being appropriately dressed.

She was still impressed by this young man, not uttering one word for fear of saying something silly. Uma, who had realised something was up from the look on her sister's face, started to kick her under the table. Gwennie was discreetly trying to get her to stop when suddenly she realised that Mister O'Sullivan had been asking her a question.

Totally missing what he had said she just smiled and said in the sweetest voice, she could muster, "Yes, that's right."

Everyone around the table began to laugh, and she did not have the faintest idea of what she had apparently just said that was so laughable. The next thing Mister O'Sullivan said made her realise just how stupid her answer had been. She flushed with embarrassment at her failure to impress him.

"I'm sorry Miss Williams, you must have misunderstood my question. I was asking how long you had been living on Ocean Island?"

With his words, his dark eyes were focused on her as though he was sensitive to her embarrassment. Gwennie realised then that he was trying to put her at ease.

All through the conversation that followed over dinner, their eyes would keep returning to each other. Her mother kept interrogating him the way she did with all the young men that ever dared to talk to her. She was asking the usual questions regarding his family background and current status. The only question she did not ask was how much money he had in the bank, but Gwennie was sure if manners had permitted her mother would have insisted on knowing.

What became apparent to Gwennie over dinner was his way of talking and expressing himself. He was a very educated man from a large family. His father was a professor who had settled in Australia from Ireland, and his mother had come from Germany.

He was a fitter and engine driver by trade and was going to work on the island on a two-year contract. She could not help feeling how ill-suited he seemed for such a profession with what she sensed was a very caring nature, and he was not brash at all. He was nothing like the men she knew back on the island. While he kept them all amused over dinner, by telling them stories of his different adventures in his cultured tones, she noticed a slight smile form on her mother's face from time to time. Uma listened to his every word; he had definitely captured her interest.

That evening, as Gwennie reluctantly retired to her cabin, she pondered over what a delightful evening she had experienced and was looking forward to Mister O'Sullivan's company tomorrow.

This was the beginning of a great journey as she spent her entire voyage waiting on any and every opportunity she could get to spend time in the company of the charming Tom O'Sullivan. Of course, her mother, who insisted on accompanying her everywhere, noticed, but despite her mother's annoying presence, the next twelve days at sea were one of the happiest times of her life, and she did not care if this sea voyage lasted forever.

Tom, as he now asked her to call him, was a perfect gentleman, and even though he possessed a casual disposition, it belied his wit and intelligence. They would sit for hours on the deck together with her mother not far away and talk about varied topics. With her sheltered upbringing, Tom would entertain her with stories of his life growing up in Hartley, a country town in the Blue Mountains of New South Wales. He was one of thirteen children, and although his family was not wealthy, his father had insisted on personally supervising his children's education; hence all his offspring except for two who had died as small children, had progressed to being professionals. Two of his sisters had already become journalists and writers while Tom himself had written various short stories and poetry.

As they sat on the deck under the stars and slowly drew closer to their destination, he would recite verses for her, while she fell even more under his spell. Her mother still was not happy with the situation, feeling he was too casual in his regard and outlook on life, especially when it came to being punctual. Tom's blatant disregard for arriving on time drove her to distraction.

"I do not know what you see in him, Gwennie. Your father won't approve, you know; he doesn't abide people who aren't punctual," her mother lectured her whenever they were alone.

"Mother, he doesn't mean to be late, he just forgets about time, that's all," she would reply in all innocence.

"How can anyone just forget about time? Anyway, he always looks so untidy."

She had to admit that her mother was right.

"But Mother, he's such a wonderful man, so caring and polite," she offered in his defence.

"Yes, I grant you he is polite and well-mannered, but you must remember that in the end all men really want is to have their way with you."

"But you've always told me it was a woman's duty to look after her husband," she protested, deciding to play her mother at her own game.

"Yes, I did, but he's not your husband."

"Well, I hope to be the next Missus O'Sullivan and to look after him for the rest of my life. That's all he needs, a female to love and take care of him."

All those old feelings of resentment came flooding back to her. It was Ata all over again. This time she was determined to stand her ground, and she had no intentions of seeing Tom disappear as Ata had.

Her mother, realising she was serious, changed tack and tried pleading, "Now Gwennie, please don't talk like that. You do not know anything about marriage and all it entails, giving birth and rearing children. Anyway, what sort of future could he give you?"

Her mother did not realise the extent of her daughter's true feelings; after all, she had never been privy to her previous heartbreak.

She also was not used to her elder daughter's open defiance. Obviously, it all had something to do with her breakdown.

"A wonderful future, and anyway, Mother, you have always taught me that money isn't everything and that happiness is more important. Look at Tea Tup and his family! Money means nothing to them, and they are the happiest family I know." Gwennie knew that she had made a good point. Surely her family wanted to see her happy at last.

"Yes dear, but they can live off the sea and their fruit trees if they have to, and you can't! You live in a different society where money does count," her mother argued. "Oh, please dear, consider it seriously. Your father and I want only the best things in life for you."

She noted her mother was now sounding almost tearful.

"Well, Mother, all I know is that I think Tom is the most wonderful man I've ever met."

Her mother sighed, not used to her usually shy daughter being so outspoken. "All right, but just remember, we will be arriving home the day after tomorrow and your father may not take to kindly to your Mister O'Sullivan courting his daughter."

"I know Father will just love him," she excitedly replied. How could he not?

She was soon to find out. After landing safely on shore, she was not only excited about Tom meeting her father, but she also realised just how glad she was to be back home. Once again, the island's charm was apparent to her as if she was seeing it for the first time. Her senses were not assaulted by the large ugly buildings rising up from the side of the hill; she was too busy admiring the vivid blueness of the sky and water, and the glistening green of the palm fronds. It all seemed such a beautiful sight. She heard the familiar calls of the frigate birds and momentarily thought of Ata as the birds circled above the water.

Her thoughts quickly turned back to the present, when she heard the happy laughter of the native children playing on the beach carry across to where she was standing. The island was once again her Eden, unspoiled by the noisy intrusion of manmade machines. She had nearly forgotten how peaceful it was.

It was at that moment that she realised Tom could hear it too. He was seeing her home for the very first time. She felt happy for him. He had asked her quite a few questions over the past few days about life on Ocean Island, and she had tried to describe it to him. How could she put into words the magic she felt when thinking of the place she called home? It was so much part of her; she felt protective towards it once more and thought just how wonderful it was to be in love.

Her father was so pleased to see them back home safe and well that she decided to try and introduce Tom to him down on the jetty. Before she got the chance; her mother had purposely hurried him away.

"I'm sorry, Tom, I didn't get a chance to introduce you to Father, but I'm sure you'll get to meet him soon."

"That's all right, Hazel." Tom had taken to calling her by her second name as she had confided in him her dislike at being called Gwennie. "I'll probably meet him at work. Now I must go and get settled in with the company. I'll see you as soon as possible; please take care." He squeezed her arm tenderly and started to turn away to see to his dilapidated luggage.

"Yes Tom, I will, and you take care. I'm going to miss you!" She did not care who heard her saying it loudly. She felt sad knowing that she was suddenly on her own again.

He turned back smiling, his arms extended.

"Not as much as I'm going to miss you." He was glad to hear she felt something for him. "The last twelve days spent in your company have been the best days of my life!" It was true; he had fallen head over heels in love with her.

"Really, Tom? I felt the same way. I wish our sea voyage could have lasted forever."

"Don't worry Hazel, there will be more wonderful times together," he promised as his eyes searched for her response.

At that moment, she did not know what came over them both, but in the middle of a crowded jetty, he took her in his arms and kissed her goodbye. Her first proper kiss; not just a peck on the cheek, and within full view of the company people working down on the jetty.

If she had stopped long enough to think about it, she would have realised it was not the correct thing to do, but Gwennie could not help feeling as if she was saying goodbye forever. They were so much in love; their hearts ruled their heads. All those days thrown together on a romantic sea voyage and not being able to touch or show their feelings had been too much for both of them as their impulsive actions were now proving.

Gwennie wondered if her fellow countrymen were going to see it that way.

* * *

"Gwennie where are you?" the voice of her father roared.

It was the day after their homecoming and her little interlude on the jetty. Up until now, her father had been in such an excellent mood and busy catching up on all the news of their last two weeks in Melbourne. Gwennie had been trying to wait for the right time to tell him about Tom. Somehow the opportunity had not yet come up, and by the sound of his voice, she had a terrible feeling she was not going to get the chance.

"Here I am, Father, what's wrong?" she called out from the hall-way, sounding as innocent as possible.

When her father was ill-tempered or cross, it was more prudent to keep out of his way. She knew he had a soft spot for her, and she always used her best little girl voice for him when she wanted to gain his favour.

"Get into the parlour now, Gwennie! Right now!" he roared even louder.

Her mother came running out of the bedroom to see what was going on.

"Darling what's wrong?" she asked.

"Gwennie knows what's wrong and I want to see her right now," he again yelled, although with her mother standing right next to him he had lowered his tone slightly.

Oh dear, Gwennie thought, he sounds so angry. She did not know if being his little girl was going to help this time as she reluctantly made her way into the parlour.

Casting her eyes to the floor, not wanting to see his angry face, she said, "Yes Daddy— I'm here, what's wrong?"

"Don't Daddy me, that's not going to save you this time."

"Save me from what, Daddy? I don't understand."

"What were you doing down on the jetty yesterday after your mother and I left, making a disgusting display of yourself with a new worker?" he demanded. "I'm the laughing stock at work. Everyone knows about your sordid carrying on with this young ruffian."

"But Daddy, that's Tom... I love him!"

Her mother realised what was going on and quickly interrupted.

"Gwennie, how could you do such a thing? You know what it's like living here in such a close-knit community. The place is full of gossips and rumours spread quickly," she berated. "You should have behaved more sensibly."

Her father by this time had realised what Gwennie had just said about being in love and was looking somewhat stunned. His voice now seemed to have lost its rage.

"Love him! Love who? Who's Tom for goodness sake?" The bewilderment clearly showed on his face.

"Thomas O'Sullivan, Daddy. I met him on the *Bulga*, he's the most wonderful man I've ever met."

Her father turned to look at her mother, trying to seek some answers.

"Ella, what's she talking about? Do you know anything about this?" He sounded abrupt, his patience wearing thin. "I left you in charge of the girls. What the hell has been going on while I wasn't there?" His voice again returned to a roar.

"Now darling, there's no need to swear," her mother reminded him, "and yes, I have met Mister O'Sullivan and I can assure you they were fully chaperoned at all times." She put her hands on her hips.

Gwennie knew her mother would not tolerate yelling and cursing in the house.

"Well your so-called supervision was obviously not enough, and to think this man would make a spectacle of my daughter on a public jetty," he retorted, embarrassed about his slip of the tongue. "He's not the sort of man suitable for any daughter of mine."

By this time, Uma, hearing her father's yelling, had sneaked into the parlour and now decided to add voice to the argument.

"But Daddy, Mister O'Sullivan's a nice man." Before any of them had a chance to say anything else, Uma innocently added, "and he's going to marry Gwennie."

Well, Gwennie thought her father would have a heart attack on the spot. She had never seen him go so red. Her mother was busy trying to calm him down.

"Of course, she isn't marrying Mister O'Sullivan dear. John, please simmer down. It's not good for you at your age, dear." Her mother tried to soothe him, patting his arm.

It did not seem to help the situation at all as her father walked closer to where she was standing and looking straight at her said, "That's it, I've heard enough. I'm not interested in hearing any more about this Mister O'Sullivan in this house."

She was still keen to try and explain to her father about her Tom, but before she could get another word in her father continued, "from now on Gwennie, you're not to see or speak to this... that... ruffian again."

"But Daddy, he's not a ruffian. He's a real gentleman and treats me like a real lady." Now she was on the verge of hysteria. "And I'll die if I don't see him!" she added dramatically.

Her father stood there unmoved, her very own sweet father who usually spoiled her rotten. He was not listening to one word she said.

"What a lot of rot, no gentleman would take advantage of my daughter, let alone any lady, on a jetty in front of his fellow workmates and employees. End of discussion! Gwennie, you're not to see him again, and I'll personally see that Mister O'Sullivan gets the message." Her father was so adamant, she knew it was useless to try and plead with him.

By this time, she was hysterical, and her mother was trying to calm her. Uma was now also upset and called to her father as he stormed out of the room.

"Daddy, how can you be so mean?"

Gwennie knew that was it. Her life was over. It was like Shakespeare's story of Romeo and Juliet. She had finally found an acceptable man to love only to lose him again, this time to her father's scorn. She really did not want to live without him, and God only knew what her father had done to her poor Thomas. He had a lot of power on this island when it came to the workers, and she knew how he could make Tom's life miserable.

Her mother, who was so opposed to Tom, initially could not bear to see her so depressed, but she was loyal to her husband and would not go against his wishes. To her mother's credit, she tried to make him understand her liking for Tom but to no avail.

* * *

That year, as Christmas and New Year arrived, Gwennie attended all the hectic social occasions. She never saw Tom at any of the functions, and after talking to one of his fellow workmates, who was an old friend of the family's, she discovered he was working mostly nights and double shifts every time a social event was organised. It was one of the most dismal periods of her life to see so many people happy and celebrating over the festive period when her heart ached for Tom.

New Year's Day was the big annual Sports Day held on the oval up on the plateau. This had always been one of Gwennie's favourite events and this year all she wanted was to catch a glimpse of Tom.

Everyone attended the Sports Day, including the Banabans, the Chinese and the various Kanaka workers, including the large Gilbertese contingent. Even the government officials, together with all the company's people, participated. For once, all work stopped long enough for the event. Everyone was expected to compete, including men, women and children. There were foot races, high jumps, pillow fights, tug-of-war battles, egg and spoon races; every race imaginable so that no one was left out, including the natives who had no competitive sense at all. But they did have a wonderful sense of humour and to have them on the sidelines was always a bonus and a highlight of the day.

While she searched the crowd looking for Tom, to no avail, she wondered how it was possible for her father to keep him away. Finally, her father insisted on her entering the various events he had nominated for her. He, of course, had no idea who she was looking for. She had not spoken of Tom and her feelings for him since her father's orders, and she was sure her father thought she had forgotten all about the notorious Mister O'Sullivan.

Her heart was not in any of this today as she competed in her events. Finally, on her last event, the long jump, she took off down the run-up and half-heartedly leapt into her jump. She landed halfway down the sandpit, landing on the side of her ankle as it twisted under her. The pain was excruciating, and she moaned in agony while the officials ran over to assist her.

With all these men gathered around her in their white suits, Gwennie heard a familiar voice.

"Excuse me, let me through here please." It was such a commanding voice that the gathered officials let him through.

There he was, her Tom, standing over her.

"Are you all right, Hazel?" he asked, crouching down beside her. "Here, let me take a look at your foot."

Gwennie was in a haze; the pain did not seem to matter anymore as he touched her bare ankle. She could feel herself almost melt into the ground around her. She did not hear the mutterings going on around them or the other authoritative voice that was coming their way.

"Gwennie, Gwennie, are you all right? Here let me through!"

"She's all right, Mister Williams, just twisted her ankle," came the soft voice of one of the officials standing overhead.

She did not know if the concerned official was trying to warn her or calm her father down, because she and Tom heard none of it. They were too busy in their own little world where other people did not exist, but suddenly they were brought back to reality.

"Get your dirty hands off my daughter!"

They both looked up to see her angry father standing above them with his hands on his hips.

At that moment she thought he was going to kill her poor Tom, who, seeing her irate father explained hastily, "Haz... er Miss Williams has only twisted her ankle, sir, she will be fine in no time."

Tom stood to greet him only to confront his angry gaze.

"Sir, you must be Mister Williams. I haven't had a chance to meet you formally, sir. I'm Tom O'Sullivan." His voice faded as he noticed Williams' gaze turn more threatening.

Such a brave man, Gwennie thought, to calmly stand there and introduce himself formally to her father when it was apparent, he wanted to strangle him. She was not going to let Tom's bravery go without trying to give him some assistance.

"Yes, Father, Tom... I mean Mister O'Sullivan, has had a lot to do with racehorses and knows a lot about leg injuries," she explained hurriedly.

This was a complete lie, but the first thing that came into her head.

Tom suddenly turned to stare at her in disbelief, and one of the officials interrupted.

"Here, Miss Williams, let's help you off the field."

This indeed saved the day, and of course, her father was not the type to stage a scene in front of all the staff.

Tom attempted to take her right arm while one of the other officials took her by the left arm.

"Thank you, Mister O'Sullivan. I can look after my daughter now, thank you very much."

"Yes sir, only too glad to be of assistance," Tom replied humbly, knowing that John Williams had the winning hand.

"Humph!" her father grumbled as he took her by the right arm and helped her make her way off the field. She kept turning around to try and see where Tom was, but again he was gone; disappeared from sight. Oh, how she wanted to see his face.

That episode would set the pattern of her life over the next months. A fleeting sight of the man she dearly loved and a father at home who was exceedingly grumpy and off handed with her. The loving and adoring father, who had always been there for her to offer support and look after her every need, was now hostile. Her mother said it was only the pressure of work that was making him morose. As often as possible, she took long walks, sometimes with Uma, or Tetabo in tow.

Her mother had even called in the island's new Catholic priest, Father Pujabet. He was a Frenchman who had a liking for good music and good wine, and her mother knew he could be trusted with the family's secrets. This was always a problem on a small island like Ocean Island, with such a large and varied cultural population. It also did not help with her father being the Head Overseer. The Williams family always had to maintain a certain standing on the island.

Father Pujabet became a wonderful confidant and adviser to Gwennie. They would sit and talk for hours, and she would take him around the island and introduce him to many of her Banaban friends. He listened to her tales of loneliness in her earlier years, and her strong belief in God merged with her Banaban spiritual beliefs she had grown up with. He had always been there to talk to her. She would tell him of the terrible mishap, things that she had not even spoken of to her own mother and of course she spoke to him about Tom. Father Pujabet never became judgemental; he listened and assured her that God would not abandon her. The Lord would always be there to protect and guide her on her way through life, and she must hold on to her faith, and she did. She just did not have the heart to tell Father Pujabet that she also still believed firmly in Banaban *kouti*, magic, and their ancestral spirits.

But the good Father's words of support helped strengthened her resolve to be with Tom. Little did she realise the central role Father Pujabet would play in her future with Tom O'Sullivan.

CHAPTER NINETEEN

DIVINE INTERVENTION

Sacred Heart Mission - Tabwewa Village 1922

The pace of life on Ocean Island was one of extremes. While the white staff worked the hard and long hours demanded of them by the company, the Chinese and Gilbertese indentured labourers put in the tough manual work of mining and loading the phosphate rocks. When not at work the company staff was at play, either on the cricket field or at their local tennis club or one of the many other sports clubs that were available to them on the island. Life for the Banabans was now at a much quieter pace with many of the daily routines of fishing and food gathering significantly altered by the provisions supplied by the company store.

There was one day of the week when even the company's workers had to rest. Sunday was the day when all Ocean Island residents, except for the Chinese staff, went off to worship at their perspective churches. It was the one day of the week where God was called upon to bless and protect them all.

Gwennie, being a good Catholic girl and like the rest of her family, spent her Sundays worshipping at the Sacred Heart Mission at Tabwewa. With only fleeting glimpses of her beloved Tom over the months since their last meeting at the Sports Day, she had made a point of checking the outgoing passenger lists, just to make sure her father had not succeeded in sending him away. She had a nagging fear that her father was determined to see him off the island as soon as possible. He had already made sure he kept him busy working, but the following Sunday at church service all that would change.

Tom was there in the congregation. She could not believe it. Her Christian God had answered her prayers. He had been on the island all this time, and she had never seen him at Sunday service before. With his Irish surname, she should have realised his religious denomination. After service, Father Pujabet was there to greet everyone personally as he usually did. The priest walked over to where Gwennie was standing with her family and greeted them all. On noticing the smile on her face, the priest gave her a slight wink of the eye in that typical French way of his. It was then that she realised he knew about Tom being there. Suddenly, out of nowhere, Tom appeared, heading straight towards them.

Father Pujabet casually said, "Oh, by the way, John, I'd like you to meet a young friend of mine."

With that, her father, who had his back turned to Tom, swung happily around with his hand extended already to greet a friend of Father Pujabet. He was caught in the most awkward position as he stood in silence, finding it difficult to find the appropriate words. He could not believe the audacity of the young man standing before him, while at the same time, he did not want to offend the priest. He had no choice but to shake the young man's hand even if it was with reluctance.

"Good morning Mister Williams, we really haven't had the opportunity of being introduced formally," Tom stated with his usual wit.

John Williams, by now, recovering from his initial shock, was trying his best to keep up appearances in front of Father Pujabet. That was until the young man spoke up again.

"I've been here for at least nine months and haven't had much chance to meet or see anybody yet. The company definitely knows how to keep you busy."

He could not hold himself in check any longer; he was not going to let some brash young ruffian show him up in front of his family.

"Yes, well, an employee doesn't come to Ocean Island for a rest camp young man!" he retorted, emphasising the word *employee*.

"I'll certainly agree with that, sir, it is more like a slave camp at times. Surely a man has some free time to himself?" Tom replied, not backing down.

"Of course he does, young man," Gwennie's father replied indignantly.

"Yes, well, it's taken me all this time to finally attend Sunday service. Thank goodness Father Pujabet came to my rescue, or I'd still be back at Uma servicing the crushers." He gave the priest a grateful smile.

"*Mon Dieu*! Yes John, a terrible situation when a young man can't even have time off for Sunday worship. I'll have to have a word with your company's officials," Father Pujabet suddenly interrupted. "It's almost inhuman in this day and age to make a man work on God's Sabbath." His hands accentuated his every word as the priest became more excited at the thought of such an injustice.

John was embarrassed. He was a tough man when it came to company matters, but when it came to his faith, he was not one to argue with a man of the cloth, especially his own parish priest. He looked slightly astounded and uncomfortable.

"Yes, Father, I'll talk to the management and see what I can do for you!" he quickly replied.

"Marvellous! Thank you, John. So kind of you to offer your services."

The good Father smiled, seemingly satisfied with Williams's suggestion. "Now, how would you all like to join me back at my presbytery for morning tea?"

"That would be lovely, Father," Gwennie's mother replied in unison with the rest of the family. All that is except for her husband, John.

"Oh no, thank you, Father, I have to go over some work."

The crafty Father Pujabet quickly picked up on Williams's reply. "Now John, you have to set an example to the rest of the men at the company and rest on the Sabbath and have time with your family to worship God."

John was trapped in a corner he could not get out of this time.

"I won't take no for an answer! Now come this way everyone, Sister Ignatius has a lovely morning tea waiting for us."

They all went, with Tom bringing up the rear.

The morning tea conversation between Father Pujabet and Tom proved so entertaining with them exchanging ideas and stories that John Williams was forced to join in. Gwennie sat back in her chair, listening to Tom's every word, while her mother occasionally joined the conversation.

Uma went off to play with some of the native children that lived near the mission. In the middle of their conversation, after her father had begun to relax slightly, Tom turned to him.

"Mister Williams, would you allow me to court your daughter, sir?"

This question stunned everyone at the table, including Gwennie, as she spluttered, almost choking on the cup of tea she was sipping. Her father was speechless, while Father Pujabet sat there smiling knowingly.

"Ah, John isn't it grandee to be young and in love!" The priest smiled broadly at the young couple. "Our Hazelette and a good Catholic hard working boy."

"Yes, but... Gwennie's too young to..." Her father stuttered, trying to think of a right answer to give the clever priest. He looked deflated.

That was the moment when he realised that he had been tricked and had just walked into the trap.

"John, Hazelette is a beautiful young, healthy woman who should be thinking about settling down and starting her own family, as God would want her to do," the priest said, insisting on calling Gwennie by her other name, which was accentuated by his French accent as it rolled off his tongue.

"Yes Father, but she's led such a sheltered life growing up here."

"Well she has to learn about life eventually, John, and I'm sure Tom is enough of a gentleman to respect her morals, and of course, nothing is stopping you insisting on them being chaperoned," Pujabet replied, seemingly with an answer for all of Williams's excuses.

After a very eventful and sometimes uncomfortable morning tea, Tom was permitted to court Gwennie at last. This paved the way to make them inseparable. Miraculously, Tom's work schedule had seemed to ease and now allowed him some free time to visit his adored Hazel. They could even attend official functions and dances with her mother in tow. But at no time were they left on their own.

Gwennie had other ideas. For the first time in her life, she wanted to be alone with a man.

Tom, being the gentleman he was, tried hard to control his passions. The situation was not helped when Gwennie whispered her intentions in his ear one night while on the dance floor. Tom's face turned a bright shade of red, and after composing himself, he quickly glanced around for eavesdroppers.

Her words were like a hot branding iron being dangled close to his loins, and he knew the consequences could have the same fatal effect.

"Hazel, you know that's not possible until we get married, and I promised your parents and Father Pujabet I'd respect your morals," he said, trying to convince himself of what he had just said.

"I don't care about morals. I just know I love you and want to be with you in a way a man and woman should." From the look on his face, Gwennie knew she was making progress.

Tom again blushed and adjusted his tie in a nervous reaction, feeling the heat intensifying. Gwennie could tell he was flustered now and made a point of pressing her breasts gently against him again, leaning over to whisper in his ear.

"I can't wait any longer."

She could actually feel him tremble when she placed her hand on his shoulder as if to confirm her intentions. Poor Tom was about to burst. Gwennie knew what she was doing was wrong, but she could not help her love for him. Her parents had said they would have to court for at least a year before they would even permit them to become engaged and she did not really trust her parents enough to believe they would not find another excuse when the time came. Whatever happened, she had no intentions of waiting that long.

18. Pathway through Tabiang village Ocean Island early 1900s

19. Tetabo (houseboy) with wife Nei Meri and son Nete Ocean Island.

CHAPTER TWENTY

BANISHMENT FROM EDEN

Ella 1922

It had been a trying past few years with conflicts in the Williams's home, and Ella believed a lot of it had to do with Gwennie being raised here on the island. She asked herself whether this all would have been happening if they had lived back in normal society. Maybe John would have handled things a little differently and not been so protective, and Gwennie probably would not have been as naive and sheltered as she was… although all the company people here claimed the opposite, saying that children grew up too quickly on the island.

Well, Gwennie definitely had not! If anything, she knew she had been over-protective and John, being the Head Overseer, had terrified all the young men who had shown any interest in their daughter over the years. Now, at the age of twenty-two, she had fallen hopelessly in love with Tom O'Sullivan. He was everything they believed not suitable for their daughter. Ella had to admit he was well educated and well-mannered and somewhat good-natured, but Gwennie had no idea of education. She had only attended the local mission school and, except for essential reading and arithmetic, was not trained in any other areas. Tom was so casual and nonchalant in his attitude to life. He was the sort of man who would not do anything he did not want to do, and that included being on time.

They lived in a place where the local Banabans had no conception of *time*, but the company ran everything to schedule, and so did John. Their whole life revolved around time. Time for breakfast, time for morning tea, time for lunch, time for afternoon tea, time for dinner and even time for supper. Ships' schedules, flatcar schedules and work schedules… Tom was more like a Banaban, to whom time meant nothing. She still had not worked out how he got himself organised to attend work every day. Hence Tom and Tetabo became good friends and seemed to have a lot in common.

His dress sense was deplorable. Ella knew a high-spirited young bachelor living on his own would find it hard to care for himself, but they had always believed that 'clothes maketh the man'. Tom was clean and always wore his Californian Poppy hair oil; he just never wore his tie straight. Most times, he threw it over his shoulder. Tom disliked wearing a hat when going out except when he had to work under the island's scorching tropical sun. Ella supposed it was a relief in one way because she was sure he would not have known how to wear it straight on his head anyway. Everything about him was askew, not neat and tidy as it should have been; everything seemed crumpled. She had even offered to arrange one of the native Janes to organise his ironing.

"Oh, that's very kind of you Missus Williams, but I really can manage."

Manage! That was an overstatement. Ella had to agree with Gwennie in that respect; he did need someone to look after him and what a job for any poor woman, especially her daughter. Her daughter had never done any home duties in her whole life. Even now, Ella herself had not dealt with routine household chores since virtually the day she had arrived here, some twenty years ago. It was still clear in her mind how tedious it was, what with washing and ironing and taking care of a husband.

Oh, her poor Gwennie; she had no idea, Ella lamented. The only hope she had was to live the rest of her life here on the island and have everything done for her by servants. She would never cope, otherwise.

John himself was so particular about the way the girls dressed that he insisted they look their best at all times. That was the way their girls had been raised.

How could Gwennie cope living with an untidy wretch? Ella knew her husband would never adjust to his prospective son-in-law and some of his careless ways, but she supposed that was part of falling in love. Father Pujabet had tried to remind them both what it would have been like when they first met. She had not admitted to Father, but at the age of seventeen when she had met John, she knew nothing of love and worldly things. She only knew she wanted to escape from the endless chores and work involved in being the firstborn child in a large family of twelve.

She knew it sounded terrible to think of it now, even though she had dearly loved her parents and family, she had always wanted some time for herself, something of her own, especially a home. She had become sick of sharing everything she had in the world. John had come along and offered her an escape. She didn't know then about the other duties she would be expected to perform once she was married. Even with her mother's warning, it still was a shock. Ella knew she had to prepare her girls properly for married life.

After those first few trying years, she eventually fell in love, but it had taken many years to establish a proper relationship, especially seeing he was hardly at home in the beginning. During their time here on the island, they had become inseparable and now relied on each other. John was known on the island as a tough man, but with her, he was different. He was a soft, gentle, considerate soul, who would have done anything for her and the girls; a good husband.

She had to admit that Tom truly adored her Gwennie. She only hoped it would last as he did not have much else to offer her. Ella knew he wrote Gwennie poems, and she thought they were just fantastic. She was so entangled in the romance that she was not practical about things. Her life revolved around her Tom. If he had told her the world was flat, she would have believed him. Thank God the Almighty Tom was a staunch Catholic. God had at least seen to that, and maybe if she said enough prayers, he would help them in other ways. Until then, she would do her best to discourage their marriage.

Over the past months of their courtship, she'd tolerated but never accepted Tom. John felt the same way. Between the two of them, many a prayer was offered up to the good Almighty asking for some of his divine intervention. As the months of courting moved on, their relationship seemed no closer to waning. John had told them they would have to court for at least twelve months before he would consider permitting Gwennie to become engaged. John was no fool and knew that Tom's contract would run out in March of the following year, making it even harder for them to arrange an engagement and marriage date. Also, the question of Tom being given a new contract would apply, and without it, he would have to return to Australia. This subject, of course, was never openly discussed though Ella was sure her husband would use this as a last stand if the time came.

Ella felt a little sorry for Gwennie when she realised John's intentions, knowing how difficult it would be for her. Even though she knew she did not want her daughter to marry Tom, she could not bear to see her hurt. Gwennie deserved to be happy.

But Ella was in for a shock. For all John's shrewdness and her own best wishes, Tom and Gwennie were prepared to outfox them in the worst possible way.

The day Father Pujabet arrived on Ella's doorstep unexpectedly after John had left for work was the day, she thought God had forsaken them all.

"Good morning, madame, so sorry to come calling uninvited, but something untoward has arisen. Do you mind if I come in for a moment?" he asked in that delightfully accented voice of his.

"Not at all, Father," she replied, slightly taken aback.

Unannounced or uninvited visits on the island were unheard of and definitely not the correct way to do things.

"You'll have to excuse the way I look. I was not expecting visitors, Father," she hinted to make him realise that he was calling unannounced.

"Oh, thank you, madame, you look lovely as usual, and my, your garden is a picture these days." Obviously, Father was trying to make small talk in that charming French way of his.

Ella was very anxious to ask him why he was here, though good manners and breeding would insist on the appropriate small talk taking place first.

"Yes, Father, it's amazing when the droughts finally break how the gardens just go wild. Would you like to go into the parlour? I will arrange with Tetabo to bring us some morning tea."

"That would be joyful, madame. You are so... so... considerate. I won't take up too much of your time." He smiled and made a small bow before stepping aside for her to pass.

Finally, after settling down in the parlour and arranging with Tetabo to organise a quick morning tea, she waited for him to speak.

Father Pujabet became unusually quiet until after their tea had arrived before voicing what was really on his mind. She looked up at him as he suddenly became serious.

He cleared his throat nervously. "I'm sure you realise, madame, that I have come here to talk to you personally... unfortunately, something untoward has arisen!" He paused, his eyes suddenly turning skyward as if he was calling on some divine guidance to assist him.

Ella's patience was beginning to wear thin, waiting for the priest to get back to his little story when he suddenly turned his attention back to her and began to speak slowly.

"I also realise your John is at work and I thought it might be better if we have a little chat first, just the two of us." He was speaking more softly now. She almost felt that she was in the confessional receiving absolution, even though his words for some reason sounded more forbidding.

Ella could not hold herself back any longer and blurted out, "Father, what is so untoward? What brings you here like this?"

"Oh, I am sorry, madame, to frighten you in this manner, but your beautiful daughter Hazelette has asked me to assist on her behalf."

Ella began to laugh as she suddenly realised the reason for his visit, "Oh Father, I understand, Gwennie wants you to help persuade her father and me to allow her and Tom to marry."

His face began to turn rather solemn again as he bent towards her and placed his hands over her hand. His voice was low, she had to lean forward to understand him.

"I am sorry, madame, I wish it were so, but unfortunately Our Lord works in the most unusual ways. You see my dear, the good Lord has blessed your beautiful daughter with the gift of life."

Completely confused by his last statement, she said, "Father Pujabet, I do not understand what you are saying, I know the good Lord has blessed her with the gift of life... but?"

Before she could finish, he declared, "Madame, Hazelette is with child. She is *enceinte!* She and Tom... were indiscreet. They could not withhold their feelings for each other."

The silence was deafening as she sat there stunned, trying to comprehend his words. Father tightened the grip on her hand and again repeated the words, "She is with child – *enceinte,* madame."

His words washed over her like the crashing of the surf down on the distant reef below.

"Madame, do you hear what I am saying?" Father added quickly, and he called for Tea Tup to bring her a glass of water.

All she could think of was the fact that the priest was mistaken. He could not be speaking about her Gwennie.

Tetabo arrived, looking anxious, but the priest nodded reassuringly, took the glass of water, and waved him away.

"Here, madame, please just take a sip of this drink, and you will feel much better." He looked concerned, holding the glass of water up to her lips.

Ella did precisely as he ordered, almost in a trance. He spoke again.

As if hearing him for the very first time, she murmured incoherently.

"Madam, did you hear what I said? Do you understand me?"

She nodded weakly, trying to speak. "A child... my Gwennie, how...?" she uttered.

"Now madame, you must pull yourself together. Hazelette will need all your love and guidance, and I'm sure you realise the ramifications this will bring on John's position with the company." The strength of his words sounded a stern warning.

She heard him very clearly now, especially when he mentioned the word *ramifications* and John; he now had her utmost attention.

"Oh, Father! Oh no… I can't believe it!" She was shattered, her hands shaking as she began trembling all over.

Father Pujabet murmured, "My dear lady, you have my sympathy. You cannot know how guilty I feel about Hazelette's er... indiscretion and the part I played in their being together. But I am at a loss to explain how Our Lord has seen fit for this to happen. I'm sure you will agree that it would be preferable if I told your husband. You know how he feels about his Hazelette and Tom. I'm most concerned about how he will react to the news."

He could see the relief in Ella's eyes when he suggested that he be the one to break the news to her husband. She was happy if one could feel that way in such a terrible situation, to let Father take over control. She would certainly not relish the idea of being the one to have to break the news to John.

"Madame, I need you to listen very carefully. I have asked God for His guidance in this matter and feel that Our Lord would want them to be married as soon as possible."

Ella just nodded in agreement as he spoke.

"You must realise, madame, this new life growing in your daughter is a gift from God, regardless of whether the poor child was conceived in sin."

She winced at his last words, 'conceived in sin...' at the thought of Gwennie pregnant with Tom's child. How could this be happening to her family? The scandal would be the talk of the island.

Father continued, "Now, I have spoken to Tom and Hazelette and heard their confessions, and they realise that they must pay the price for their sin."

Ella looked up at him again, realising that there was more to come.

"Tom and Hazelette will have to leave the island, which I can assure you is a great price to pay for their sins. I will marry them in the second week in September so as not to raise too much suspicion, and Tom has said that they will go back to his mother's home in Sydney to await the birth of their child. You can see that this is the best solution for everyone."

Ella pondered over his last words. The impact of what he had told her seemed to stab her like a knife in her heart. The sadness and pain were all-consuming as she realised the price she would pay for her daughter's sins and her own failure as a mother.

Turning her attention back to Father Pujabet, she replied, "Thank you, Father, for all your assistance in this matter, but I am so greatly saddened. I have dreamed of the day when Gwennie would finally marry and have a child of her own, and now it will all happen in Sydney, and I won't be there for her." The very thought of Gwennie leaving them seemed too much to bear. Her eyes began to fill with tears.

"I know, madame; it is most unfortunate. Our Lord does work in mysterious ways, so maybe the gift of this child has been sent to test us all. Now I need to arrange with you to have a meeting set up with John post-haste." He looked relieved that she had not given strong objections to his plan.

Ella tried to push her emotions to the background while she made arrangements with Father Pujabet to have John go over to see him on the pretence of discussing the building of the new chapel. Tetabo hovered around in the background while the priest was there, and she could see the worried look on his face, as he too realised the seriousness of the situation. Talk of his Missy Gwennie was very much his concern as he had been so involved in her life.

Father Pujabet finally left once he was assured Ella had collected herself. After he left, Tetabo could not contain himself any longer and rushed into the parlour to speak to her. Ella felt his presence when he entered the room and looked up to meet his gaze, tears rolling freely down his cheeks.

"Our Missy; she is going to leave us?"

"Yes, Tetabo, I am afraid she is."

"But I do not want our Missy to go away! She is to have a *tetei* then she must stay at home so we can look after her," he sobbed.

Ella had to agree with her dear friend, Tetabo. A full-grown man and all he was worried about was losing his Gwennie. Scandals and morals did not even enter into his way of thinking. His only concern was for Gwennie, and her *tetei* and the thought of her leaving home and moving away from her family was just unthinkable to him. His people valued their families so much. How could she ever try and explain to him the workings of the white man's culture and what society would decree at the mere mention of a child conceived or born out of wedlock?

"Come and sit beside me a moment, my dear friend, for I too am very sad."

He sat down beside her on the sofa as he had been directed. Ella also began to quietly sob, and at that moment, the different colour of their skins and cultures meant nothing as they sat huddled together on the sofa reaching out for one another's hand.

* * *

Ella really did not know how she coped with matters over the next few days with John not knowing of her anguish. Facing Gwennie when she came home was also one of the hardest things she had ever had to do on her own. Gwennie now realised what the ramifications would be, and even though she loved Tom, she was terrified at the thought of leaving them all behind and making a new life for herself with Tom and a new child to raise, so far from home.

They rallied themselves together and started to make plans as John was going to see Father Pujabet that night, and they would have to prepare themselves for his wrath. Ella organised for Gwennie to stay over with Ellen Lewis, who was the manager's clerk and a young single woman. They had become close friends since Ellen's arrival two years ago and a night at her bungalow would not cause John any suspicion. Uma was over visiting the Olsen family for the weekend. Frederick Olsen was one of the stevedores down in Uma, and his young daughter and Uma were the best of friends. This would leave Ella alone in the house to cope with her husband when he arrived home after speaking to Father Pujabet.

That night, as Ella watched the hands on the clock, they seemed to take forever to move. It was as if time was standing still. More likely, it was the fact that she dreaded the moment John would come walking through the door. Finally, at 10 p.m., she heard the faint scuffle of footsteps coming up the front stairs and decided to go to the door to greet him and face the problem head-on.

Opening the door first, she caught him unawares, and her shock at his appearance was something she would never forget. John stood there on the doorstep with his head bowed, a dejected man. His face flushed and the usual confidence and strength he projected were nowhere to be seen.

"My darling, are you all right? Here come inside, and I'll fix you a cup of tea."

He slowly made his way into the parlour as if in the same trance she had experienced herself only the other morning. He too was stunned into the same shocked silence. She quickly made him a strong brew and rushed back into the parlour. After handing him his tea, she took his free hand and held it.

"Darling, I know how you feel it is a terrible shock." She waited a moment before continuing. "I'm sure Father Pujabet explained it all to you. I just want to say one thing my darling, and that is the fact that regardless of what our Gwennie has done, I still love her."

He turned his head towards her and lifting her hand to his face, spoke softly. "I love her too, she will always be my little girl," he murmured. "I only ever wanted what was best for her. I never meant for this to happen." The sadness was apparent in his voice.

"John, this isn't your fault. You did the very best any father could have done; maybe our only fault is that we both loved her too much." With those last words, she gently kissed the top of his brow. "Come on now sweetheart, I think it's time we retired to bed; it's been a very trying day, and nothing we do now will change it. It's up to both of us to rally around her and give her all our love and support. She's definitely going to need it, and we mustn't forget that out of all this disappointment we will have a beautiful grandchild who never asked to be born."

John lamely followed Ella into the bedroom. That night as they lay in each other's arms, sleep was not forthcoming. Their minds were racing over all the conflicting emotions that were raging within them while the one forbidding thought kept haunting them. Gwennie was leaving them.

20. Left to right: Uma, Gwennie (standing), Ella and John Williams aboard ship travelling back to Ocean Island c.1919.

21. Te I-Matang wedding ceremony Ocean Island early 1900s

CHAPTER TWENTY-ONE

TE I-MATANG'S WEDDING

Tetabo 1922

Tetabo stood there in a *te I-Matang* suit that Madam had given him. The sound of the surf breaking below carried up over the side of the cliffs. He glanced across to Miti Tom standing beside him who appeared to be very *raraoma*, or tense. Standing under the *taai,* or sun, the air was still while the perfume drifted up slowly from the blooms scattered all around them and the sound of the frigate birds soaring in the sky above was almost as if they too had come to honour the special guests.

Tetabo slowly scanned his eyes across the gathered crowd seated before them. They were all there; the Banabans from all the villages together with the *I-Matang*s and a handful of special guests from the various labour groups on the island. Suddenly a searing pain shot up from his feet. How could the *I-Matang*s wear these terrible shoes? He could not wait to be rid of them, but for the moment, he would join the rest of the *I-Matang* and their strange ways standing here before the grotto at the Sacred Heart Mission patiently waiting with Father Pujabet for the moment when Missy Gwennie would arrive.

The day had finally come, the *I-Matang*s had said it was called the 14 September 1922. They seemed to have a name for every moment they called *time*. To Tetabo, time was more a simple thing like the arrival of the spirits who daily came to greet them. The Virgin Spirit of the Dawn; they called her Nei Tengaina, Au was the rising sun-hero and Bue their sun-hero. Their lives revolved around these spirits and the start of each new day from the moment Nei Tengaina came upon them, and Bue would take his leave. They felt truly blessed with their presence. But this day would be special, for his beautiful Missy Gwennie would marry in the *I-Matang* way. It was one of the first weddings of its kind on their island. Everyone was very excited, including his own people. They had never seen such a thing but realised it would be the cause for a big celebration and feast.

Miti Wiriami had been here with them for many years now and was a good man, his *raraou,* or friend. He had been with the Wiriami household since Madam had first arrived with Missy Gwennie. He felt very close to them all. It had been such a busy period leading up to the wedding. Madam Wiriami had made the most beautiful white dress for the occasion, saying that all *te I-Matang* brides dressed this way. He too was busy helping Miti Tom get organised. Madam had asked him to lend his assistance, believing he needed some guidance. Tetabo was given the real *I-Matang* honour of being his best, number one man and felt very proud.

He liked Miti Tom very much. He was also a good *I-Matang,* and Tetabo knew he would take care of his Missy Gwennie. He tried not to think about why she would be taken away from them. The longer he lived with the *I-Matang,* the more he could not understand their strange ways. No sooner did they have their *tetei* in some cases when they were already so old, *te unaine*, they would send them far away. He just could not understand how they could live this way.

His people would only give their *tetei* away when they had too many and then usually it was to other family members within their clan who had no *tetei* of their own. This helped everyone in the village to have someone to care for them when they were in their old age.

At that moment, he heard the murmurs from the gathered crowd. White faces sat near the front right-hand side of the gathering, while all the dark faces were on the left-hand side. At the very front sat the elders from the various villages. The *kambana* flatcar was slowly making its way towards them, although this time it looked very different. Not only were the village children running beside it, which was usually forbidden, but the two big Gilbertese boys who poled the car were dressed in the *I-Matang* way. Madam had made them their new clothes as well.

As the flatcar drew near, it was covered all over with palm fronds and strewn with frangipani and hibiscus flowers, a sign of great honour and celebration. Sitting up on the seat of the car was Miti Wiriami, dressed in a new white suit and looking very proud. His arm was entwined with his beautiful daughter, Nei Gwennie. She looked like an angel from the *baibara*, or bible. She was covered all in white and looked so pretty with a large white cloud draped over her head and surrounded with white *uri* blossoms. She carried a handful of flowers, and underneath the clouds, he could see she looked *tikiraoi,* so beautiful.

Father Pujabet suddenly spoke. "All right gentlemen, our bride has arrived. Please stand over here and Thomas, you remembered the ring, I trust?"

Tom immediately started patting the pockets of his suit and was beginning to shake his head when Tetabo suddenly drew the ring from his pocket while Father Pujabet just quietly smiled.

"Thank you Tetabo, good man!"

Missy Gwennie and Miti Wiriami made their way toward them, walking through the arch of palm fronds and flowers especially prepared by the people of his own village in honour of such a great event. His people had also created a pathway through to the grotto covered in a variety of blooms. Little Missy Uma began walking ahead, tossing flower petals into the gathered crowd. At that moment Sister Ignatius and her choir began to sing, and to their credit, it was one of their own Banaban songs, Missy Gwennie's favourite.

They watched Gwennie slowly make her way towards them. Miti Tom had a big smile on his face. All the Banaban people had begun to join in the singing, and Tetabo's heart swelled with pride at the honour his people had bestowed on the young couple. Madam Wiriami, who had been quietly at the front of the crowd, began to silently dab at her eyes with her handkerchief. She must be truly proud.

On reaching where they were standing, Miti Wiriami handed his daughter to Miti Tom, and after saying a few words, joined Madam at her side. Missy Uma went to stand next to her big sister as Father Pujabet began to speak and call on his God to bless them all.

He could not believe his hearing when the good Father asked if anyone gathered here today had a reason why this couple should not be married. He immediately glanced back over his shoulder at Miti Wiriami, waiting for him to stand up and protest. Miti Tom had begun to tug on the bottom of his jacket, while he looked at him, wondering what was going on.

"Don't look at him; it's all right, Tetabo," he whispered in his ear.

Tetabo nodded in relief and turned back around to face Father Pujabet, who seemed to be also looking very *raraoma*.

Strange people these *te I-Matangs*, he thought. One minute the good Father is asking people to complain about the couple getting married and Madam Wiriami had been so ardent when she had told him not to tell anyone about Missy Gwennie's *tetei* saying it was a most delicate matter; yes they are very strange people indeed when it comes to babies.

He turned his attention back to listen to Father Pujabet's words. The good Father was once again talking about God and calling on him to bless all the people gathered here today. Now he was asking Missy Gwennie if she would take Miti Tom as her husband in sickness and health, for richer or poorer, until death do you part.

She answered in such a little voice, "I do!"

Miti Tom also said the same words and then placed the ring on her finger. Father finally called on God again to bless them.

"You may now kiss the bride."

Miti Tom lifted the white clouds from her face and kissed her on her lips. Tetabo could not help smiling and clapped with excitement as every other Banaban in the crowd took his lead and began to cheer and clap. The *I-Matang*s just sat there, some smiling, most of the women weeping. He could not help thinking about the funny ways of these *I-Matang*s. Father Pujabet just stood there, nodding and smiling at the same time.

When Miti Tom drew away from his new bride, the choir once again began to sing. Missy Gwennie looked all red in the face, and Miti Tom began to straighten his tie. With his arm around her waist, they both turned toward him, and Miti Tom honoured him in front of all his people by shaking his hand, and his Missy Gwennie kissed his cheek. They turned again to face the rest of the people and walked over to Miti Wiriami and Madam where they also honoured them before making their way back to the flatcar. Tetabo took Missy Uma's hand and escorted her down the pathway after them.

The happy bridal couple, as Madam told him to call them, led the way back to the government residency where they were to hold the celebrations out on the veranda and surrounding oval. Everyone was invited to attend, and this again had been a great honour for his people to participate in the festivities. Miti Wiriami had organised all the food and drink for the feast including a big fancy cake with small figures of a bride and groom on the top. The feast went on for the rest of the day with much ceremony and speeches from all the leaders of the *kambana,* and even the village elders made long speeches. Miti Wiriami and Miti Tom also made speeches and he and Missy Gwennie finally cut the cake.

Before the dancing started, Madam asked him to remind his people of the *I-Matang*s' ways and permit the bride and groom to dance on their own first. The bridal couple quietly began to glide around in circles staring into each other's eyes as the Police Band played on. Dancing had always played a significant part in their lives, and everyone became very excited watching the happy couple dance, even if it was very slow. Miti Wiriami and Madam finally joined them, and then other *te I-Matangs* started their gliding dance.

Following their lead, his people, including the children, joined in trying to *babaka te matang,* mimic the white man. This added to everyone's great amusement. As soon as manners permitted, the Banaban men gathered in a circle and began beating out the rhythm on their wooden box drums as a *te bartere,* the Banaban style of dance began. The *I-Matang*s enjoyed their dances very much, and Miti Tom and Missy Gwennie were encouraged to join in. Now they tried to *babaka* the Banaban, mimic the Banabans.

When *taai* began to leave them, Miti Tom announced that he and his new bride must be leaving. Madam Wiriami again began to weep, as did Missy Gwennie and now little Missy Uma joined them. The three *neikos* stood huddled together, hugging and crying. He walked over to them, again reminded of the funny *te I-Matang* ways; they were suddenly happy, suddenly sad. His Missy Gwennie lifted her head when he approached and rushed up to him, weeping profusely while suddenly throwing her arms around his neck.

"Tea Tup, my Tea Tup, I'm going to miss you so much. You were just so wonderful today." Her words washed over him, and he was suddenly reminded of why they were indeed all so sad.

This would be one of their last times together as Father Pujabet had advised Madam that Nei Gwennie should leave the island as soon as it could be organised.

Missy Gwennie suddenly spoke again. "Don't cry Tea Tup, you'll make me more upset," as he felt her hand come up to his face and brush the wetness from his cheeks.

Madam suddenly joined them.

"Now come on, darling, everyone is watching; it's been such a beautiful wedding so let's not spoil it." Her voice sounded strong as she began to take control of the situation.

"All right Mother, I'm just going to miss you all." Missy Gwennie sniffed, wiping her eyes with her lace handkerchief.

"I know darling, but now you have to make a new life with your husband," Madam said with a smile, trying to rally them all.

Noticing his daughter's tears, Miti Wiriami had now appeared and stood close next to Missy Gwennie, looking concerned.

"What's the matter, darling?"

"Oh nothing, Daddy," she said, turning to hug him. "I've just realised how much I'm going to miss you all."

"Come on, Gwennie. People are beginning to stare and wonder what's wrong," Madam again reminded them all.

"Oh, it's all right darling, it's not every day one's daughter gets married, especially here, so let them stare," Miti Wiriami replied with all sincerity. "Don't worry, we all love you very much, and Mummy and Uma will be there to visit you in Sydney as soon as possible. I'll have to wait till I get my leave due, but I'll be there as soon as I can sweetheart," he assured her.

"I love you so much, Daddy! I'm sorry I caused you and Mummy so much trouble."

"No more of that silly talk. It's been a wonderful wedding for my special girl, and I know Tom will take good care of you."

He was pretending to be a little gruff, but Tetabo knew that he too was sad about Nei Gwennie leaving the island. He also noticed Madam going over and placing her arm around her husband as he mentioned Miti Tom. The way things had been at home regarding the mere mention on his name, he was surprised to hear Gwennie's father now talk in favour of him. Miti Wiriami indeed was a very good man. Now that Miti Tom had finally married his daughter, he would accept his new son-in-law into his household. Tetabo still could not understand why they both had to leave here because of the *tetei*. Madam had told him the English word to explain the situation was morals. She said it was a word that manners decreed should not be discussed.

Now Miti Tom joined them. "Are you ready to go, darling?" he asked his new bride while she still had her arms around her father.

With reluctance, she turned to Miti Tom as he reached out to take her hand.

Madam suddenly said, "Now come on, Gwennie, you mustn't keep your new husband waiting."

"That's right Gwennie… and Tom I'm sure you will take good care of my daughter?" her father told his new son-in-law.

"Certainly, sir, I can assure you both that I love your daughter very much and will care for her with all my heart." He looked at Gwennie with love in his eyes and smiled at his new family.

With those words, Missy Gwennie suddenly hugged and kissed him, apparently forgetting all her previous fears. Even Madam and Miti Wiriami could not help smiling at their contagious happiness. Uma was now her usual excitable self while the gathered wedding guests also began to take notice of the happy couple saying their farewells. Miti Wiriami asked the wedding guests to gather around the happy couple and bid them farewell by singing *Auld Lang Syne*. This was one of the *I-Matangs*' favourite farewell songs and people joined into a large circle holding each other's hands while the bridal couple stood in the middle of the group. Once again, his people joined hands with the *I-Matangs* to bid farewell to their honoured guests.

Today would be a special day for all of them when for one day all their problems would be forgotten. Land issues for once were put aside for another day as his people stood hand in hand with the *I-Matangs*, joining in the festivities celebrating the *I-Matang* wedding, that ideal day when Bue, the sun-hero shone his happiness down upon them all.

22. Gilbertese labourers with their wives working topside.

CHAPTER TWENTY-TWO

THE TRIAL

Kabowi - Uma Village 1923

It had been nearly five months since the happy nuptials that had drawn the island inhabitants together. Gwennie had left the island without her new husband just days after the ceremony, while Tom had to stay behind to finish his contract. To the Williams's credit, Tom was taken in under their roof and made feel like one of the family. Ella and John were still coming to grips with their beloved daughter's sudden departure and clinging onto the fact that they would soon be grandparents. Ella had already made plans for herself and Uma to be in Sydney by April. No daughter of hers would have a baby without her being there.

John, as usual, threw himself into his work and suffered more than any of them over Gwennie's leaving. He, unfortunately, would not be as lucky as Ella and Uma and would have to wait another year before his holidays were due.

Tetabo went about his daily chores as usual, but somehow, he did not seem his old self. He, like John Williams, was virtually mourning the loss of a child. He had regarded Gwennie as his own daughter and felt a part of his heart had gone with her. He too, like the rest of them, waited for any word from his beloved Nei Gwennie. Meanwhile, while the Williams clan came to grips with life on their island without Gwennie, another major problem was brewing, this time from a completely unexpected source.

Corporal Teakai was the only Gilbertese non-commissioned officer in the local police constabulary and had been placed in charge of the Chinese labour force. He now was standing trial for his abuse of power and ill-treatment of a Chinese prisoner. His trial was something out of the ordinary for a man who was held in such high esteem by not only the general population of the island but the Chinese community as well.

As the sun shone down on Uma village, storm clouds were gathering on the horizon almost as an omen of things to come... The trial had begun.

"Gentlemen of the court, I would like to call as my next witness, Sergeant Major Taituse," announced the Acting Police Prosecutor who also happened to be Acting Commissioner at the same time; Arthur Grimble.

As the Sergeant Major stood to give his evidence in the assembled *Kabowi,* the accused sat to the left-hand side of the proceedings, his head hung so low that it was impossible to make out his face.

After Taituse had taken the oath on the Bible, Grimble said, "Now Sergeant Major Taituse, would you please tell the court what you saw happened on the twelfth of March 1923 between the accused, Corporal Teakai and Mister Fong."

"Yes, sir! Corporal Teakai, because of his good nature and eleven years' service with the police force, was the sole officer in charge of the Chinese prisoners, sir. His work party had been working down on the beach, collecting rocks and then bringing them up to the prison yard."

"Yes, Sergeant Major, and then what actually did occur when you came across his party?"

"Well sir, as I said, Corporal Teakai was the sole officer in charge, and he was not expecting me to call down and visit them," Taituse replied firmly, no emotion showing on his face.

Grimble sighed in mock exasperation. "Yes, Sergeant Major, we understand, but what did you actually see when you did come across Corporal Teakai and his work party... unexpectedly as you say?"

"I really do not know how it all began, sir, but for some reason I'm sure... Corporal Teakai began to flog Mister Fong, sir! And..." The Sergeant Major paused, lost for words.

"Yes! Yes!" Grimble spoke up again. "Sergeant Major, is it correct in saying you actually saw Corporal Teakai flogging Mister Fong?"

"Yes sir, that is correct!" Taituse finally answered, looking at the accused.

"And is it also correct that at the time of the flogging, the poor slightly built Mister Fong was carrying a large load of sand on his shoulders?"

"Yes sir!" the Sergeant Major replied, almost reluctantly.

"And is it furthermore correct in saying that this poor Mister Fong at the time of this sad occurrence, was trying to climb up a very steep part of the track up from the beach?" Grimble lifted his eyebrows, waiting for the witness to answer.

"Yes, sir! I—"

"Speak up please, Sergeant Major!" called Eri, who as the Banaban leader of the *kabowi,* was officiating as Magistrate.

"And what was Corporal Teakai using to flog Mister Fong with?" Grimble asked, pressing on with his line of questioning.

The Sergeant Major hesitated then replied, "Well, sir, it was a tarred rope-end."

"A tarred... rope-end?" Grimble repeated his statement, adding emphasis to his words. "Yes, er... well now as you said earlier, Sergeant Major, as far as you know from your powers of observation, there was no actual provocation. Is that correct?"

"Well, sir, there is always the usual abusive behaviour the Chinese seem to have towards the Gilbertese."

"But you're not a Gilbertese are you, Sergeant Major?" Grimble asked. He was aware of the supposed racial prejudices at force here among the indentured labour force.

"No sir, I'm not, Corporal Teakai is the only Gilbertese NCO in the Force here, sir."

"Well, would I be correct in saying that there were obvious tensions between Corporal Teakai and the Chinese prisoners?"

"Not really, sir. I have the opinion that the Chinese knew Corporal Teakai was a man of gentleness; if anything, sir he is greatly respected among the Chinese community here, sir... in my humble opinion."

"All right, Sergeant Major; that is all, you and your humble opinions may sit down," Grimble said.

"I would now like to call Mister Lee-Loone to give evidence," Grimble told the court.

As Lee-Loone stood with the Chinese interpreter to take the oath on the Bible, no one seemed to notice or care that Mister Lee-Loone was swearing an oath, to tell the truth on a white man's Bible that meant nothing to him at all; not that he did not have every intention of telling the truth.

"Now Mister Lee-Loone, would you please tell the court what happened on the twelfth of March 1923," Grimble asked, slowing his words somewhat to allow the Chinese interpreter to translate his question.

With the lengthy process of translating every question and answer, the small stature of Lee-Loone seemed overshadowed by the whole proceedings. He eventually told the court in his singsong voice a similar story.

Acting Commissioner Grimble added just one last question, "Mister Lee-Loone, have you ever seen or heard of Corporal Teakai flogging or hitting a prisoner before?"

"No, sir, never Corporal Teakai."

"Thank you Mister Lee-Loone, you may take a seat," Grimble concluded.

"I would now like to call Peter the Painter before the court," Grimble stated. He looked at his pocket watch to confirm the time. He was becoming hungry.

When the Chinese man known as Peter the Painter stood to give evidence and take the oath, the interpreter also accompanied him. Grimble sighed; another witness that would need translations; it was so exasperating and time-consuming.

"Now Mister Peter, the reason I have asked you here today is in your official capacity as one of our Chinese work overseers," Grimble explained with deliberate slowness. This method of interpretation was far too arduous and not entirely foolproof, he thought. The interpreter obviously had no standard schooling.

"Would you please tell us, Mister Peter, why Mister Fong was under arrest and with the work gang?"

"Well sir, he had been manhandled by a Gilbertese labourer and due to unfair police retribution and false witness been arrested for fighting," Peter the Painter stated as if he had been rehearsing that particular statement.

"Are you implying, Mister Peter, that our police tell untruths?" Eri interjected.

Peter the Painter, being the smart man he was, realised it was not wise to question the honour of a Banaban or Gilbertese with Old Eri as Magistrate and answered emphatically, "No, sir!"

Grimble tried another way and looked hard at the witness as if he was searching for the truth of the matter.

"Would you please tell us, to the best of your knowledge as overseer, the current feeling among the Chinese labourers concerning this outburst by Corporal Teakai?"

"Well Mister Grimble, sir, my people have had enough of this ongoing manhandling and brutality we must all endure from the Gilbertese!" Peter the Painter waited until his interpreter translated his statement and stood still and silent; his impassive gaze never left Grimble who was feeling uncomfortable with Peter's defiant stand.

He cleared his throat uneasily. "And, Mister Peter, is this manhandling and brutality, as you call it, coming from the Gilbertese labourers or the Gilbertese in the Police Force?"

"Both, Mister Grimble, sir," Peter the Painter replied quickly.

"And to your knowledge, Mister Peter, has there been any reason or previous provocation why Corporal Teakai should flog Mister Fong in such an unmanly way?"

"No sir, the only time to my knowledge was the incident sometime back when Corporal Teakai first took up the position. Fong was assaulted by a fellow Gilbertese worker down at the Basket Shed, and Corporal Teakai was the policeman involved."

"Thank you Mister Peter, that is all; you may take a seat!" Grimble directed, relieved that Peter was the final witness who required an interpreter. A wearisome business, he thought as he turned to address the Magistrate.

"Your Honour, as the court is aware, the victim Mister Fong is unavailable to tell us what happened. Obviously, he was in fear of his life and fled off into hiding. All attempts by the Police to find him have so far proved fruitless." Grimble paused. "I would, therefore, like to call my last witness, the accused, Corporal Teakai!" His voice boomed as the murmurs sounded in the crowded court.

Corporal Teakai slowly got to his feet, and for the first time all day, he raised his head. He straightened his uniform while proudly making his way to the witness chair. After swearing the oath on the Bible, he turned to face the court.

Grimble immediately began his questioning. "Corporal Teakai, could you please tell the court what actually happened on the twelfth of March 1923?"

Teakai slowly recounted the entire episode up to the point of telling the court where he had hit Mister Fong. Grimble asked, "Now Corporal Teakai, you do admit hitting Mister Fong?"

"Yes, sir!" Corporal Teakai answered solemnly.

"And is it correct in saying that the poor Mister Fong was laden with a heavy load of sand on his shoulders and under extreme physical disability was climbing one of the steepest grades on the path?"

"Yes, sir, that is correct," Corporal Teakai replied, with apparent signs of discomfort on his face.

"And is it also correct in saying, Corporal, that this poor defenceless Chinese did nothing to provoke such an attack?" Grimble sneered.

While the murmurs again rose from the gathered crowd in the court, Corporal Teakai, looking very distressed, turned to face Eri the Magistrate and then looked back over to Grimble. He seemed lost for words when Grimble said, "Corporal Teakai, may I remind you, you are under oath and would you please answer the question for the court."

He could tell by Teakai's eyes that he was ready to break.

Teakai seemed to become more disturbed and in a sudden outburst so unlike him, turned to the Magistrate as he called out, "The *Curse of Nakaa*!"

As the impact of his words sounded throughout the court, Corporal Teakai now had the undivided attention of every native in the court.

Grimble, thinking that poor old Teakai was indeed suffering madness, quickly asked, "Corporal Teakai, may I remind you of the fact that you are now in His Majesty's Court where we deal with facts. Not some native superstition! Would you please answer the question correctly and in a proper manner?"

Before Corporal Teakai, who now had fire in his eyes had a chance to reply, Eri, the old Banaban Magistrate, interjected.

"Just a moment please, Mister Grimble; I would like Corporal Teakai to explain what he means about the *Curse of Nakaa*!"

The Court suddenly became quiet as Corporal Teakai turned to Old Eri. "The man walks with the evil spirit Nakaa and brings Nei Terang, the Spirit of Madness upon our children."

Grimble again interjected, feeling annoyed at the use of superstitions being used as evidence.

"Your Honour, as you can see, Corporal Teakai is under terrible strain. I feel it would be wiser to let Corporal Teakai have some time to receive attention from the company's doctor."

"Yes, Mister Grimble, I understand your concern, but now would you please let Corporal Teakai tell us of the incident," the Magistrate ordered.

Turning to the accused, Eri asked, "Now Corporal Teakai, would you please finish your story."

"Yes sir, I am sorry for my outburst and lack of manners, but I have been most upset to see the evil of Nei Terang brought down upon our children here on the island," Teakai apologised in his best English. He felt slightly ashamed at his lack of control under the eyes of officialdom.

"Yes, keep going Corporal, carry on. Tell us how Mister Fong is walking with Nakaa and why Nei Terang has brought madness down on our children," Eri said, encouraging the big Gilbertese.

Teakai, now more under control of his emotions, spoke slowly. "This evil man Fong gives our young people a strange medicine and tells them to smoke it in a pipe, and it makes them go mad."

The court was suddenly awash with gasps, especially from the Europeans in attendance when they had realised the significance of Teakai's evidence.

The native contingent, including Eri, not realising the full meaning of what Corporal Teakai had just said, was still more concerned about their evil spirit Nakaa and their spirit of madness, Nei Terang, being involved.

Grimble, realising the significance of this news, again rose to his feet. "Corporal Teakai, is this the real reason for such a vicious attack on a poor defenceless man and the provocation for such hostile actions?"

"Mister Grimble, sir, on the day of the assault, after receiving further information, I questioned Mister Fong with the interpreter present about his evil ways and the selling of this madness powder to our young people. I then threatened to take him to the *I-Matang* authorities..."

"Please go on, Corporal!" Grimble demanded.

"Well sir, he just laughed and sneered at me saying that the *I-Matang* knew all about the madness powder and he would sell his powder to my own son if he wanted to."

This was the last answer Grimble had expected to hear or for that matter wanted to hear.

He decided to make his explanation simple and in a matter of fact manner. "If I may speak, Your Honour, I now realise that Corporal Teakai is referring to a Chinese medicine called opium, sir."

"Opium, Mister Grimble?" Eri had never heard of this thing called opium. Suddenly an uneasy feeling came over him.

"Yes, Your Honour, it is just an old Chinese remedy they use now and again, sir. It's also sometimes found in white man's medicine, but not often," Grimble explained.

"Well, Corporal Teakai says it brings madness, is this correct Mister Grimble?" Eri pressed on.

"I've never really heard of it bringing on madness, Your Honour. The Chinese do not seem to be to affected by its use."

"And is it true, Mister Grimble, that the *I-Matang* know all about this madness powder being sold to our people?" Old Eri asked with a very stern look on his face.

"Well, Your Honour, I can assure you as His Majesty's representative here on Ocean Island, that yes, I have heard of the medicine called opium, but I have never heard of the Chinese selling or giving it to the natives," Grimble said with much indignation.

"Very well, Mister Grimble, we will stop for the noon meal and then I will come back and give the judgement on Corporal Teakai...

while you, Mister Grimble, can tell me during our meal all about this thing that brings Nei Terang and her madness."

Old Eri dismissed the Court and Grimble joined him with reluctance.

Grimble and Old Eri sat under the thatched roof of the *maneaba* nearby with the other court officials while the women of Uma village served the men their meal. Eri had waited until after the meal had been eaten and then, after loudly belching to show his appreciation, he turned to Grimble.

"Now Kurimbo," he said, using Grimble's name given him by the Banabans. Old Eri preferred to keep this name for more personal meetings and not in court. "Why is it that you do not seem to know what is going on here on this island when you as Acting Resident Commissioner and the man in charge of Police should know these things?" Old Eri's keen eyes took in Grimble's discomfort.

"I'm sorry, Eri, but it's very difficult to know everything that is going on, and you must remember I have so many other things to contend with here, just not the Chinese."

"But surely you must be concerned with Teakai's accusations. You have a responsibility as representative of His Majesty to protect us against such evil," Eri scolded.

Grimble gave a false laugh.

Eri was not fooled by Grimble's behaviour.

"That is if you can believe all that Teakai is saying! I really believe he needs a good rest. If anything, it's my fault for putting Corporal Teakai in charge of the Chinese... just too much resentment between the Gilbertese and Chinese." Grimble was becoming impatient with Old Eri's lecturing.

"Kurimbo, I speak as a friend. You know Teakai is not the type of man to lie. He honestly fears for our people, and as a friend, I ask you to protect our children from this evil that Teakai talks about," he pleaded.

"All right Eri, as a friend, I will make sure no evil or madness comes to your people's children, and as a friend, I ask you to please help me end this case against Teakai as soon as possible and for everyone's benefit dispatch Teakai off this island. Otherwise, not only your people and the Gilbertese but also the *I-Matang*s will have the whole Chinese workforce wanting a lot more than just Teakai's blood," Grimble replied.

After the court had returned from the lunch session, Old Eri called the court to order. Corporal Teakai stood before him while he spoke; once again, his head was bowed.

"After much consideration, I have found Corporal Teakai guilty of flogging Mister Fong. He will be given a choice on the punishment he will receive."

More gasps were heard throughout the court, while the Chinese onlookers seemed satisfied with the outcome.

"Corporal Teakai will have the choice between dismissal with three months' imprisonment or reduction to third-grade constable with a flogging from his Sergeant Major." Old Eri's eyes searched for any objections.

He did not give the man more than a few seconds to decide his fate. "Corporal Teakai, what is your decision?"

"The reduction of grade and flogging, sir," he replied. The usually proud man's shoulders were bent low. The disgrace of his sentence was almost too much to bear.

"Very well, Corporal Teakai, Mister Grimble will see that your punishment is carried out."

"Yes sir," Corporal Teakai murmured, his head once again held low in utter shame.

As Corporal Teakai was being led out of the court to face his punishment Eri said, before officially calling the court to a close, "And Mister Grimble, as Acting Resident Commissioner of Ocean Island, the court requests that your government takes a further look at what is going on within the Chinese community." He looked hard at Grimble. "You and your government have been careless in the handling of such an incident that could endanger our children." Eri's last words were more a private reprimand, and Grimble did not take kindly to being addressed this way in public.

Holding his thoughts in check, he meekly acknowledged, "Yes, sir!"

* * *

Corporal Teakai had taken his punishment the very same day as his trial and by the next day was transferred to Tarawa, another island in the Gilbert Group, with instructions never to be returned to Ocean Island.

Fong, on the other hand, had finally been discovered after being missing for a week. Unfortunately for Fong, his discovery had not been soon enough. After fleeing from Corporal Teakai and being terrified of being found, he had escaped to one of the remotest parts of the island, the old dugout minefields. Here he had fallen and lay bruised and battered among the razor-sharp coral pinnacles for at least five days. As he was unable to move, the sun had shown no mercy and turned his bruises gangrenous. The day he was discovered was the day he had died. This immediately sent the Chinese community into a state and after going out on strike they had sent their interpreter to advise Acting Commissioner Grimble of their demands.

The Chinese had decreed that they would stay out on strike until they had all been repatriated back to their homeland unless the government agreed to their terms. Firstly, the Chinese requested that the entire police force, as a gesture of contrition for the murder of Fong by Corporal Teakai, should follow the dead man's body to his graveside with uniforms stripped of all buttons, badges, stripes or distinguishing marks. Secondly, they asked for the recall of Corporal Teakai from Tarawa, and that he be made to stand trial for murder.

While Grimble was reading the note of terms, a large crowd of around seven hundred striking Chinese massed in front of the government residency. Grimble, very much outnumbered and realising there was no way of meeting the demands, spent the next two hours arguing the government's case. The only solution he could think of was that of a personal gift, the offering of all the fireworks he could find to help make for a happy funeral for Fong.

Peter the Painter, who had given evidence at the trial and seemed to have some control over the crowd, suddenly surged forward throwing insults at Grimble. Then, just as suddenly, he screamed to the crowd and began running down the hillside with all but two of the Chinese in quick pursuit. The two remaining men then calmly agreed with Grimble on his terms with the fireworks. A shaken Grimble could not believe the men had accepted the offer. As for the seven hundred screaming Chinese, they were last seen galloping down towards the village. They all returned to work on the same day.

Whatever Peter the Painter had screamed was satisfactory to Grimble.

Over the next few days, Fong was sent on his way to eternal rest with Grimble's assistance and one of the biggest displays of fireworks ever seen on Ocean Island. Grimble hoped he had finally heard the last of these goings-on. He had to turn his mind back to more important things like the Banaban land issues that just would not go away.

23. Ongoing conflict between the Gilbertese and Chinese labourers Ocean Island.

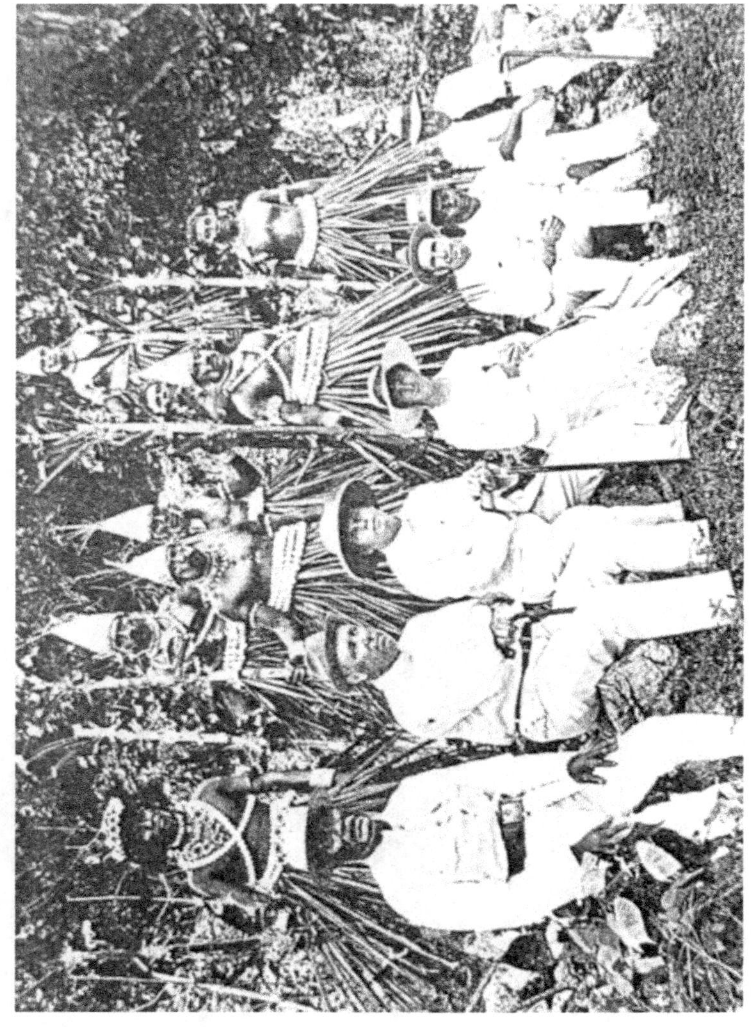

24. Banaban Magistrate, Eri (left) with European staff and Banaban dancers on Ocean Island early 1900s.

CHAPTER TWENTY-THREE

END OF A DREAM

Port Melbourne, Australia 1923

He tried to control his anger while he stood patiently waiting for the ship to finish docking at the extensive Port Melbourne shipping facility. The area was a hive of activity, as the stevedores expertly moved around the weather-beaten timber wharves, safely securing the ship's vast bulk to the sidings.

It was one of those stifling hot summer days that only Melbourne could produce and the people were busily scurrying to find cooling relief in the shade of buildings surrounding the wharves. He revelled in the hot weather and stood on the edge of the pier silent and alone, seemingly lost in his own thoughts and enjoying the scorching noonday sun. His muscular physique was clothed in the best-tailored three-piece woollen suit that money could buy and even with the sweltering heat his deeply golden tanned skin did not seem to perspire. The gleam from his hand-made black patent leather shoes glistened along with the sheen of his jet-black hair.

As the workmen finally secured the gangway, he slowly moved closer to watch the people disembarking from the ship. His hostility and mixed emotions were carefully hidden beneath his calm and well-manicured exterior. People were quickly making their way past him now, rushing to meet their loved ones and friends coming down the gangway. His striking appearance had not gone unnoticed by several of the women passing him, and they made a point of turning back. His bright piercing blue eyes contrasted with his dark good looks.

It had always been this way since he had arrived here and he had never realised they were, in fact, admiring glances. The word vanity was a word he was unfamiliar with, and as the years had passed, he believed people only stared at him because he looked so different. Even though he had grown accustomed to their unwelcomed stares, it only added to his feeling of alienation here in his adopted homeland, Australia.

He scanned the faces of the people leaving the vessel but knew the man he was waiting for would be one of the last to leave the ship. Today was one of the most important days in his life, the day when he would finally confront him. The man he waited for had all the answers, and he knew today was the day when he would finally insist that he tell him the truth. There would be no more lies.

Suddenly, his attention was averted to a flock of squawking gulls that were now circling overhead. Glancing upwards, a smile formed on his lips and his mood immediately lightened thinking of these creatures as his friends. He watched them dive all around him, dropping down out of the clear blue sky to pick up any scraps of discarded food while his mind was transported back to a happier time; a time and place were his life had been so simple and complete. It had been a place with only happy childhood memories and where he knew he really belonged.

Yes, the birds had always been such a happy part of his life back then, such an idyllic time and one filled with only love... but now everything was different.

His thoughts were drawn back to the unhappy present by the sound of a man's deep voice.

"Arthur! Arthur lad! I'm here... over here, lad!"

His anger once again flared when he turned to face the familiar voice. Holding himself in check, he walked calmly towards the large imposing figure coming down the gangway.

"Hello, Captain, it's good to see you again," he greeted the man, formally shaking his extended hand. He had made a point of calling him Captain; the word Father just would not form on his lips.

"Good to see you lad, you're looking so well," the big man replied. He was obviously happy to see him and placed his arm around his shoulder.

His emotions were now a mixture of anger, frustration, and a special bond that he had always tried to ignore. Every time he was in this man's presence, he could not help feeling terribly uncomfortable.

The two of them slowly made their way down the long stretch of wharf leading back to where he had parked his car; seeming in no rush they were oblivious to their surroundings locked deep in conversation.

"There has been no word for all these years. Why haven't my letters been answered?" he pleaded, the frustration apparent on his chiselled face. He did not usually lose his demeanour in this way, but now part of him could not hold himself in check any longer.

"I'm sorry lad, I can only tell you that I do not have the answer," the older gentleman replied, trying to sound indifferent to the young man's pleas. How could he ever tell him the truth?

"But something is wrong. I know it is!" Ata said in his cultured voice, suddenly stopping. He was not going to let the matter be pushed aside as it had been previously whenever he tried to hold these discussions. "What did she say the last time you saw her?" he pleaded. "Just tell me the truth... please!"

"I haven't seen her for quite a while, in fact, so I can't really recall." The big man was trying to sound as vague as he could. "I've been busy travelling with work, laying new moorings at Nauru and then over at Christmas Island." He cleared his throat. "I haven't been back on Ocean Island for quite some time." Again, he tried to sound casual, hoping this would ward off any further questioning.

Ata caught the older man by the arm to gain his full attention. "I know there is something wrong. She promised she would wait for me," he protested. "There must be a reason why she hasn't written, and if anyone has the answer, it would be you." What more could the Captain want from him? He had done everything that had been asked of him.

The older grey-haired man turned, the piercing blue eyes of his young counterpart struck him, and a sudden terrible feeling of guilt seemed to consume him. How could he ever explain what he had been doing all these years? How would this wonderful, intelligent young man feel towards him if he knew that he had never delivered those letters that had been entrusted to him? Would he ever believe the truth behind his actions and the deep feeling of love he felt towards him... his own son? Could this young, successful man who stood before him ever understand that he had done it all to help him get on with his own life and career? Would he ever believe it had all been for the best?

"Arthur... er, Gwen... Gwennie is married and already has a child," he blurted out, suddenly feeling very old. "I didn't want to have to tell you such news... I knew you would be upset," he implored, trying to justify his own unwillingness to discuss the matter. But before he could say another word, the look on Arthur's face was one of utter disbelief.

"You're wrong! It can't be! Gwennie loves me," he stammered, shaking his head in despair.

"Arthur, try and pull yourself together. You must remember you've been away a long time and people change. You and Gwennie would never have been permitted to marry... you must know that" he said, in all honesty, realising what he had just said aloud.

"But look at me, Father," he demanded. "I'm a *Matang* now. Am I still not good enough for her? I've given up my own people and homeland to become a *Matang,* and now you're telling me that Gwennie could not even wait for me."

"Please son, please do not be too hard on Gwennie. It's not her fault." His feelings of guilt overcame him again. "And you are a *Matang*, you're my son, and you must understand how proud I am to have you as my son." He could not hide the emotion from his voice.

His son stood there silent, seized by the memories of his past life and the anger he felt towards them all.

"Look at you, lad. You have everything a man could ask for," his father pleaded. "You're a young man of influence and growing importance here in Melbourne with a wonderful career that will secure your future, a car of your own and I thought we could look at the new plans for your house you're building?"

As Arthur slowly lifted his head, the look in his eyes startled his father. He began to speak in his cultured tones, slowly and precise, but the words were that of his old native tongue. His father had not heard him speak like this since he had brought him here to Australia.

"Yes, Father, I have everything a *Matang* could desire. All the trappings of wealth and privilege, but on the inside I have nothing... my heart is dead!"

Each word was carefully and correctly formed in his old dialect, his father translating the words in his head.

"I always promised my people I would return one day as an important man," he said bitterly. "Well, how can I ever be an important man, if I feel nothing?" His eyes were now focused on the expanse of water out across the bay, his mind deep in thought. He suddenly turned to look back at his father again, forcing himself to smile as he murmured, "and I will always have nothing... for I do not have Gwennie." He turned and quickly walked away, trying to hide the tears forming in his eyes.

His stunned father stood speechless, watching his son stride off, searching for the right words. Any excuse to call him back. But no words would come... what could he say?

As the lone figure of the handsome young man moved on away down the wharf, a flock of crying gulls circled above him.

CALL IN THE TROOPS

John 1925

"Mister Williams sir, I have an urgent cablegram for you. The office asked me to come up and give it to you personally." His voice sounded excited and a little out of breath after the walk from the office at Uma up here to the diggings on the topside.

"Thank you, Charlie," John replied. He took the envelope from his brown fingers, anxious to know the contents. "Off you go now in case they need you back in the office."

Charlie was their latest addition at the office and even though a Banaban lad, he had come to work for the company with his father's full blessing. His father wanted his son to learn the ways of the white man. Most of the Banabans over the years had seemed to become more remote towards them, the company staff. This was especially the case when it came to the younger generation. Many of the noble old inhabitants were now gone. The ravages of a hard life and earlier deprivation on the island had finally taken its toll with the passing of the years.

John quickly opened the cable, hoping for good news. Knowing it was more than likely from his Ella in Australia, he scanned the contents quickly, suddenly feeling the smile rise on his face.

"Boys! Boys! My daughter Gwennie has just had a baby girl," he called across the diggings, to any of the men who could hear or understand him.

He had been up on topside inspecting the mining's progress and also watching the different work gangs in action. Being the head overseer, he was responsible for supervising the various work parties and the individual overseers that led them. He enjoyed keeping a keen eye on the operations and lately things had become a little strained as far as the Gilbertese and Chinese were concerned.

The problem was not new. It had been going on for years, but since they had that last big strike about eighteen months ago over that Chinese fellow dying, things around here just were not the same. It was not that they were not all working, but something just did not feel right.

John supposed he could be cynical and say he was becoming as superstitious as the natives, but, even though there was nothing he could really put his finger on, something was amiss. At least he felt relieved knowing Ella and Uma were in Australia with Gwennie while she had the latest baby. Worrying about their safety was one fewer problem he had to be concerned about.

He had only sat down the night before in the staff mess rooms with some of his fellow senior staff discussing the island's latest problems after dinner. They had reminisced about their good old pioneering days, and they had all agreed that things just had not been the same since the takeover of the British Phosphate Commission.

John knew he had his own share of problems, especially with Gwennie marrying Tom. That had been a truly stressful time and one he did not ever wish to repeat. The one consolation was a beautiful grandson he had the pleasure of meeting on his last leave in Australia, and now a new baby girl. The place had lost some of its charm for him with Gwennie gone. He had never mentioned this to a living soul, including Ella, but he noticed that she too was looking for any excuse to visit Australia to see Gwennie and the family. Hence, he was left alone to fend for himself. The grandchildren were having a lot more of his wife's attention than he was.

He finished his inspections of the topside diggings and made his way back on the train through to the eastern mining area to see if the work was up to date. Feeling in a happier frame of mind after receiving the news about his new granddaughter, he continued to broadcast the information about Gwennie and Tom's new baby to all he could. It was not until someone made a comment that they had never seen him so excited that he realised he was acting out of character.

It probably had something to do with Gwennie's first baby, Brian, being such a close kept secret until the time was right. John could tell everyone about this new baby without causing a scandal now that she was respectably married. He went about his work, but he was reminded of Gwennie and how much he missed her. They had not mentioned a name in the cable, so probably had not decided on one yet. He knew he must give Tetabo the news or he would be terribly offended if the rest of the island knew and not him.

"Mister Williams! Mister Williams! Please, sir, come quick!" Charlie called, running towards him up the hillside.

"What's the matter, Charlie?" he asked, wondering what would be so important to send the poor lad scurrying up from the office again.

"Sir, Mister McLintock asks that you come down to his office quick," he pleaded.

"All right, Charlie, I'm coming." There was no arguing with an urgent message from the island's manager.

On making his way down to the office as quickly as he could, he heard yelling and shouting coming from the other side of Home Bay toward Tabiang village. It sounded ominous, giving him a sense of foreboding. When John reached the manager's office, he noticed that it was crowded with almost all of the white staff gathered around, anxiously waiting.

"All right, gentlemen, quiet, please! Resident Commissioner Grimble would like a few words," shouted the island's new manager, Mister McLintock, over the loud din.

Grimble waited for the men to quiet down before he spoke.

"Right, gentlemen, we have an extreme emergency on our hands. An all-out riot has broken out between the Gilbertese and the Chinese," he boomed to the gathered crowd. "Each of you gentlemen will be issued arms, and it will be your responsibility to protect the lives of your fellow workers, their families and Her Majesty's property. I can report that the Chinese have actually taken up arms against the Gilbertese this time. I'm sure I do not have to tell you the gravity of the current situation."

The crowd murmured anxiously for him to continue.

"I have issued orders for the married men and their families to be moved into the visitors' quarters and to be equipped with a machine gun for protection. The rest of the single men will be formed into an Island Defence Force."

Grimble went on to issue orders with the assistance of Mister McLintock, and John was put in charge of an armed party and ordered to go back up to the mining fields with authority to place all

Gilbertese and Chinese labourers under house arrest. Grimble had no intention of allowing them to join in with the other rioters.

After Grimble left, the word from McLintock was that the riot was a bad one this time, with men killed on both sides. At the moment, though, no exact numbers could be given. As a result, he placed certain heads of departments in charge of various armed parties, realising that this could be an all-out war. Thank goodness Ella and the girls were not here to see it, John told himself.

As he made his way back up to topside with his party, John reflected that Grimble had sent other groups off to guard the powerhouse, the explosives shed, the radio room and government residency building together with the Commission's stores building, which housed the island's entire food supply. McLintock, on the other hand, was more concerned about protecting the company's interests and sent further armed parties off to secure the jetties and other key facilities that were imperative in keeping production of the phosphate going.

John had no idea then that this latest riot would take nearly two months to quell. Grimble had already arranged for a warship with a contingent of Marines to be dispatched from New Zealand. The High Commissioner in Fiji had organised to send his secretary, Mister Pilling, to meet up with the warship so he could conduct an inquiry on the island as soon as the ship landed.

John also was not aware at the time that Grimble was refusing all offers of help from General Griffiths and eighty of his armed police from nearby Nauru. Grimble was more concerned with the political consequences of bringing a semi-military force onto a British possession to enforce law and order. He was prepared to wait for the warship with only fourteen of his own armed police to assist him and a handful of white government staff. Luckily, he had about fifty of the company's staff to back him up, because he was facing between six hundred Gilbertese and four hundred Chinese. In John's opinion, it was not a case of bravery or worrying about creating a political incident but more like stupidity.

Once again, it had all begun over a minor incident that the white labour inspector called a family squabble. Ironically it had started back in the old basket shed where once again a Gilbertese and Chinese working together had an argument. This time, after the Gilbertese struck his Chinese workmate, the Chinese man came back with thirty of his friends who promptly assisted in breaking the offender's arm. Next, this incident escalated as more Chinese workers mobilised back at the Chinese quarters where firearms of somewhat ancient origins were being brought out of hiding. The group then advanced on the Gilbertese camp, where luckily their first assault was driven back by rock-hurling Gilbertese.

While John was busy rounding up all the work gangs, the Chinese had spent the last few hours busy planning a more organised assault. Now they had several hundred men massed back at their quarters, mostly armed with knives, sticks, revolvers and some even with elaborate homemade dynamite bombs. They stormed out of their area, marching to the sound of drums and cymbals as they split into three groups.

John was not aware of these details at the time, but the din could clearly be heard on the topside. Realising something was wrong; he immediately left two of his men to guard their gathered work gangs while he hurried back down the hill with the rest of his men.

They arrived down near the Gilbertese camp to find Grimble trying to stop a battle between the two factions. His men had joined ranks with Grimble's who had then led them on a charge straight into the affray with all their guns at the ready. John did not know whether it was the terrified looks on their faces or that the warring factions had realised that the *I-Matang*s had gone mad and really meant business this time. Now that their own people and families were at risk, they had no hesitation in going into battle.

John supposed Grimble had counted on this, knowing that the Gilbertese especially did not want a confrontation with the Europeans. His move succeeded as they drove the warring parties back to their camps.

Then Grimble organised the removal of injured men for medical treatment. Six Chinese and ten Gilbertese lay injured while one of the Chinese was found dead among them. He quickly directed his men to guard the two camps, not permitting anyone to leave. Grimble followed this order by directing his officers and the BPC head of departments to meet at the staff mess rooms as soon as possible.

"Gentlemen, we've been successful in driving the Chinese back to their camp. Now it's a matter of keeping them apart and making sure no more are hurt or killed," Grimble instructed, trying to gather his composure. John had never seen the man with such a wild look in his eyes. Most likely, it was the look of fear. They probably all had a similar appearance.

"We'll have to disarm those Chinese, sir, before anyone else is killed, including one of our men," McLintock said, stating the obvious.

"I feel it is more dangerous at the moment to try and enter their camp and force them to give up their arms. It could even escalate problems," Grimble replied. "We're terribly outnumbered, and the Gilbertese will expect me to take their side and protect them against the Chinese." He glanced over his men, obviously trying to judge their reactions.

"Sir, what do you want me to do with all the men I've presently got under house arrest up on topside?" John asked.

"Just hold on to them a little longer until after I've had a chance to go in and talk to the leaders in each camp," Grimble replied. "It would be wise to try and start negotiations as quickly as possible."

John thought this man was either the bravest man he had ever met or else quite mad. Here they were on a remote island in the middle of the Pacific with over one thousand Chinese and Gilbertese men rioting, or should he say warring, and only fifty of them standing between them wanting to kill each other. Grimble thought it was more dangerous to try and disarm them but was quite happy to walk into a camp of armed killers and have a chat. He would probably be inviting the ringleaders back to the residency for high tea if he had his way.

"What if they won't negotiate? We can't leave one hundred Gilbertese and Chinese workers under house arrest up on topside. It's almost impossible, and how do we feed them?" McLintock asked.

"Is there anywhere we can hold them, so we do not have to let them back to the main camps?" Grimble asked. His eyes seemed to be turning skyward. Maybe he was asking for divine intervention.

"Nowhere secure, sir, and they will have to be fed. The native and Chinese hospitals must be nearly overcrowded at this time, so I don't think they would cope with any more, that is unless you take them up to the police yards!" McLintock exclaimed in disgust.

"Well, let's wait and see what happens after I speak to the leaders, and if it looks too dangerous, I'll lodge them there as a last resort. So obviously, Mister McLintock, I'd expect your people to organise food and provisions." Grimble's air of authority hinted at his stubborn defiance.

"Yes, sir!" McLintock replied. John could see he was more than reluctant.

"Now gentlemen, whatever happens, we have to hold out until some assistance arrives," Grimble ordered.

"Well, that could be a while," McLintock replied sarcastically.

"Sir, what about getting some quick help in from Nauru?" Captain Cozens asked.

"Gentlemen, do I have to remind you this is a British Colony and the British handle their own affairs. We do not want foreign troops on our soil." Grimble was adamant.

John thought about the stubborn British and their ill-fated stands and glanced at Cozens, together with the rest of the company staff. They turned to look at each other and silently agreed. The majority of them were Australians, and the old colony philosophy did not wash too well with them any longer. He was sure his old mate Cozens had asked such a question just to get Grimble's back up. The Aussie sense of humour always had to rear its ugly head regardless of the situation, and old George was an expert. They all loudly answered Grimble almost in unison.

"No, sir!"

McLintock, realising they were having fun with Grimble, quickly asked, "Any idea, sir, how long before a ship arrives here with some troops?"

"Not yet, but I'm sure to let you know as soon as I hear anything," Grimble replied. "Now gentlemen, if you secure your posts and keep those men up there on topside from joining in, I will go in and try and negotiate with our friends," he added.

He was cut short by young Charlie arriving with a new message from Grimble's second in charge, his District Officer.

He quickly read the message and sighed in exasperation before speaking. "Well gentlemen, another new problem has come to hand. Apparently, the Chinese have taken twenty Gilbertese as hostages."

"Then we are forced to try and start negotiations as soon as possible, sir, before anything else happens. That is, straight away!" McLintock apparently did not care about offending Grimble.

Grimble left hurriedly to start negotiations while McLintock stayed behind. Grimble did not want any more problems with the company people getting more stirred up.

McLintock sent all his men back to their original posts after they had verified the security arrangements at the guest quarters where the women and children were gathered. The machine gun was prominently mounted on the front veranda with the men barricaded behind it. The sight of the gun pointed towards anyone walking up the path towards the building was rather daunting.

As the day slowly drew to a close, word finally came through for John to escort his work gang down to the police yards. Obviously, Grimble still was not taking any risks. That night as he made his way back to the staff mess rooms where the single men were bedding down, he realised he still had not had a chance to see Tetabo and tell him his good news. After they had something to eat, John asked Charlie to quickly take a message up to his house for Tetabo. None of the men were permitted to have any beer rations, and he did not know if it was exhaustion, fear or no beer, but the men seemed rather quiet. He suddenly remembered he had not told most of his workmates the good news about Gwennie and Tom.

"Gentlemen, I forgot to tell you the news," he shouted, "my Gwennie and Tom had a baby girl back in Australia!"

They suddenly all brightened, coming over to pat him on the back, shaking his hand and congratulating him. The way they carried on he could have almost sworn they were the proud fathers them-selves. Gwennie was so well known among the old staff; many of them had been sweet on her over the years. Tom also seemed well-liked and remembered by the men who had worked with him.

"What a shame we can't wet the baby's head, John," Jack Miller called out. Jack had been another old friend from the early days, spending most of his time over at the settlement of Tabwewa. His wife and children had been friends of the family and Uma seemed to spend a lot of time over at their house.

"Yes, and I suppose you'll all have to wait for a cigar for a while," he replied as they all laughed.

"I remember the time we gave you a cigar when Uma was born, and you were ill for a week," George Cozens teased. His sense of humour outweighed the grave predicament they were in.

While they all laughed, the men began to reminisce and retell the good old stories and yarns they loved to hear. It did not matter how many times one listened to the same old yarn, they still laughed and remembered what great times they had all shared. John really be-lieved they all had to have been a little crazy to come here in the first place.

This was their first night of many they would share until the riot had finally been quelled. The amazing Grimble, true to his word, did negotiate, mostly with the Chinese, as the Gilbertese stood firm on the notion of not returning to work until all the Chinese were shipped back to China. The Chinese agreed to release their hostages if they were kept in the administration gaol until the warship arrived. The word around their quarters was that after a few days into the riot, the high-ranking Chinese staff had disarmed their unruly workmates and thrown their weapons into the sea.

Ten days after the riots had begun, His Majesty's sloop *Veronica* arrived and sent a landing party ashore to help. Just their show of men had helped enforce Grimble's standing. The warship *HMS Laburnum* finally arrived two weeks later, this time with plenty of marines to secure the place. Mister Pilling, Secretary for the High Commissioner in Fiji, also arrived and began his enquiry as soon as he landed. This kept them all busy for a few days giving evidence. Meanwhile, phosphate mining was at a complete standstill. The entire facts of the riots ended up as a fifty-page report with Grimble's action of courage and disregard for personal safety duly mentioned.

Pilling could not believe how it was common knowledge among the white staff that a riot was imminent and the BPC Commissioners had not acted accordingly. The Chinese workers had finished their contracts and were waiting to be returned to Hong Kong. The company was having trouble obtaining ships to take them out as there had been a shipping dispute in Hong Kong. Meanwhile, the Chinese just seemed to be stranded on the island with no word of when they would be returning home. This only added to their unhappiness.

Grimble had tried to persuade the company's Commissioners to use their vessel the *Nauru Chief* to return them, but they felt this was not appropriate as the crew was Gilbertese and they needed the ship urgently for mooring work on Nauru. The Gilbertese had still refused to return to work until after the Chinese had finally left. The only solution was to ship these men out who refused to work and start again with new recruits. Therefore, most of the Gilbertese were shipped home. They didn't realise then that it would not be so easy to recruit more to take their places.

From the enquiry findings, the Commissioners were directed to relocate the Chinese and Gilbertese camps to new positions where they would not be situated right next to each other. They also had to build a high fence between the old camps with an armed party from the warship left behind until the job was done.

Another event happened around this period. Grimble had been the Acting Resident Commissioner during all this time, relieving for Douggie McClure while he and his wife were on extended leave. Poor old Resident Commissioner McClure had gone and died on them, and Grimble was promoted to his position, becoming one of the youngest Resident Commissioners of his time.

Now, as things started to settle back to normal, except they now hardly had any Gilbertese or Chinese staff left to work the phosphate, John sent a message through to Ella that it was safe for her to return. She finally arrived home three weeks after the warship had landed and it was one of the happiest days of his life to see her step off the ship. He almost felt if he was a young man again, like a newlywed. He had not been this excited in years. He had even organised to take her down to the beach house for a couple of days, just the two of them. She had been away for nearly eight months, and he had missed her terribly.

25. BPC staff enlisted to quell the riots Ocean Island 1925.

26. Gilbertese police capturing Chinese rioter Ocean Island 1925.

IMPORTANCE OF FAMILY

Ella 1927

Ella now travelled mostly on her own with her younger daughter, Uma. However, this journey was a little different from the usual. John had been granted an extended three weeks of leave after all the riot and troubles back on the island. She knew he was also finding it harder to be away from not only his beloved elder daughter but now his beautiful grandchildren.

As Ella boarded the train in Cairns situated in the far north of Australia, Gwennie and her little ones were there to say farewell. Tom, Gwennie's husband, had joined the Queensland Railways since returning from Ocean Island and was now a relief driver on one of the remote outback railway lines. Tom loved his job and would be away for weeks, working as far away as Normanton, a small town in the remote Gulf region and north to Cooktown in the wilderness area of Cape York Peninsula. She was relieved that he had the good sense to leave Gwennie and the children back in Cairns, but poor Gwennie was terribly homesick and missing her family.

Ella had stayed on for an extra month after John had to return, and she was leaving Uma behind with Gwennie to keep her company and give her a hand with the children. Uma was now sixteen and such a delight. Always happy, never lonely, she was almost the complete opposite of Gwennie at that age. Uma delighted in travelling and spending time with her big sister and her little ones.

John had arranged to pay for Gwennie and the children's trip back to the island in time for Christmas. He thought a happy Christmas reunion would be just the thing so they would not be home on their own with Tom away. As Ella blew her kisses and said her farewells, they all knew it would not be long before they would all be together again.

The trip back to the island seemed to go so quickly this time, and there were quite a few of their old friends on board who were also returning from vacation, which helped to make it a pleasant voyage on the *Wongangella,* one of Ella's favourite ships. There was the added excitement as their ship came in towards Home Bay. The weather near the island had quickly deteriorated, and she knew they were in for one of those landings. There was also a large ship called the *Ocean Transport* that had run aground, apparently from the bad weather, and ended up not far from the main jetty. The Captain had assured them that the weather had abated since the *Ocean Transport* incident last week.

After so many years of ships coming into the moorings, in what all the sea captains referred to as the most dangerous waters in the world, it was a sobering reminder of what could happen. Ella thought that with around forty ships visiting every month, one tended to take these situations for granted. As they all made their way off the

Wongangella, it seemed a rather quiet affair. All the old-timers could not help feeling sad at the loss of such a beautiful ship. Even though they were all hardened seafarers, *Ocean Transport* stood so helpless, like a beached whale washed up on the shore with the huge blades of the prop sitting exposed on top of the reef.

Ella could just make out John standing on the end of the jetty waiting for her. She felt very grateful for another safe passage and to have a loved one to meet her.

"Darling, how are you?" she called as soon as she was within hearing distance, waving frantically from the surfboat as they made their way nearer the wharf.

"Even better now," he shouted across the water with a grin.

As usual, John was happy to have her back. Over the past few years with her spending more time with the family in Australia, her husband was like a silly schoolboy and usually had something special planned every time she arrived home.

The other men around him did not dare say anything at his antics, especially concerning his affection for his wife and family. They kissed and hugged politely. John was not about to make a complete spectacle of himself in front of the staff and quickly gave orders for her luggage, ushering her off to the flatcar he had waiting to take them up to the house. Up close, John seemed to have aged since she had been away. She did not know if it was just that she had not seen him for six weeks, or she was only realising for the first time that they were not youngsters any longer.

Tetabo, Meri, Nete and Meri's sister Jane and the children were all there at the house to greet her. It was a wonderful time arriving back home.

Later that evening over dinner, after Tetabo was fussing over her, they caught up on all that had been happening. Of course, Tetabo would not leave until he heard all the news about Gwennie first.

"Tetabo, the children will all be here for Christmas."

"Oh, so happy… we all ver… ee happy," he excitedly replied, now smiling like the old Tetabo she knew. "I miss my Gwennie so… so much," he added.

Obviously, John had not given him the news, and now Tetabo made his way out of the dining room, leaving them to finish their dinner. The spring was back in his step, and over the clanging of dishes and chatter when he reached the kitchen, they could hear him singing.

"Darling, I've planned for us to have the weekend at the beach camp," John announced.

"That will be lovely!" She always enjoyed spending time at the camp.

"Yes, it seems strange not having Uma here at home."

"Well, in the beginning, there was only the two of us. I suppose being on our own again will take a bit of getting used to," she replied. "Anyway, she'll be home at Christmas, and the break living with Gwennie back in civilisation will do her a world of good." Ella patted his shoulder.

"Just as long as I've got you. I missed you so much." He smiled, and tenderly kissed her hand.

"And I missed you. I'm just so glad to be home. You really do need taking care of; it looks as if you've lost weight," Ella joked, leaning over to kiss his face. "I'll have to ask Tetabo and Meri what they have been feeding you while I've been away."

"Now don't make a fuss, I've been so busy with work that eating hasn't been one of my priorities."

"I'm not fussing, John, I'm just worried about you! Now come on, let's retire for the night, it's been such a hectic day, and I want to cuddle some of those old familiar bones of yours."

"Come right this way, Missus Williams." He smiled and pulled her to her feet. "Oh, how I missed you."

That night after they retired to their bedroom and she snuggled into him, she was shocked. He insisted on leaving on his bedclothes and even though it was a hot evening, he would not remove his pyjama top.

Ella did not want to spoil her first evening home, so she made light of the situation.

Next morning, however, as soon as John had left for work, she took Tetabo and Meri aside and asked them what had been happening.

"Madam, we have given Miti Wiriami much food while you have been away," Tetabo protested.

"Yes, Madam, I too have noticed he is looking poorly and made him all his special dinners, but he isn't eating all his dinner," Meri answered in that little girl voice of hers.

"Madam, I think Miti Wiriami so sad without you, and Missy Gwennie. He cannot live on his own," lamented Tetabo, always so full of sentiment.

"I'm very grateful and so glad that you two have been looking after him. I'll have to give him some extra special attention," she vowed. Her two old friends smiled at her; their worries eased.

Over the coming days, Ella gave him plenty of attention and their weekend at the beach house was enjoyable even though the weather was still terrible and blowing a gale. John was still rather tired, and they could not go swimming, so she just pampered him as much as she could and let him catch up on some well-earned rest.

Ella had also begun to notice since returning home that John was not enjoying his food even though he pretended to eat heartily. When she challenged him, he said it was indigestion, so she had been administering bicarbonate of soda to ease his discomfort.

Except for these few small problems, everything was just perfect. John seemed to try and spend as much time with her as he could and seeing they did not have Uma at home, they were still behaving like newlyweds. Tetabo was indeed a happy man. Ella was sure one of his greatest delights was to see her and John happy. Even Meri, who was usually rather quiet, seemed to be doing a lot of giggling lately.

Nete, their son, was now seventeen and a handsome young man. He had just arrived back from the terraces where he had spent the last few years learning the ways of men from Tetabo's elder relatives. Tetabo and John had often spoken about a job for Nete. Ella could not understand why John had not offered him a position in their household, as he would be perfect for helping her with the new vegetable garden she was building.

On arriving home one evening, John called Tetabo in to see him.

"Tetabo, I have just heard that Mister Maynard is looking for a house boy and I thought Nete would be just right for the position," he suggested.

"Yes sir, but I do not know this man."

"No, Tetabo, he lives on Nauru and is the Manager there." John smiled. He knew that the news would impress his faithful friend.

"Oh, the Manager, he very important man on Nauru," Tetabo said almost in awe. He certainly looked pleased.

"That's right, Tetabo, and a very important job. That's why I mentioned Nete for the position. His English is good, and I know you have trained him well." John added, "And I can always organise for you and Meri to visit him on Nauru, and Mister Maynard comes to

Ocean Island quite often, so Nete could probably visit you at the same time."

Ella knew John had mentioned this to put Tetabo's mind at rest as the thought of losing his one and only son would play heavily on his mind.

"It would be a wonderful opportunity for Nete and your family to look to the future, Tetabo. Madam and I will not be here forever," John continued.

"Of course, Miti Wiriami you are right. I will tell the boy and his mother of our decision," Tetabo replied.

His trust in John's wisdom was not questioned, even when it involved something as crucial as his only child. He knew John would only be interested in his son's best welfare.

Over the next few weeks, while waiting for the dreaded weather to improve again, everything was organised for Nete to go to Nauru and start work. Tetabo thought it wise to send his mother with him to make sure Mister Maynard's house was organised correctly before leaving Nete on his own there.

A few weeks after finally saying farewell to Nete and Meri had returned from settling him in on Nauru, Ocean Island was in the grip of a bad strain of influenza. Doctor Gould immediately reacted, trying to prevent influenza breaking out into a full-scale epidemic by placing the four Banaban villages in quarantine. This was imperative to protect the spread among the Banaban population, especially the children and old people who were the most susceptible to the disease. The only quarantining that could be carried out among the Chinese and Gilbertese labourers was after they had become sick. Of course, the mining had to be kept going regardless. When the sick were taken to their perspective hospitals, they were put into quarantine compounds and closed off from the rest of the community.

Over the twenty-two years Ella had been on the island, she had seen these epidemics take their fatal toll before. The European population seemed to have a higher tolerance and were usually the carriers as people returned from vacations abroad. Ocean Island, having been so isolated by its geographical location, also missed out on most of the diseases and ailments that affected other places. That was until the arrival of the *te-I-Matang* bringing their diseases with them.

The island had experienced droughts for the past few years, up until the rains finally came this year in spasmodic bursts. Now the island was suffering from the opposite weather patterns. The weather had been so adverse that it had reduced the shipping so dramatically that they were starting to run out of supplies. John said the same thing happened around the time of the riots and they were really beginning to suffer as their mainstay of tinned bully beef ran out.

This all seemed to take its effect as Doctor Gould, and his assistants worked day and night to control the outbreak. It spread with such a vengeance that even the white population was now being affected. John had been in bed for the last two days, and Ella was feeling rather poorly. Father Pujabet was so concerned with the high mortality rate among the Gilbertese labourers and their families that he began a campaign to educate them about wandering down to the sea when they felt fevered. The logic for their actions was to cool down their fever-racked body, but instead, they would quickly succumb to pneumonia and die a quick death.

Father Pujabet, with never a thought for his own welfare, began a soup kitchen, with the help of Ella and the other ladies. With the assistance of the Chinese who used strange herbal medicines made from various plants and weeds growing wild on the island, he began to feed the Gilbertese his special brew. Whatever it was the Chinese were using for medicinal purposes, it seemed to be working for their community. Father's belief in his healthy soup paid off, together with his faith in God as the sick Gilbertese began to recover. Everyone on the island of all persuasions and race knew they had this wonderful man to thank for their wellbeing.

During this time the daughter of Captain Preece, the harbour master, became ill. It was believed she had succumbed to the fever and she was immediately treated for such. When her condition deteriorated rapidly, and she seemed to be in terrible pain, it was realised that her condition was not influenza but appendicitis. As Doctor Gould rushed to operate, she died. A beautiful girl of nineteen was lost and the European staff were immediately enveloped in a veil of sorrow that pervaded the whole island.

John and Ella were terribly affected. Irene Preece had been a girlfriend of Uma since her parents had arrived a few years back and to make things even worse, the Ross baby had become gravely ill. This reminded them of their tragic loss of their own son all those years ago.

As the epidemic abated and they buried their young friends, the community very slowly returned to normal, although the air of depression could not be denied. The management directed that in future, people returning from vacation should take every precaution not to knowingly bring any colds or flu back to the island. It was not as easy as it sounded when the Commissioner's Medical Officer in Australia was only too happy to make sure you did not miss your ship and take unnecessary sick leave.

As Christmas drew closer and the weather had finally cleared, John slowly recovered from his fever. He was looking forward to Gwennie, Uma and the grandchildren arriving. He still was not looking his old self, and his eating seemed to be a problem, especially his daily indigestion. Ella's bicarbonate did not seem to be working, and she had asked him to see Doctor Gould about some new type of antacid, which might be more effective. John just kept on telling her he would and then changing the subject.

One morning, only six weeks before Christmas, he woke up feeling very poorly. As soon as he tried to get up out of bed, he became violently ill. When Ella realised he was not even capable of getting out of bed, she sent Tetabo off to fetch Doctor Gould immediately.

After he arrived and examined John, he made arrangements to send him up to the hospital straight away. Ella was so terrified of the apparent severity of his sickness that she insisted on knowing what was wrong with him.

"Now calm down, Missus Williams, I need to take him up to the hospital for some further tests," Doctor Gould answered.

"But John's never been that ill he could not get out of bed," she insisted. "He'd go to work even if he had two broken legs."

"Please stay here, Missus Williams, and I'll send word down to you as soon as I finish the tests."

While she sat at home that day with Tetabo by her side and Meri not far away, it seemed to be one of the longest days of her life. Her mind ran over all the past deaths and tragedies that had happened. Being such a small community and with John's position as head overseer, they had always felt it their responsibility to personally advise and look after the bereaved families. Most of the families were living far away in Australia, so they always took the time to write to them and tell them about their loved one's life here.

Now Ella felt it was her turn. Life had always been so good to them, and she felt their family had been so blessed with good health that now it was her turn to pay the price, just as the price she had paid over Gwennie. As these terrible thoughts kept rushing through her mind, there was finally a knock at the door. Charlie had come down from the hospital with a message for her, and she was almost too frightened to read it.

'Mrs Williams, could you please come up to the hospital to see me. Yours sincerely, Dr Gould.'

Tetabo, realising her distress, insisted on accompanying her to the hospital. John seemed to be sleeping peacefully when Doctor Gould ushered her into his office. This time she left Tetabo sitting next to John's bed.

"Please, Doctor, what is the matter with him?" she asked.

"Well, Missus Williams, my original diagnosis seems to be correct. Your husband is suffering from a partial obstruction of the bowel."

"Doctor is that serious?" she asked, still terrified.

"What it means, Missus Williams, is that your husband is unable to eat or absorb any food properly and he will need an operation to correct the problem," he answered. "And yes, it can be quite serious if not treated quickly."

"Will you operate on him straight away?"

"I'm sorry, but he will have to be sent back to Australia and have the operation there. It's rather a major operation and too risky to do here. Now don't worry, I have already arranged with the management to get him on a ship leaving for Australia tomorrow morning and to cable the hospital in Sydney of our expected arrival."

"I can accompany him, surely?" she asked.

"Of course, Missus Williams. The management will organise it for you."

"Oh... thank you, Doctor, for arranging John's travel and hospitalisation. I am so grateful. Can I see him now?"

"He's been heavily sedated for the pain, and I suggest you go home now and get yourself organised for your trip tomorrow," Gould advised.

Ella was disappointed, but Doctor Gould was right. John was sound asleep and would never hear her.

That afternoon, as she rushed home with Tetabo, she knew she would have to organise an urgent cablegram to Australia to tell the girls the news and arrange accommodation for them all in Sydney. She had a lot to do.

After ten days at sea, with John heavily sedated and Doctor Gould at his side, they arrived in Sydney. The company had organised everything ahead of their arrival, and John was rushed to Prince Henry Hospital. On arrival, Ella was delighted to find the girls with the grandchildren there to meet them. John, even though still heavily sedated, knew they were all there with him, and the second day after their arrival, he was operated on.

The operation proved to be very successful, though rather extensive, and John would take two months to recover in Sydney before returning to work. Gwennie and Uma and the children stayed with them the whole time, and Ella was sure this had aided in her husband's recovery. Even though the family had missed the Christmas celebrations on the island, John was still keen to have Gwennie and the children return with them for the holiday he had promised them. After Gwennie contacted Tom, it was agreed that she could accompany them on their return voyage home.

The Williams family of Ocean Island was finally all together again. John was on his feet and starting to look like his old self, although still rather thin. Uma was, as usual, a breath of fresh air, and Gwennie was her happy old self with the excitement of going back to her home, as she still called it, with her two young children. Their trip aboard the Commissioner's vessel *Nauru Chief* was nostalgic for all of them. It was a very sentimental journey and Ella once again felt she had been truly blessed, revelling in seeing her family together again and returning to the family home they all loved.

27. Young Banaban girls early 1920s. Ocean Island.

28. Panoramic view of Home Bay with surf boat bringing ship's passengers ashore.

CHAPTER TWENTY-SIX

WHAT ABOUT OUR LAND?

Tetabo 1928

"Madam, we are not allowed out of the villages between 6 p.m. and daylight. How will I be able to fish at dawn?" he asked Madam Wiriami.

"What do you mean Tetabo, not allowed out of the villages?"

"Kurimbo say all the Banabans now have to stay in their villages from 6 p.m. to daylight and we must stop our dancing," he explained.

"Tetabo, what you are actually saying is that Resident Commission Grimble has placed a curfew on the Banaban villages and has also stopped the nightly dances as well?" She had stopped her work and was waiting for his explanation.

She realised by the look on his face he did not know the meaning of the word curfew, so she explained. "Curfew, Tetabo is a time ban, the 6 p.m. to daylight restriction placed on the village."

"Yes, Madam… yes, Madam, that is Kurimbo he done, de curse-few Madam," he answered, excited with Madame's understanding of his news at last.

"Well, Tetabo, it shouldn't affect you personally because you live up here at the house and I'm sure Miti Wiriami can sort things out, but why would Mister Grimble do this to the Banabans?"

"Madam they no agreement, elders no sign, no sell de land. My family say *no*… no more land."

"Is that the agreement that Mister Gaze drew up when he was here in July?" she asked.

"Yes, Madam, *te unimane* Tito says if Empire want de phosphate, de pay five pounds der car for it."

"Well, Tetabo I know nothing of the money details regarding this agreement, but I am most concerned with Grimble being vindictive towards your people. I will talk to Miti Wiriami and see what he can do."

He did not have a clue what the word vindictive meant, but Madam had been good to them. He knew she would try to help.

"Thank you, Madam, I not talk to Miti Wiriami and de problems… he not like land talk in de house," he answered, glad to have the moment to discuss this problem with Madam alone.

"No, you're quite correct Tetabo, but he is a fair man, and I'm sure he doesn't know about this latest curfew business." She looked at the clock on the wall in which the sticks moved around to tell when Miti Wiriami would be home from work.

That day after work, he asked Madam to give him permission to visit Uma village. She gave him a personal note to carry, saying he was delivering an urgent message for her if the police apprehended him. The strict new law was hampering their freedom. He did not care for this curse-few business. The police were indeed enforcing it, and without Madam's note, he would never have got through to the village. He made his way to Tito's *mwenga,* noticing how sad everyone in the village seemed. Not allowing a man to dance was indeed evil, Tetabo told himself.

"Kona mauri, te unimane!" Tetabo called, standing under the eaves of Tito's house asking for admission.

"Enter, enter Tetabo!" Tito called back.

After making the usual Banaban pleasantries that manners insisted upon, he told Tito that he had asked Madam Wiriami to speak to her husband. Tito knew that Miti Wiriami had a lot of influence with the company and had asked Tetabo to see if he could try and enlist his help.

When the days passed and Madam had not said anything more on the issue Tetabo again asked her for help.

"Madam, Banabans still have curse-few," he said, looking worried.

"I'm sorry, Tetabo. I tried to speak to Miti Wiriami about it. Unfortunately, he won't discuss it with me," she replied. "He seems quite annoyed about the whole subject. I just can't get him to speak about it." She knew that Tetabo was well acquainted with Miti Wiriami's moods and his stubbornness.

"Should me ask Sir help us?"

"Well, Tetabo, you know what he is like about company matters," she replied with a shrug.

"Yee see Madam, but he is good *I-Matang*."

That night when Miti Wiriami arrived home, Tetabo quickly followed him into the parlour.

"Miti Wiriami, Sir, de had der good day?" he asked, trying to assess his mood. The poor man was tired as usual; he was now a *unimane*.

"Rather exhausting, Tetabo, I'm glad to be home." He smiled at him.

"We glad you home, Sir." He gestured to the kitchen from which tantalising smells were already drifting. Tetabo had remembered to organise Sir's favourite meal for the evening.

"Thank you, Tetabo. Now, if you don't mind, I'd like to get changed for dinner."

"Ye…ees Sir, me sorry, Sir, but I need talk, ver… ee big news, Sir," he pleaded.

"Well come and sit down here and tell me what is such big news," Miti Wiriami instructed as he pointed to the chair opposite the sofa.

Tetabo awkwardly seated himself. He always felt so ill at ease sitting on *Matang* furniture and balancing on this soft sofa did nothing to settle his nerves.

"Sir, I know you, good man, I ask for de help, Sir," he stammered.

"What's the matter Tetabo, that you must ask my help? Is Nete all right?"

"No, Sir Nete is very good. No Sir, it old man *Tito*. He ask, all *te unimane,* ask you help us… Kurimbo has curse-few on our villages," he replied. "Our people feel very badly, so does Missus Wiriami too."

"Tetabo, I have already spoken to our manager, Mister McLintock, about this matter and he too is not happy with Grimble's actions," Wiriami answered, "but you must understand even Mister McLintock cannot tell Resident Commissioner Grimble how to run the island."

"Sir, what we do, de people now de prisoners. The good King George will not treat his loyal peoples dis way?"

John sighed heavily. "Tetabo you are so right and as you know my loyalties must lie with the company, but on the other hand, I cannot condone what the British government is doing. You have to understand that I now talk to you as your friend... you must be aware that the government will not let your people hold up the phosphate mining." He watched Tetabo's eyes cloud over.

"But Sir, our Good King George if he know what Kurimbo is doing he will stop him." He was desperate to have Miti Wiriami fully know how unhappy his people were with the curfew and its results.

"Please try and understand what I am saying. If your people do not sell their land and sign that agreement, the government will just take your land." He was so solemn that Tetabo suddenly knew that he was serious. This awful business could happen. His people without their land was unthinkable to him.

"Tis our land!" He shook his head, finding it hard to believe what he had just heard.

"Now look, Tetabo, I tell you all these things as a friend. The word around the office is that the British government will make a new law to take the one hundred and fifty acres mentioned in the agreement if you don't sign it." He spoke clearly so that Tetabo could fully understand. "I can tell you I don't like any of it, and neither does Mister McLintock. But we are only employees of the BPC. We cannot stand up against the entire British government, and neither can your people," he said unhappily.

"Sir, no, I know you are good man… you are Tetabo's friend, and you give the truth."

"I've also heard quite a bit of talk around the office that your people are thinking of moving to another island." Miti Wiriami looked sad.

"Yes, Sir, they talk about that in de *maneaba*. The women angry and cry, No let Kambana mining more de lands. Our old ladies refuse to leave and tell our men must fight for de land," he answered, feeling stirred by emotion.

"I suppose I can't blame them, but I've got to tell you it doesn't look good. There is too much money and phosphate at stake. You must warn your people and ask them to keep my advice secret. It will not help them if Grimble finds out I have advised you."

Miti Wiriami was right. He would be in serious trouble as well.

"Thank you, Sir, I will tell them."

Tetabo quietly passed on Miti Wiriami's words to *te unimane* Tito and the other elders who were really shocked at the idea of the British government making a law to take over their land. His people could not believe that the government of the Good King George would ever be so dishonourable. Tito, on the other hand, believed they should heed Miti Wiriami's words. After many years of seeing how the original Pacific Islands Company and now BPC had always used their lawyers to get what they wanted he knew the only chance the Banabans had was to employ a lawyer of their own. Tito still believed that if they could just get to England to meet with the Good King George in person, he would stop the injustices against his own honourable people.

Meanwhile, the curfew stayed in place, and during that time, a man arrived on Ocean Island that they believed might be able to help them in their search for a lawyer. He was a young anthropologist whose name was Harry Maude. Ella Williams had tried to explain to Tetabo that an anthropologist studied the ways native people lived in their past and present lives. He had arrived on Ocean Island to register land settlements. His work was to record exactly who owned what in the Gilbert Islands Group and he travelled to each island on the government boat. He seemed to understand the Banaban people well, and Tito saw him as the opportunity they needed.

Believing that all *te I-Matangs* needed money, Tito gave Miti Mauto, as they called him a bag full of gold and kindly instructed him to please find a good lawyer that could help them.

Maude was stunned to find the bag laden with gold sovereigns, and on his late return to the Government residency, Grimble questioned him. He had no other option but to convey the instructions he was given by Tito. Grimble immediately went into a rage and told him if he wanted to remain in his current position with the Foreign Office, he would not become involved in government and company business and instructed him to hand over the money.

A few days later, Grimble took great delight in handing the gold personally back to Tito who now seemed to be the leading spokesman against the company and their land matters. Grimble was becoming increasingly angry with the Banabans because they still resisted all efforts to buy more land. In August, Grimble wrote letters to Tito and other landowners using their own native language to insult them. He said they had shamed the Chief of the Empire and they would have to make up their minds whether they would bring 'Life' or 'Death' to their island.

By 'Life', Grimble meant that by signing the new agreement it would bring long term advantages to their people and by 'Death' he implied that the mining would be carried out with no guarantees of protecting the people's land or paying them money for it. He also wrote that they would be responsible for choosing suicide, and he could no longer help them when he had done all that was possible to save them.

Tito tried one last time to get word through to good King George by writing a letter to the Secretary of State in London. In the meantime, Grimble signed a compulsory purchase order, thereby allowing the company to begin mining the new area mentioned in the agreement. This was Tito's ancestral village in *Buakonikai*, the most fertile part of the entire island.

When the terrible day arrived, the women draped themselves around the coconut trees as the bulldozers began their work. They were prepared to die with their trees. Grimble had organised for the Gilbertese prisoners to be made acting policemen and instructed these men to remove the women from the trees. So, with guns in the acting policemen's hands, the women were removed from the diggings and destruction began. Old man Tito realised while the work went on that they, the company, had already dug up two pieces of land that were not on the agreement. On his way down to see the *I-Matang* at the BPC office, Grimble's men stopped him and would not let him pass. If it had not been for the elders' words of advice under Banaban custom that to shed blood was prohibited on the island, Tito and his friends would have willingly died that day for their land.

As the news spread through the island, Tetabo realised Miti Wiriami had said from the beginning they would do it. It still did not make it any easier to believe such evil actions could be committed against his people. But from such evil, the Banabans' determination to stand up against the BPC would only grow. Tetabo knew Wiriami and Madam were part of the *kambana,* but he would always remain loyal to them. They had always treated him like family. He felt no loyalties to the *kambana,* even if they did employ him and now Nete to work for their people. He knew he could no longer stand back and see such evil.

Tito, believing in the white man's Christian ethics, was more determined to fight the BPC the only way he could, and that was to go to London himself if he had to and visit the Good King George in person. He knew the Good King was a man of God and leader of the church, and he would not allow such things to happen. He also believed now, more than ever before, that the Banabans needed a lawyer and they would need the *I-Matang*'s money to pay for it.

The Banabans stood behind Tito's proposal, and they started to put aside part of their royalty money and go without; especially food. While they saved their money, their determination grew as they watched helplessly while the BPC continued to mine the new area, now unchecked. Their hearts seemed to cry with every bucket of their beloved land that was taken away.

29. Banaban land left destroyed by phosphate mining Ocean Island early 1920s.

CHAPTER TWENTY-SEVEN

FALLING IN LOVE

Uma 1930

"Please, Fah can I work as a stewardess this time? Mother thinks it's a good idea."

Uma Williams was now nineteen years of age. She was pleading with her father, who calmly sat on the sofa in the parlour with not an ounce of expression on his face. Uma was asking his permission to allow her to work as a stewardess on their up and coming voyage to Australia.

The ship, *Nauru Chief,* was the BPC's own vessel and Captain Rhodes, the ship's Master, was a good friend of the family. Uma knew her father trusted him. The Captain also knew she was looking for some employment as she'd discussed the matter with him over dinner at their house the other night.

"It will only be until I get to Sydney; around ten days at the most... please, Fah?" she again pleaded, using her pet name for her father, trying to soften that hard exterior of his.

After sitting silently for a few more minutes, he finally spoke.

"Uma, I still can't see why any daughter of mine wants to be a stewardess on a ship. It's nothing but a— a... glorified waitress. Do you think your mother and I worked hard to see you end up a waitress?" he asked, with a hurt expression in his eyes.

"But Fah, I need to be able to do something, earn money for myself," she tried to explain.

"I may be old fashioned, but I thought all young ladies were kept busy preparing their glory boxes and trousseaus for the day when they married, not out working, God forbid!"

"Please Fah, but it's now the thirties. There is nothing wrong with a lady wanting to earn some money and be independent. It doesn't mean I won't get married."

"Well, I'm not keen on my daughter being a woman of the world."

"Yes, but you know Captain Rhodes won't stand any nonsense on his ships," she pleaded. "Anyway, you and Mother will be on the same voyage, so I'm not exactly on my own." She was hoping he could not think of any more excuses.

"Very well, I'll give you permission. It doesn't mean I totally approve, so tell Captain Rhodes you are permitted to work this voyage only, all right?"

"You're wonderful Fah... I love you dearly," she yelled, rushing over to throw her arms around his neck.

Her father could not help laughing as she threw herself all over him. That tough old crusty exterior of his hid a sweet soul underneath and to be completely honest, he did not stand a chance when she worked her charm on him.

On the 5th of May, the happy Williams family sailed off into the vast blue Pacific. Her parents looked their best in expensive travelling clothes and were pleased with the prospect of seeing Gwennie and the grandchildren. Life at sea was always such enjoyment for all of them. It was the freedom of pulling away from land and sailing into the unknown that lay ahead until finally reaching Australia, usually ten days' sailing away.

Uma had been travelling on ships from three months of age when her parents had taken her back to Australia to meet the relatives. Sea voyages were such a natural way of life that she was lucky that she had never experienced seasickness.

This voyage would change all those past pleasant memories. For a start, Uma did not have the usual family cabin that she had so often shared with her parents. Seeing that she was now part of the ship's crew, she was designated a cabin that she could only describe as being in the bowels of the ship.

The *Nauru Chief* had always been such a beautiful ship. It was what the Commissioners called their showpiece since they had her especially altered and equipped for the company's requirements. She was capable of carrying large amounts of phosphate and several passengers to and from the island. Up until this time, Uma thought she had explored every inch of the vessel as a child often did in those days. But she had never encountered the crew's cabin or more like the cell, that she found herself in now. It made her feel quite ill just to enter, let alone the idea of sleeping in it. She swiftly moved her belongings back into her parents' cabin, where at least she could be comfortable.

While she quickly fell into the pattern of everyday ship's life from a stewardess's point of view, she had never realised how hard it all was. She spent long hours working day and night on her feet, only to collapse at the end of the day in total exhaustion. Her mother was terribly concerned and wanted her father to speak to the Captain.

Her father just sat back and calmly stated that it was not possible as Uma had already signed a contract and would just have to wait until they arrived in Sydney. She was too exhausted to argue, usually falling asleep in the middle of their discussions. She knew Father was gloating, so she was even more determined to prove him wrong.

By the fifth day, she was beginning to become more accustomed to being on her feet. She was not going to let her exhaustion stand in the way of proving she was a good stewardess. She moved efficiently through the dining saloon, serving everyone with a smile. She did not want to give her father the satisfaction of telling her he had been right, and she had been wrong. Uma even overheard Captain Rhodes telling her father across the dinner table that he thought she was a good worker and he could do with a few more like her.

"Yes, a bit of hard work never hurt anyone," her father replied, loudly enough for her to hear, smiling in her direction.

A bit of hard work indeed! Uma told herself. Her father did not even think a woman, let alone his daughter, should work. Now he was telling Captain Rhodes a bit of hard work never hurt anyone.

Day ten finally arrived; ten days too late for her liking. She virtually crawled her way to the Captain's cabin to receive her discharge papers, dreading to think what he would say.

"Miss Williams, come in, my dear!" he said as soon as she announced herself at his door. "It's been a real pleasure to have you work for us," he added as Uma squirmed, "and I want you to know that there is always a job here for you if you'd like one."

Uma was lost for words. She could hardly believe what he had just suggested. Then she thought that she would not be surprised if that father of hers had put the Captain up to this.

"Thank you, Captain, but my father doesn't want me to work. He doesn't think it's ladylike," she answered.

"Well, that's your father's prerogative, and I'd never interfere with his decisions, but please don't forget you'll always be welcome to work aboard this ship should you choose," he replied, and patted her arm. "Good girl!"

"Thank you, Captain, I really appreciate your words." She was feeling very pleased with herself.

"You'll also notice on your discharge papers I've stamped it with 'very good service' for the records."

"Thank you, Captain, I do appreciate it."

"Thank you, Miss Williams. I suppose this means I can call you Uma again?" He laughed.

Over the years when Uma looked back on that epic voyage, she would always treasure those discharge papers she well and truly earned. Her father might have gloated at her initial shock at the realities of work, but he could never deny her the fact she had not disgraced the Williams name.

This same journey to Australia would also prove to be a turning point in her young life. Gwennie and the children had joined them in Melbourne, and they had all spent a wonderful time, doing what they usually did. The theatre, ballet, movies, dinners, luncheons, the museums; all those things Melbourne was renowned for.

On returning one afternoon to their guesthouse, there was mail waiting for her. It was one of the strangest letters she had ever received. Addressed to Dearest Lady, it was from a gentleman who said he was a secret admirer and who had fallen hopelessly in love with her from afar. The letter went on to say some ridiculous things about Ocean Island and what this gentleman had heard about the way the natives were cannibals and the phosphor, as he called it, was laid by hens dropping their eggs all over the island.

The letter was entirely ridiculous, and obviously, someone was having fun with her. Whoever it was seemed to know a lot about her. He knew her father was one of the bosses, as he called it, and he hoped he might assist the writer with a job there. The gist of the letter was one of an unknown admirer, admitting his love for her and telling her he was going to follow her back to Ocean Island so he could be with her. He finished the letter by adding he would wear a red rose when he got off the ship so she would know who he was. Until then, he signed it Ernest Blackbottom, with dozens of kisses at the bottom of the page.

Gwennie thought it exciting for her sister to have a secret admirer. Uma thought it was just a friend having fun, while Gwennie and Mother, who was her usual protective self, tried to think of every man she had met since arriving in Melbourne, which was not as easy as it sounded. With their hectic social life, dance partners came and went. She had spent her entire life as the centre of attention among the male population on the island and had grown up with the notion that all men were the same and liked to show off when a lady was around. Of course, being the only single woman on the island had led her to this opinion.

Her father was not too pleased regarding the letter business. He did not take kindly to someone writing all this rot, as he called it, and not signing a proper name. The letter ended up being put aside when nothing more was forthcoming, and they said their goodbyes to Gwennie and the children. The trip home was far more pleasurable than the previous voyage. Her father seemed to be in one of his silly moods, making jokes about the working arrangements on board the *Aymeric* and how the ship could greatly do with her services. Uma could not help telling him she was too busy working on her trousseau to think of working, which would see her father collapse in laughter.

On returning home, they all quickly fell back into the island way of life, and as far as Uma was concerned, it was the only way to live. The invitations started arriving as soon as they were home. A farewell dinner, a mess room dance, an afternoon tea at the Residency, and a formal dinner at the Manager's house. It was all so much to organise, especially with new dresses to be made. Mother always insisting on indulging in a new creation, feeling it was not acceptable to be seen in the same dress too often.

Uma could not blame her mother for her ideas on dressing. If anything, her father was the one who insisted his women should always dress their best. He was still giving Gwennie money every time he saw her, just to make sure she could dress properly.

One evening, when she was attending the Manager's Welcoming party for the latest new BPC arrivals, she was busy signing her dance card as the young men lined up before her. It used to embarrass her once, but over the years as she had grown older, it just seemed natural to have a dozen men standing before her trying to get their names on her card. She realised when you looked at what the poor young chaps had as an alternative, older married women, most of them with children and quite a few with jealous husbands to dance with, there was not a great deal of choice.

She smiled at Tommy Gower as he signed her card. He had been given the first dance, and they joked at how he had accomplished such a task. She wondered if working under her father had helped in any way.

Next was Maurie Tough who looked after the catering and happened to be in charge of the meat supplies. His job held quite a position of power, especially among the married women who looked forward to their weekly meat order. She could not help wondering if her mother had used a bit of influence this time.

As the third chap stepped forward, she nearly fainted. He was the most handsome man she had ever seen, and he looked faintly familiar.

"Miss Williams, how do you do? My name is Wilfred Cooper. Would you mind if I signed your card?" he asked in a smooth, sophisticated voice that made her melt.

"Certainly, Mister Cooper," she replied, almost jauntily. She could not help herself. He was something a female could only dream of, and he was asking her permission to dance... she just could not believe her luck.

"Thank you." She smiled as the other chaps standing behind him, patiently waiting, cut him off abruptly.

When he turned to leave, she noticed a dried red rose buttonhole in his lapel. Her mind went into a whirl as the next young chap stepped forward.

"Good evening, Miss Williams, may I sign your card?" a deep voice inquired.

She did not even know who she was talking to as she automatically let him sign her card; her mind was elsewhere. She slowly had to go through the whole process of getting her card marked and then having her first two dances with Tommy and Maurie. She tried to catch a glimpse of the mystery man Wilfred Cooper before his turn finally arrived.

"Good evening Miss Williams. I believe this is my dance," he said, breaking in on Maurie just as their dance finished.

Poor Maurie did not even get a word in as this mystery man whizzed her away. Uma felt as if she was gliding on a cloud for his dancing was just great. His shoulders were square, like the shape of his face with his strong jaw and his dark eyes. His black hair was short and brushed back with oil, revealing all of his handsome face.

His hand was secure and commanding around her waist as he masterfully guided her around the floor, not like the other poor chaps who always seemed a little nervous of her on the dance floor. She was sure this man knew what he wanted and, judging by that poor faded rose, she hoped it would be her.

"Please call me Bill," he said when they glided to the middle of the floor.

"All right, Bill, but I hardly know you," she replied somewhat nervously.

"You do know me," he said, again so direct and yet mysterious.

"Do I? I thought you looked familiar," she replied, trying to stop from giggling. What was happening to her?

"Yes, in Melbourne."

"In Melbourne? I'm sorry..."

"Yes, you were dancing at the Town Hall with a good friend of mine, Tom Hudson."

"Oh, Tom. I'm sorry. I don't think we actually met, did we?" she replied, now feeling confused.

She had danced for quite a while with Tom, but she did not recall him introducing her to this suave charmer; she was sure she would have remembered. When she attempted to ask him more about Melbourne, her next dance partner interrupted them. Apparently, the dance had just finished, and she had not even noticed. Bill Cooper reluctantly let go of her, making a point of squeezing her hand.

"Miss Williams, I look so forward to seeing you again."

She could not believe it. He was so debonair, and as she turned to begin the next dance, she still felt as if she was dancing on clouds. She did not even know what her new partner thought of her, on that wonderful night when Bill Cooper danced his way into her life.

30. Uma Williams with fiancée Billy Cooper (right) outside Williams house before leaving Ocean Island 1931.

CHAPTER TWENTY-EIGHT

NEW ARRIVALS

New Year's Eve - Ocean Island 1930

While the wind and the rain unleashed its full fury on the island, the staff's New Year's Eve dance was in full progress. The partygoers did not seem to notice the tumult going on outside or, more likely, did not particularly care. It was amazing how a few drinks and some good company could take one's mind off things.

One particular partygoer that evening, a man named Joseph White, however, *was* affected by the adverse weather conditions. He was a relative newcomer to Ocean Island who had begun work only six months earlier as an assistant under John Williams.

The island had been experiencing this terrible weather for the past eight days now, and it did not look likely to abate for a while yet. Now, as he stood there among his cheery workmates and their families, his thoughts drifted out across the wild sea to his wife and children, and he wondered what they would be doing at this moment.

It had been six months since he had last seen them and now they were all sitting out there on that hostile ocean aboard the *Nauru Chief*. They had left Melbourne over sixteen days earlier and for the last six days, had spent the time drifting offshore waiting for a lull in the weather to come in. The seas were still so high that the waves were breaking over the main jetty and actually flooding the boat sheds. The old *Ocean Transport* wreck was screaming as the winds pounded her hard onto the reef and the surf broke more iron plates away from her hull, sending them adrift on the wild waves.

He had so looked forward to having them all here tonight at this dance where they could have celebrated their reunion.

"Mister White, why don't you come over and join us?" The voice of Williams's wife broke his reverie.

"Oh thank you, Missus Williams, but I'm really not very good company tonight," he replied.

"I can understand your concerns and can assure you that our hearts go out to you and your family," she said sincerely.

"Thank you, Missus Williams." He gave her a weak smile.

"I can also assure you that after nearly thirty years of travelling on these seas, they are in wonderful hands with Captain Rhodes. He knows these waters better than anyone," she assured him. "How old are your children?" She was curious to know more about one of John's newer staff.

"Joseph Junior is nine, and my Maureen is turning six on the eighteenth of January. I hope she can at least celebrate her birthday on dry land," he said, his voice lifting as he spoke of his children.

"We will just have to make sure she has a good birthday party," Ella said. "I'm so looking forward to meeting your wife. What is her name?"

"Letitia." He sounded more enthusiastic, brightening up at the mention of his wife.

"Isn't that a coincidence! She has the same name as Mister Maynard's wife." Ella smiled at him.

"Yes, I suppose it is," he replied, turning around to gaze at the clouded window and the unabated fury that was still raging outside.

Ella realised she had just lost his attention; his mind turning back to the predicament his family was in.

"Come on, Mister White, please join us. Your wife wouldn't want you to be all alone on New Year's Eve. Just think how wonderful it will be when they get here," she urged.

He slowly turned back to address her, realising his rudeness. "Of course, you're right, Missus Williams. Would you kindly allow me the pleasure of the next dance?" He had appreciated her conversation, and there was no point being so miserable. He could only look forward to the new year and a new life for all of them here on Ocean Island.

Turning towards the lively crowd on the dance floor, Joseph White, as the perfect English gentlemen he was, tried hard to forget. There was no doubting these people when it came to their intentions to enjoy themselves. Gale force storms were not going to interfere with their fun. Maybe once his own family arrived, he too could really enjoy the spirit of such occasions.

The party continued into the wee hours of the morning with the revellers seeing in the New Year. Some were so severely intoxicated that they probably would not even remember this New Year's Eve dance at all.

The days passed on and some of those weary heads returned to normal, but the weather took another two weeks before it started to abate and *Nauru Chief* quickly made her way to shore.

* * *

"Quickly men, we have to go now before the tide turns. It's now, or never; she can't hold out much longer. Our supplies are just about finished, and we don't know how long this break in the weather will last." Captain Cozens, the island's harbour master, was becoming almost frantic. His usual calm composure was taken over by a feeling of alarm, and he did not want his excellent record blemished.

"But the waves are still breaking over the end of the jetty. It's still highly dangerous, and there are women and children aboard that ship," replied McLintock, the BPC's manager.

"Come on, sir, I know what I'm doing, and I've picked out the best boys I have to crew the surf boat." Cozens was not used to having to justify his actions. He had been doing this job for thirty years now, and he was the one man here who knew the island's waters better than anyone.

"I think it's too dangerous, but then again, you're the one in charge of the shipping here, so I trust you will take full responsibility if anything, God forbid, goes wrong!" McLintock was beginning to lose his trust in the once able Captain.

"You want to hope nothing does go wrong, and if it does, it will be God willing, because my boys won't be at fault," Cozens shouted, with his crusty old hackles rising.

"Very well, have it your way!" McLintock shrugged and went on to obey Cozens's orders.

As word spread on what all the inhabitants called the Island's Telegraph, referring to the quick rate at which gossip would spread on the island, that the *Nauru Chief* was finally coming in, a large crowd of native and Chinese workers and even the white staff gathered on the wharf. The *Nauru Chief* had been the topic of conversation around the island as she drifted for the last few weeks and the island's inhabitants did not want to miss the excitement of watching her poor passengers finally land.

When Cozens and his handpicked crew took to their small surf boat, everyone thought he was mad. The sea was still wild as the men pulled hard on the oars. The hardest obstacle that lay ahead was navigating past the *Ocean Transport* wreck without being driven back onto it. Cozens had already seen to having its large propeller removed because it posed a real danger to all shipping, standing right out of the water so close to number one jetty.

The small boat bobbed on the churning white water as they slowly pulled past the wreck, dwarfed by its massive superstructure. The passengers of the *Nauru Chief* were already up on deck waiting to alight and were quickly becoming more terrified while they watched the small boat draw closer.

The ship's crew tried to reassure them, telling them that going back into shore was not as difficult. It was coming out against the tide and wind that was the real challenge. The men on the oars rowed with all their might, their muscles rippling, with faces set in grim determination, using all of their amazing strength to fight the incoming surge. Once they cleared the wreck, they came out towards the leeward side of the *Nauru Chief*, the ship's bulk protecting the small craft from the wind. As they rowed quickly up to the side of the vessel, the gangway was lowered, and the passengers rapidly bounded onto the boat.

Cozens immediately assured his passengers, especially the two young children, that everything was fine. He was such a large man that he arranged for the children to be seated right next to him and kept reassuring them with his jovial manner.

"All right everyone's aboard, let's go!" he ordered before anyone had a chance to say anything.

The surfboat left just as quickly as she had arrived, except now she sat lower in the water. The men put their backs into the oars, straining against the weight of their new load of terrified passengers. The boat began to speed through the water, and with each wave, the small vessel was pitched upward. Up, up and then down, down, down she sped, cutting through the surf, the tight-lipped men timing their strokes with every wave. There seemed to be an understanding between them as they timed one another's every move, rowing with team-like precision.

Once again, they made their way directly across in front of the massive wreck, courting certain death if they had been sucked into the huge gaping hole of her hull which was now so apparent from the seaward side. With the large swell running, there was no way they could attempt to land at one of the jetties. The surf was still breaking right up on the edge of the boat sheds and Cozens steered her in towards the only small patch of beach that still remained above the water level. He timed the last wave perfectly, riding right up over the coral reef and straight up on to the actual landfall of the island. As the wave receded, the boat was stranded high and dry.

"Hurry please, ladies and gentlemen. Would you please get out of the boat as quickly as you can!" he roared.

The passengers did not want to be sucked back out into that cauldron, and they ran as fast as they could. The onlookers had come down to lend their assistance to the new arrivals. Joe White, who had been nervously waiting on the shore, quickly gathered up his family and bestowed them with kisses of welcome.

Ella Williams eagerly moved toward them.

"Welcome to Ocean Island, Missus White," she said, presenting her with a garland of flowers. "We're so glad to have you and the children safe ashore at last."

"Thank you so much; we're glad to be here." She gave a peculiar laugh. It was one of relief and happiness. Ella was reminded of her own feelings all those years earlier when she had experienced a similar fate. Even though Letitia White looked half drowned at the moment it was clear she was a real lady of style with good bearing, and a beautiful English rose complexion. Ella took an immediate liking to her and was already looking forward to enjoying her company.

"I've bought some towels down for you and the children. I thought you would be drenched," Ella said, as she dabbed at Missus White's sodden hair.

"Thank you, Missus Williams, I do appreciate your kindness." Joe White could hardly believe that Letitia and the children were here at last.

The White family were quickly led away to begin their new life on Ocean Island. Ella felt an affinity with them. She didn't realise on that day what important events in the island's history would revolve around this family in the years ahead.

31. Resident Commissioner Arthur Grimble in his office Ocean Island early 1920s.

CHAPTER TWENTY-NINE

BETRAYAL

Ocean Island 1931

"I must make it clear! I am not here to upset Resident Commissioner Grimble's judgement over the enforcing of the Ordinance covering land acquisition," stated the Consul for Tonga.

The Consul, Mister Neill, had come to Ocean Island at the request of the High Commissioner for the Western Pacific to arbitrate on behalf of the Banabans. Now that Grimble had used the powers given to him under the Ordinance of 1928, to simply enter into possession of Banaban land and then lease the new areas to the Commissioners without the landowners' consent, it was mainly only a question of compensation that had to be settled with the Banaban landowners.

Harold Maynard of the BPC island staff was selected to represent the Commissioners.

"I also must express the view of the British government by informing the Banabans gathered here today at this meeting that nothing can be gained by opposing decisions made in their own best interests and for the general benefit of the Empire." Neill's voice carried across the room.

The Banaban elders sat there patiently hanging on his every word as the interpreter translated the diplomat's speech. As his words and their meaning were finally understood, the Banabans' faces reflected their sudden change of mood. It had already become apparent with his opening words of his findings that this meeting was not going to end well at all.

"After looking at all aspects of this new land acquisition, I am of the opinion that the payment of 150 pounds an acre offered by the Commissioners is clearly excessive. I also must add that I cannot in any way defend the rate of compensation for trees as asked by the Banabans," he continued.

The Banabans now realised they had no ally in this man, another so-called representative of the Good King George. They sat quietly as manners decreed, enduring his every word.

"After hearing all sides to this dispute, I am further of the opinion that Resident Commissioner Grimble has negotiated a satisfactory price with the Commissioners and that any opposition regarding this matter has mainly come from only one quarter led by Tito," Neill continued.

On hearing his name mentioned, Tito, with his basic grasp of English, knew he was going to be made the main focus of the Banabans' bitter fight for justice.

"I find Mister Rotan Tito to be somewhat offensive and an insolent young man who seems to have been a victim of some misguided advice or even in possession of excessive personal vanity and responsible on the whole for stirring up problems within a small group of the Banaban people." Neill's speech had now become a tirade as his interpreter nervously tried to convey the appropriate words to the gathering.

While the interpreter conveyed the last of Neill's words to the Banabans, the rumblings of disquiet filled the room. Even the Banabans' good manners could not hold any longer as the meeting was quickly being drawn to a close. Rotan Tito had been publicly discredited, and the other young, rising leaders of Rotan's stature had no intentions of accepting this pompous Englishman's decree.

If anything, his words had only drawn them all closer, with previous petty squabbling quickly forgotten. They were now united, for they realised it was up to the new generation of young men to fight for the future of their people, as they genuinely believed that they, the Banabans, had become the victims of a horrible conspiracy.

* * *

While all this had been occurring in the native courthouse at Uma, another decree was being handed down. This time, it was of a more personal nature and involved the tall, middle-aged man slowly making his way from the door of the Island's European hospital.

"Thank you, Doctor, for being so candid with me," he said gratefully, shaking the young doctor's hand.

"I'm sorry to have to give you such news. Would you like me to speak to your wife?"

"No, Doctor, I would not!" he retorted, his face ashen. "I must request that you keep this information to yourself."

"Well, you know I have to report my findings to the company."

"There will be no need for that!" he replied sharply. "I will make my own arrangements, and I might remind you of the oath you have taken as a doctor to protect my privacy first."

"Very well," he hesitantly replied.

As the older man turned and made his way towards the path leading back to Uma village, his overall demeanour belied the new fears that were now raging within.

32. Tetabo (back) with wife Nei Meri (right) with son Nete (front) with extended Banaban family Uma Village Ocean Island.

CHAPTER THIRTY

LAST FAREWELL

Ella 1931

"Darling, that was a lovely dinner. Would you mind if we took our tea into the parlour? I would like to have a private word with you," John said, quickly glancing in Tetabo's direction.

"Not at all, darling," Ella replied, smiling, knowing it was virtually impossible to have a private word in the house. The walls always had ears and Tetabo and Meri missed nothing.

John had brought home a large, locally caught, lobster for supper tonight and some fresh blueberries that had just arrived by ship from New Zealand. These were a real culinary treat, and it had been a lovely meal for just the two of them. Uma and her current beau, Bill Cooper, were over at the Stevens's house at Tabwewa for supper.

Since John's emergency operation nearly four years ago, he had not fully regained his appetite. Food was now a constant source of indigestion problems, which the doctor had described as quite a typical aftermath from such extensive surgery. Ella was overjoyed to see him arrive home with such delights. She hoped now he would start to gain some weight.

They settled down in their favourite chairs in the parlour, and as they began to sip their tea, John spoke.

"*Tetabo, Meri,* would you both come here for a moment?" he called.

"Yes, Sir, I am here," Tetabo quickly replied, obviously not too far away.

"I here Miti, Sir," Meri replied somewhat later.

"I would like you both to have the evening off. Go and enjoy the dances down in the village," John instructed with a smile.

"Miti Sir I no do washy up," Meri replied in her distorted English.

Tetabo added in his cheerful voice, "Sir, I have not fix-up dining room or your bed!"

"I know, but I want you both to go off now and enjoy yourselves. Madam and I want to be on our own."

"O'key Sir," Tetabo replied, suddenly understanding. The glint in his eye did not go unnoticed.

Tetabo quickly ushered Meri out of the room as she began removing her apron, chattering so quickly in their native tongue that even John and Ella could not catch the words.

They heard the back door shut, and John turned to her.

"Now, we shall be able to have a private chat for a change."

"John, what is so important we need to send Meri and Tetabo off like this?"

"Well, in one way it affects them both, and I do not want to worry them in any way," he answered.

"What affects them? I don't understand what you're talking about." She was a little mystified.

"I'm sorry, darling, I do not mean to alarm you at all, it's just that I want to have a private conversation with you and not the entire island."

Ella laughed at her husband's reference to the island's Coconut Wireless.

"It's just that I've had a few things on my mind lately and I really need to discuss them with you," he added.

"All right, darling, out with it. What are you trying to tell me?"

"Well... my darling, what would you think... if I did not renew my contract at the end of July?" he stammered. "And we went back to live in Australia?" he continued with a rush of words.

"What, you mean to leave the island forever?" she asked, stunned.

"Well, darling, if I leave the company we have to leave the island, you know that."

"But Australia and the rest of the world is in the grip of a depression! How would we survive over there?" she asked, not knowing what else to say.

"We're not getting any younger, and it's about time we looked towards our retirement, and I do miss the children so."

"Oh, so do I, John. I just didn't think you would want to leave the island just yet, that's all!" She could not imagine John even contemplating the idea.

"We have Uma falling all over this new beau of hers. It brings back so many memories of those terrible times we had with Gwennie, and I don't think I could face it all again," he said, sounding drained.

"Why didn't you tell me you felt like this? Anyway, Uma's nothing like our Gwennie."

"It's not just Uma or missing Gwennie and the children for that matter, it's the whole way things are being done on the island now. It makes me so angry."

His face was now becoming flushed as he continued, "I can't abide what they're doing to those poor Banabans, taking more land all the time from such decent people. Why, it's almost criminal except that the bloody British government has written a new law to legalise their crimes." It was not like John to be so critical of matters affecting the politics of the island.

"John, please— there's no need to explain. I thought I was the only one around here that seemed to take any real interest in the Banabans' plight."

Before Ella could say anything else, he continued on this angry note. "And you know what makes me feel even worse? The fact I've been one of the main culprits blowing up the darned place. Who would have ever thought all those years ago that it would end up like this? Remember how beautiful this island was, Ella? Surely you can remember." He placed his hand over his eyes as he lost himself in his thoughts.

"Darling, it was nearly thirty years ago, but I will never forget just how beautiful it was and you mustn't feel it's all your fault. You were doing your job and looking after us, your family."

"I just never realised it would come to all this," he murmured, shaking his head.

"I hate to see you talk like this. You know I'd only be too happy to follow you to the ends of the Earth if I have to and going back to Australia to be with our family is something I've only dreamed about."

"Have I been that mean to you all these years keeping you away from them?"

"John, you wouldn't even know the meaning of the word 'mean'. You have only ever tried to do what has been best for all of us," she replied. "Now come on, we have a lot of planning to do," she added as cheerfully as she could.

How could she tell him she was terrified at the idea of leaving her beloved home and oh no! Tetabo and Meri! They could not possibly go without them.

"John, you wouldn't mind the idea of taking Tetabo and Meri back to Australia with us, would you?" she asked.

"Well, I hadn't actually thought..." He must have just seen the look of despair on her face for he added, "of course not, anything you want."

"No wonder I love you so much," she said, throwing her arms around his neck.

"No wonder I love you, Missus Williams," he replied, embracing her in return and kissing her tenderly. "Now that's enough talk. We're going to bed."

"You know I'd follow you anywhere, my dear." She laughed as she grasped his hand and led him down the hallway. "The bedroom sounds just the right place for our first stop." She gave him a resounding kiss just as he began to laugh at her remarks.

That night as they fell into each other's arms, Ella felt the deep love for her husband as it was in those wonderful old days; the times when they spent weekends at the beach house and when she had arrived home after months away. She would never forget that very first night spent on Ocean Island and even her early aversion to sex had seemed to mellow with the years, while their love and commitment for each other had overcome everything. It seemed just like yesterday as the two enjoyed the closeness of being together. Tomorrow they would face the outside world and all the new problems that lay ahead, Ella told herself, but for tonight nothing else mattered but just the two of them.

The following morning as John dressed for work; she quietly took him aside and reminded him. "Darling, please do not forget to get all the necessary papers and information regarding Tetabo and Meri."

"Don't worry, I won't," he reassured her.

"And please don't say too much about our leaving just yet until you've had a chance to speak to Tetabo and Meri," she suggested in a whisper, looking around to make sure they were alone.

"Don't worry, Ella, I was thinking the same thing myself," John answered in a stage whisper.

They both laughed and hugged, realising how they always thought alike. Ella was at least relieved that his state of mind had improved from last evening's upset and he was laughing again.

That morning as Ella followed him out to the door, she gazed at him making his way slowly down the path that led from their house. She wanted to cherish the view of him and relish something that had become familiar to her over all the years. While she stood on the doorstep savouring the moment, her heart seemed to just skip a beat, and suddenly the tears welled in her eyes.

The thought of loss was all-consuming. What had come over her? She was laughing and fine just a few minutes ago when John had been here. The sharp sorrow that she felt had given her that overwhelming sadness and the sudden realisation of leaving her island and what it would mean. No more brilliant island sunsets, no more sea breezes coming up the hill from the Pacific Ocean. No more natives singing or dancing or even the clanging of the rail cars as they went down the hill to offload their prized possession - phosphate! No more sounds of the great ships' sirens as they pulled away from the island and hardest of all was no more heady smells of saltwater mixed with the exotic perfumes of the frangipanis and the *uri* blossoms that seemed to rise with the heat of the day. She turned around, dabbing at her eyes, feeling like a foolish schoolgirl.

"Madam, what is matter?" Tetabo asked in a worried voice. He was standing in the hallway with a cloth in his hand.

He was concerned about seeing the tears in her eyes. After all these years of living with her as her personal servant, it was impossible to hide her thoughts from him.

"Nothing, nothing Tetabo, I'm just thinking that's all, you know daydreaming, thinking of my family back home," she lied, realising that talk of her home would strike a chord with him.

"Oh Madam, you miss your *tetei* and *tibu*, grandchildren?" he said with a note of understanding in his voice.

"That's right, Tetabo how did you know that?" she answered, feigning surprise.

"Oh Madam, Tetabo knows what sorrow it brings a father's heart not to live with his son," he replied, almost in answer to his own feelings. He was referring to when his Nete had lived away on Nauru. Luckily, now Mister Maynard was living on Ocean Island, and Nete had been reunited with his parents.

"Yes, Tetabo, my heart feels sorrow," she replied.

"You come, Madam, for de cup of tea. You no be alone. We take care of you, brighten your heart," he said.

Being alone had always been the subject of great concern for her dear friend.

That night as they again finished their meal, John and Ella retired to the parlour early. Uma was at a dance over in the mess rooms with Bill Cooper who seemed never to give her a moment alone. John asked Tetabo and Meri to join them both this time.

Ella could see the worry on their faces. They could sense that this event was to be something out of the ordinary. While John slowly explained to them his story about leaving, they were so aghast that Ella had to interrupt.

"Please, darling, you're frightening them. Please explain to Tetabo and Meri our idea for them," she urged.

John went on to explain their proposal of taking them with them, and their faces turned to looks of excitement, especially when John had told them he would look after them in their old age and they would become one big happy family. He also explained, if they came to Australia with them first, he would try and make arrangements later to bring Nete and Jane and her family also. He was sure Ella's large family back in Bundaberg would be only too happy to employ some of their relatives. After much discussion, they all retired, ready to face a new day and all the new arrangements that must now begin.

It took until the next evening before finally getting Uma to stand still long enough without the ever-present Bill Cooper to tell her of their decision. Her reaction was somewhat unexpected as she went into a flurry over leaving the island.

"But Uma, we'll all be back home together with Gwennie and the children, not to mention all our family back in Bundaberg."

"You don't understand. I can't leave Bill behind. He loves me!" she cried, storming out of the parlour, her face awash with tears.

Ella could see this was all too much for John. The mere mention by Uma that 'he loves me,' was enough to turn his face ashen.

"Don't worry John, I'll talk to her. You know what Uma's like, she loves everyone," she tried to reassure him. But he did not even reply; it was all too much for him to try and cope with. This time she would handle things her way.

Over the next few days, John's plans for retirement were put into motion, first advising the office and then notifying their friends of their decision. Farewell parties were already being planned and the date set for John's official farewell dinner. Ella had sent a cablegram over to Gwennie to let her know the news, which she knew would cheer her. Letters were also sent to Ella's elderly parents, advising them they would be coming home with the hope of settling back in their hometown of Bundaberg. She asked for their assistance in finding a house to buy so they would have a home to move into.

John had sent the necessary government papers away to the Australian Immigration office applying for permission to take Tetabo and Meri back to Australia with them. Everything was going to plan, and Ella was so busy organising everything she did not have much time to think.

But some new events were about to occur that would make both of them stop and think seriously about the future.

* * *

The night Uma and Bill Cooper asked to speak with them both after supper was the moment Ella told herself, 'not again!'

"Sir, Missus Williams, I would like to ask you both for your beautiful daughter's hand in marriage." Bill Cooper's handsome face was solemn, a rare expression for him. "We love each other so much, and I can't bear to lose her." He gazed at Uma with love in his eyes.

Ella's mind was racing; she could not understand why on earth Bill Cooper would want to marry her daughter. He was a man of the world and Uma, even though very happy and outgoing, was not his type. She was sure Uma was only one of many women who had crossed his path and to be completely honest, she believed he was a bit of a cad. While her imagination flew into a panic, another sudden thought came to mind. Oh no, she has not snared him into marrying her? Ella had not even stopped to think how all this news was affecting John when he suddenly spoke.

"Well, Bill, I appreciate the fact that you love my daughter, but you have only known one another for a short time," he said to the young man, his voice sounding calm.

"Sir, I realise we haven't known each other for a full year yet, but Uma has swept me off my feet."

"And when did you plan to get married?"

Ella sat there, aghast. She could not believe John was condoning all this. Uma just stood there hanging on to Bill's every word like a lovesick puppy.

"Well sir, with your permission, the first Saturday in August. It's the weekend before you and Missus Williams plan to leave," Cooper answered swiftly. It was apparent that all this had all been pre-planned between the two of them.

"So you want to marry Uma before we leave and have her stay behind with you as your wife?" John asked.

"Yes, sir, that's correct," Cooper replied, smiling at Uma, obviously happy with John's understanding of the matter.

Ella sat silent, feeling more surprised than she expected. Uma would probably be born, raised and die here and never have a chance to meet all those thousands of eligible young bachelors that were far more suitable for her.

John suddenly spoke again.

"Well, Bill and Uma, I speak now on behalf of both of us..."

What did he mean by *both of us*? Ella hadn't said a word yet, and there was no way she was about to condone this arrangement.

"...Missus Williams and I believe the best thing for Uma is for her to return home with us."

Uma was already starting to protest when John slowly went on, "...and then after a few months if you and Uma both feel the same way about each other you can marry her back home in Australia with all her family and for that matter, all your family attending as well."

Thank goodness John had shown some sense, Ella told herself. She still did not completely believe that a few months would make much difference, but at least he had come up with a good compromise. Once Uma was home in Australia who was to know what would happen, and Ella would definitely make sure she could do everything possible to change her mind. If her impressions of this young man were right, there would be another girl to take Uma's place as soon as she left the island.

"But Fah, why can't we get married in August?" Uma pleaded.

Ella suddenly found her voice. "Darling, I think your father has made a wonderfully sensible suggestion, and if you really love each other, you will wait. I'm sure Bill thinks you're worth waiting for, don't you, Bill?"

"I'd wait the rest of my life for Uma if I had to, Missus Williams," he replied.

Ella thought how smooth-tongued he was. Uma's naivety was no match for this man's charm.

"So, you won't mind if we get engaged before Uma leaves?" he asked.

"If you both promise to wait at least six months after Uma arrives back in Australia before setting a wedding date," John answered confidently.

That night after Bill had left, John quietly took Ella aside and asked her not to say anything to Uma about Bill. On finally retiring, he explained to her that confronting Uma would only cause them to do something rash. Ella knew precisely what he was talking about and obviously feared that they would have another Gwennie incident on their hands.

"I'll do whatever you ask and trust your judgement. I suppose an engagement is far better than a wedding at this stage," she joked feebly.

"Trust me," John replied as she noticed how drained and washed out he looked.

"Are you feeling all right?" she asked.

"It's been a big day. I'm a little tired."

"Well, I want you to drop in and see Doctor Young tomorrow and get a good going over," she instructed.

"All right, Ella, now let's get to bed," he replied, changing the subject as he always did.

* * *

Their departure date drew nearer, and the days seemed to speed by. There was still no word from Australian Immigration, and John sent off an urgent cable to see if matters could be sped up. Their social life was hectic, and they finally found themselves attending John's official retirement dinner. They were all there from the Commission, and Grimble attended in his full dress uniform, representing the British government. Since Uma was now officially engaged, she was accompanied by Bill.

They saw all the old faces that seemed more like family members than workmates. Some of them were the roughest of men, and for this special occasion, they had all donned their best apparel to bid their farewell. The leaders of the Chinese community had come with their interpreter, who had worked so closely with John with them. The Kanaka work supervisors were there to represent the mainly Gilbertese community and the smaller Ellice labour contingent. John's face was flushed with pleasure at seeing them there to pay their respects and bid him farewell.

Ella was proud of her husband when he had insisted on Tetabo, Meri, Nete and the rest of their extended family being there together with the elders of the Banaban community. Those old familiar faces all seemed so much older now, and many of the old-timers had already passed away. Ella thought that while their faces and bodies showed the expanse of time, their minds and hearts seemed young again that night.

After the band played and people danced, the official speeches were finally made. Ella knew John had been well respected by the island's community, but it still came as a shock to see the genuine show of respect they felt for him. After McLintock, the BPC manager, made his farewell speech to both of them he presented John with the most exquisite 22 gold carat fob watch on behalf of the Commission. It was intricately engraved with his name on it. John was truly touched, and for the first time in her life, Ella witnessed him overcome with such emotion that he found it difficult to stand up before his peers and reply to the manager's speech.

His old mate George Cozens, on realising his dilemma, immediately began to toss jokes at him and rallied the rest of the staff and their good sense of humour to save the day.

John finally spoke. "Thank you, gentlemen. I do not know how I will manage without my daily dose of humour once I leave here. What I can tell you all is that it has been an honour for me to have known you all and an absolute pleasure to be associated with such wonderful people, and I mean all the people of Ocean Island or Banaba as my old Banaban friends would say. Regardless of the colour of our skins and our different backgrounds, you have made me a very proud man to have the privilege of living here with you all. Even though we will be leaving here in two weeks, I can assure my Banaban friends that my heart will always remain here with you all and my thoughts will often return to the best years of my life spent here on the island." While he gave his thanks, he smiled at Ella.

"On behalf of my family and myself I say thank you, *kam raba!"* he added for his native friends.

After the speeches, the band started up again and people gathered on the dance floor. Ella was busy talking to their various friends when Doctor Young joined their group.

"Good evening, Doctor. I'm so glad you could attend John's dinner." She smiled at him.

"I'm sorry I'm late; it took me longer than expected to get away from the hospital."

"I do hope everything is all right?" she asked.

"Oh yes, just the usual last-minute emergency," he replied in an off-handed manner.

"I hope my John has been to see you?" she asked, trying to make conversation. He was almost taciturn.

"Oh, so he has told you?"

"Told me what?"

"Oh, nothing Missus Williams... I thought..." he stammered, shifting his feet nervously.

"Thought what, Doctor Young?"

"Sorry, Missus Williams, I'm very tired. I must have made a mistake with someone else," he replied. He, no doubt, was a poor liar as he tried to avoid looking at her.

Ella took his arm. "Doctor Young, can I have a private chat with you for a moment?"

"I'm sure you'll excuse us for a moment; we won't be too long," she told her friends gathered around them as she led the doctor to the corner of the room where it was more private.

"Now young man, what's going on with my husband?" she demanded. "There is something he has been keeping from me?"

"I'm very sorry, Missus Williams, but I'm not permitted to breach your husband's confidence."

"Young man, if there's something wrong with my husband I demand to know and if you don't tell me in the strictest confidence, of course, I will have no other choice but to tell my husband you have already breached his confidence by informing me about his visit," she threatened. "I'm sure you wouldn't like me to do that, would you, Doctor Young?"

"No! No! Missus Williams, I can assure you that it is not necessary, but you must give me your word you won't divulge what I am about to tell you. Mister Williams was very insistent about that," he replied nervously.

"Very well. I can assure you that I will abide by my husband's wishes, so trust me, please. Now, what is the problem?"

"I'm very sorry to say, Missus Williams, that your husband is, er... is dying," he replied with the greatest reluctance. He gazed at Ella, judging her reaction. Perhaps he had been too brutally honest.

The blood drained from her face while her thoughts raced, thinking of all that had been happening over the past months. She realised now it all made sense. Why had she not suspected that there was more to this retiring business?

"Is it the same problem?" she asked calmly, almost not really wanting to hear his answer.

"It's stomach cancer, Missus Williams, and yes you could say it's a result of all those earlier problems," he replied.

"Thank you, Doctor Young!" she answered shortly. "Would you please excuse me now. I must return to the party." She turned and walked back to her small group of waiting friends.

"Everything all right?" Agnes Cozens inquired.

"Everything's just fine, just fine!" she replied, forcing herself to smile. She could see John busily chatting and laughing with some of the chaps over near the refreshments table.

She was sure he had not noticed her little chat with Doctor Young. It was now up to her to stand by him and his wishes for privacy. She was not about to spoil that stubborn pride of his.

Over the next few days, she had to carry on regardless while her heart was breaking. She did not know why John had not told her, but she supposed he just wanted her to spare her from worrying more.

Five days before their departure date, another event also drastically changed Ella's life. John arrived home with a letter from the Australian Immigration Department regarding Tetabo and Meri's upcoming trip to Australia and read the letter aloud to her.

"...it is the current Australian government's policy under 'Immigration Act 1924' to reject your application for entry for the following persons, Tetabo and Nei Meri, natives of the said Ocean Island, for the Gilbert and Ellice Islands Group, Central Pacific..." Ella and John were absolutely devastated, and so were Tetabo and Nei Meri.

John was sure with the recent amendments to Australia's Immigration Restriction Act, commonly called the 'White Australia Policy', that restrictions had been reformed and would allow Tetabo and Nei Meri to come back to Australia with them. They didn't realise that this amendment had only made immigration laws more difficult, especially in regard to what the Australian government deemed as indentured labour from nearby South Pacific Islands.

As the flood of tears came, Ella could not drop her guard and admit to John that she also knew his secret. Her whole life seemed over as all the thoughts collided in her mind. From the moment she left the island, things would never be the same. She would have Uma and Gwennie for a time, but Uma would surely want to come back here and marry Bill Cooper. Gwennie was still living in Cairns, and her parents were now in their advanced years back in Bundaberg. Thank goodness she would have her brother and sisters in Australia.

The next morning, John made his way off to work after apologising profusely for the disappointment and telling her it must be a mistake. He insisted that he would do everything possible to get the matter reviewed, but she could see he was severely affected. Ella was sure he had probably known that Tetabo and Meri would have taken good care of them when the time came. When Tetabo came out to the veranda to farewell John, she could see the emotion etched on his face.

"Come, my friend, it is I who will make you a cup of tea," she said, leading him into the kitchen.

Once inside, he took hold of her hand and suddenly burst out in tears. Her heart went out to him, this big burly grown man, her best friend, who stood before her and unashamedly cried like a small child. She threw her arms around his shoulders, something she had never done before, realising just how much he meant to her at the thought of losing him.

Overcome with grief she stammered, "You know, Tetabo, even though we all can't be together, I will always love you like my brother... no one will ever take your place." She did not have the heart to tell him about John, as he was so distressed as it was. "You will always remain in a special place in my heart," she said in between her sobs.

Finally, their last day arrived, and Ella's sorrow was all-consuming while she still was doing all she could to maintain an outwardly happy disposition. John deserved that from her. John and Uma obviously had their own thoughts to deal with as the day finally arrived. Uma was almost physically sick at the thought of leaving Bill and Ella did not have the heart to tell her about her father. John seemed a lot quieter than usual.

The moment the furniture was packed and their belongings were on the way down to be loaded at the jetty they said the hardest goodbye of them all to Tetabo and Meri.

"*Tia kabo* my friends. You will stay here with me always," she said, as she patted her chest. Ella then rushed to both of them and hugged and kissed them, not wanting to let go.

John took her arm while he took Tetabo's hand and said, "*Tia kabo* and goodbye my good friend and *ko raba,* thank you for all you have done for my family and me," he said, trying to keep his emotions in check. "I will never be able to thank you enough." He could not contain himself any longer as he now stepped forward and hugged his friend in a brotherly embrace, his eyes clouding over with moisture. He slowly pulled himself away to embrace Meri.

"Please take good care of this lovely lady," he said, as he tried to smile, addressing his friend, "...and don't worry. I will do everything I can once we get to Australia to change Immigration's ruling."

Trying to bring his feelings under control, he pulled an envelope from his pocket and placed it in Tetabo's hand. They had already given Tetabo and Meri all the utensils and fittings from the house that they could use. John now gave him money that he hoped would help him and Meri stand on their own two feet once they were gone and help them survive in the days that lay ahead.

"*Tia kabo* my friends... until we meet again!" were the last words he uttered before he turned and quickly made his way down the front steps. He never once turned back.

Again, after tearfully bidding farewell and hugging her two dear friends, Ella reluctantly pulled herself away and fled after John, joining him and a weeping Uma on the flatcar that was waiting to take them down to the jetty. John never lifted his head on their last trip down to the wharf.

* * *

The three of them stood there out on the deck of the Commissioner's new ship the *Triona* when the dreaded moment finally arrived. Their Banaban friends had all come down to the jetty to see them off, garlanding them with masses of flowers. Tetabo and the other men had even come out towards the ship on their *te waa* which they had covered in flowers. The colour was everywhere, as were the tears that were being so freely shed by their Banaban friends.

Ella looked back down on such a beautiful spectacle, her mind drifting back to the first time she had arrived here. She still could remember the sun shining down on their golden skins, made smooth and glistening with oil. The memories of listening to the laughter and the excited cries of all those beautiful people as they welcomed them, the new *I-Matang*s to their shores; at least she had those memories.

Her mind was drawn back to the present as the voices now united in song and carried up to where they were standing on the deck of the ship. It was a song of farewell and love sung in their beautiful native tongue. She could make out some of the faces standing back there on the jetty. Meri, Nete, Jane, Agnes and George Cozens, Letitia White and her two young children now waving as her mind again began to drift back again to her first day and her arrival to her beloved island. Making her way on up that path covered in a canopy of beautiful coconut palms as they filtered the hot sun above; such a magical place, their island home, so untouched and perfect in those wonderful early days before all the destruction had begun.

The sound of the ship's siren blaring broke her reverie. The three of them had increased their waving when they heard the anchor being drawn up. Ella turned to John and noticed the misting of his eyes as he stood so stoic and solemn, his arm waving almost mechanically. How hard it must all be for him, she realised. Uma was unashamedly crying and blowing kisses no doubt to her Bill. Ella stood there with the tears slowly flowing down her cheeks. The ship's engines suddenly stepped-up pace, and began to turn the ship seaward, away from the moorings. They all tried to savour that final moment of farewell for as long as possible.

Ella could see Tetabo frenziedly paddling his *te waa*, trying to stay with them for as long as he could... their ship suddenly pulled away. The stricken look on his face at that very moment would remain burned into her soul forever.

Recovering her composure after a few moments, she swallowed her tears and discreetly dabbed at her eyes. Turning to John, she placed her arm around his waist and, gathering all the strength she could muster, she quietly said, "Come on, darling, I think it's time we went inside."

POSTSCRIPT

As the lives of the Williams family of Ocean Island, Central Pacific would come to an end, the Banabans' fight to save their homeland would just be beginning. What did become of Ella and John, Hazel and Tom and some of the other characters, especially Ata?

John Williams safely settled with Ella and their newly engaged daughter Uma back in Ella's old hometown of Bundaberg on Queensland's Central Coast. Within nine months, he was dead, suffering from what the family described as the rare tropical disease of 'elephantiasis', which is a disease that causes massive enlargements and swelling of the legs and other parts of the body. Tragically, in John's case, it was his stomach that was most affected, and over his final year, it had caused continued debilitating complications. The year was 1932, and he was sixty-three years of age. I never had the pleasure of meeting my great-grandfather, as he died over twenty years before I was born. His treasured gold fob watch from the island is my only tangible link to him and his incredible life on Ocean Island. I wear it with great pride.

After John's untimely death, Ella soldiered on alone, becoming increasingly more independent and more eccentric as time went on. After years of living in the tropics, her face grew heavily lined and her small, slender body slowly arched with age. Her long dark tresses became heavily streaked with grey but still remained knotted in the familiar chignon on top of her head. I can remember her striking green eyes even though in later years she would become virtually blind with cataracts, while refusing to let any doctor touch her. This strange phobia had something to do with her earlier life spent on the island, and she insisted on treating herself with the herbal remedies and medicines taught to her by the Banabans and the Chinese. Her back garden became home to many of the old plants and fruit trees that grew back on her beloved island.

By the end of 1940, Ella had plans already in place to realise her dream of returning to visit the island, but her dream would be shattered when war erupted in Europe, and the Japanese bombers dropped their deadly load on Ocean Island as they returned from their surprise attack on Pearl Harbour in the Pacific.

While war raged across the world, she lost all contact with old friends, especially Tetabo and his family. This whole incredible episode is covered in the second book of the LAND OF MATANG series, titled CURSE OF NAKAA. In fact, even though the Williamses are no longer the central characters of this terrible episode, the results of the war and its tragic effects on Ocean Island seem to be the catalyst that would again significantly change the Williams family's lives forever.

As the years passed, Ella became greatly saddened by the terrible events that would transpire back on Ocean Island, blaming everything on the British government. The large mounted photograph of the island was Ella's only visual reminder of her previous life, together with her tales of those wonderful early years and the beautiful Banaban people whom she loved and admired deeply, she would happily reminisce for hours. But somehow her mind would always wander back to the British government and launch her on a tirade of how they had destroyed her beautiful island and the Banaban people.

Except for her memories of the past, Ella would spend her final years living simply and happily on her own, almost blind and virtually deaf, her faithful dog and a handful of chickens her only companions. She would go to bed when her rooster crowed and rise with his call at the break of dawn, spending her days tending her garden. These were also the delightful days I remember as a child wandering around her high set Queensland style home. She did not believe in electricity, telephones or any type of modern technology, and because of her simple lifestyle, never saw a need for them. Her house was a treasure trove of items from the past and, like Ella herself, unique. She passed away peacefully and suddenly in August 1968. Ella Williams was ninety years of age.

Uma Williams, my great-aunt and the youngest of the Williams clan returned to Queensland with her parents as promised, never knowing her father was dying. His untimely death would affect her future plans to marry her beloved Billy Cooper and the life they were planning back on Ocean Island. The second book of the Land of Matang trilogy covers this episode of Uma's life.

Hazel Williams, or Gwennie, as she was christened, was my grandmother and a central figure in my life. Of all the Williams clan, Hazel was the one most affected by her earlier life raised on what she perceived as an idyllic tropical island. As a child, hearing these stories seemed a fairy tale to me and as mentioned at the beginning, more like a childhood fantasy. It was not until after Uma's death in 1989 and the discovery of her battered tin containing her island treasures that the impact of this story would change my destiny and lead me on a search for the truth. But what did become of Hazel and her exile back in Australia with Tom?

Tom, or Grandpop as we affectionately called him, was one of nature's true gentlemen. A highly educated and clever man, he was at the same time a sensitive and artistic soul. The only thing he ever lacked in life was ambition. He was a humble man who never realised his full potential, and for that matter, never wanted to be anything more than what he was and that was a train driver on the Queensland Railways.

At one stage in their early married life, he would become the relief driver on one of Australia's most historic rail routes through the remote far North Queensland outback track to Normanton in the Gulf. My grandfather was not only a writer but also a poet, an artist and a wonderful storyteller when it came to recalling his adventures.

Hazel, on the other hand, was never at peace with her life back in Australia and with Tom. As the tragic events would unfold back on Ocean Island, especially during the war years, Hazel became increasingly bitter. My poor grandfather also seemed to bear the brunt of much of her frustration as she found it extremely hard to settle down to married life in Australia. Her yearning to travel never left her and she was her happiest when moving house or travelling to new places.

She could not face any type of cold weather, and even a mild Brisbane subtropical winter was too much for her. Every year she would move back to Cairns in far North Queensland or in the earlier years, back to the island she loved with her young children, and after the death of her father, she would travel back to her mother's home in Bundaberg. Hazel always remained very close to her mother, and after her mother's death seemed to step up her pace and her quest for travel.

Tom and Hazel's meeting had begun as a true love story with what she always referred to as, 'love at first sight', but sadly, it never lived up to her high expectations. Maybe her early upbringing among the Banabans had ill-prepared her for the hard realities of life back in civilisation. By the time she married, she had been so well travelled and experienced a lifestyle so unbelievable, that anything else could only ever be an anticlimax. My grandparents always seemed ill-matched, and in the final years of their lives, Hazel strangely decided to legally separate from Tom to free herself for more travel.

Tom was taken in by his youngest daughter and young family and spent his last days happily surrounded by his loving family. He died from a sudden heart attack only eighteen months later at the age of eighty-two. After his death, Hazel seemed more lost than ever, continually speaking of the wonderful years they had spent together, seemingly only wanting to remember the 'good times' and of course Ocean Island. Her travel plans once again seemed to increase, and it was while away on one of her adventures that she would suffer a fatal stroke and die far away from home doing what she loved most. Hazel had survived her Tom by less than two years. She was seventy-five years of age.

It was only after studying the full extent of their story that I began to realise what led to my grandmother's unsettled and at times, unhappy life. Her early years were idyllic, even though she always referred to her loneliness. She also told me how she climbed those tall palm trees so she could speak to God and the birds. It is only now that I realise the full meaning of her words that seemed so strange at the time. Just like the 'birds' she so often spoke of soaring high out over the sea, I understand now that her spirit could never be caged or contained. My grandmother's spirit and soul have finally been set free.

It was not until this story was thoroughly researched that I would discover the true extent of how much Ocean Island had affected all of their lives. They all went to their graves, believing that the Japanese had murdered their beloved houseboy Tetabo. Somehow, with my family's belief that Tetabo and Meri were dead, together with the murder of the family's favourite priest and personal friend, Father Pujabet, the past and idyllic days seemed to die with them. Hazel especially became very bitter towards religion and the church, believing that God had not helped the good priest and his innocent congregation of Banabans against such evil. Ella could not overcome her guilt and grief over the Australian government's refusal to allow Tetabo and his family to immigrate to Australia, leaving them behind to be murdered by the Japanese. This would haunt her for the rest of her days and only add to her distrust of government authority. The story of Tetabo, Meri and Father Pujabet also continues in the next episode.

What did become of Ata? Ata, or Arthur Cozens', existence was only discovered after work had begun on this book. His name was never mentioned in the family home, but Hazel often spoke of her friendship with the Banaban children.

In my research, I found myself speaking to a delightful old Ocean Island character, Captain Norman Anderson, who was ninety-four at the time. He was the one character still alive who vividly remembered all the Williams family. He even divulged he had been a suitor, as he called it, of my great-aunt Uma and had a crush on her at the time. He remembered John and Ella well and told me the story of George Cozens and his Banaban son, Arthur.

He told me during the interview that the story was a scandal and never openly discussed. He related how someone's wife on the island had informed Captain Cozens' new Australian spouse about her husband's notorious past. Captain Anderson recalled how he had run into the young lad, Arthur, many years later in Melbourne, Australia, and he had become a successful architect, he believed. He had lost track of the lad over the years and also George and Agnes Cozens had died in Adelaide years earlier.

At the time of our interview, I was preparing to make my first visit to meet with the Banabans. I asked Captain Anderson for his advice, and he was adamant that I should ask the Banabans all about the story of Arthur. He kept saying, 'they will tell you the story'. Captain Anderson would die the summer following our interview. Ironically, he had told me that he had settled in Adelaide to escape the heat. He died during one of Adelaide's extreme heatwaves.

His words turned out to be accurate in regard to the Banabans. After arriving on the island, I was befriended by a young Banaban man, Kaiea Bakanebo. His great-grandfather, Temate, had been one of the elders who had signed that notorious document with Albert Ellis in 1900, giving the company the rights to mine the island for the next 999 years. Suddenly I found Kaiea asking me if I had heard the story of Arthur Cozens and telling me there was an old lady on the island who wanted to meet with me.

After being led to her humble home with the old Williams treasured photographs in my arms, I was welcomed in and greeted by the old lady and her younger descendants. Unfortunately, due to her poor eyesight, she was unable to identify photographs of the person we believed could have been Arthur in the Williams' Collection. She was able to tell me that Arthur had ended up marrying an Australian woman and, sadly in Banaban eyes, had never been blessed with children. He had indeed become very successful, making and drawing houses as she described it through our interpreter and also, she sadly told me that Arthur's mother had died a few years earlier. The old lady was Arthur's aunty.

She went on to describe how Arthur had always promised to return but never had done so. He would often spend time down at the wharves in Australia waiting for one of the island's ships to come in. He yearned to hear stories of home and especially his mother and family from the young Banaban seamen on board ship. Arthur would send letters and gifts home and promise time after time that he would return. His aunty informed me that word had come through to them about four years earlier that Arthur had passed away. Every effort I have made since that meeting to find someone that remembered Arthur in Australia or even knew the name of his wife has been unsuccessful. But somehow, I have a feeling that the story of Arthur Cozens or Ata is not quite over yet and one day, the rest of the story will come to light.

All the great things my great-grandmother, Ella and my grandparents, told me about the Banabans were accurate. I shall be eternally grateful to my family for passing on their knowledge and love. I only wish they were here today to hear the truth and clear up some of their eventual misunderstandings. At the beginning of this story, I just had a battered old tin filled with hundreds of unnamed photographs and handwritten letters and documents. As each piece of the jigsaw puzzle started to fall into place, I had strong feelings of what I believed really had happened. It was almost as if I was being compelled to write it. What was more amazing was when I assumed a theory or a particular line, my hunches usually proved correct.

An excellent example of this was the writing and description of Hazel and Tom's wedding. A photograph would come into my possession months later that showed the event precisely as I had described it in such detail.

My life and that of my family has now become entwined with the Banabans, and I believe that fate and the spirits of our ancestors have somehow brought us all together. It was almost as if the events leading up to my meeting with the Banabans and the journey I now find myself on had all been pre-planned. While many of our other Banaban characters mentioned in this tale have passed away, they have left behind many descendants. Who would ever have foreseen that five generations or one hundred years later that the descendants of the Williams family and the Banabans involved in this story would end up united in marriage? Now in the twenty-first century, a sixth generation has been born, creating new family bonds and blood ties, but of course, this is another story waiting to be told.

What I have realised since my life became involved with the Banabans is the level of spirituality and understanding that I have developed. It is something that cannot be easily explained but a knowing or unspoken word that exists deep in my heart in relation to the Banabans' ongoing suffering. Whether much of this story had stayed buried deep in a child's subconscious or whether this was always part of my destiny, I do not know. What I do know is that somehow the spirits of all of them live on in me today and I have been given the task to help the Banabans continue their struggle... after all, it is what they all would have wanted!

THE END

Author, Stacey M. King with Banaban Clan spokesman, Raobeia Ken Sigrah at their home in Australia 2004.

They met on Rabi Island, Fiji in 1992 and came together to write the first history book from a Banaban perspective in 1997.

But you will have to wait for Book Four in the **Land of Matang** series to learn more about their story.

As they say, *"the rest is history…"*

GLOSSARY

I-Kiribati	English
A-nte Rua-rua	below the pit
aba	land
aba ni butirake	land of the asking
abo	fishing line
ae	that
aii	coconut crab
aika	which were
Aka	first hamlet
ana	belonging to
anti	spirits
anti n aomata	half human, half spirit
anti ni mate	pounder made of wood or coral, used for preparing pandanus
ao	and
Ao kabiram te ba	and of oil for your anointing
Ao kanam te am-arake	and your right to partake of the food
Ao kanam te ika te urua	and your right to eat the stranded fish (travelly)
Ao katikani koran	and of drawing the measuring cord
aon te aba	across the land

Ao mwaem te kaue	and your right of garlanding the stranger who arrives
Ao ruoiam	and your right to direct the rouia
Ao taekan aon te aba	and to decide on land matters within your boundary
Arana am Kainga!	Name your hamlet!
ati ni mate	pounder made of wood or coral, originally used as a weapon, now used for pounding pandanus leaves
atia	things that have been done
Auriaria te Tabu	Auriaria the Holy
ba arom ni bane ai-kai a bon tiku iroun teuaei	for all these your customary rights indeed remain with this man
ba e uotia ba te mane	for he takes them, being a male
bakarerenteiti	the lightning strike
bana	boxing gloves, woven from coconut sinet with spikes on knuckles
Banaba	land of rock
bangabanga	water cave
bangota	ancestral shrine
baobao	tall wooden frames for frigate birds to sit on
bareaka	canoe shed
bata	sleeping house
batere	cultural dancing
bau	headpiece worn for Banaban dancing
baurua	large ocean-going outrigger canoe
binobino	coconut shell water containers

bonito	skip jack tuna
boti	sitting place in the *maneaba*
bua	lost
buki	Kiribati style of swaying hip dance
Bukiniwae	forerunner clan for the elder clans
bunna	sacred garland made of certain leaves
bure	belt made of plaited pandanus leaf and shells, worn for Banaban dancing
Burita	war canoe of te Aka clan
butirake	asking of special favours for social standing or to inherit land
butu	thumb thrust stance in Banaban boxing
bwaa	coconut oil
bwaai	things
bwaene	plaited coconut leaf baskets
E maoto naona!	His waves have broken!
Ea baka karaun Nei Kabuta!	Kabuta's rain has fallen! (an idiom for 'Life is back again!')
enta	neck piece with amulet, worn for Banaban dancing
fatele	Tuvaluan style of dance
I bukin	because of
I nanora	in our hearts
I-Matang	European
ibi	hardwood tree, native to Banaba
ikabuti	smaller fishing scoop for catching schools of sardines along the seashore
inaki	sitting places in the *maneaba*
Inaki ni Buiniwae	sitting place of the forerunner, right-hand man to the elder

Inaki ni Karimoa	sitting place of the eldest
iroura	us
itau ni Banaba	Banaban boxing
Itimoa	name of canoe of protection for te Aka clan
itimoa	first lightning
itinikarawa	heavenly lightning
kabwane eitei	frigate bird snaring
kaekeko	acting on behalf of an elder
kai ni katua	oblong shaped hand throwing weapon for men made of wood or rock, now used as weight for the game of *katua*
kai-ni-karemotu	tossing stick used by women in the game of *karemotu*
kaimatoa	Kiribati style of set pattern dance
kain roa	fishing pole
kainga	hamlet consisting of family dwellings
kaitau	special word of thanks
kakii	neck piece made from human hair, worn for Banaban dancing
kakoaki	bleaching process
kakoko	first shoot of the coconut leaf
kakuri	Kiribati game
kamakama	sea crabs
kaneati	stalactite fishing hook
kaoti n Engiran	uprising of England
kaoti-n aine	woman's arrival
karanga	war spear dance
karanga are e uarereke	short stick war dance

karemotu	tossing the stick game
karetika	Kiribati style of throwing of babai plant stems
Karia	lowland in Tabwewa district
Karia te ang	waiting of the wind
Karieta	upland in Tabwewa district
karo ten	style of braiding used especially for fishing lines
katabara	open stance in Banaban boxing
Katea rikim?	What is your genealogy?
kati	Kiribati game of bow and arrow shooting
katua	putting the weight game
kaunga	slave
kaunrabata	Kiribati style of men's wrestling
kauoua n raeaki	second partitioning of Banaba
kauti	rituals to evoke magic
kibena	fishing scoop net for catching flying fish
koro karewe	cutting coconut toddy
kouti-n aine	small mat worn around the shoulders
kua	porpoise
kunkun	*Terminalia catappa*, wild almond
mai	breadfruit
mai	from
maie ni kauti	dancing magic ritual
makauro	hermit crab
malo	Polynesian word meaning a short skirt of leaves strung around the hips
manai	land crab
maneaba	traditional Banaban community meeting house

mangko ni Banaba	wild mango
mao	*Scaevola kownigi*, bushy shrub found amongst rocks around the shoreline
mata-bou	a new face or eyes
matoa	Continuous or strong
maunei	dried treated grass skirt, worn for Banaban dancing (on Rabi)
motu	coconut markers used in the game of *karemotu*
mwemweneitei	upward flight of the frigate bird
mwenga	House
Na Areau	male spider god
Na Tabakea	male turtle god
naki toki	forever, non-stop
nati-n-atei	adopted child
nei tere	head marker in the *karemotu* game
Nei Tituabine	female stingray god
ngea	*Pemphis acifula*, coastal bloodwood useful for tool and weapon making
ni	for
non	*Morinda citrifolia*, commly called Noni throughout the Pacific
oon tabakea	a certain species of turtle
oreano	Kiriabati style of ball game
ramwane	crosspiece ornament for men, worn for Banaban dancing
ren	*Tournefortia argentea*, plant
riri	dried coconut leaf skirt, worn for Banaban dancing
roa ati	tuna pole fishing

rouia	Kiribati sitting dance
tabakea	a certain species of turtle (also name of Kiribati totem)
tabo ni kauti	private terrace for magic ritual
Tabo-n te Rengerenge	edge of the cliff
tabunea	performing of sorcery
Taeka	word
tairua	foreigners or outsiders
taitai	tattooing
takataka	a piece of coconut
tangiraki	beloved
tani Bekan	pagans
tani Kiritian	Christians
tatae	fishing for flying fish
te	the
te Aonoanne	That place! (other name of te Aka adopted by newcomers to Banaba)
te ati ni kana	Kiribati custom of hair cutting and offering ceremony
te be	cloth wrapped around lower half of body also known throughout the Pacific as sarong or lava lava
te Burita	an enchanted place in te Aonoanne district
te moa n raeaki	the first partitioning
te moa ni kainga	the first hamlet
te rii ni Banaba	the backbone of Banaba
te waa	outrigger canoe

Te wa-ni-Kaiowa	the canoe that accompanies the two boarding canoes from the Karia clan
Te Wantieke I	canoe which takes out the elder who boards foreign vessels from the Karieta clan
Te Wantieke II	the other canoe which takes out the elder who boards foreign vessels from the Karia clan
tei	uphold
Te itai	*Calophyllum inophyllum*, also known as the ship tree by the te Aka people
Tera taum?	What is your family's inherited role?
tia itau	boxer
tia kabo	goodbye
tibu	grandmother or grandfather
tibu babako	great-great-great-grandmother or great-great-great-grandfather
tibu mamanu	great-great-grandmother or great-great-grandfather
tibu taratara	great-great-great-great-grandmother or great-great-great-great-grandfather
tibu toru	great-grandmother or great-grandfather
tie	Kiribati style of swinging game
tiribenu	shadow smash stance in Banaban boxing, used by women only
toa ma I-matang	foreign giant or giant from Matang
Toka ni Mane	seat of the man
tou	pandanus fruit
uea	king or high chief
uma	home stance, in Banaban boxing

uma n anti	spirit house
uma n roronga	young man's sleeping quarters
uma n teinako	house for menstruating women
uma ni kanaiai	cooking house
unaine	old women
unimane	old men
uri	*Guettarda speciosa,* plant with small scented white flower
uringakia	for their remembrance
urua	type of fish (travelly)
utu	immediate family or next of kin
wawi	death magic

ABOUT THE AUTHOR

Stacey M. King is a businesswoman with commercial interests in the natural health industry and indigenous arts throughout Australia and the Pacific. She is an author and historian who specialises in Banaban Colonial history. Her association with the Banabans is more than a casual interest. Four generations of her family were involved with the early mining industry of Banaba (also known as Ocean Island) from the discovery of phosphate from 1900 to 1931.

In 1991, she began research on her family's history in 1989 for a historical novel based on their lives titled – **Nakaa's Awakening**, the first in the **Land of Matang** four-book series. From her first meeting with the Banabans in 1992, she has worked extensively on aid projects to try and assist the Banaban communities on Rabi and Banaba Islands. She went on to become the founder of the Banaban Heritage Society in 1995 and during this period she was involved in the research and coordination of various Australian and international television documentaries including:

Exiles in Paradise, 60 Minutes, Nine Network, Australia (1993),

Banaba – Grief for an Island Home in the South Pacific, Foreign Correspondent, ABC, Australia (1995),

Paradise Lost, NHK Network, Japan 1997,

Coming Home to Banaba, BBC OUL, United Kingdom (1997).

She has also written various articles on the Banabans for worldwide publication over the past 30 years. In 1997, she formed a personal and collaborative partnership with Ken Raobeia Sigrah, a Banaban Clan historian and spokesperson. They both soon discovered their shared passion for seeking justice for the Banaban people and to see the rehabilitation of the Banaban homeland left destroyed by the mining. Together they have built one of the largest private collections on Banaban history from a European and indigenous perspective.

Her other publications include:

Books:

Te Rii ni Banaba (2001), (2nd ed. 2019), Banaban history written from an indigenous perspective and endorsed by Banaban Clan elders.

The Banaba-Ocean Island chronicles. Chapter 17, *Hunting the collectors.*

Papers | Abstracts | Presentations:
Legacy of a Miner's Daughter (2004)
The Cultural Identity of Banabans (2004)
Australia-Banaba Relations; the price of shaping a nation (2006)
The Banaba-Ocean Island chronicles: private collections, indigenous record-keeping (2006)

King and Sigrah share the belief that their lives and destiny are intertwined, bringing them together so they could try and right the wrongs of the past. They are converting much of their writings and research findings into publications for future Banaban generations and for a broader audience keen to learn more about the plight of the indigenous Banaban people in the modern world.

Where to find Stacey King online

Website: banabanvision.com
Facebook: Banabanvision
Blog: Banabanvision
Linkedin: stacey-king
Email: stacey@banaban.com
Banaban Official Website: banaban.com

To hear more on Stacey and Ken's story go to:
(Banaba: The island Australia ate), ABC Radio National, Australia -podcast.
The Black Knight and the Iron Maiden, ABC Radio National, Australia story.